Praise for the Novels of E. E. Knight

The Age of Fire Series

Book One: *Dragon Champion*

"Knight, best known for his Vampire Earth mass-market series, makes an auspicious trade-paper debut with this smoothly written fantasy told from the point of view of its dragon hero . . . a bloody, unsentimental fairy tale."

—*Publishers Weekly*

"An enchanting story of a young dragon's search for answers to help him understand what it is to be a dragon. This is a heartwarming story full of adventure where good deeds and friendship always succeed. The characters are wonderfully endearing, and the adventures that Auron experiences as he grows into an adult dragon are exciting and entertaining. A superb introduction to what I hope will be a wonderful series."

—The Eternal Night

"The author of the Vampire Earth series has crafted a series opener with a refreshingly new protagonist who views the world from a draconic, rather than a human, perspective. A fine addition to most fantasy collections."

—*Library Journal* (starred review)

"Knight did a great job of hooking me into the story. . . . This concern and attention to the details illustrates how strong the overall feel of the book is—Knight clearly is building something more in this world and the amount of backstory to the characters and creatures is very impressive. . . . Very entertaining, the characters were genuine and the world full of depth. With the ending Knight gave us, I am very interested to see where he takes these characters next."   —SFFWorld

"E. E. Knight makes the transition from the science fiction of his Vampire Earth series to a fantasy saga with an ease that is amazing but not surprising with someone with his enormous amount of writing talent."   —Paranormal Romance Reviews

continued . . .

The Vampire Earth Series

Winter Duty

"The series is always fun."

—The Weekly Press (Philadelphia)

"The plot contains shockers and twists as E. E. Knight provides a powerful, thought-provoking suspense thriller that will keep fans up late into the night."   —*Midwest Book Review*

"Mr. Knight uses his impressive eye for detail to reinforce and expand this well-built world. *Winter Duty* is a combination of genres and has a story line set in a war-ravaged and imaginative future."   ——Darque Reviews

"Gritty and realistic, Knight's series provides consistent high-quality adventure. . . . Excellent battle scenes, strategy, and descriptions take readers further along this epic journey."

—*Romantic Times*

"Knight's latest effort really gives you something to savor while taking you for a ride through the harsh landscape of a war-torn world and man's fight for survival."

—Fantasy Literature

"Another rousing success. . . . Knight brilliantly continues world building on a monumental scale, while adding complexity to the personality of his multifaceted main character, Major David Valentine. . . . E. E. Knight is uncompromising in detail and continues to present the picture of a world that is both believable, as well as frighteningly plausible. He molds and develops characters that are sympathetic, layered, and mysteriously familiar. Valentine, the main protagonist, is compelling on so many levels, and has grown steadily from novel to novel. Eight books in, and I still want to spend precious time reading about his further adventures."   —BSCrview

"The author continues to build on this fascinating world, making it one of my favorite ongoing series."   —Buried

NOVELS BY E. E. KNIGHT

The Vampire Earth

Way of the Wolf
Choice of the Cat
Tale of the Thunderbolt
Valentine's Rising
Valentine's Exile
Valentine's Resolve
Fall with Honor
March in Country

The Age of Fire

Dragon Champion
Dragon Avenger
Dragon Outcast
Dragon Strike
Dragon Rule

Dragon Avenger

BOOK TWO OF THE AGE OF FIRE

E. E. KNIGHT

A ROC BOOK

ROC
Published by New American Library, a division of
Penguin Group (USA) Inc., 375 Hudson Street,
New York, New York 10014, USA
Penguin Group (Canada), 90 Eglinton Avenue East, Suite 700, Toronto,
Ontario M4P 2Y3, Canada (a division of Pearson Penguin Canada Inc.)
Penguin Books Ltd., 80 Strand, London WC2R 0RL, England
Penguin Ireland, 25 St. Stephen's Green, Dublin 2,
Ireland (a division of Penguin Books Ltd.)
Penguin Group (Australia), 250 Camberwell Road, Camberwell, Victoria 3124,
Australia (a division of Pearson Australia Group Pty. Ltd.)
Penguin Books India Pvt. Ltd., 11 Community Centre, Panchsheel Park,
New Delhi - 110 017, India
Penguin Group (NZ), 67 Apollo Drive, Rosedale, North Shore 0632,
New Zealand (a division of Pearson New Zealand Ltd.)
Penguin Books (South Africa) (Pty.) Ltd., 24 Sturdee Avenue,
Rosebank, Johannesburg 2196, South Africa

Penguin Books Ltd., Registered Offices:
80 Strand, London WC2R 0RL, England

Published by Roc, an imprint of New American Library, a division of Penguin
Group (USA) Inc. Previously published in a Roc trade paperback edition.

First Roc Mass Market Printing, May 2011
10 9 8 7

PUBLISHER'S NOTE
This is a work of fiction. Names, characters, places, and incidents either are
the product of the author's imagination or are used fictitiously, and any resemblance to actual persons, living or dead, business establishments, events, or
locales is entirely coincidental.

The publisher does not have any control over and does not assume any responsibility for author or third-party Web sites or their content.

TO JOHN RONALD REUEL AND ANNE INEZ,
WHOSE DRAGONS BIT ME, BUT GOOD

Travels
of

Wistala

Avenger
of the
Clutch

THE CESPINE

Barbarian
Lands

Blacklake
Kark
11

INLAND OCEAN

Hilpatian Empire

RED MOUNTAINS

5 4 6
2
10
12
1

Thallia
Vippian

Krakenoor

Shryesta

Bant

Ghioz

Mapshop
Thomas
Manning

9. Vesshall

8

BOOK ONE

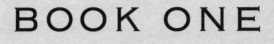

Hatchling

BETTER SEVEN RAGING DRAGONS AS YOUR
ENEMY THAN A SINGLE PATIENT DRAGONELLE.

—*Islebreadth*

Chapter 1

The cloudscapes and air currents, so pleasant to drift across, darkened. Her glittering green scales turned dull and slag. A vast black mass rolled overhead.

Thunder hit her ears, pounding thunder, relentless, unnaturally regular, pursuing her like hoofbeats.

She tipped her wings, dropped, tried to flee the storm, but the darkness overtook her. The feathery dimpling of the clouds below disappeared, replaced by a wet mist of confusion . . . suffocation. The darkness shot down her nostrils and into her lungs.

Out, out of this weather!

She tried to straighten her neck, form her body into an arrow, to dive out of the storm and take shelter, but her limbs wouldn't cooperate. She twitched, confused, fighting, unwilling to draw a breath of the storm's thick air.

Crack!

Am I lightning-struck? she thought.

Then the air came and she breathed, a gasp that infused her with new life, her limbs with strength. The mists faded, except for the booming thunder; she realized the noise in her ears was her own hearts. No clouds, no storm, no choking mists, just cramp and wet and a maddening irritation like insects biting under her scales.

She twisted, stretched, as though each of her four limbs,

neck, and tail were in a contest to get farthest away from the others, and then the world gave way—

—and she found herself on her side. Terror struck. *My belly is exposed!* and she fought to roll. Then her nostrils smelled it, a rich musky scent that set her at ease. Something sharper in the background, blood . . .

Blood! The smell of appetite and danger.

Dimpled, irregular surfaces all around, but hard and dark, quite the opposite of the clouds, an agonized squeaking near her . . .

Come out, Wistala, or Auron will have your breakegg meal.

I am Wistala.

She rolled her eye, tried to raise her *sii,* her tail, but instead of coiling ropes of muscle that could fell young trees, she saw stubby deformities trapped in bits of viscous-sided egg clinging to her like a net. Next to her, another green face, pale-pink fringe rising from her skull-ridge and folded this way and that as it descended along the neck. Her sister had her own problems: a head hardly out of her egg.

Too hard, Momma. I-Jizara cannot get out. The thought-words confused Wistala. Had they come from her? No, from the other green hatchling still trapped in her egg.

Jizara, Wistala, you must come out of your eggs. This is your first test, and you'll learn a valuable lesson. In any crisis, the first scale you must bite through is your own. Master your spirit, apply your mind, harness your body—then you will be able to break through difficulty.

Mother, big enough to be a world herself, rested against a curving wall of stone. She could not be taken in with a single glance. Wistala had to assemble her out of impressions: her endless tail, deep rushing heartbeat, mountainous haunches, softly whooshing breaths, folded wings, arching neck, elegantly fringed head with its shining golden-yellow eyes cut by deep black slits. A loving *prrum* started deep within Mother's throat, a drum-roll encouraging her daughters.

Wistala quit trying to go in six directions at once. She

employed all four limbs and her tail to get out of the con-
fining egg.

Tch-crick-crack!

And she was away from it.

But down again.

Her rear legs couldn't get purchase. A wet mass that
wasn't quite her and wasn't quite egg, attached at her underside, entangled newly uncurled toes. She let out a frustrated squawk.

She dragged herself, wanting that blood-smell, using her
cleared front legs, pulling foul anchor and bits of eggshell.

Wistala, how strong you are! Mother thought.

The smell also meant death. She saw a red-scaled hatchling lying dead on its side, blood still trickling from its torn
throat and stomach, brief life over already.

She knocked an empty broken egg out of her way, freed
one hind leg. She could see more of the cavern now. Her
mother rested on a ledge halfway up the side of the highest
part; the rest was like a dragon's muzzle, narrowing with
teeth in the form of dripping stones meeting, though in a
haphazard fashion when compared with a dragon's regular
rows.

Something moved at the edge of the precipice, and it
took her a moment to recognize it as another hatchling.
With its head down over the edge and its gray, black-
shadowed skin, her sibling resembled a heap of oddly
shaped stone.

It had no scales. A moment later she got a mind-picture
of a mighty grown gray dragon flying over a mountain that
hugged ice between its vast arms—some dream out of the
past or from her brother's future?

Her sibling turned on her, baleful red eyes under his
shieldlike eye crest wild and staring. He cocked his head at
her and tested the air with his tongue. With that, he strode
up to the corpse as though he owned the shelf and dug at
the succulent fresh flesh.

The fire left his eyes.

If he thought anything of, or at, her, she could not tell.

Help, Momma, please help, her sister thought.

Wistala wanted a mouthful of that feast, but suppose the gray hatchling objected? She looked behind, saw her sister still struggling against her egg. Jizara had managed to get her head and neck out, thanks to the sharp prong on her snout—*why, I have one, too*—but hadn't so much as cracked through with her back.

Too hard!

Wistala turned, slipped on the drogue still attached to her belly, and pushed herself clumsily sideways, still learning what her legs could and couldn't do, until she stood alongside her sister.

Come, Jizara, come with me to the blood-smell! A fine feast is disappearing down our brother's throat.

Jizara gave a dispirited peep, managed to break a little more eggshell with her neck. At this rate, nothing would be left!

Wistala felt her tail whipping back and forth, seemingly in a nasty mood of its own. She redirected it, and struck the side of her sister's egg—hard.

The egg cracked.

After that first opening, it was easy. Three sharp blows, and the whole side of the egg clung together, thanks only to a thin translucent membrane beneath. Her sister broke free, lay gasping and squeaking with the effort.

I see what you mean about the smell, her sister thought.

Jizara slunk forward, unable even to raise her forequarters and neck off the ground. The mass of broken egg still wrapped half her scrawny long-necked body.

Can you open your mouth?

Yes, her sister thought back.

Then hang on to my tail.

She felt the prick of tiny sharp teeth biting through the hardly-there scales. Using her forelegs and the untangled rear, Wistala pulled her sister free and toward the meal.

Her brother raised a blood-smeared snout, egg horn trailing bits of viscera, and cocked his head in that funny way of his. He let out a satisfied gassy noise that echoed off the egg shelf wall and trotted down to a trickle of water running down the side of the cavern wall. Wistala followed its musical path to a pool at the base, which was rimmed with thick growths of blue-green lichen. The lichen glowed like her brother's eyes, but in a far more soothing fashion.

But he left the feast to them.

Wistala tore into it. Better than any dream of flying, the smells and tastes and textures of meat transmitted by her own buds and nerves made the confusion of her hatching fade. The odd sensation of rended flesh sliding down her throat and the pleasant sensation of a filling belly mattered.

A coppery flash and blazing eyes landed atop the corpse. This hatchling held a bleeding forelimb tight to its narrow chest.

Wistala slid next to her sister, tripping on the cursed thing hanging from her belly, and the closing jaws of the copper just missed the air where her nose had been a moment ago.

She flattened herself against the rock, instinctively covering her vulnerable spots. The copper hatchling pounced on her sister, claws and teeth searing as it tried to drive her away from the meal Jizara was too weak to abandon.

Help, Mother! Wistala didn't know if the call came from one, both, or all three of them.

Wistala let out a challenge, but the battle cry of her dreams came out as a thin peep. It still startled the copper into turning.

It was fast, even with its wounded leg, and didn't have the wretched umbilical sac slowing and tripping it. She put her head down and butted him as hard as body mass allowed.

At least he left off attacking Jizara.

He opened his mouth, glaring at her from behind rows of teeth, and every instinct told her to retreat. Her back end showed its strange tendency to act of its own accord, and she backpedaled—but she showed her own teeth, giving as good as the copper had done.

He turned his head, grabbed a piece of the carcass's tail, and ran.

Her feeling of triumph vanished as her gray brother bounded up, coiling and uncoiling his body in a way

Wistala envied, covering ground in a run that was more a series of elastic leaps than footwork.

The copper scrambled off the egg shelf, clutching his meal.

Her scaleless brother screeched down at his opponent, long tail lashing back and forth so that it threatened to catch her across the nose. When he returned to the feast, he sniffed at Jizara's neck—What would she do if the gray male tried to make a meal of Jizara?

Wistala extended her neck—not so long as either of her siblings'—and began to lick her sister's wound.

The gray hatchling gave a snort and returned to his meal. He didn't seem to mind sharing. After eating, Mother lulled him off to sleep with a song, and Jizara dozed, bits of shell and membrane still on her limbs.

Wistala's sharp ears picked up the sound of claws and scales on rock. She crept to the edge of the egg shelf and looked down.

The copper rooted around in the waste near the trickle at the far end of the egg shelf. He appeared to be hunting. She wondered if he'd try to attack her siblings while they slept.

That's a male for you, Wistala. They're always satisfied with a win, even if the victory's incomplete.

He worries me, she thought back.

You're ahead of your brother and sister already. How well-formed your thoughts are! And the way you pulled your sister out of her egg. That ability will help you in the Upper World, when it comes time.

Pulling Jizara with my tail?

No, the ability to improvise.

Wistala wasn't sure what that thought meant. *Tell me about the Upper World. Is it like my dreams?*

Yes and no. But you should rest, little hatchling. Leave the worrying to me, for now.

The copper stared at her from the garbage pile. If Mother could see the hatred in his eye—

But sleep beckoned. And Wistala hoped that with sleep would come more dreams of flying.

Chapter 2

H atchlings! Your father has arrived. Come and know your sire."

Jizara left off complaining to Mother about having to eat her eggshell—Mother insisted it helped grow healthy scale, and Jizara claimed she just said that to get rid of the messy broken bits. Auron dropped Wistala's tail-tip, which he'd been biting.

The hatchlings smelled Father first, so quietly did he approach the egg shelf. The air around Mother smelled oily but comforting. Father's scent had a harder point as it went into the nostrils.

Wistala listened to the scrape of his scales and realized he was approaching the egg shelf in a back-and-forth manner, as though inspecting the cavern. She caught a gleam as he passed a thick growth of cave moss hanging from a crack in the ceiling.

Dwarves'-eye, Mother had called it.

Then she saw her father's head, six horns, bronze scales a blend of liquid gold and blood. So wide, even with wings folded tight against his spine, he made Mother look like a drakka. He walked oddly, limping, holding one leg up against his chest. Had he been maimed in his youth like her copper brother?

"AuRel, meet your hatchlings," Mother said, inclining

her head. "Auron, Wistala, and Jizara, out of their eggs in that order."

Next to her, Auron quivered when Father gave a snort as he sniffed the hatchlings. He barely acknowledged her or her sister. He ground his upper and lower jaw, setting his teeth clattering.

"Wistala is speaking already," Mother said.

"Which is she, again? The thick one?"

Thick one? Yes, she was bulkier than Jizara, who was all neck and tail.

"Greet your Father, hatchlings."

Auron extended his neck and peeped, a bit clumsily in his twitchiness.

"Hello, Father," Wistala said.

"Wel'ome home, Faszer," Jizara added.

"Was your hunt successful?" Mother asked, to break the silence.

"Not very. A sheep and a tired goat. I'm going to have to try in the foothills east."

"That means men," Mother said.

"I remember," Father said.

He reached out with his foreleg and dropped the carcasses. "You have the sheep, Irelia. The hatchlings can divide the goat."

"I'm full up on slugs," Mother said. Wistala only remembered Mother eating one slug, the slimy creatures that ate the cave moss, bat droppings, even dragon waste. "Let them eat. Eat, you three."

The hungry hatchlings tore into the bled-out feast. Not a trace of warmth was left, but their appetites were such that it didn't matter.

"I'm for sleep," Father said, winding himself around a towering stalagmite. But his tail still thrashed and his teeth ground.

"What's the matter?" Mother asked. "I've no appetite, honestly."

"It's not that."

"What, then?"

"There weren't any grays on *my* side of the family," Father grumbled.

With that they fell into an argument over Auron's merits.

Wistala couldn't think of many, unless being a nuisance counted as a merit. Mother changed his mood by praising him for siring two males—the skulking copper counted, as he seemed to be surviving on his own somewhere in the cavern. As Wistala understood it, all the males fought after their hatching until one became the champion of the nest. She and her sister were afterthoughts.

Auron finished his gorge and then, hearing the copper at the base of the egg shelf, jumped down to chase him off.

Perhaps Mother read her mind. She brought her head close to Father's, began to clean him behind his *griff,* the armored fans that descended from his horn-crest.

"Oh, of course," Father said. With that he disappeared into the darkness beyond the moss light. When he returned, he had a bulge in the side of his cheek.

"Here you are—"

You can do better than that! Wistala overread Mother think.

"—my little treasures," Father continued, a little lamely. He dropped some things before them that rattled as they fell. "Gems for my gems."

They glittered enticingly. They were stones of a dozen different colors, cut and polished to catch light and throw it back broken into dozens of pieces. Jizara squealed in delight. Wistala thought them marvelous, and she joined her sister in placing them into colorful spiral patterns.

Father sagged with weariness, his smell no longer sharp and strange but a comforting shield between them and the forbidding shadows of the cavern. She would grant the Gray Vex that much: he plunged into the darkness readily enough, despite his lack of protective scales.

She and Jizara encircled the dazzle their father called *gems,* lying snout to tail-tip to form an unbroken wall of hatchling between jealous world and hoard. As they nodded off, Mother sang:

> *Daughter, daughter, shining bright*
> *Precious jewel within mine sight*
> *Oh, if I could soar with thee*
> *As you seek your destiny.*
>
> *To see with you the caves and skies*
> *Vistas grand beneath your eyes*
> *Taking wing to horizons new*
> *Let us wonder who waits for you.*
>
> *A dragon bright?*
> *A dragon dark?*
> *Victor of duels with battle mark?*
> *A dragon strong?*
> *A dragon keen?*
> *Singer of honors and triumphs seen?*
>
> *Red, Gold, Bronze, and Blue*
> *To your lord you shall be true,*
> *Copper, Silver, Black, and White,*
> *Who will win your mating flight?*
>
> *For in your hearts our future rests*
> *To see our line with hatchlings blessed*
> *And for those who threaten clutch of flame,*
> *To feel the wrath of dragon-dame.*

Chapter 3

The last fragments of eggshell disappeared, and in time the gems did, as well.

Mother neither ate nor slept, as far as Wistala could tell, save for a slug or two, and a whole horse Father brought back along with a dirty-smelling monster Mother insisted was a human. To Wistala he smelled like a two-day-dead sheep not properly bled and gutted. Auron got the honor of hunting and eating him.

Wistala watched the Gray Vex disappear with Father. "Auron's crest must be made of gold, the way you favor him," Wistala said to Mother.

"Don't whine, Tala," she said. "You and your sister have a whole horse to share. That's ten times a man or more." Mother had already consumed hers, and was licking the last runnels of blood from her teeth and lip-line. She sighed, and her golden eyes brightened. "Eat those metal rings from the saddle. They're good for you."

"I'd rather be hunting that man," Wistala said.

"You'll be hunting on your own soon enough," Mother replied. "Practice on slugs."

"They're a bore. Tell us more of the Upper World," Wistala said. "Fish leaping at waterfalls!"

"I want to hear about Father's mating song again," Jizara said. Jizara liked to imitate the tunes, and even Auron admitted that she had a gift for song. "Did he really cause an avalanche?"

Mother's stories always entertained. She mixed words and pictures and sense-memory so skillfully, Wistala felt as though she were living it.

"No, you shall have a lesson."

Both sisters drooped at that. Lessons came only through Mother's words, and one had to form one's own imagery and sensations. Learning about The Hatchling Who Cried "Dwarf" or The Geese That Saved the Seven-Egg Clutch couldn't compare.

"Since you've both seen and smelled a man today, I'll tell you about the Great Betrayal. A man had a hand in that."

Jizara closed a nostril at Wistala. She stifled a snort and tried to clear her thoughts so she might summon her own mind-pictures.

"As you know, the Age of Dreams ended when the ravenous Blighters appeared. The Four Great Spirits of Earth, Air, Water, and Fire each gave a gift to Dragons to make them supreme over the Upper and within the Lower Worlds to tame the foul Blighters. But while fighting over their reward for this deed, they created the Dwarves, Elves, and Men who now come to kill us. Men are the worst. Men, who breed so fast that a single female in a dragon's lifetime can produce a nation, like a small rock falling from a mountain's height can knock two that send six rolling that create a landslide. All of that horde seek to kill us.

"But it wasn't always so.

"For a time, the hominid races were just as terrified of us as the blighters were. Now back in the Age of Sky-Kings, all blighters did was grovel and worship before dragons, but the other hominids helped the dragons build great palaces and towers. The greatest dragon hall of all the kingdoms was Silverhigh, built out of leftover pieces from the creation of the Moon, so white it shone night and day.

"Now the Dragons of Silverhigh were oh-so-pleased

with themselves to be living in such glorious palaces. The older, battle-scarred dragons who remembered taming the blighters and cowing the men, elves, and dwarves became fewer and fewer. Their hatchlings grew up thinking the luxuries Silverhigh offered were theirs on account of their being born such fine fellows, forgetting that anything worth the having is worth the effort. They painted their scales and wings in magnificent designs but hardly ever flew anywhere with them, as there was no finer place in the world than Silverhigh.

"Flying off to fight battles and so on does interfere with stuffing oneself with grain-fattened swine and golden coins brought in tribute. So the later Dragon Kings of Silverhigh looked for someone else to do their fighting for them.

"Blighters are quarrelsome, and only a skilled leader can unite them. Dwarves, though resolute fighters, are stumpy and slow moving, and are not given to taking orders without a good deal of backtalk and complaining, and only by the harshest measure can they be cowed for a brief time. Elves, though dragonlike in their intelligence, will stop in the middle of a campaign to feast and sing and praise each other for deeds they've still to do, and forget about battle altogether. But men are easily trained and pop out young like heated corncobs, so they are well-suited to fill armies.

"Thus the Dragons of Silverhigh trained a grand army of men to go and do their fighting. This gave them even more time for play.

"Now there was one man who was particularly useful to the Dragons of Silverhigh. His name was Prymelete, and he was not a famous warrior or a great builder or even a man skilled at bringing delectables from near and far to tempt dragon appetites. Prymelete was a soothsayer. He praised the Dragons of Silverhigh even more than they did each other. Many a high vault and gold-walled nesting chamber saw his presence, as he read flattering oracles predicting future greatness.

"Prymelete's tongue arts admitted him to the deepest councils of the Silverhigh Dragons, places no famous warrior, great builder, or clever trader were allowed. They even gave him a seat at the Firepit. Now I'm told the most renowned of the Silverhigh Dragons spat fire into the Firepit when making judgments and rules to show their mind had been made up. So much dragonfire went into the Firepit that it burned night and day. Of course, Prymelete outdid himself with praise for the dragons who met around the Firepit; his tongue left them so muddle-headed, they didn't know tailvent from nostril.

"Then one day Prymelete lingered, watching the fire after the dragons left. He took from his vast cloak a thick steel vessel such as human warriors wear on their heads and dipped it in the dragonfire. Then he ran like a hoard-filch. He left Silverhigh and went to a dark council of men, elves, and dwarves, carrying his dragonfire.

"The dragonfire had cooled by the time he met this evil gathering, and he filled the wine cups of the hominids assembled there. They all drank from it, and it put dragonfire into their hearts that made them brave enough to challenge the dragons. The hominids marched on Silverhigh and threw down its perches and vaults and galleries, and suffocated its deeps and wells and chambers."

"Why didn't the dragons fight?" Wistala asked.

"Some say it is because they'd forgotten how," Mother answered. "Others say Prymelete returned from his trip and put more folly in their heads, pronounced doom and despair at the approach of warlike men, elves, and dwarves, so that they did not go and fight with the parts of their grand army of men who remained loyal to their oaths. Then when the abandoned men were destroyed, Prymelete redoubled his predictions of disaster. The dragons were so used to abiding by the soothsayings of Prymelete that they panicked and fled, or hid in deep holes to be hunted and killed one by one."

"What happened to wicked Prymelete?" Jizara asked.

"There are different stories, but I shall tell you this one: Other dragons from the far side of the world heard about the destruction of Silverhigh and came to seek after their relatives. Finding them slaughtered, they learned the story from some blighters and sought out Prymelete. Since he places himself above dragons, they took him to a high mountain and hung him there by his fine girdle to be pecked at by the great carrion birds who ride the winds of the thin-air heights. When his body fell apart and went down the mountainside, they brought the bones back to the high ledge to give the carrion birds another meal, and there they sit, cold and exposed."

"Tales and terrors, that's a horrible story, Mother," Jizara said. "Dragons hunted and killed in their own homes. I'm scared."

"I tell it to you so you will always be on your guard. Ever since that awful day, the hominids have had fire in their hearts to kill dragons. And so it will be until the happy day, as my mother used to say, when all the hominids kill each other off and the dragons may return from hiding. But I fear that day is far, far off. That is why I'm always listening."

Chapter 4

I f you're patient enough, and keep still, out of sight and smell, the prey will feed itself right up to you.

Mother's words echoed in Wistala's memory as she waited for a slug above the cave moss. According to Mother, it was spring aboveground, and snow was melting and finding its way into their cave, feeding flush new growth of moss. And with the moss came more slugs.

She clung, upside down, content to just roll her eyes as she searched for a pale, slow-moving back. Sometimes you could hear the soft slurp, like dragon tongue against the roof of one's mouth, but with water dribbling and dripping into the cave from a hundred inlets, hunting by ear was impossible. With so many old trails crisscrossing the cavern floor, the nose was useless unless one came upon a still-slimy trail. So that left watching.

Of course, she had more to worry about than being able to properly push off, turn, and land near enough to the slug so she could catch it on the drop or the first pounce. The Gray Vex was prowling and snuffling around near the waterfall whose pool fed her slug. It would be just like him to come blundering through in that off-kilter leaping style of his, scaring every slug away until the next scale-shed.

"With every day closer to drakehood, he'll be more

restless," Mother had said. "Then he'll wander out and never return. Or your father will drive him out."

"How many more days?" Jizara had asked, probing the hole left by a missing scale where Auron had pounced on her.

"You'll think differently when he's gone. I know I did with my brother Culekin—Wind Spirit knows what's become of him."

Drakka usually stayed closer to their home caverns until a new clutch of eggs came, or so Mother predicted. But Mother needed at least a year in the Upper World to get her strength back, during which she'd teach them much huntcraft. Then she'd fly with Father—

Snick-snick-snick-snick came the sound of Auron's claws as he tore through the moss patch, nose held to the ground and *griff* half extended. Probably following the copper's scent again.

So much for hunting.

She aimed, kicked off, and dropped. Twisting as she fell, she landed in a patch of cave moss with half a mind to pounce the Gray Vex, but by the time she gathered herself, his tail-tip had disappeared toward the pool. Whatever else might be said of her brother, he *was* fast.

Wistala turned, and froze.

Two hard eyes the color of flowing blood stared into hers. The copper!

They stood nose-tip to nose-tip, the copper a trifle smaller and a good deal lighter. His scales had come in small and crooked, and his maimed *sii* had turned in toward his body, though he propped himself up by the forejoint.

He lowered his *griff* a claw-breadth or two, pulled back his lips to reveal his rows of teeth. She backed up, sidestepped, and he advanced, matching her, nostrils opposite hers as though she were playing a game in the cavepool, trying to outwit her reflection.

"What's my name?" he asked.

The question, put in simple Drakine, stunned her so she hardly understood what he said. He may as well have spoken one of the more obscure Elvish dialects to her.

"Wha—?"

"What's my name?" he asked again, and this time she found an answer.

"I don't know."

"Out of my way or I'll kill you," he said.

His eyes kept flicking in the direction Auron had taken. Wistala didn't know what he expected to accomplish. He was smaller than she, and Auron was bigger still, at least in length. Auron had bested the copper in every contest they'd had. She should bleat a warning, scream and have Auron come running as he did when they came out of their eggs.

But the Gray Vex had a big enough head. A bite or two would do him good.

She ate a few dead dropped bats on her way back to the egg shelf, upset for some reason. They made slugmeat taste like fresh horse, but her gut needed something to work on beyond vague worry.

She climbed up onto the egg shelf. Jizara was matching herself against Mother's tail-tip, standing up when it stood, rolling when it rolled, a *prrum* in her throat.

"Mother, I was hunting slugs, and—"

"Earth Spirit," Jizara said. "You get any thicker, and your tail will disappear!" Jizara proudly displayed her long, lean tail, and she never tired of matching her extremities to those of her stumpier sister.

"Jizara, don't tease. Wistala, you're all latent wingbone, as I was, and short limbs are the stronger for it." Mother, despite the more plentiful meals since the melt began, was breathing audibly from the effort of the tail game.

"Mother, the copper is after Auron."

Mother stared, long and slow, out into the depths of the cave. "I'd hoped he'd left. Auron may kill him. Your father never knows when to back down either."

"Maybe they'll do each other in," Jizara said. "We'll have more food and a little quiet."

"Every hatchling is precious," Mother said. "There are few enough left, and it's the rare drake who grows to dragonhood these days."

"If there are fewer drakes, that means fewer songs sung to dragonelles," Jizara said.

"Well, in the North—"

"Mother! Mother! Mother!" came a hatchling's shout. "Others! Assassins, dwarves, here in the cave." Auron jumped clean to the egg shelf, his stripes hard and black against his skin and blood running from behind his crest. Wistala heard metal ring against stone somewhere in the cave, felt her scales rise.

Mother swept her tail around Wistala and her sister, putting her body between whatever approached and her daughters. "We are discovered?"

Auron turned this way and that, going in three directions at once. "They're here. With spears, Mother."

Mother looked out into the gloom of the cavern. "No! I'm faint with hunger, and the winter's been so—"

Mother reached up with her long neck and put her mouth about a loose stalactite. She wrenched it free, and Wistala felt air move. "I hope you aren't too big for this, my hatchlings. Auron, take your sisters and go to the surface. At once! Climb, my love, climb." She shoved Wistala up the wall with her nose.

Wistala climbed toward the patch of shadow with the faintly new air flowing down from it.

Wistala looked down at the egg shelf, where chaos ruled. Jizara clung to Mother's leg, all eyes and bristling scales and fluttering *griff*. Auron stood at the egg shelf, tail twitching, crest-shrouded eyes fixed on ranks of approaching mounds of metal and muscle, short-legged fellows with beards that glowed like fire. Had they drunk some latter-day dragonfire before charging into the cavern?

She almost lost her grip with her *sii* as she counted the numbers. Behind the dwarves, she saw what she took to be an exceptionally tall dwarf or broad man in black armor. The tall figure wore a winged helm and gestured with a broad-headed spear that sparked and glowed as though it had a life of its own. He pointed it toward the egg shelf, and dwarves bearing some kind of wood-and-metal con-traption on their backs hurried up a broken stalagmite.

With his other hand, he held the straining lines of a pack of hairy-backed dogs the size of ponies.

Mother, her head level with Wistala and imploring Jizara to release her grip, must have seen them, too. Wistala got a brief thought—*Him! Gobold has sold us out!*—before Mother reached down and picked Auron up by the base of his neck. She threw him into the air toward the hole. Auron twisted as he flew and struck next to Wistala at the opening. Wistala reached and held him as he found his grips. As he breathed, Auron's ribs moved so fast, they were a blur.

Dwarven climbing poles struck the egg shelf with a *klank!*

"Climb! Auron, climb!" Mother called.

Jizara, we're up here. Climb with us! Wistala thought, but her sister retreated behind Mother's hindquarters as the first dwarf-helm appeared over the rim of the egg shelf. Jizara looked up at her, stupidly, not even recognizing her. *Sister!*

Scrring came the sound like an arrow in her ear. She saw blades flash silver in the lichen-light as they were drawn.

Auron drove his crest into her side, and the tenuous connection vanished. *Wistala, up and away!* came Mother's last frantic thought, and with it a horrible, clawing fear that blinded and deafened. Wistala fled upward.

Ku! Ku! Kuuuuuu! came the war cries from below. The sound traveled through rock and ice.

Dead lichen, ice, and loose rock gave way, dropping onto Auron, who was following below. Vague flashes came through—*Blood—spears—Wheel of Fire Drakossozh—Yellhounds! Jizara!*

Death cries and madness pursued her up the shaft. Up she climbed, up until there were no more sounds echoing from below, up until *sii* and *saa* both burned and quivered and the hatchlings had to cling to each other with tail and mouth, up until blood-taste coated their tongues with each breath and the hammering in their neck hearts made their ears ache. Wistala pushed through bone and dead dry pine needles in utter darkness, no longer climbing but not walking either. The darkness unnerved her. Not even dragon eyes could pick out detail, and at every moment she feared the terrible sound of blades being drawn.

She fetched up against something cold and wet—an ice flow blocked the tunnel. She could still feel air moving from a crack at the top, a crack that could hardly fit her snout. What little remained of her ebbing strength vanished.

"Auron, we're trapped," she said, hardly able to get the words out. A last hope flickered: perhaps the dwarves and that tall wing-helmed man had been defeated. "We have to go back down. Perhaps Mother and Jizara—"

"No," Auron said. Dully, she observed that he was hardly panting, though he moved stiffly. Of course, he was lighter, being scaleless. Auron sniffed at the clean, cold air coming in over the ice flow. "Fresh air. We're almost there."

"That's why you don't want to go back. Your thin hide—"

Auron shoved her aside. Her brother simply went mad. There was no other word for it. He began to pound the ice with his tail. Pieces, tiny pieces of ice compared to the mass, flaked off and slid down to the bones at the bottom of the tunnel. She wondered if this was the raging fighting fury that Mother said took over young drakes. He bit and clawed at the ice whenever he shifted position.

When his tail began to spray blood at each swipe, he spat at the ice. The spittle hissed as it struck, and it ran into fractures, raising a sharp odor of bat urine.

"Wistala, spit!"

"I've no fire yet—"

Excrement and excuses. *It is melting the ice,* she realized. She tried to squeeze her fire bladder behind her breastbone. Nothing.

"Spit, Wistala!"

"Can't!"

Then she could see. A faint pink light came through the ice flow. It must be the light of the Upper World, the sun.

Two cracks ran up the ice flow, parallel and in a shape

oddly reminiscent of the man with the spear's winged helm. She pictured the helm at the base of the cracks—Something spasmed behind her breastbone, and she found she could spit. Found she could—she had no choice. Her tongue pressed itself against the roof of her mouth, and her jaw opened wide—

Out it came, until she felt as though her vertebrae from shoulder-pivot to tail-tip might be running up her neck and out her mouth. An orangish light filled the cave along with the acid smell, stronger than ever.

She collapsed, spent in an entirely new way.

Auron gathered himself, curled tight, and exploded toward the orange glow like a projectile from one of the dwarves' war machines.

He broke through in a shower of yellow-white shards—

And disappeared straight over a ledge.

Wistala struck out from her shoulders, extended her neck even as his tail-tip whipped for a hold. She sank her teeth into it, tasted her brother's blood in her mouth. His momentum dragged her forward, toward the ledge. Impossible distances stretched off in every direction, out, to either side.

Especially down. Her head went over.

A drop, a thousand times greater than that of the egg shelf, lay beneath. The vast distance seemed to reach up and touch her between the eyes. Her head swam. . . .

Her teeth, however, gripped all the tighter as her short legs found purchase. She arched her thick back, claws dug into ice, rock, and hardened snow, setting every haunch against her brother's weight.

Auron found a grip, and his weight vanished. She didn't release his tail, though, until he rolled beside her on the ledge.

The two hatchlings shivered against each other, panting in the thin air of the Upper World.

Chapter 5

*D*on't think about this big, empty, howling chaos that is the Upper World, Wistala told herself for the beyond-countingeth time. *Or how much you miss Mother, even her endless lessons. Or dwarves. Or eager, straining hounds. Don't think beyond the next meal. Just find food, and then rest. Find food, and then rest.*

They made it down the mountain, thanks to Auron. His light weight allowed him to test holds for her, and they'd come off the horrid, cold mountaintop and into a slightly less horrid, slightly less cold tree line, where Auron promptly scared away some feeding goats by leaping at them at first whiff. She had no luck hunting after that, and it was only after they developed a system where he'd drive game to her, or she to him, as his skin naturally changed color to match whatever he rested against, that they were able to eat.

Auron had a plan to find Father. She went along with it. Having a goal, "a star to fix on," put hope in his hearts and stopped him from crying in his sleep at night. She listened, learned to find Susiron, the unchanging star, by following the nose-tip of the Bowing Dragon.

Wistala suspected that, small as they were, it was just a matter of time until something got them. The only question was what—and where and when. At one point she thought Auron had died in the night, taken by the frigid wind on his scaleless skin, for when she woke, he was white and cold, until he stirred and she realized he'd just been mimicking the snow.

She hoped that as they traveled west around the shoulder of the mountain toward the main entrance to the cave—Auron had some idea of the topography, thanks to mind-pictures from Father—they'd find a quiet mountain lake where they could spend the coming spring and summer, feeding on frogs and fat bottom-sucking fish. Perhaps they could find a hollow log and enough muck to hide their smell. When one didn't have a cave, one had to improvise. Without a safe refuge, it was only a matter of time before something got them.

"Quit saying that," Auron said. "We're doing all right. We've adapted to the Upper World, at least what we've seen of it."

Auron trotted fearlessly through the Upper World, turning from brown to green to white as the surface he paused over changed. Wistala felt that every step she took was through an endless arena under thousands of eyes peeping at her from treetop and slidepile. Voices relayed what the eyes saw, berry-brained birds tittered about the hatchlings passing beneath, not caring a dead twig whose ears might hear of their movements.

Having every field mouse know of their passing bothered her.

Then there was the dirtiness of the Upper World. As she passed through thickets, pine needles and branches caught under her scales; pebbles had an uncanny knack for working themselves inward rather than out, resisting any but the most determined effort of tooth and tongue to extract them. She lost scales in pursuit of biting and stinging insects, stopping to probe and dig for them as Auron stamped impatiently. His leathery skin couldn't turn arrows, but it kept out the flies admirably.

Then the storm hit. Winds screamed up from the southwest, pursued by lightning and thunder, more terrifying than ten thousand stamping dwarves on the march. They found shelter, if the notch between two boulders could be called shelter, and waited it out.

Auron talked her into trying the rainwater. Its clean taste seemed to clear her mind and wash away the thoughts of danger and doom. It was the first sensation in the Upper World she enjoyed. She stuck out her tongue and let the water run off the boulder, onto her tongue, and into her jowls, where it could be easily swallowed.

And—Sun-bless the Water Spirit—the rain washed her scales clean. She stretched and rippled and lifted her scales to the invigorating flow. *Take that, sticky pine sap! Better luck next hatchling, bloodbugs!* Even the faint sparking smell in the air from a nearby lightning strike gave her hearts new life.

The rain left the valleys to the south and west clear; individual branches stood out in the storm-washed air. Anything was possible. Finding Father, even. Then the dwarves would taste their own blood and tears.

The rain slackened, and the hatchlings found plentiful soft worms driven to the surface by the moisture. Auron tried to snap his up, but Wistala found that they went down faster and easier if one simply inhaled with one's lips tight around the worm. Auron thumped his tail in appreciation as she showed him the trick.

"Clever," Auron said, giving a faint *prrum*. "You know how to find a meal's weak spot."

"Father will boil those dwarves in their own skin," she said, more of a mind for vengeance than compliments.

"To do that, he'd have to dig them out of their own holes," Auron said. "I have a mind-picture of a dwarf fortress from Father. It's all sheer rocks and towers and gates and arrow-slits."

"Father shared more with you."

"And Mother more with you."

"Think of it. Think hard. I'll try."

Auron's eyes screwed up in concentration. Wistala got a flash or two, grim towers around a mountain lake, an overhanging rock, a pounding sound, craft on the lake like water beetles—and then it left.

"Now it's going fuzzy," Auron said.

"Stop trying. I got some of it. Who are they?"

"They're some dwarves Father saw at some point. To the north of the cave."

"Dragons must kill them one day. Or they'll come into other caves."

"The only day we can count on is today," he said.

She nuzzled her brother. She'd never felt this close to Jizara, and even Mother had been more presence than person. Perhaps it was the way they depended on each other.

She settled down next to Auron as he made himself miserable and tore up the turf with his *sii*. She formed a resolve—perhaps a silly one, with her being so young, but she would grow, and the resolve would not die unless she let it. Auron would have to take care of their line. She'd protect the lines of others:

> *And for those who threaten our ancient fame,*
> *To feel the wrath of dragon-dame.*

The horse smell the next day made Wistala hungry. But they weren't wild horses. They came with blankets and saddles and lines and other accoutrements of the hominids. She also smelled a cold fire, which could only mean hominids—dragonflame, even old, had a greasy smell. Auron counted better than thirty horses in a high meadow, and they decided to climb to avoid the chance of running across sharp-eyed elves in the mountainside forest.

By Auron's calculation, they were on the same part of the mountain as the western entrance Father used. They moved, taking extra care, staying low behind brush or fallen timber. That approach limited their vision of the landscape, but more important, it also limited their enemies'. As the sun set, they crossed another high meadow, bellies tight to cool earth.

"Nearly there, Tala," Auron said when she tired. "See that point of rock? Like a claw held out? The cave mouth's just on the other side."

Wistala saw Father first, high to the north, his bronze scales shimmering in the sun.

"Auron! Auron . . . *look*," she gasped.

With limp four-leggeds clutched in his *sii*, Father tipped his wings and began to descend, floating down through the air like water feeding into a cavern crack.

Auron let out a glad cry and leaped away, dashing for the stone prominence. Wistala stood and waved her neck, trying to catch Father's eye, but the dragon kept his head to the dangerous dark just inside the cave mouth, examining his landing spot from a variety of altitudes and angles. Why wouldn't he just look round?

She caught up to Auron in time to see him sag against the outcropping, neck and tail drooping.

"Father didn't see me."

Wistala choked back a wail.

The cave mouth showed signs of ancient construction, ruined battlements and cracked towers about wide creeper-hung mouth. Father must have considerable flying skill to land inside without disturbing the overgrowth.

Spilled rock covered the whole mountainside beneath the cave mouth. Moss grew thick out of the wind between the rocks.

Betrayed! The Wheel of Fire!

The power of Father's mind sent a shudder down her long spine. Not so precisely modulated as Mother's mind-speech, Father's was all emotion and imagery. Auron's mind-picture of the dwarf hold, though this time as clear and painful as naked sunlight, burned into her brain. A roar she felt through the rock as much as she heard emerged from the cave, as though the mountain itself were screaming from its broken-toothed mouth.

After the roar came the dwarven battle cry she'd heard before: *Ku! Ku! Kuuuuu!*

Father's pain and need came through to her, as hard and bright as his gemstones they'd thoughtlessly gobbled. She felt wounds as Father emerged, a dwarf with legs set tight against his neck, hacking at Father's scaly spine with a bloody ax as though trying to cut a tree dodging out of the way.

Off, off my back, you klut!

Wistala could feel the dwarf on her back, winced at the blows. She threw herself off the rock, rolled in the meadow as battle horns blew in the valley below.

"Above you!" Auron shouted in a voice louder than she'd have given him credit for. Then Auron, too, gave in to Father's pain, and he rolled himself into a ball.

Flee!

She saw Father flapping north, plucking spears from his hide, got another flash of the dwarf halls around the lake. He couldn't mean to go into battle again!

In the valley below, from hiding places in the mossy rocks, elven heads watched him go.

"Wistala, lie flat!" The words came fast as Auron told her to let him lead the elves away. She would go north and find Father.

Her hearts almost ceased beating at the thought of her brother leaving her. "Blades and raids, let's run. I want us to be with each other, no matter what."

"One of us has to make it, Wistala. You hunt better than I. You have a chance of making it alone in the wilderness."

"I don't know the way!"

"Follow the mountains north. You can't miss this lake—it's on this side of the mountains and very big." He gave her his fuzzy mind-picture again, but it didn't matter. She'd never make it—

Auron touched her nose, managed a choking *prrum* as he pushed her into a crevice.

He listened to the hoofbeats of the approaching elves. "Go to Father. Follow the Bowing Dragon. Follow Susiron. Father is there!"

"Auron, I can't—"

"Yes, you can. Don't waste time."

Auron hurried into the meadow, in the open for everyone to see. High above, wheeling hawks altered course and moved to fly over him. They cried out, and were answered by horns from the valley.

He can't be leaving! He can't he can't he can't . . .

She called to him with her mind, called him brave and good and sent all the love she couldn't find words for, reaching to touch his mind if not his soft gray skin.

"Good-bye, sister."

He'd never called her sister before.

He never would again.

Wistala cried, alone, and not one living thing in the Upper World cared.

Chapter 6

arkness settled on the mountainside before Wistala moved again. All the time she waited, she had to choke back little peeping hatchling cries. A day ago, she would have put her neck on an oath that she couldn't keen like a still-wet hatchling anymore, but the sight of her brother leading the elves away from her and to his doom brought the sound—whether she liked it or not.

She waited until long after dark, hoping that Auron would return, galumphing out of the mountainside mists with eyes ablaze and a tail-thumping story of outwitting the elves.

She looked into the valley in the direction Auron had disappeared. Campfires dotted the area around the meadow where they'd come across the unsaddled horses. She heard no baying of hounds, saw no torches in the trees indicating a hunt still on. But Auron was quick, perhaps—

No. You're alone now. They're all assassinated.

Except Father. Gone north, to some dwarven fortress by a lake. The clouds thickened; another storm might be working up.

She couldn't just leave. She and Auron deserved some mark to show they'd lived and breathed and seen. She went to the ledge where they'd watched Father fight the elves and dwarves. She extended a thick *saa*-claw and scored a pair of marks into the lee side of the stone.

Though she took her time, the result certainly didn't match the fabled artistry of Silverhigh—it looked like something a bored blighter might carve into his cave wall: two dragons, mirror images, circling each other as though guarding the other's back.

"We'll always be together here, Auron. This stone won't forget."

She crept up the hill, moving away from the rocky prominence.

Going up a mountain can sometimes save you travel around its base, but that wasn't the case for Wistala. Without a second pair of eyes to keep watch as she moved, she had to pause every hundred lengths or so, to watch and listen and pick a route for her next creep.

The cave also drew her from the heights. This time, instead of screaming, the mouth of the cave seemed to call to her. Home ... home ... home, the egg shelf, the trickles, the patches of moss and easily caught slugs.

And she had to know.

Perhaps at the last moment Mother had shoved Jizara into the chimney, the way she tossed Auron. Or both sides, having torn each other to pieces, had retreated to lick the blood from their wounds.

She hazarded an entry by the roof. The elves and dwarves would be less likely to watch the top. While difficult and tiring, it would be infinitely safer to go that way.

Once closer to the mouth of the cave, traveling through knots of creeper where a hominid could barely crawl and cling, she examined the ancient battleworks. Dwarves or blighters had broken up pieces of mountain and rebuilt them into walls and chambers, sealing them with something that felt—and tasted, she explored a crack with her tongue—like long-dried mud, only harder.

The view from the top of the cave mouth made her dizzy and disoriented. Not so much from the distance she could see even in the dark, for dragon eyes opened wide, or from the height to the rock spill below, but from the sense that she'd seen this view before. Sensory impressions from Mother, no doubt.

Below and at the bottom of the rock spill, a tiny camp-fire guttered with hominid forms sleeping around it. Woven bags containing some kind of prize gleaned from the fight—perhaps dragonscale? The nets were too widely woven to hold Father's gems from the small hoard Auron had told her about and which she and Jizara had played with before greedily devouring. If a sentry watched the cavern, he was well concealed.

She reversed herself and entered the cave at slug speed. There were no end of grips for her probing *sii* and *saa,* and if her tail wasn't so long as Auron's, her rather stumpy limbs were a good deal stronger than his. The great hump of muscle on her back that would one day power her wings—assuming she survived the passage of the season-circles—took over when she clung to just rest.

Detritus of a battle could be smelled below. Dragonblood—dwarf *loathsome reek!*—and fainter scents like bruised mint-herbs that may have been elf.

The cave twisted and turned, and at one corner, she descended to the cave floor to pant and rest her muscles. She might have become lost on the way down, as the cave branched out twice, but thanks to the spatterings of dragonblood, the trail was easily followed. When she started to come across cave moss again, she returned to the ceiling.

She let out a hatchling mew—the noise took her by surprise—as she entered the cave, a tiny skulking shadow of one of Father's glad returns with *sii* full of feast for his hungry hatchlings.

Alarmed at the noise, she spent a long time looking, listening, and smelling. Except for the odor of dragonblood and the faint foreign smell of dwarf, the cave smelled no different; indeed, it was achingly familiar, so much so that it was all she could do to keep from running to the egg shelf.

The familiar patterns of the faintly glowing cave moss pulled at her. How could the splashes of light remain unchanged when everything else had? It should re-form itself into spear points and daggers and arrows and—

Something lay on the egg shelf.

She lost her grip, didn't even right herself as she plum-
meted, and only a patch of cave moss saved her serious
injury.

The egg shelf shielded what lay up there. Most of it,
anyway. She crept, mindlessly as a slug, toward the shelf. A
broken ax-blade slid as she trod on it, and she froze, listening. Nothing but her own heartbeat answered.

She climbed up to the egg shelf.

It wasn't Mother. It was mother's size, certainly, but
mother had skin, glowing green dragonscale that changed
color as it rose and turned according to mood and body
temperature.

Mother also had a head. And *sii*. And *saa*. And tail.
And great leathery wings that could cover the whole egg
shelf when extended. Not tendrils of cave moss exploring
and thriving on what it found as it crept up her back.

She stood in the cave moss consuming Mother, engulf-
ing her like a growing, grasping soft claw.

Wistala's body no longer obeyed her. It jerked and
shook as she walked, walked away, turned her back, and
shut her nose to the sickly-sweet smell, tripping clumsily
like a hatchling fresh out of the egg. She hurried to the
trickle at the end of the egg shelf, sat under it, let water fall
and wash her scales clean.

Then she saw her sister.

They'd done the same to Jizara, then tossed her on the
dragon-waste pile. The thing that had been her sister was
mostly obscured by devouring cave moss, but even moss
couldn't hide that the tail she'd once been so proud of, her
lovely elegant tail. . . .

A shrieking, whistling cry came up her throat, and she
didn't care if the dwarves came again. Once her head was
off, she'd have no more images of this, this *butchery*. How
could her mind carry this for the remainder of her life?

She ran all the way to the egg shelf, where it turned into
hardly a ledge, drove herself against the cave wall, vaguely
aware of a racking sound coming from somewhere deep
in her chest. She rubbed her fringe against a sharp rock.
Some old scales were coming loose up there, and it would

be just as well to be rid of them sooner, and the pain wasn't bad at all; in fact, it was a bit of a relief as—

"Sister?"

Auron?

She looked off the shelf, heart leaping and body ready to join it—

And saw the copper. Thinner and more haggard than ever. The copper stood, leaning a little as he balanced on his crippled limb's joint.

"They killed her, Jiz—" His voice was only superficially like Auron's after all; he still had some hatchling inflections.

"I'm Wistala. You're no brother to me. You had a tooth in this." She felt her fanlike *griff* expand. Though she had no crest to rattle them against, they could still flutter angrily, she found.

"They lied," the copper said, but she launched herself off the ledge, jaws agape and *sii* reaching for him. "A bloody cave, no hoard—"

He dodged as she landed, took advantage of her being off balance to throw himself across her neck. "We need to overcome this, put it behind. Unite. The past can't be changed!" he said.

Wistala squirmed, couldn't break free. She gathered her limbs under her body. "No. But it can be avenged." She lifted herself with all four limbs and her tail, pushing forward.

The copper tipped.

And she struck him, *sii*, teeth, even dealt shoulder blows, trying to tip him so his vulnerable underbelly would be exposed, *gutted and thrown on the waste heap to feed the lichen!*

She tried to claw at his eyes, but her *sii* just rattled off his crest and *griff*. She found something soft, drove her digits in with claws extended.

The copper squealed, so loudly that it shocked her into releasing him, vague memories of wrestling with Auron during one of his attacks triggering instincts—

Face smeared with blood, the copper scrambled away,

striking her between the eyes with his tail as he turned so that she saw dragonflame explode for a moment. She shook her head to clear her vision, and he was gone.

Liquid gurgled and pulsed behind her breastbone, and she spat after him. Her fire bladder bile had a sharp, unpleasant smell, like vomit and sulfur.

She sniffed out the blood trail and followed it. The dribbles led her to the biggest of the cave pools, the one with the waterfall next to it. A fissure in the wall had been widened, and she saw a forgotten spike or two still resting in a piece of wall that had come down and fallen into the pool.

Had he gone to get the dwarves?

I'll meet that cripple and his dwarves again when I have real dragonfire, instead of bladderbile.

But until then, she had to survive. She took a deep drink of the water from the pool; her brother's blood could just be tasted on it. Or perhaps it was simply a loosened tooth from the fight. Wistala turned and left her home cave forever.

Chapter 7

Wistala used the walls and ceiling again on her way out, now sure of the route and good places to rest. She wasn't afraid of being taken unawares by pursuit; the bloody-handed dwarves might as well bang their shields against the walls for all the noise they made.

She feared and hated them. It would be hard to say which emotion was the stronger—perhaps her fear, that she would end up another headless, *sii*-less, *saa*-less corpse robbed of life and skin itself.

Her body wasn't equal to the anger she felt. It hung above her, vast and thick, like a storm cloud. One day she might be able to inhale that cloud, take it into her body and use it to fuel her vengeance for a butchered family.

One day. When I am strong. I'm too weak now.

Weak wasn't the word for it, more like exhausted, drained . . . Every muscle in Wistala's body ached as she climbed out of the cave. She inched forward as she emerged, not knowing what sort of help her brother might have summoned. Furtive creeping was her only defense. She wouldn't be able to put up any more of a fight than a slug, thanks to her weariness and the cold despair in her hearts.

The smell of fresh air steeled her limbs and gave her a last burst. As she climbed up through the creepers at the mouth of the cave and squeezed into an old crack in the battlements, she felt as though her body was sloughing off her limbs to puddle beneath her. She joined it, slid down a rushing slide of fatigue, and slept.

Wistala awoke to alarm that she couldn't smell Auron. The events of the previous day came back in a rush, along with the tumult of emotions. Not true emotions, rather echoes of them. The fear, the anger, the disgust, the despair all felt cold and dead and dark, leaving her spiritless.

Was it just yesterday she had lost one brother, and fought another?

I'm done for. The world's too much for me. It'll have me, too, in the end.

She would have laughed at the dreams of were-blood taken from the dwarves were it not too much effort. Never to smell Mother's rich, comforting scent, spin gemstones on the egg shelf with Jizara, listen to Father's approach with awe and a little fear at the bloody odors . . .

A beetle probed the dirt of a crack in the battlement above her eye. She could pick it with a flick of her tongue and crunch it down, but it still sought sustenance with the determination of one who knew only instinct. It knew nothing of doom or enemies or the vast indifference of this uncaring, friendless world.

"I shall be you for a time, beetle."

The beetle hunted so that it might eat, unaware of its own near destruction. And so should she.

She crept out of the cold crack. Everything on her hurt, especially the gripping maniples of her *sii*. She got behind an old wall, or perhaps it was a paved path; it was wide and low, and thick brush almost turned it into a tunnel.

It was morning on the other side of the mountains, she guessed. Here the land lay shadowed and cold under a purple sky. The clouds above slowly warmed, and she took advantage of the twilight to explore a broken tower. From an arrow-slit next to a stony ledge, she examined the approaches to the cave.

No campfires. No dwarves. No hunting dogs. No men. Elves you wouldn't see until their bowstrings sang your death. Some wide-winged birds circled above the woods and meadows; others sat on bare tree limbs with a good view of open ground, preening or keeping watch. Their behavior was regular: they didn't suddenly change course or startle or cry out, as they would if hunters were prowling the woods. To the north, more mountains, a long line of them, snowy tops tinged with morning gold. Father was up there somewhere, but he wouldn't even be a dot at this distance.

If he still lived.

Wistala sniffed the air, smelled mountain goat droppings in the grassy interstice filling the bottom of a rocky runnel. The beetle would no doubt find the clumps tasty. She preferred the source.

Wistala followed the smells at a slow stalk with a thoughtless—but not senseless—appetite.

Wistala didn't need to follow the Bowing Dragon during the day, since the mountains appeared to run more or less north. She kept to the dead area above most of the trees but below the snow. Brilliant green moss the color of her scales covered every rock, evidence to some play of wind and weather that meant mists at these heights almost every morning and night.

While moving in open sunlight meant she could be observed, she'd rather see trouble from a distance than worry what might be around the next scraggly pine tree.

Water was plentiful—the mountains were shedding their winter weight of snow, and it came down in innumerable streams. The streams carried more than just refreshing water and bits of bark and leaf on a long journey down the mountain; they were full of tasty frogs that wiggled delightfully as they went down Wistala's long throat.

By evening she'd crossed over two shoulders and had to face a decision. The mountains curved away west before going north again, and she could save herself a good deal of time by cutting across the valley, going the same distance in a quarter of the dragon-lengths. But it would mean plunging into thick forest. Trees could mean men, or worse, elves.

But trees also meant warm-blooded, furry, four-footed feasting, marrow-filled bones to crunch, and juicy eyeballs for sucking.

Appetite and the desire to hurry north, hopefully to find Father somewhere plotting destruction to the dwarves, won out over caution. She descended into the valley.

Patient trees waited for her. Soon she could see only slivers of sky around the tops of pines.

"Grounddragon look look!" a blue jay shrieked. It fluttered to a lower branch to scream at her: "Nestraider! Nestraider!"

Birdspeech made hatchling babble seem sophisticated.

"News! Dragon lives?" a swift answered from a nearby tree. Wistala couldn't see it.

"Lives, lives, the grounddragon lives," the jay called back.

"I won't raid your nests," Wistala said. "Why would it be news that I live?"

"Such news! News! Sparrow say grackle say thrush say elf-hawk say elves kill grounddragon," the swift called.

"Nestraider! Nestraider!" the jay insisted.

"I will raid your nests if you don't shut that thorn you use for a beak. When was this grounddragon killed, swift?"

"Not-today," the swift answered.

Perhaps birdbrains had room for only two concepts of time: something that happened today and Everything Else. Auron might still live, somewhere. The birds might be gossiping about a killing in the area from weeks and weeks ago.

But she wondered—and her fire bladder went cold. Could birds keep a thought in their singsong heads that long?

Mother said some elves understood birdspeech. Wistala didn't want her comings and goings sung about through the whole forest. She knew she couldn't convince them to lie. Then she'd have to come up with an alternative truth they could understand. "Good riddance. We not-dragons don't like them."

"Nestraider! Nestraider!"

"You look like a dragon," the swift said, and Wistala finally spotted him sheltering in the notch between two thick branches. She'd seen him only because he raised his whitish chin to speak.

"No, I'm a not-dragon. Though we look a lot like dragons and are often mistaken for them, that's why we hate them so."

"Nestraider! Nestraider!"

"Not-dragons don't raid nests!" Wistala said. She marched off into the forest, tail held high, exposing her vent to the still-screaming jay.

"I've met a not-dragon," the swift bubbled. "The sparrows must hear of this!"

The next day she cut through another wooded valley and crossed a low rocky ridge in the middle of the forest. It was honeycombed with caves of assorted sizes and, unfortunately, empty nests. There was good snake hunting in the rocks. All she had found to eat in the forest was a white-eyed possum, which had been wandering around in the daylight in a muddled daze. It stank like disease, but she still ate it. Mother had said that the illnesses that plagued mammals wouldn't affect dragons.

Snake hunting was all quickness, and it appealed to Wistala. One good thump behind the head, and a snake's back was broken, leaving a thick feast that fit neatly down one's throat. She got one bulging black-cave serpent that had recently eaten a large rat or a baby raccoon, judging from the size of the bulge in its midsection, thus giving her two meals with one jump.

She felt dirty, and found a rock where she could bend and stretch and extend her scales to the afternoon sun. Sunlight cleaned the crevices around the scale-root almost as well as water but felt a sky's worth warmer, especially with a snake dinner inside.

A *prrum* might even have been forming in her throat, until her memories betrayed her: Auron would have been a fine snake-hunter, quick as he was. Why couldn't he be with her?

Stop it, Tala. Auron is in the past, gone save for a scratch on a rock and your memories.

Except for his head and his claws, perhaps. What sort of wretched hominid ritual are they being incorporated into? Mother said the hominids used dragonkind for medicines and magic, if they were lucky enough to get one down.

"Stupid hearts. Give him up."

Or did they know something she didn't?

Wistala looked to the sky, to the late afternoon sun, now disappearing behind a bank of clouds. There'd be a rain tonight, if not a storm. She should nap on the ridge, and then shelter from the storm in one of the caves.

And lose half a day finding Father.

She picked her route down the ridge.

Wistala would have avoided the great claw-shaped cave, for it smelled like bears—but for the sounds wafted up from it. A breeze blew *out* of the cave. Perhaps it was another chimney from the Lower World, similar to the one she'd climbed with Auron.

As this one didn't have to travel most of the way up a mountain, the path to the Lower World must be shorter. It conducted sounds, strange rhythms that couldn't be natural, unless the air was moaning on its way up thousands of individual channels.

She ventured into the cave, found a bone-strewn ingress that had been collecting odds and ends since the forming of the world. But a trio of cracks sent air and sound up from below.

Voices.

She couldn't pick out individual words, and indeed she could hardly swear that the voices she heard weren't in her imagination rather than some trick of wind. But the rhythm repeated itself again and again every hundred heartbeats or so.

A song.

No dragon song—that, she'd be able to comprehend. Probably dwarves, singing as they worked or buckled on helm and shield to go kill more hatchlings. This was not a light, glad sound like that of a bird happy to get the morning dew off its feathers; this was a dirge such as a mother dragon might sing over empty, broken eggs. She hoped Father had given the dwarves reason to lament.

Dwarf voices meant dwarf tunnels, chambers, and mines. She must be getting near the tower-girded lake.

And Father.

> *Sing-song a dragon's dead!*
> *No more wingwinds, no more dread,*
> *Sing-song, a firestarter's dead!*

The song awoke Wistala from her predawn nap beneath a fallen tree. Some surviving branches still held up part of the bole, and a fresh start emerged from one of the roots—a testament to the resiliency of oaks—and she'd taken shelter beneath it, waking to find fresh spiderwebs all around and the birds cheering.

Wistala's chest heart shrank to the size of one of the wrapped flies in the web by her nose.

Curse the birds and their tinder-dry nests. "What news?" she called in birdspeech.

"Great news, giant log-turtle," a grackle chirped. "A dragon's down by the river-gorge."

"I don't believe you."

"Look under the buzzards, then. Already they gather."

Wistala came out from under the log, and the birds went silent. She heard some tiny frightened peeps.

A tall pine stood nearby. She ran to it, climbed its regular, neatly spaced rungs as high as she dared. She saw mountains and many treetops and butterflies and an overcast pushed up against the snowcaps but—

No. There they are. Oh for my wings, for just one hour's use of my wings!

She went down the pine recklessly, headfirst, in a series of controlled falls, letting the springy wood and interlaced branches catch her, not caring how the needles stuck or the sap clung to her.

She landed with a *thump*.

Wistala hurried through the forest, crashing through bramble and sending dead leaves flying, leaving a trail a blind elf could follow by touch. The first hot rush wore off, and she settled into an agonized dogtrot, her breath now louder than her footfalls.

The ground became treacherous and thin soiled, with pines and beeches clinging to strips of earth between rocks flattened and rounded and moss-bitten. She jumped, reached a prominence where she could see through the scattered trees, and corrected her course across blue-green stone with sharp edges that bit her *sii*.

Dragons aren't built like horses or wolves, though their legs can get them over short distances at speeds that surprise—and kill—the unwary. They walk over long distances easily, resting tail and head on the ground frequently with weight otherwise divided between their four powerful limbs. But they are poor runners beyond the limits of a dragon-dash.

Wistala, though thick-bodied and strong, was no exception. After the first burst, all she had to give in her run was determination. She matched it against the fire in her lungs, the pain in her high-joints, the fatigue in her muscles. Her field of vision shrank until she saw the forest as though through a long dark tunnel. Hearing was gone save for the sound of her hearts pounding; all she could smell was blood-tinged saliva flowing from her mouth, thanks to stress-ruptured vessels in her long lungs.

White froth hung from her dry mouth.

She hit the gorge first, crashing through bushes, scattering berries that bruised into sickly scent. Only a quick *saa*-dig saved her tumble down the hillside.

Steep-sided, fern-covered fells flanked a river of frothing white and mist. Just beyond a rainbow created by the rising water, the river threw a wide loop around a prominence that resembled the upper half of hominid leg bone. A long wall of rock ran out to a knoblike point, surrounded on all sides by water.

The carrion birds circled above the stony bulge. Every now and then one would dip its wings and go lower and the others would follow; then it would rise again, but never quite so high as when she had first marked them.

Just when her body needed to hurry most, it betrayed her. She tripped, she stumbled, lost in a yellow-and-pink fog that played tricks on her vision.

Then she stood on the peninsula, the river rushing in opposite directions a dragon-length to either side, the peninsula riven and notched like vertebrae. Her run became a stagger on stones treacherous with green slimes and gray lichens.

Then to the knob, a scarp like a castle keep with ferns clinging to the side as though they were freshly hatched spiders drying themselves on the egg sac. The birds no longer whirled above.

Wistala smelled dragonblood, and the mists cleared. Ancient irregular steps were cut into the side of the rock prominence, but ferns had taken over. She climbed the stairs on a carpet of green.

The rock was somewhat flatter at the top, stonework like that of the battlements outside the home-cave crowning it. Three mighty toothlike obelisks stood upright, rough hewn, with lichen blurring glyphs carved into the sides facing each other. Had they all been standing, they would have made a roofless cage, but the rest had fallen with broken pieces strewn all about. They lay on their sides, half-covered by jagged pines all leaning upstream.

The ruin of her father lay in a depression in the center, his own blood in a pool all around. Feathered spikes thrust into riven scales covered his back like fur. He had but five horns now, one was broken off at a great notch in his crest, and he couldn't fold one *griff* thanks to an ax-head stuck in it. Blood ran from under his *sii*.

"Father!"

Brown-and-white carrion birds, perched at the tops of the obelisks, took wing at her cry.

She dashed to him, licked at a dimpled wound under one closed eye that hardly even bled. She didn't begin to know how to manage the rest.

His other side was just as bad. The hilt of some mighty

weapon, notched like an arrow but the size of a spear, projected about the length of her tail from his side. The back was attached to a chain, and the chain to a heavy round ball that had cracked the ancient stone where it landed. Had father flown dragging that?

"Ayangthe, I've hurt myself on the slate pile. Jumped too far down. Is Mother asmelled?"

"Father, it's Wistala. Wistala."

Father grimaced. "You're a star, Wistala—I saw you twinkling beneath dear Irelia last night. You, Auron, and Jizara all in a row. I'll be up there soon. Wait."

"Do open your eye, Father."

"Can't. Light hurts."

"What do you think you're doing?" one of the condors croaked. "He's done for."

Wistala ignored the judgment, though she admired his birdspeech. It had a loftier tone than the grain-brained bush-hoppers.

"You're only making it harder for him," the condor continued from his high obelisk.

What had Mother told her to do with wounds? Oh, it was in one of her Lessons. The hatchling and the wounded tiger, of course! Dwarf's-beard! It loved rotting old logs, especially damp ones.

"Father, I'll be right back. I'm going to help you."

Novosolosk, the little black dragon, had just ventured above ground. . . .

She looked up at the condor: "Fair warning! I see any of you pecking at him, I'll be venting feathers for a week."

"Perish the thought." The condor fluffed up his feathers and settled. "I'm eager to see how you manage this."

While hunting rock rats, Novosolosk found himself trapped atop a low jungle kopje by a great tiger. The tiger prowled round and round the base of the kopje, growling and panting.

She looked off the east side of the knob at the river-turn. Sure enough, masses of logs had washed up against the rocks at the base of the peninsula, wetted by the constant spray of white water. Along with more mundane lichens, tufts of gray hung from cracks and knotholes in the logs.

Novosolosk tried to bargain with the tiger for safe passage out of his territory, but the tiger just spat abuse in return. He noticed an arrow through the tiger's neck, broken shafts sticking out either side of his coat, the orange and white gone brown with blood and green with pus.

"Tiger, tiger, I can extract that arrow. . . ."

Hope gave her tired body new life. She eschewed the cut rocks for a quicker climb down the side of the knob. Going down would be easier than coming back up. . . .

Novosolosk went to the swamp, the tiger padding along just behind, its hot breath on his tail and drops of saliva falling like rain. He expected the tiger to jump at any point . . .

Sure enough, a few of the logs had thick growths of dwarf's-beard. The plant appeared to like broken-off ends, for some reason, or split trunks. It spilled out of the rotting black wood in a thick thatch of gray, interlaced and layered and almost woven in a way that made it difficult to tell where the growth began and where it ended. It reminded Wistala of the hair shirt from the man Father brought back to the cave for Auron to learn hominid-killing. One final test.

As the tiger groaned away, Novosolosk broke a piece of the moss at a thick joint. It was joined by a whitish band. He blew on the band. It stretched and waved in his breath but did not break. . . .

She tore off two hunks of moss, carried it in her mouth back up the stairs, feeling a bit like a bullfrog she'd seen croaking away in a stream with his windbag expanded under his chin. She took the stairs in a series of leaps.

Novosolosk crushed the moss in his sii *and pulled out the arrow with one quick motion. The tiger yowled and swatted him across the crest, but he pressed the mass to either side of the hole the arrow left. Dwarf's-beard both staunched the flow and cleaned the wound, so powerful is its magic, and the tiger's angry fever came down. . . .*

She listened to Father's heart when she crept under his wounded *sii*. Father would not move his limb; she had to wedge herself into the gap between body and arm like a river clam and then flex her back so she could get at the wound.

The ugly red gash gave off a pulse of blood from one end, a steady flow from the other. She packed the wound with dwarf's-beard, crushing its laced branches with her *sii* until they were sticky with the whitish gunk. It had been a brave dwarf that came so close to his *sii* to open the bronze dragon's breast with his ax.

Father looked relieved as soon as she wiggled free of his armpit, although whether this was from instinct at being able to press the wound closed again or comfort brought by the dwarf's-beard, she couldn't say.

The stream of blood feeding the pool Father lay in slowed.

Wistala sank to her joints.

"Thank you, Novosolosk."

Chapter 8

I still say he's going to die," the condor insisted.

Most of his cousins had left by the time the sun set, but a few still circled far above. The old yellowbeak chuckled every time Wistala limped up the long, long staircase, bearing another mouthful of dwarf's-beard.

Wistala worked from nose-tip to tail, crushing the growth and placing it atop Father's wounds. Sometimes it fell out again right away, and every time Father shifted his position, he exposed new wounds.

"Prophecies and fallacies, I'm starting to enjoy proving you wrong," Wistala said.

"Ah, but there I've got you, if you'll take the high view. There's no hole so deep or airs so lofty for any of us that old Father Death doesn't visit. He's more reliable than even your fire. We, his humble retinue, clean up after him. How about giving us a taste and letting me warm my chilled grippers?"

"I've no fire yet, and even if I did, I wouldn't waste it on a grouser like you."

"Grouse! I'm a High Mountain Condor, hatchling. Barring your kind, no one matches my wingspan save the lost Rocs of the east. And once you dragons are gone—"

"What's that you say?"

"Please, take no offense. We carrion birds value our manners. If I spoke on a delicate subject—"

"I should have asked you to explain yourself. Do you mean once Father and I leave the river, you'll be the skyking?"

The condor clacked his beak. "I rarely see a dragon anymore. In the time of my father's father's father's egg, I'm told your kind were thick in these mountains, and there was good feasting on the remains of your kills, for kind dragon lords always offered fresh, delectable heads with eyeballs intact to us of lesser wing."

Wistala wondered how many other caverns hid butchered, moss-covered families. "Who is driving the dragons away?"

"Perhaps you should ask your father that, if he ever speaks again."

"You must see everything. I've seen you soaring as high as a dragon."

The condor straightened a little; birds were as vain as dragons sometimes.

"So who can master dragons and bid them depart?"

"The hominids, I suppose. They do shape the world to suit themselves, don't they?"

"The world wins back, in the end," Wistala said, thinking of the toppled, overgrown battlements around the home cave.

"We condors look to the day of the Last Swancall. Do you know what a swancall is?"

Wistala twitched her nose. "No."

"It's a great metal thing shaped like a dragon's neck, and it makes a call as loud as the white swans you see on the lakes of the north. The hominids blow them before slaughtering each other. We carrion birds wait upon the war of the Last Swancall, when all the hominids kill each other off; then there'll be the vast battle feast in celebration and the world will be given over to we of talon and feather again."

She sniffed at the wound around the great shaft. It

smelled evil. While waiting and dreaming of the condor's last swancall might be pleasant, she'd have to venture along the slippery banks of the river in search of more dwarf's-beard.

A clear morning sky brought rainbows to the waterfall up-river. If Wistala weren't so weighted down with worry, the bright colors would have made her hearts glad. But Father still seemed to be worsening.

"Wistala, I'm so thirsty," Father panted. "I'll perish of it before I can move again."

River, river all around, and not a drop within reach. Father chose a good location to collapse, for it would be difficult and dangerous to cross and climb all the slippery rocks for a hominid bearing arms, but he couldn't reach the river swirling below as it bent back around the knob.

"But you must move!" She didn't have enough digits to count how many times she urged Father to move. The blood around him had dried into a brown stain, still claw-deep and sticky under his scales.

Father pressed his back against a horizontal slab at the center of the knob, not a fallen obelisk but obviously a cutting of some importance, judging by how it stood on a little platform. His claws slipped against the stone. He rolled a little, got his claws under him.

Wistala had to look away; she couldn't bear to see Father's limbs trembling under him again. Father's mighty head fell.

Gluck-glk-glub . . .

Is Father crying?

"He must have water," Wistala called.

The watching condor looked at the sky, checking for rain clouds, perhaps. "Were you speaking to me?"

"No . . . yes."

"Water flows up to down, not down to up. What you need is a train of pack-dwarves carrying waterskins."

"Waterskins?" Wistala asked, thinking it was some sort of plant.

"Hominids make them. They scoop out the insides

of sheep and lambs and fill them with water to drink on journeys."

Hominids must have stomachs stronger than the condor above to drink water stored inside rotting flesh. Disgusting creatures.

Why did the condor spew such a useless detail? He might as well have said, "You need a good rainstorm," or "A spring bubbling up through these rocks would help." She wouldn't begin to know how to scoop out a dead animal and fill it again with water. They had nostrils, throats, tailvents, never mind the holes one made while killing it. If she could reach up and grab the condor, she'd be tempted to try it with him . . . squeeze it out like Mother bringing up a tenderized sheep for hungry hatchlings.

Would that work?

She hurried down to the river, gulped down mouthful after mouthful, felt her stomach swell until she became sick with the fullness. . . .

The water came back up easily enough, a little sour-smelling, thanks to her empty belly.

But it worked.

She filled herself even fuller, until it seemed as though she could hardly draw breath from the liquid in her stomach—dragon innards were built for gorging—and learned a lesson when it came back up of its own accord on the stairs.

She took in less for her third load and made it all the way to the top.

"I've got something for you, Father," she said.

He opened a weary, bloodshot eye.

She cast about and settled on the central slab Father braced himself against when he tried to move. It had a gutter running down the center, perhaps designed to catch and hold rainwater? She hopped up onto the edge, and with a loudish belch almost filled half the trough with water.

Father sniffed. "Tala! You're a miracle!" He lapped at the water. "You are your mother's hatchling, no doubt about it," he said on the second trip.

"This is doing me wonders," on the third. All the gorging and retching were exhausting, but she pressed on.

As she filled her stomach a fourth time, she felt a little woozy; the climbs up and down the rock were trying. She needed a meal. Would fish live in water this rough?

It turned out they did. They liked to wait behind the bigger rocks, sitting in the calm, waiting for a meal to be swept to them by the current. But they scattered when she dived in after them and disappeared into the bubbling water.

She thought it over and tried steering herself through the current. This was far trickier, but with a little practice, she found she could shoot into the calm waters with water-lids lowered and snap down a fish quick as thinking.

But if her stomach was digesting fish, it wasn't helping Father. He had blood and scale to make up. The juicy fish would help. Weren't they shiny little bags of water, after all?

She dived into the river upstream, and after a wild ride round the reversal at the knob—and a bloodied nose on an unexpected rock—she had five fish in her belly. She took her time climbing the steps.

Father was asleep. Was his breathing less labored? Hard to tell. Wistala decided against waking him for a meal; the fish just felt too good in her gorge. Besides, they'd give her strength for more fishing. When Father woke, she'd try a few trips with a belly full of fish.

Two days—and a countless number of trips with fish swallowed whole—later, Father wasn't his old self, but he could reach the river on his own in order to drink and wash the clotted moss from his wounds.

They'd extracted the oversized spear—Father called it a *highpoon* and told her dwarven war machines fired it to weigh down a dragon and bring him to earth. At one point, he'd had two in him and was plunging toward the lake around the dwarves' battlements, when luckily the second tore free and he could just fly with the other. . . .

"They got me on that great bridge between those towers of rock," Father said as he spat gobs of fire onto the chain links, which Wistala pounded with an edged rock under Father's instruction, feeling that her shoulders would give way long before the chain. "There are caverns big enough for a dragon to get in at them, but they had the war machines concealed in decorative galleries, all woodwork and flower beds and curtains. I was hit before I heard the roar of the chains. Clever blighters."

Finally the links gave way, and Father drew the high-poon out his other side, where it projected from his scale—the barbs on it made any other kind of extraction impossible.

Wistala almost swooned during the gory extraction. How did Father manage the pain?

Flying was beyond him, of course. He crept ever so slowly down the knob, shuffling his *sii* and *saa* and keeping grip with three while one explored the next step. Wistala fretted as he moved—this was almost as bad as seeing him lying in a pool of his own blood. An honorable death after battle had a twilight dignity to it. Seeing her strong, confident father, lord of her home cave, reduced to a slug's pace down the gentlest slope of this rock pile brought new anguish.

The trip back up took all afternoon, it seemed.

"I never knew there could be such a fight," he said as the sun set behind fire-edged clouds.

The old condor still waited above, looking a little droopy. Wistala wondered if he was molting at the thought of his feast living on day after day. She liked his companionship, though, and brought him a whole dead fish she found washed up on the riverside.

The condor didn't mind the ants.

"The Wheel of Fire?"

"Where did you hear that?"

"Mother and Auron."

Father bowed his head, nostrils shut. "I saw her. What happened to Auron?"

Wistala told him. The shouted warning . . . the elves chasing him . . . the story came slowly. She tried to give him mind-pictures but had to fill in the fuzzier parts with words.

"And here I thought he took after the grandsire on his mother's side. That sounds like something my father would have done. And you, scales so thin they hardly keep out the raindrops, went on alone?"

"Yes."

"You might have done better to have found a nook in the home cave and waited another year until you had your flame. A mouthful like you would be easy pickings for wolves, leave alone the hominids. But perhaps the wolves have been driven from these woods, too."

"I wanted to find you. We're all that's left." She didn't—couldn't—mention the copper and his betrayal. Father had grief enough.

"Perhaps," Father said. "Some pair. A hatchling and a half-dead dragon. The hunt's probably on already, you know."

"In this wild country?"

"There's no country too wild if there's a wounded dragon down. I tried to confuse them by flying hard south and then circling around through cloud layer, but my wings gave out. An elf will pick up a piece of bird-gossip or those hounds will find me. That dragon-hunter will have a new piece of scale for his harness, and our line will go unavenged."

"I'll avenge it, Father, if it comes to that."

"Were-oaths and corpse-curses are for drakes and dragons, daughter. Dragonelles get their vengeance by seeing clutches of eggs laid to take the place of the assassinated."

"I told you that you should have left him be," the condor said.

Father blew his nostrils out at the condor. "Only thing that'll change the mind of a dragonelle of Irelia's line is herself, Bartleghaff," Father said.

"You know that old buzzard?"

Bartleghaff squawked: "Condor!"

"Know him?" Father snorted. "He's my oldest friend."

"Friend? You were waiting to eat him!" Wistala said to the condor.

"Of course he was," Father said. "I wouldn't want some

stranger getting the best bits. Who better than an old sky-mate to serve the dragon-wake."

"What a feast!" Bartleghaff said. "And my son's got a hatchling of his own now, first year in the sky. Such a gobble we'd have, we'd all be too fat to fly for a week. You'd have been remembered fondly at every cliff-sit for a hundred years. We were gathering to see you off properly." He fluffed his feathers again. "Till she came along."

"For someone who dines on lips and vents, you offer complaints a plenty," Father said. "That legendary politeness of your kind—if it ever existed—is on the wane as your years advance."

"Tell me about the dwarves, Father. Why do you say they betrayed you?"

"They broke a bargain they struck with your mother. Strange, for of all the hominids, dwarves are the only ones who can be trusted to keep their word without crabbing. Serves us right for believing legends. Perhaps dwarvish honor, like so many of the other old truths, has been brought down by poisoned arrows." He sent a significant glare Bartleghaff's way.

"What was the bargain?" Wistala asked.

"It came from our need for a decent cave. Your mother and I had already seen our share of tragedy. For our first clutch, we were too high in the mountains and in too shallow a cavern. A bitter freeze took the eggs. Your poor mother. The next cavern had a seep of bad air, odorless, clinging to the floor. Again, no hatchlings stirring after the first weeks. I was inconsolable at that and gave up hope— all those years of searching wasted. While flying the southern reaches of these mountains, we came across a band of blighters, half of them hurt, and made an easy meal of them. While I chased the survivors off south, your mother nosed through their belongings for digestible metals.

"Up popped a dwarf. Your mother thought him well scarred from battle and a stout, strong sort, even for a dwarf. Now had I been there, I would have made an end to him, but your mother knew we were strangers to the mountains this far from the sea, and she conversed with him. He gave his name as Gobold of the Wheel of Fire clan.

" 'You're unusually bold for a dwarf abovegrounds,' your mother said.

" 'I'm in your debt,' Gobold said, pouring out the contents of a small purse he carried. There was a goodly mouthful of silver for each of us to be had. Just the thing we needed to put the sparkle back in our scales after the long flight.

" 'Silver and salivation, what service have we done you?'

"Gobold replied: 'You've finished a battle commenced days ago. The blighters outran us. Yea, they even outdug us.'

"Your mother let him talk, and he spoke of the decay of the human empire that once circled the Inland Ocean the way cave moss circles a pool. They'd given up their outposts in the southern mountains, and blighters filled some of their old caves and tumbles. The blighters were plaguing the dwarves' trade routes and taking over mines.

"When he spoke of how the blighters filled several caves at the end of the southern mountains, closed them off from the dwarvish tunnels and roads in the Lower World so that the dwarves couldn't get at them, your mother began to hatch an idea of her own. She told the dwarves that in return for six chests of gold and twelve of silver, we'd drive the blighters from those caverns and see that they never returned.

" 'Such a deed would long be sung at our Memorials, Queen of Dragons,' Gobold said.

" 'I must consult with my husband before formally pledging tooth and claw to bargain. Perhaps you should seek the agreement of your clan?'

" 'That will not be difficult,' Gobold said with a chuckle.

"In the end, the bargain was formally struck with many words and an etching on a silver war-shield. She had the dwarves pay us half in small sums as we brought back heads for counting. When it came to dealing with hominids, your mother was fond of the old dragon-saying: *Trust, but keep an eye open.*

"So we fought the dwarves' war for them. I would have just forced my way into the cave and set fire to all within, but your mother demanded a more patient war that allowed us to build our strength even as we weakened theirs.

"We attacked their herds and their flocks, burned their Upper World crops, and took such blighter parties as were easily consumed by two dragons hunting by day or night. Such feasting we had—"

"Oh, yes . . . ," sighed Bartleghaff.

"And when they sent out hunting parties or tried to trick and trap us, we got away without too much difficulty, and sometimes got a chance for our own tricks and traps, for your Mother has—had—a fine mind for that sort of thing. Many of the blighters left in despair, but a hard few stayed within their cave, scratching a living from the Lower World. Soon we made them afraid to cast a shadow outside their cave."

"Did you destroy the battlements around the cave, then?" Wistala asked.

"Oh no, daughter, time is fiercer even than dragons. Hatchlings think the world began when their egg cracked—eh, Bartleghaff? Those old works date from the Age of Wheels, when the blighters first ruled the world before dragons tamed their appetites."

"You must have gone in the caves eventually."

"When we were fat and strong with full fire bladders and fresh iron-fed scales, we challenged the blighters in their own caves and drove them out. In a deep chamber, we found a place that fulfilled all our hopes.

"The blighters had diverted melt and underground springs to feed cave moss plantations and slug herds. It was deep enough to be out of any weather. Even a nice shelf in case of bad air! We let nature take its course and didn't even object to a few bats' helping fertilize the cave moss."

"A triumph," Wistala said, but wondered why there was no light in Father's eyes, the way there had been before, when he spoke of his battles.

"Save for some hard words with the dwarves. Gobold sent some shifty bargainer who showed up with one chest of silver and one chest of gold and a great bag of gems and jewelry. His name was Quizzilick and he was a *pogt* if I ever met one. He gave us treble praise and precious little metal when we spoke to him on the shores of that great icy moat that guards the approaches to their twin halls.

" 'O dragons mighty, strong, sure, fierce (this went on for some time, daughter, until you began to hear the bats drop of boredom), your work shall be rewarded beyond even our bargain, for we bring you not monies but riches.'

" 'Riches to some, dross to others,' I said. 'A few gems are always welcome to a dragon's appetite. They make for healthy, shining scale, but what we need are soft metals to replace scales lost in our joined war.'

" 'And our hatchlings must have some,' your mother said. Her desire must have unguarded her tongue, for I'd never heard her make such a mistake when talking to dwarves. For even slow dwarvish minds might start turning at the thought of families of dragons being bred on their borders.

"In the end, Quizzilick slightly increased the amount of gold and gave us more jewelry that had rich strands of it, and a great deal of silver besides, but there was no end of grumbling. But we'd kept our part of the bargain, and when we quit them, we never troubled the dwar-lands."

"How do you know it was the Wheel of Fire and not some other group of dwarves?" Wistala asked.

"I did not lose my head and attack the nearest dwarf-works, Tala. The etchings on their round shields and helm-circlets told me their tale of betrayal. The Wheel of Fire take pride in showing their flame-winged eagles."

"Ironic," Bartleghaff said. "So eager are they for eagle feathers and heads, they've killed off almost every one in these mountains. I'm glad they don't have condors perching atop their standards."

"Happy thought," Father said. "I'd hear fewer complaints. But why bring up iron? Fault them for much, but not for the quality of their weapons. Finest steel, as I know too well."

Bartleghaff preened his neck-tuft. "How can such wingspan be powered by so small a brain, you scaly sheep-roaster? I meant their insignia is ironic—*irony,* a form of elvish humor. Like having your tail burnt by your own fire."

"Come to your perch, if you have one," Father said. His eyelids drooped and his eyes were dull. Just telling a story had worn him—or perhaps old emotions had drained his hearts' blood.

"I'm told by the battle-crows, curse their nest-pillaging feathers, that the flames signify dragonfire. Some story lost in the mists of time."

"Whatever they learned of dragons they must have forgotten, to go murdering hatchlings," Wistala said, but neither of the pair appeared to hear her. She could almost hear Mother's voice above as she sang:

> *And for those who threaten clutch of flame,*
> *To feel the wrath of dragon-dame!*

Father yawned. "Time for sleep. *A dragon must rest* and all that. Daughter, I've had my fill of fish. See if you can catch something red-blooded unawares for breakfast, would you?"

Chapter 9

A week's worth of breakfasts later—mostly fish, unfortunately for Father's blood-hungry appetite—Wistala smelled smoke in the evening twilight of the forest west of the river gorge.

Game had become scarce in the area around Father and Bartleghaff, who seemed to do little but befoul his perch and goad Father into burning him up like a feathery candle.

Smoke in the forest, with the wood so wet from the constant spring rains, could mean only one thing—hominids. No other creatures save dragons wielded so dangerous a weapon.

With luck, she'd have hers in a few more months. Coming aboveground early had its terrors, but she had to admit she was thriving on the variety of food to be found.

And speaking of variety of food—as she rolled the smoke smell around in her nostrils, she got the mouthwatering scent of charred flesh, which she hadn't had since Father brought home a burned sheep to the egg shelf what seemed like a lifetime ago.

The smoke smell was as easy to follow as a bright moon on a cloudless night through the trees. After a little casting back and forth, she came to a wide hollow.

It was an unnatural sort of place, like a dry creek, only

the bottom was filled with tiny broken stones all roughly the same size, and the overgrown banks carried no smell of running water, though every rill for miles was brim-full with the rains. The hollow bent around the peak of the hill as though a claw like Bartleghaff's obelisk had scored the hillside. But from the heights, one could both see either end of the streambed-like cut for a goodly length and be out of the wind.

A dwarf had chosen to camp here.

"Great things have small beginnings," Mother used to like to say when she and Jizara compared their minuscule size to her bulk.

Her vengeance would begin here. As a bonus, the dwarf had a string of ponies. Surely she'd bring down one or two and be able to carry several limbs back to Father before the birds made off with it all.

She stayed downwind in the smoke smell. Examining each *sii-* and *saa*-hold as she crept up, she reached a pounce point in the cut of the bank. Perhaps two bounds to reach the dwarf, and if he had an ax, he didn't keep it beside him. . . .

The dwarf wasn't even helmed, though he did have a sort of mask across his face and just a few scraggles of beard showing. Her store of dwarf-lore was not great, but she knew that a dwarf without a full beard was either very young or some kind of criminal. The only thing remarkable about him was his riding boots, which rose all the way to his hips.

The dwarf carefully set his frying pan down and stood.

Wistala froze, waiting for him to reach for a weapon.

But he wasn't looking in her direction.

She tried to follow his gaze, but all she could see was the string of tasty-looking ponies, chewing their meals in bags attached to their noses.

One of the middle ponies had no interest in his meal; instead he stood miserably with one hoof tipped forward.

The dwarf went to his little two-wheeled cart and returned with a bag. She watched the dwarf lift the pony's hoof and shake his head. He scratched it between the ears, grumbling something in his tongue, and went to work.

Wistala had gnawed at enough horse hooves to know that men sometimes put iron soles on the bottoms of their *saa* to save their beasts sore-footedness. Perhaps one had come loose. In any case, the dwarf carefully cleaned the pony's hoof, extracting a sizable rock with a long device shaped like a dragon's snout, and applied some kind of tart-smelling salve from a covered clay pot. Then he pounded in a fresh shoe, driving nails right into the animal's foot. The pony didn't like the hammering, but placed its foot on the ground, happy to rest its weight on all fours again.

Still grumbling, the dwarf refilled the nose bags from a sack and returned to his now-cold meal. The dwarf mopped up a little congealed grease with a lump of bread and left the rest.

The desire to leap and kill left Wistala. Any sort of creature that would leave his own dinner to see to the comfort of a four-legged brute didn't seem the type to slaughter hatchlings in their cave. Besides, he held no helm or shield with flames; as far as she could tell, he had no sort of insignia on him, unless you counted the strange angular design like the gems Father gave them to play with on the rear doors of his cart.

He removed the nose bags on his ponies and posted them so they could nibble at the grass and growth on the banks or lie down. The nose bags intrigued Wistala, Bartleghaff's story of men carrying around water in the bodies of animals had stayed with her. They seemed just the right size for fish.

The dwarf cleaned his tools and then sprayed a sweet-smelling liquid on his short, thin beard using a bag that hissed like a hatchling as he squeezed it.

The dwarf turned in. Once she heard snores, she crept up and licked the contents of his pan. Then she picked up two of the nose bags in her mouth. The startled ponies shifted and whinnied in alarm.

She shot into the brush as the dwarf came awake, still with the grease on her tongue. Once out of hearing from the dwarf's camp, she dropped the nose bags and licked her teeth, searching for lost tidbits. Delicious.

*   *   *

Father didn't like her playing with the nose bags: "The Four Spirits gave dragons everything they need to survive, and your mother's wit will fill any gaps." Once dragons started relying on hominid artifice, they'd be painting their scales and wing tissue again like the decadent dragons of Silverhigh.

But Mother's wit told her to improvise. The nose bags were big enough to hold rabbit and pheasant or several fish. When she dumped a meal of squab—oh, the thrill of leaping on them as they took wing—out for Father, he bent so far as to say that circumstances permitted a temporary utilization of the nose bags.

They were so clever! Leather straps designed to hold them on the ponies' heads had little brass latches like dragonclaws poking through holes punched in the straps, and a rope drawstring closed them like the leg coverings she'd examined on the man Auron ate. Wistala, after a good deal of trial and error that was more error than trial, fixed the straps so they hung across her shoulders just where the neck-dip began. They swung about a little, which was a bother, and snagged on her scales. She wished she could find that dwarf again and convince him to fix the bags together somehow.

"Tell me again about burning the bridges at Sollorsoar," Wistala urged her father.

"You've heard that one before," Father said.

"I like the part where the elves either must jump into the river or burn," Wistala said. It was easy to place the faces of wide-eyed elves who rode after Auron upon the group of warriors trapped at the center of the bridge.

"You're an odd sort of dragonelle, Wistala. Those saddlebags, and now war stories. Even your Mother only asked for my battle anecdotes when she wanted to be lulled to sleep. You gobble them like gold."

"She's a young Ahregnia, or imagines herself one," Bartleghaff said.

Curse that condor! Every time he mentioned Ahregnia,

Father went into one of his lectures. She felt her *sii* extend as Father cleared his long throat.

"My sire knew her as sister, Wistala. A bitter female, consumed by revenge for her lost mate. Scarred she was, poisonous of mind, with tongue as sharp as her claws. Leave battles to dragons, and save your hearts for husband, hatchlings, and home cave."

"Jizara, Auron, and Mo—"

"Are mine to avenge, daughter. If I can ever get aloft again."

Father spread his wings, wincing at the pain in his ax-hacked neck and shoulders. He beat his wings, stirring hardly enough wind to blow Wistala's fringe to the other side of her neck. One long black fringe-point dropped to the corner of her eye, and she reached up with her left *sii* and snipped it short with her claws.

"That's a terrible habit, Wistala," Father barked. "A long fringe means a healthy dragonelle."

A failed attempt at flight always leaves Father irascible. But his tone still stung, no matter how many times she told herself that.

"You're just wearing yourself out," she said. "I smelled deer spoor in the woods. I'll try to find you a yearling."

"What I really need is some metal. Look at these scales coming in! A snake would be ashamed."

"Deer wouldn't carry gold and silver," Bartleghaff said.

"I saw a . . . a . . . ," Wistala said, searching for the word, ". . . road. Might riders carry gold?"

"They'd carry weapons, as well," Father said. "I thought I saw some ruins in the forest to the southwest, probably Old Hypatian. There might be iron to be plucked. I'd settle for nails. You could carry them in your neck contraption."

"How far?" Wistala asked.

"Too far for you to find it on foot. You'd spend weeks searching," Bartleghaff said.

"Exactly," Father said. "Listen, old vulture, you're getting fat on all those fish heads. Fly and guide her so your wings stay in training."

"Why?" Bartleghaff asked. "I need nails like I need a captive hawk's hood and tether."

"Call it a favor to an old friend keeping an eye on his daughter. Two, if you can spare a glance down now and then."

"High flier! Not an errand-wing," Bartlegaff cawed.

"Smoldering pile of feathers for taking advantage of her hospitality," Father said. He spat a globule of fire off the steep rockside facing the river, watched it fall and hit the froth in a hiss. It rode the waves for a moment, still burning, before succumbing to the white water. "She's been catching and hauling fish for you for weeks. And you fair bubbled with gratitude last night over that rabbit. Or did the gratitude get coughed up along with the bones?"

Bartleghaff worked his trailing wing feathers with his beak. "Oh, very well."

"Have a few mouthfuls of metal yourself, daughter. You're growing, and you need your ferrites. If you come across any quartz or fine sand, a mouthful or two wouldn't hurt. Scours the teeth and aids the digestion."

"So you and Mother have told me. Over and over," Wistala said. But she couldn't hide her excitement at the errand.

Bartleghaff's guidance consisted of a few visits throughout the day, mostly to tell her she was heading in the wrong direction. He always picked out landmarks that she couldn't see, even by climbing a tall tree! She'd follow a ridge he put her on for an afternoon, only to have him swoop down and tell her she'd been making too easterly for hours, and she had to veer back south. She felt her fire bladder twitch at some of the abuse he employed—birdspeech had no end of colorful calumnies.

"You could come down and correct me more often," she said, her fire bladder pulsing in time to her angry hearts.

"You could rest in a clearing now and then so I might see you through these confounded trees."

She guessed it was a young forest. Now and then she

passed a stone wall that led nowhere and divided nothing but its mossy side from the bare. She found a tall brick building on a bank. Someone had gone to considerable trouble to divert the stream years ago so that it flowed close to the building; now all was overgrown and inhabited by raccoons who retreated to tight holes in the bricks and bared their teeth when she sniffed at them. According to Father, where one man came, soon there would be ten and then hundreds, but whatever men had lived here, they'd long ago abandoned the land to the thriving trees, leaving the waterfall and pool they'd crafted to tasty frogs and fish.

She chased some smaller crows away from a dead groundhog and decided the meat was too noisome to interest her, but Bartleghaff thought it palatable.

Greenstuff filled every nook and cranny of the ruins, but where wind and water contested the mosses and lichens, marble still gleamed. Wistala crept to the edge of the forest, swarmed up a tree looking out over the ruins, and tried to put a mental map together.

Wistala watched men graze their sheep in the wide grassy lanes of what must have once been a city as their women and children gathered nuts and berries. Dogs, more interested in disturbing the cats sunning themselves atop ruined walls or in the gaps between decorative friezes, trotted from man to sheep, learning whatever might be discovered in each other's tailvents.

The fallen city had three clusters to it, each atop a hill, linked by low walls between, like three spiderwebs sharing a hollow log. A marsh stood at the very center of the three hills, but ancient vine-wrapped columns projected from it, showing that it hadn't always been a wetland. The village of the men stood a few dozen dragon-lengths off, outside a fallen gate that admitted a stream into the ruins. The stream fed the marsh.

She decided to hunt and rest for the day, and then explore the ruins at night. Metal would smell the same day or night, and she'd just as soon poke around after the men had retreated to their hearths. She just hoped they didn't loose dogs in the rubble.

She released Bartleghaff. Retracing her steps would be of no difficulty now that she knew the landmarks. She could find the brick ruin by the stream, and from that the ridge, and from that the wall corners, and from that—

"Keep clear of those men," Bartleghaff warned. "If you smell stewing lamb, just shut your nostrils. 'Temptation hatches instigation which hatches assassination!' "

The old condor had perched over Father too long: he was starting to sound like a dragon.

"Tell Father I'll be back in a day or two."

"Wasted air. He'll send me back to watch you," Bartleghaff grumbled. He took to the skies, wings wider than she was long beating the air as he rose.

Wistala flattened some tall grass and let the sun clean her scales. As twilight fell, she found a pile of old timber riddled with termites and tore open the pieces with her claws, taking up the crunchy tunnelers three at a time with her tongue.

Insect eating, once started, is difficult to stop, and it was a very lucky termite that escaped into the fallen leaves. The next thing she knew, the sun had disappeared in her silent fall, and the night belonged to her.

It was a warm summer night, with red clouds purpling overhead. The air had a thick softness to it that promised a hot day tomorrow.

Wistala started her search, mostly following her nose from corner to alley to stoop.

She found a few nails, almost unrecognizable for their rust, and found it was easier to break up the wood where they still lay than it was to pull them out. She ate one—it tasted almost like blood. She found what might have once been a cutting tool beneath some broken shards of pottery. It smelled like bad steel.

She chased a smell down and dug at the base of a wall, but found only bits and pieces of mixed metal and glass.

"What-t-t on earth-th-th are you?" a voice said to her in rather breathy birdspeech.

A pair of yellow eyes, slit like hers, watched her from a deep shadow.

"A scaled snaggletooth. Are you a cat?"

"Look, learn, and give in to the awe!" the owner of the eyes said. Wistala found her easy to understand, her body and throat issued patterns sisterly to dragonspeech.

The eyes came out into the moonlight, walking along the wall. Wistala read the thin orange-striped silhouette from whiskers to long twitching tail. "A word of advice: Never ask a softstalker whether she's a feline or not. If she is, you may admire at leisure. If she isn't, you'll just shame her. My name is Yari Sunwarm Fourth Orangedaughter, born this spring here in Tumbledown, and I've never seen anything dumb enough to swallow metal before. Even dogs are brighter. Did you think it a beetle?"

"No. I have strange appetites."

"I'll say," Yari Sunwarm Fourth Orangedaughter agreed. "Have you a name?"

"Wistala. Here hunting metals."

"I prefer rats, myself."

"I don't smell blood on you."

The cat licked one of her black paws and rearranged the hair on her ears. "The moon hasn't smiled on me yet tonight. I'm a free spirit. All the big males have the best spots staked out for their mates and kits."

The cat seemed terribly thin to Wistala. "I hate rats. My brothers could swallow them whole, but those tails . . ." She shut her nostrils and changed the subject. "You must know these ruins, then."

"Of course."

"Do you know where I can find more metal?"

The cat turned a neat circle, looked Wistala up and down. "You've got short thick claws. Almost badgerlike. How are you at digging?"

"I—I don't know. I've clawed through ice."

"The rats have a place under Tumbledown here. They call it Deep Run. A network of tunnels. Not built by them, of course. Supposedly there are outlets in the swamp, but no self-respecting feline will traipse around in there for

fear of the channelbacks. I know a hole that leads to Deep
Run. If you enlarge it, I'll show you some metal coin. It's
old and crusty, but metal nonetheless. Nice little mouthfuls. Of course, you'll have to dig again. I don't think you'd
fit."

Wistala considered. At the rate she was going in the
ruins, her improvised nose bags would take days to fill. The
men had obviously picked the surface clean of anything
useful.

Anything worth the having is worth the effort, Mother
used to say.

"It's a bargain."

"It occurs to me," the cat said, "that once underground,
you could make a meal of me."

"Can you keep something from the birds earthbound
and ditch-gossips?"

"Of course. Felines are full of secrets."

Wistala drew herself up on her stubby legs. "I'm a
dragon, feline, and I give you my word as Wistala Irelianova that I'll keep a fair bargain if you will."

Whiskers twitched. "And what would a dragon be?"

Wistala froze for a moment. The cat seemed perfectly
worldly, well-spoken and felicitous of fang. Apart from the
chopped-short neck and face, she was almost drakine after
Jizara's elegantly limbed fashion. How could she not know
what a dragon was?

"We are old, falling between mountains and man, gifted
by the Four Spirits with strengths to order the world."

The cat's back rose in a graceful arc. "Order? Order is
the enemy of the feline. We thrive on chaos, and if there's
not enough about, we instigate some. I hope you haven't
come to bring order to Tumbledown."

"Nothing like."

"I should think a creature meant to bring order to the
world would be bigger."

"I'm young."

Yari Sunwarm Fourth Orangedaughter turned her
alarmed pose into a casual stretch. "Make me this hole,
Wistala Irelianova, and I and my kits will be in your

debt and keep your secret that a dragon has come to Tumbledown."

"Bargain."

"Then let us touch whiskers . . . errr . . ."

Wistala extended her *griff*. "Will these do?"

"How beautiful! Yes, of course."

The cat approached and stood nose-to-nose with her, then put her head alongside Wistala's. Wistala felt the cat's whiskers tickle as they flicked along her scales and probed the gaps. They *prrumed* at each other, and Wistala felt a warm affinity.

"I fear I shall have to like you for your mind, Wistala Irelianova. You are too hard to perch on for a comfortable nap and smell like that furnace the men use to cook their metal."

"It's Tala to my friends."

"Then I'm Yari-Tab to you. Follow."

The cat jumped away, tail flicking this way and that in excitement. Dragons and felines must be related somehow! Even their naming customs bore some resemblance.

"What's catspeech like, Yari-Tab?"

The cat spoke from deep in her throat: *long garble garble hrrr hunt and fair garble garble hrr blood.*

Why, felines used words of Drakine!

"Beware blighters bearing gifts," Wistala said back to her in Drakine, quoting an old dragon-proverb.

"Watch out for—ummm, dirty presents?" Yari-Tab said, as she trotted up a leaning column that reminded Wistala of a windblown tree on a mountainside.

"Close. That was dragonspeech."

"Well, I never! I feel like I've got a new *tchatlassat*."

Wistala thought she knew the word. "A . . . clutchmate?"

"More like a—umm . . . cousin. A distant blood relation who is also a friend."

What was the word for that in drakine? Ah yes, kazhin. "My mother never told me about felines."

"Mine taught me to hunt, and that's about all. But that's felines for you. Great at telling their own tales and looking out for same, indifferent to anyone else's. We've got to find that basement now. Ahhh."

Yari-Tab jumped down from the column to a protruding branch, then to a broken windowsill, and then to the ground in a sort of controlled fall. She landed a good deal lighter than a dragon.

"Can you fit down this, Talassat?"

Wistala looked down what appeared to be an overgrown hole. Brambles trailed over an overhanging pile of rubble.

Yari-Tab ventured in and turned so her eyes glittered from the darkness. Above it three ancient arches, all broken open at the top, hosted a tangle of spider-legged plants.

"It widens out a little way down. Can you smell the rats?"

Wistala stuck her head in, smelled the rat urine mixed with old leaves and wormcast. The gap yawned bigger than it looked; it was mostly closed off by roots and their attendant mosses and trapped leaves. She pushed her head down and through, catching bits of lichen and dry air-root in her scales.

She found they were on stairs, Yari-Tab already down and through another hole, a half-filled passageway.

She tracked by smell and sound—the cat's footfalls were as silent as morning mist, but Wistala could hear her breath and sniffing.

"I wish I had my fire," Wistala said.

"Fire?"

"Yes, dragons can spit fire. I don't like not being able to see. A *torf* here and there makes all the difference."

"That's part of the fun, hunting by ear and nose. Though all this talking has sent the rats running."

"Sorry. I like being underground—I just want to explore thoroughly so I can feel safe, and unless dragons live long out of the sun, their eyes can't work on nothing."

"It's light you want? Want to see a bit of magic?"

"Cats and rats! You can do magic?"

Yari-Tab purred. "Oh no, but I'm fond of pretties. See this, my all-nose-and-no-smellsense-*tchatlassat*."

Wistala heard the cat scamper up a wall and more *prruming*.

A faint glow, like an angry dragoneye, threw a faint amber light across the chamber. With a modicum of light to work with, Wistala could now see the passageway they traversed.

She reared up and sniffed at the light source. It was some humble gem, perhaps enchanted in a fashion, for it held a glowing liquid within. As her nostrils breathed on it, the light grew brighter.

Yari-Tab extracted a clump of dirt from her paw and a cobweb from her whiskers. "There you are, Talassat. Some bit of forgotten magic—they're here and there in odd corners in the underground. The men have stripped them from the chambers they can get at. No one's found this one."

"How do you know about it?"

"My mother showed me this chamber and the trick, and I imagine she got it from hers. Rats aren't very clever—if you put a little light in a room, they're far braver about traveling the shadows than they are when it's holefill black."

"Did your father ever teach you at all?"

"Never knew him." She made another light descent and trotted to the far corner of the passageway. *"One of a dozen possibles and not much for hanging about* goes the feline proverb."

Wistala tried to imagine what the home cave would have been like with other hatchlings and mother-dragons about. Other male hatchlings pouncing her—she got a pang as she thought of Auron.

So much less to eat!

Wistala found herself liking Yari-Tab, though once she began talking, she was like a mountainside stream on a warm spring day, running always.

They entered an arched chamber, dead-ending in a collapsed cascade of dirt and masonry. The cut-off passage was about the size of Father if you didn't count his neck and trunk, cobwebbed above and rat-fouled below.

"You're sending the rats running," Yari-Tab said, hearing scrabbling sounds from a series of holes at the edge of the room. They were choked with dirt, broken stone, and everything from bits of bark to twigs.

She paused at one that stood under a crack in the wall where a good deal of masonry had fallen away, showing dirt behind mixed in with chunks of man-cut stone, both enlarging and blocking the passage. "There are bits of tunnel beneath this. Lots in other places are filled with swamp water, but this one has so much rat-scent coming up out of it, I think it's got to lead to the Deep Run."

"How do you know the Deep Run exists?"

"The rats squeak it to each other when they're being chased."

With every word, it became easier to understand the cat. Wistala wasn't sure if they were speaking Feline or Drakine or some simplified version blending the two. Their slit-pupiled eyes regarded each other in the darkness.

Wistala sniffed at the blockade. Only the tiniest glimmer of light came from the stone in the other room, but it was enough for her eyes to work on. "The rats have dug a hole. Why don't you just enlarge it?"

"A feline? Dig?" Yari-Tab flipped onto her back and rolled around in delight, batting at a bit of old cottonwood seed that had drifted down somehow, fighting it like an enemy. "Digging's for the rodents," she said as she sat and reset her fur.

Wistala thrust her snout into the hole, widened it enough for her *sii,* and went to work. Soon she sent showers of dirt in either direction, extracting or shoving the bigger pieces out of the way.

Yari-Tab found a perch out of the way of the digging and settled down to watch.

Her claws struck metal, badly rusted. Some kind of bars had been set into the tunnel, which trapped sticks, which collected leaves, which stopped dirt and blockaded the inlet.

The bars vexed her even after she dug her way through. Though rusted, they were too hard to bite, and all her claws could achieve against them were a series of scorings. Just beyond, a mound of dirt blocked the inlet, but a rat path ran up toward the top of the sluice. She backed out of the tunnel.

"Finished already?" Yari-Tab yawned.

Wistala blew dirt out of her nostrils. "See if you can get through the rat hole now."

The cat disappeared down the hole and returned, mud tipping her whiskers. "You're almost there. Beyond the bars is a hole, and beyond that I smell fresher air and hear lots of water drips."

"Except I can't get beyond those bars."

"Surely your neck can get through," Yari-Tab said, cleaning herself.

"I can't dig with my head."

"Well, don't look at *me*."

Wistala's tail swished of its own mind, and she crawled back down the sluice. She put her head through the bars and felt around with her nostrils. At the bottom joins, the water had worn away masonry, and it was quite crumbly on the other side. She extracted her head and went to work with one of her claws.

When she cleared off chunks all around the bricks holding the bar, she pushed again, but still it wouldn't yield.

"Stone and bone, what a bother!" Muscles convulsed in her chest, and she spat at the bar. A rope of spit clung to it, as ineffectual as her claws. But it gave off a sharp, hot odor.

Am I getting my foua *this early?*

She heard a rat make a *yeek*ing noise and scuttle.

If she could only part the bars a little so they'd offer more room, like—

Wistala remembered sleeping between Auron and Jizara. Jizara always took the warm spot against Mother, and Auron would sleep to the outside, leaving her cramped in the middle. Sometimes they pressed so close, she could hardly breathe. When they did that, she turned on her back and used her short, strong *saa* legs to part them.

She wedged her hindquarters sideways, pressing her tail

through the gap, and backed as far as she could between the bars. She pressed with her legs at the center of the bar, just as she used to do at the center of Auron's back.

It bent!

With that achieved, she repositioned herself between the bars facing the other way. She bent that one, as well. Now she had enough space to really put her legs and back into it—

Craaak!

The sudden release of pressure shocked her into thinking she'd broken her back instead of the bar for a moment, but sure enough, the bottom join had broken free of the rest of the clawed-away masonry. With half its strength gone, she could get down on all fours under it.

Ten heartbeats later, it was done—she could get through.

"Done it done it done it!" she called up to Yari-Tab.

"I knew you would," the feline called back, sounding half-awake.

With the bars out of the way, clawing earth seemed like pushing through nothing more than a pile of fallen leaves. She spun as she dug, all four limbs working once and tail helping shove out the loosened earth, and then she got through. Her nostrils filled with fresher-moving air.

And the smell of rats.

A smooth-sided tunnel yawned beneath, water and muck filling the bottom. Other arched-off tunnels branched off it, some dry, others trickling a bit of water and algae. A green lichen grew at the rim of the water, some weak cousin of the growth from the home cave. Or rather the stuff living in the lichen—Mother had told her that the lichen itself didn't glow; rather, the light came from tiny creatures that thrived on its fuzzy surface.

"Come and have a look, sister," Wistala said.

Her water-lids fluttered up and back down when she realized what she'd said.

Yari-Tab crept easily between dirt pile and a tangle of roots holding the earth that hadn't fallen.

"Such scents! Such hunting! I'll never suffer an empty

belly again." Her tail stood straight up as she looked out over the water-bottomed tunnel. Walkways big enough for a man stretched to either side of the main channel; other passages branched off everywhere.

"Watch yourself. They can be savage when cornered. If they're anything like cave rats, that is."

"Oh, to be sure."

"The coin?"

"But, of course."

Yari-Tab tore herself away from what Wistala suspected were dreams of bloody rat livers and climbed back up the sluice. This time she went to the glow-room, reignited it by rubbing herself round the stone again, and took off down another passage. She passed under a low arch and came to a badly cracked wall.

"Someone took a lot of trouble to seal the metal behind this wall and make it look like just another stretch of passageway. It's just inside that hole at the bottom."

Wistala could smell metal through the hole. She thrust her nose in, following an instinct that wasn't quite hunger and wasn't quite lust.

But nothing but dusty darkness met her exploring tongue—though the dust did taste of refined metal.

"Where is it?" she asked, withdrawing her head.

Yari-Tab bunched up in the darkness, eyes widening.

"Where's what? The hole's full of it!"

"No, it isn't. What kind of trick is this?" She felt her *griff* drop and begin to rattle, and the cat backed away.

"I wouldn't play a trick on a *tchatlassat*! Never!"

"Take a look," Wistala said.

"I . . . I can't seem to move."

"Fears and tears, I'm not going to hurt you."

Wistala lay down in hungry despair, feeling frustrated. After a long moment, the cat padded to the hole and entered.

Yari-Tab reemerged. "The rats. Wouldn't you know it."

"What would they use coin for?"

"I've never made it past wondering why they eat tail-stinkies that are better off buried, myself."

"Well, might as well ask them."

"Ask who?"

"The rats, of course. They took it."

Her ears went flat. "The rats? Are you frothing? They can only just vocalize. Hardly more sense than mouse-jibber."

Wistala picked herself up and started back for the sluice. "Are you coming?"

"Do you even understand Rodent?"

"Err—"

Yari-Tab bounded after her. "Then I'm coming. Someone sensible ought to come on this expedition. This story will be worth yowling till it echos, if you pull it off."

They returned to the opening to Deep Run. They heard rats flee ahead of them as they climbed the dirt pile.

"Inspecting your claw-work."

"Where to next?" Wistala asked once they climbed down to the pathway beside the muddy water. She saw glittering red rat eyes on a high ledge that ran near the top of the tunnel.

"I don't know. You instigated this dogbrained hunt. Follow the strongest smells until we corner some."

This underground felt wrong to her; everything was even and proportioned and unnatural. She felt vaguely tense and unsettled as she explored.

They came to an outpouring of water from some above-ground entry. The fall was about as wide as she was long and fed a swampy mass of tangled water plants, here and there sending out buds on long stems like dragon necks.

"Can you jump that?" she asked, looking at the water-fall. The rats slipped through it under a low, wet overhang of fallen-away masonry.

"No. Too long," Yari-Tab answered.

"Then hang on to my back. You're going to get wet."

"Oh, bother," Yari-Tab said. Wistala winced as she felt claws dig into the base of her scales.

Wistala plunged through the spray and came out the other side into a join of passages.

Yari-Tab hopped off her back and made a great show of

flicking her tail this way and that and kicking up her rear legs as she shook off the wet, a good deal of her grace and all of her dignity gone. She was even bonier than Wistala had imagined, obviously—

A ripple broke the pool, and the water exploded as a blur of a long-nosed shape lunged for Yari-Tab. Wistala saw snaggly yellow teeth and open mouth—

Once when Wistala was just out of the egg, a stalactite had cracked in the home cave, and Mother came to the edge of the egg shelf in a flash, putting her scaly bulk between the hatchlings and the gloom of the cave before the echo faded. Mother explained it later as "the fighting instinct," and something very similar must have happened in some same depth of Wistala's brain that kept her hearts beating.

Wistala jumped forward, threw herself into the jaws, felt them close on her scales and belly. An irresistible force dragged her into the water and under into darkness.

Whatever had a hold of her was perhaps surprised at her size, for it tried to shake her, but managed to only wave her back and forth in the black water filled with tiny strings of water roots. Wistala clawed with both *sii* and *saa*, lashed with her tail, brought her head round, and bit whatever held her at the join of its jaw. She got one *saa* into the teeth and tried to pry the jaws apart.

The pressure vanished, and the beast rolled, pulling her around it like a constricting snake as she left its jaws. It was perhaps the weight of a pony, though all jaws and tail, limbs smaller even than hers—

Since it had released her, she returned the favor, and it swam off into darkness. As she broke the surface of the water, she saw a thick tail with a serrated fringe like leathery teeth swirl the water and capsize the podlike blossoms of the water plants.

Wistala hugged ground and pulled herself up beside Yari-Tab, spat out a loosened hatchling tooth.

"That was a channelback!" Yari-Tab said from a perch at the top of the wall. For a half-starved cat, she was quite a jumper. She hopped down and landed softly next to Wistala.

"It fled. I was too big a mouthful anyway."

"If you miss on your first pounce—," Yari-Tab said.

"Try, try again elsewhere," Wistala replied, paraphrasing an old dragonelle proverb. A creature that lived by hunting could ill-afford fights with prey; a lost eye or a broken limb could mean death by starvation.

"Thank you, *tchatlassat*," Yari-Tab said. They turned and climbed away from the tunnel lake to a drier path, only to be attacked again.

Wistala felt a pull at her *saa* as she saw a trio of rats leap down from the ledge above—she lashed out instinctively with her *saa* and swished with her tail.

Two rats landed on her back, one on her head. It went for the eyes, and she panicked, whipping her head and rolling. Yari-Tab squealed as her body weight rolled over the cat.

She felt a bite in the naked flesh under her *sii*-pit. She whipped her head down, pulled the rat up by her teeth as she might a tick, crushed it, and flung it back into the channel water. Something bit at her hindquarters again, and she kicked—

Then they were gone as quickly as they'd come. She smelled blood and rats thick all around.

Yari-Tab had one pinned, both claws digging into its shoulders as it kicked out. The feline opened her teeth—

"Wait!" Wistala said.

"Whyever? The foul beasts bit my—"

"I want him to show us to the coin."

The rat squeaked in fright.

"Ask it," Wistala urged. "Ask it where the shiny metal is."

Yari-Tab squeaked out something, and the rat chattered back.

"He says he knows just what you mean and that there's lots. Don't believe a word, though. Rats will say anything once you've got your claws in them."

"I'll take the chance. Tell him to show us."

"He'll bolt down the first hole or dive—"

Wistala bent down and took the rat in her mouth. She

held her jaws just open enough for the rat to see the tunnel through her rows of teeth.

Yari-Tab purred. "That'll keep him in line." She squeaked up at the rat.

"He begs you not to swallow."

Wistala tried to form words but couldn't. She tilted her head and rapped a claw on the stepstones.

"Oh. Of course." She squeaked out again. "He says straight ahead for a while."

To any rats, or perhaps cave toads or bats lurking in the tunnels, they must have made a strange procession. Wistala walking with her head aloft, jaw set in its grimace, a rat nose protruding from between prominent fore-fangs. An orange-striped cat walking beneath, hopping over mud and rat droppings, occasionally rising up on its hind legs to squeak into the hatchling's mouth, in and out of mottled moss-light.

Eventually they climbed up a pile of fallen brickwork and into a chamber roofed by the remaining masonry and tree roots. The tree roots ran down the sides of columns, rose out of statues of human figures like bizarre hair braids, explored crumbles and cracks and dark ends of holes.

Rats filled the chamber, not in a smooth sea but rather in little puddles of brown fur, constantly shifting according to whim. Wistala had found some piles of bat droppings in the home cave that smelled worse—but not by much. Light came down from above in a pair of shafts, large and small, through some kind of half-clogged well in the roof.

The rats retreated from their entrance, disappearing into innumerable holes and cracks in a flurry of naked tails. The stouter-hearted bared fangs at the cat from beneath piles of fallen brick.

Wistala spat out the rat. It scampered away, shaking saliva from its hind feet.

"Better hop up on my head," Wistala suggested as a braver group of rats gathered on a pile of rags and bones at the center of the room.

It wasn't easy to hold the weight of the cat at the end of her neck, especially with the taste of rat in her mouth—the hairy beast had fouled her tongue in its terror—but she did her best to raise Yari-Tab up.

"Tell them we come to make a bargain, if there's any such word the rodents use."

Yari-Tab *yeek*ed out something.

That set up a storm of chittering like crickets.

More questions and answers passed back and forth. Wistala hoped Yari-Tab wasn't committing her to driving the men away in exchange for the coin or anything mad like that.

Her head swam, and she lowered it. The rats backed away and returned, easily frightened, easily encouraged.

"Just a moment—they're calling for someone," Yari-Tab said. She made a pretense of nonchalance, licking mud from her paws, but her tail twitched.

Wistala stilled it with a *sii*.

A creeping, cloud-eyed rat appeared, white all around the eyes and snout. The other rats jostled it as it came forward. A big brute of a rat dashed from the shadows and bowled it over, before scampering around them in a quick circle.

Wistala felt Yari-Tab instinctively lunge after the rodent, drawn by the motion, but held her back by the tail. The cat let out an outraged hiss.

The cloud-eyed rat would not be discouraged. It approached and *yeek*ed.

"What did he say?"

"I can't make nose or tail out of it. I know we were called *nightstalkers*."

"Just say what I say: I've come to claim coin rightfully mine, mistakenly taken by the rats."

With a great deal of halting and repeating, Yari-Tab chirped out the message. More rats had gathered, until they surrounded the pair like a gray-brown field.

The big rat that had jostled the cloud-eyed one stood up on its haunches and chattered. Wistala noted that the brute had a patch of fur missing from its shoulder, pink scar tissue with a few spikelike hairs had replaced brown fur. The older rat *yeek*ed in return.

"Well?" Wistala asked.

"What do you suppose 'finders keepers' means?" Yari-Tab asked.

"They have it, anyway. Ask them what they could possibly use hominid coin for?"

"Oh, my aching head." Yari-Tab chattered back. After that, only the cloud-eyed rat spoke, and at length.

Yari-Tab stopped to scratch the back of her ear. "I think I'm getting a perch on this. The rats seem to think if they get enough coin together, men will come and fight over it and leave bodies strewn about as they did long ago, and the rats will have great feasting."

"Tell them—tell them it does no good to just gather it if the men don't know about it. If they'll return the coin from behind the false wall, only enough for me to fill my bags, I'll spread rumors among the men about their hoard. Then the men will come and fight."

Yari-Tab *yeek*ed, but was cut off by the big rat, who ran up to her and stood nose to nose, baring his teeth.

"You've just been called a lying every-name and then some."

"Tell them this: I intend to find or replace my coin. I'll dig and I'll dig, looking for more. Who knows how many holes I'll open up, and then these tunnels will be crawling with cats."

Yari-Tab's eyelids went so wide, Wistala feared her eyeballs might roll out of her head. "We might not want to threaten—"

"Just say it," Wistala said, widening her stance and lowering her belly as the feline translated.

At that, the big brute rat screeched and jumped. It had courage; Wistala had to grant it that. It landed on her back and started to clamber up her neck, all awful sensation, rat claws digging into the base of her scales.

Yari-Tab disappeared under a wave of rodents as others jumped on. The feline let out such an earsplitting yowl, the mass of rats around them froze for a moment.

That worked so well, Wistala added a roar of her own, not so sharp to the ears, but a good deal louder—even if it

came out as a strangled cry. The tide of rats turned, save
for a few locked in combat with hatchling and cat. The rat
sank its teeth into the soft flesh beneath her jaw. Wistala
whipped her head to and fro, but the brute hung on, digging in. Wistala opened her mouth and swung it so its hindquarters flipped up and into her mouth.

Even in death, the rat's teeth didn't relax.

Yari-Tab, blood-smeared and wild-eyed, exploded out
of the rats and jumped to the top of Wistala's broad back,
clawing up by way of the canvas bags. From there, the cat
lashed out with her paws, swatting rats even as she hung
on to the twisting hatchling. Wistala bit the rats clamped to
her friend's haunches.

It was over in a few heartbeats. Wistala and Yari-Tab
stood panting, the torn rat still dangling from the hatchling's neck like a blood-dripping ornament.

Only the cloud-eyed rat still stood its ground. Perhaps it
hadn't seen the bloody contest.

"Well?" Wistala asked it, prying the dead rat loose with
a claw. It came away with no small amount of flesh and
blood between its jaws, its scarred shoulder red with her
blood.

Yari-Tab trembled so on her back, it reminded Wistala
of the beating wings of her dreams, only hundreds of times
faster.

The rat *yeek*ed heartily.

"Did you catch that?" Wistala asked.

"What?" Yari-Tab said. "Oh. My apologies, noble rat-
hunter." A conversation ensued. Wistala tried licking out
her wounds as the noises passed back and forth. Though
shallow, the bites hurt abominably. A great forest boar
wouldn't have been able to draw so much blood with its
tusks against her scales as the rats could with tiny sharp
teeth.

"The meal of it is, he's going to give you the coin," Yari-
Tab said.

"What's his price for the rats we killed?"

"Nothing. He thinks it's good for the hotheads to kill
themselves off now and then. More room for the rest."

Wistala swallowed the remaining half of the brute rat. It wasn't so bad after all, and she was as hungry as she'd ever been eating bones and claw-thin, fresh-spawned slugs in the home cave. "Even so. No sense leaving bodies lying around to remind them."

A procession of rats led them to a dank, dark room at the meeting of two sets of stairs where a metal cistern, big enough to hold a clutch of dragon eggs, lay half on its side.

Wistala's wounds still stung, but less now, and the pain was being replaced by a warm itch that in a lot of ways was worse than the sharper hurt.

Gold and green-covered coins lay within. The spill of metal didn't shine or glitter or gleam, but even the most tarnished coin made Wistala briefly swish her tail and stand with head erect, saliva suddenly thick at her gumline. *A hoard!*

Kill the rats! Kill them all! Kill the cat! Kill anything that so much as makes an echo near my glitters!

"*Tchatlassat!*" Yari-Tab squeaked as Wistala dragon-dashed forward, bowling her over. "Sister!"

Wistala stood with hindquarters to the coin, the shadows around her dark and red and angry.

The rats scattered, but Yari-Tab stood her ground, though she stood sideways, back arched, ready to flee.

"Sister!" she repeated, sounding passably Drakine.

Wistala blinked. The red faded. She took a mouthful of metal, more to give the wet in her mouth something to work on while she set her thoughts in order. She'd never expected the glamour of gold to be so strong!

"Oh! Sorry, *tchatlassat,* I came over funny. The rat bites are making me moody."

Yari-Tab said, "Your eyes went all red and fiery. I was worried for a moment that you had the froth."

"Better now." She took another mouthful of coin, rolled it around with her tongue until it was good and slimy, then let it slip down her throat. A brief, pleasant tinkle sounded from within as it clanked into the first bit.

"Let's see how much I can carry."

The rats regathered to watch.

Within a few moments, she had both bags filled—the pile looked hardly touched. Wistala looked around the chamber. Not a bad spot, actually, with water near and ample food. In the form of rats. But a dragon vow couldn't just be shrugged off like a dropped leaf. Besides, Father needed the coin worse than she.

Wistala nodded to the rats and trudged back the way they'd come. Yari-Tab jumped on her back and rode, claws dug into the crosspiece for the bags.

"It's going to feel a long way back carrying this load," Wistala said.

"Why leave?" Yari-Tab asked. "The hunting's going to be good with that run open. Next tailswell, I might even treat one of the local lazeabouts and have a litter of kittens. Deep Run will be our little secret."

"I'm already overlong," Wistala said, as they rejoined the sewer. It took her a moment to get her bearings, but only a moment—she still had her Lower World sense.

"Will you come back for more coin? I mean someday."

"I can't say."

"You've got a funny smell and a clumsy foot-way about you, Talassat. But I must admit you're the most interesting creature I've come across since I pounced my first mouse. I'll be sorry to see you leave Tumbledown."

Wistala sniffed the passage with the glow-crystal before reentering it. Full daylight shone outside, and there'd be men up and around. Perhaps she should sleep for a while and go back into the forest by dark. Yes. She was very tired. And the rat bites itched.

"I'm for a nap."

"Always a good idea," Yari-Tab agreed.

Wistala found an out-of-the-way corner with good air carrying smells from the entrance and settled down on a patch of dried mud obscuring some kind of tile artwork.

After a few tries, Yari-Tab curled up against her belly. "Your skin's about as comfortable as a riverbed," Yari-Tab said. "Warm belly, though."

Together, they slept.

Chapter 10

Y ari-Tab wasn't much of a sleepmate. She got up and went off to prowl at least four times that Wistala remembered, then returned and made a production out of finding a comfortable spot.

But she did bring Wistala a dead snake for breakfast. Wistala had no appetite, as she felt dry and sick from rat bites. Wistala wondered that the bony feline could carry the serpent, which looked fully half her weight, from wherever she'd caught it. Unfortunately, she'd have to carry the onerous weight of the coin much, much farther.

Time to be off.

"A good jump and a full belly, Talassat," Yari-Tab said as they made their good-byes.

"A good jump and a full belly, fur-sister," Wistala replied. The cat rubbed the side of her face against her folded *griff* and gave her forehead a lick.

As Wistala sniffed her way out of the ruins, she looked back at her feline friend, who found an old headless statue to sit upon and watch her leave. Wistala flicked head and tail up, and the cat raised a paw. Far off, a dog barked at the motion, and Wistala scrambled to the other side of a fallen column to put its bulk between her and the noisy dog. She looked back once more at the bottom of the hill, but Yari-Tab atop her statue was nothing but a lump against a multitude of other lumps filling the hills.

Wistala didn't relax until she was far from the smell of burning charcoal with a forest of shadows behind her. Only then did she cast about for a meal.

She had no luck—the clanking coins atop her back sounded a warning of her approach—and she went hungry that night.

She heard the first bay from the ridgetop, her halfway-home mark, as the morning sun turned the western mountains of her birth into blood-edged teeth.

At first she guessed it to be a distant wolf cry, but when the call wasn't answered from any quarter of the horizon, but rather taken up by other canine voices behind her—quite precisely behind her, she realized with an anxious gulp—she knew it had to be dogs.

Perhaps the dogs were after some poor stag or fox. She'd kept clear of the flocks of Tumbledown to avoid a vengeful hunt, and in all likelihood, she'd roused one anyway.

But time, she had time. Time to improvise.

Keeping to the ridge had its advantages. She could hear or see the pursuit—and it was the most direct path home. But a series of lakes to the morning side and a stream to the evening side might delay the dogs. She didn't know much about canines except that they couldn't smell their way across water.

Wistala trotted along until she found a sharp-sided ravine on the lake-littered side of the ridge. She let a little urine go to give it a strong dragon scent, then slid down its muddy sides. She trotted to a reed-infested pond, scattering waterfowl this way and that. She drank deep and thought for a moment—she had to get this just right.

First Wistala loosed the rest of her urine at the pond's edge, allowing most of it to go into the water. With a little luck, it would spread and filter through the whole pond until the dogs would detect it on every bank.

She left a confusion of muddy tracks and knocked over reeds at the bank, then rolled in waterfowl droppings, smearing her *sii* and *saa* thoroughly with them. Then she backtracked and climbed the ridge to her original path at a different spot, and carefully avoided the well-marked ravine.

All the climbing made her legs weary. The heavy yoke of coins across her neck felt heavier at each step, even as her stomach felt emptier despite the water.

At the thought of the coins, her mouth flooded with the slimy drool she'd had when she first came across them. Father wouldn't notice a mouthful or two gone—and they'd carry lighter in her stomach.

Once clear of her dog-dodge, she hurried as best as she could along the ridgetop, carrying tail high and doing her best to keep from snapping branches or trotting through muddy hollows. When her breath left her, she paused and ate a big mouthful of coin from each bag, more to take the desire out of her mind and mouth than because she actually needed it. . . .

An hour later, she came off the ridge, fixing her snout on the mountain notch that marked the source of the river gorge. If she traveled hard, she'd reach Father before nightfall. The rat bites were itching worse than ever, not quite pain, but adding to her bone-deep weariness.

She tore the loose bark off a fallen tree and managed to get a few insects, but they only made her hunger worse. *Oh, for a sick porcupine or a one-winged pheasant!*

A noise behind, light footfalls . . .

Wistala caught a glimpse of a hairy back, thinner than a bear's but not much smaller. She jumped up a bank and turned into a concealing patch of milkweed.

A black dog, with foam-flecked tongue and yellow teeth, padded out of the brush. Its eyes were wide and nervous as it put its long pointed snout to the trail. It had an odd sort of fur, extremely short at its head and limbs, thick and spiked like a badger's about the shoulders and upper back. It bore no tail that she could see. A leather collar, fixed high about its neck, and studded rings showed it to be domesticated. Even more oddly, two matching red runes were painted on its flanks. They reminded Wistala of flames or lightning bolts.

It sniffed the air and turned a nervous circle.

Wistala held her breath.

The dog trotted along her trail, nose pointed down but eyes watching the way ahead, passed her little bank upwind. The dog, like most fur-bearers, smelled like a dungheap. A faint smell of blood came from it, too.

Leap on it leap on it leap on it!

But she couldn't. All her body seemed capable of was shivering beneath the white-yellow flowers of the milkweed.

The dog turned, obscenely bulging eyes with their evil round pupils fixing on her location. It gave one querulous bark and looked right and left, as though searching for allies among the tree trunks.

Wistala shot forth to the edge of the bank and planted her feet, extended her *griff* and hissed at the beast:

"Go away!"

If it understood her, it gave no sign. Instead it let loose with a deep-throated snarl and came straight at her.

Fast, so fast, it was on her in an eyeblink. They came down the bank, rolling together, the dog's long limbs tangled with her own, teeth clattering against teeth. It yelped as she landed on its hindquarters but still sunk its teeth into her *sii*-shoulder joint. The upper teeth had no luck against her scales, but the lower went home.

Wistala raked it with her rear claws and felt blood and sinew. The dying dog hung on, closing its eyes to the pain. . . .

She resisted the urge to tear it free from her skin; that would do more damage. She waited until its heart stopped and then gently pried its jaws open.

Distant dog barks from the ridge told her at least one of the canine's yelps had been heard. She nosed into the dog's claw-torn belly and found the liver. Mother always said, if you could just eat one piece of an animal, it should always be the liver.

The body twitched as she chewed and lapped at dripping blood. It was an old dog. There were white circles
about its eyes, ears, and nose. Perhaps it had become confused and broken away from the rest of the pack—

Then she licked the bite wound clean and pressed on.

Despite the meal, she'd come off worse from the engagement. Her front limb was horribly sore; she could
hardly stand to move it, so she hobbled along as best as
she could using the other three, now heading up into the
foothills of the mountains.

She found a dry gully full of thick thorny brush and
plunged into it, snaking along with half-closed eyes. The
thorns rattled and snapped on her scales, red flowers
above like wounds in the sky—those wretched dogs with
their thin-furred muzzles would be miserable following her
through it.

A tear—one of the bags had ripped open, caught on a
thorny branch that had the tenacity of an iron hook. She
turned and sniffed at the coins already falling from the
sack.

Nothing to do but eat them.

When she came out of the thornbushes she found that
her load was unbalanced, the remaining bag kept sliding
over sideways—her makeshift contraption didn't have
much in the way of stabilizing straps. She ate mouthful
after mouthful of coin from the other bag as she rested,
greedy for each deliciously metallic swallow.

She staggered on, sick with fatigue, the coins in her gut
clattering. Step after wretched step after wretched step
uphill, until she thrust herself forward using only her hind
legs, the front ones folded flat against her side.

The bags were too heavy; that was why her limbs gave
out. She abandoned them, ate a few more coins so that
they wouldn't go to waste—maybe her last pleasure in
life would be that of silver and gold rolling around in her
mouth. Besides, the men would just have them anyway,
and go buy themselves new mates or flocks or boots or
whatever it was that men did with coin.

But, Father! She tore off one tiny pocket of canvas and

spat two remaining coins into it, gripped it in her teeth as she pushed on, keeping three of her four limbs moving on into darkness.

Roaring in her ears now. She felt wet on the interior of her nostrils.

The river!

She could see the prominence ahead. The battered columns, the rocks where Father would perch and fish, the jagged spur he always used to help himself back to the sleeping spot at the old meeting place or whatever it was.

She gave a glad, trumpeting cry and staggered on—at least she wasn't leaving a blood trail anymore. She'd failed this time, but she knew where to get more coin now, she'd be trebly-careful, cross the man-road by tree limbs above, there wouldn't be rat bites next time . . .

Wistala limped out onto the peninsula, climbed up to Father's prominence.

He looked dispirited and sleepy; blood seeped from a reopened wound. Perhaps he'd tried to fly again. "Father!"

"Tala! Back so soon? Bartleghaff's only just left to see how you were doing in the ruins. But perhaps he marked you—here he comes."

"I . . . ," Wistala managed to gasp. Her throat felt too dry for words.

Your contraption didn't survive the trip, I see.

Wistala squinted against the setting sun. The old condor waggled his wings this way and that on the confused air currents of the gorge as he approached.

A baying like a thousand wolves broke out from the banks of the river, louder even than the sound of water crashing into rock.

"What's this?" Father asked.

Wistala could manage thought-pictures: "Some dogs smelled me. I killed one."

Bartleghaff swept low over the peninsula but didn't land. "AuRel: it's the Dragonblade and his pack!"

Father blinked, let out a deep breath. "So he's found me," he said to no one in particular.

"The Dragonblade?" Wistala asked.

"The dwarves would hire him, I suppose." His wings drooped a little farther, and he searched the banks. Wistala saw black shapes bounding through the thick mist-washed ferns. Hunched shapes moved in the lengthening shadows of the woods beyond.

"They're coming off their horses now!" Bartleghaff shouted on another low sweeping pass.

"Fathered by a wolf and mothered by a bear, it seems, with the memory of a tortoise to boot, for his sire was killed by dragons long ago, and he's been seeking vengeance ever since."

"Do you suppose he was at our cave?" Wistala asked.

"Dragons must land sometime, and he always finds their refuge," Father said.

He straightened and got to his feet, a new light in his eyes. He cocked his head at Bartleghaff and flicked a *griff* up and out. "Go gather your relatives for that feast, old croaker."

Wistala didn't like any of this. Father's words set her trembling with the worst fear she'd ever known. If only she weren't so small, fireless. *Useless, useless, useless.* "Father, I did find you some coin." She spat out the canvas bag-bottom; her spit made it smell faintly of oats. She nosed out two tarnished coins: one of gold, the other of silver.

"Marvelous, daughter," Father said, nuzzling her fringe. "A pair, alike and yet not twins. Like you and Auron." He took them up with his tongue, carefully placed them to either side in his mouth.

The dogs let out another joined cry.

Must get away . . . "Are we going to run from the dogs?"

"Tala, I'm never going to fly again, in the air or on land. This fellow's killed more dragons than you have teeth, but he's never tried his luck against me. If I can—"

"Let me help you. I'll draw off the dogs."

Father stamped the ground, hard enough to cause Wistala to bounce.

"NO!"

His roar echoed off the gorge walls, louder than the rushing water, louder than the baying dogs.

Frightened, she tucked her head down into her wounded joint.

"Tala, you're too young for this fight. The best way for you to avenge your brother and sister is to have clutches of your own. Each hatchling of your own who lives to breed avenges them thrice over."

"The dogs—they'll bite and hold."

"I'm not afraid of the dogs or anything else that walks or crawls or swims. Now go."

The dogs must have caught a fresh scent, perhaps Father's blood on the wind, for they set up an eager clamor.

She stood there, shaking. She'd led them right to Father! That was why they'd sent a single old dog to nudge her along! "I won't. I can't."

"Promise me, Wistala. Clutches of your own. Lots and lots of hatchlings."

He nosed her over the edge of the precipice and looked once more down on her. His eyes crinkled, and he no longer looked fearsome and angry.

Love. Wistala'd seen it before when he gazed at Mother as she slept.

"Thank you for the coins, Tala."

With that, he turned. She saw his tail whip briefly overhead, its bronze catching the last of the setting sun. She heard him growl something to Bartleghaff, but couldn't catch it over the churn beneath.

No. She'd climbed up and escaped before. She wouldn't climb down this time. Not even the pain in her dog-bitten *sii* could stop her.

She slipped over the lip of the cliff and wormed between two pieces of fallen masonry. From the crack, she watched Father advance down the ridge of the narrow peninsula, choosing a rocky outcropping difficult to approach.

Dogs ran toward him in a mass of limbs and white-rimmed eyes and teeth. Behind the dogs, a file of men approached, led by a tall, broad figure in black armor. He was carrying a spear in one hand and a great sword in the other, helm with wings reaching up and almost touching above his crown.

The Dragonblade?
As the dogs approached, Father roared:

> *Foe and friend 'tween cave and sky*
> *All hear me now before I die*
> *Fire and blood this night will see*
> *When filial vengeance I take of thee!*

If any of the assassins understood his death song, they showed no sign of it.

Father ignored the dogs as they swarmed around him, leaping to reach his joints and claws. Barbed shafts flew from the archers and broke against his crest and scales. Father sent a great jet of fire up and across the crest of the peninsula, striking man and pine woods beyond. As the trees exploded into flame, she heard men's voices cry out. Wistala saw flaming figures fall down the steep sides of the pathway.

The dogs—all alike and bearing the same painted design on their sides as the old one she'd killed by the bank—jumped and bit and hung from Father's belly and limbs, planting their feet and pulling, arching their backs as they tugged at his flesh. Father was screaming in pain and turned into a whirlwind, biting and lashing at the dogs with his claws. But there were so many, and new slavering beasts jumped up to take the place of each one he killed.

The man in the black armor advanced, raising his spear. It sparked and flashed like distant lightning, lighting his armor and throwing shadows all around.

A hot lump burned in Wistala's breast. Father couldn't kill the Dragonblade with dogs pulling at him from every direction. She dragon-dashed forward, squeaking out a roar.

She'd never smelled such a thick blood odor in her life, if anything made sharper by the oily smell of burning dragonflame.

Mad-eyed dogs came at her, and she recoiled, but as her head came up, muscles in her breast took over, and she spat. A thin jet of flame arced out at the dogs, but they jumped aside or over the pathetic puddle of flame.

The dogs, moving so fast they seemed shadow rather than flesh, piled on her.

A white-tipped spear erupted from Father's neck, and he turned, mouth wide and roaring at the black-armored figure who stood atop a rock, silhouetted against the burning trees behind. Arrows that glowed as they flew struck Father all about the neck and jaw and burned there.

Wistala staggered forward, feeling the dogs pull at her. She spat the last of her flame at dog haunches clustered at Father's back leg and pulling him over, and was rewarded by agonized yelping above the snarls of the three dogs dragging at her.

Father rolled, crushing the dogs, sending others spinning off into the darkness, the spear lodged in his throat like a great bone. The Dragonblade leaped forward and slashed at Father's belly, opening a wound fully the length of Wistala.

Other men stood at some kind of machine on the peninsula. It sent an oversize arrow into Father's side, punching through scale as easily as her claw-tip could go through a leaf.

"Father!" she cried.

The Dragonblade ducked under Father's bite and swept up with his sword. Father's head and neck crashed down, almost severed.

Wistala forgot the pain, forgot the dogs trying to pull her limb from limb.

She looked into Father's eyes as the battle fire faded and they went dry and glassy. AuRel, Bronze of the Line of AuNor, had joined Mother in the stars above.

Wistala wailed out her pain to the sky.

The Dragonblade knelt and kissed the pommel of his sword, and his men broke into some manner of song.

Wistala bit into a dog, exchanging pain for pain. It howled, and the Dragonblade's men left off his victory song and turned toward her.

Other men, some carrying two-handled saws, gathered behind.

She wouldn't end up on these rocks, her head and claws

sawed off. Wistala gathered what remained of her strength and managed to stand. She tottered a few steps toward the edge of the cliff, dragging dogs at every step. The dogs pulled back, at war with her body.

Perhaps the Dragonblade read her intent. He ran forward, bloody sword held out, waving on the others, who stood gaping at Father's bloody wounds.

The two still-living dogs snarled and fought her every step, their muzzles covered with blood, the spiky hair on their backs standing straight up. They dragged her back, away from the ledge, toward the Dragonblade.

"You shan't have—," Wistala grunted. She swung her tail, knocked a dog off its feet, and lunged at the ledge. She got the claws of one *sii* over. Now she had some real traction.

Tearing—pain.

Fly! She'd fly once before she died.

She got a *saa* at the edge, and the dead dog fell over the side, its jaws finally relaxing. Freed of its weight, she coiled her spine and jumped.

Wistala felt light as one of Bartleghaff's long tip-feathers as she spun through the air. She struck the prominence Father used to climb up from the river, rolling over on a growling dog and hearing a snap, and felt free air one last time before she plunged into the cold, roaring river.

BOOK TWO

Drakka

WHOSOEVER SAVES A SINGLE LIFE HAS SAVED A WORLD.

—*Hypatian Low-Priest Proverb*

Chapter 11

D rifting, flying, but the air—so cold. Impossible to see through the clouds.

Tiring—so she glided. A hurtful pull in the back—had a wing joint slipped?

Now she could see.

A hominid bent over her, face shadowed. Can't raise her claw to strike it—

A sound, sharp and regular *tap-top-tap-top,* movement in time with the beats, lulling her, and she slept. . . .

Fighting for breath—cold. Nose must be kept out of water. Drowned dog pulling me under, if I don't get free, I'll die. Bite! Tear! Rushes of warm blood in the cold. Nose up! Nose up! One more breath before I go under!

Wistala stretched, unbelievable warmth and well-being suffusing her body, dreams fair and foul gone.

She opened an eye. She lay stretched out on hairy fabric that caught in her scales. A vast presence, white and curved like a huge dragon egg, gave off heat from a mouthlike opening in its side. *Woof-woosh woof-woosh woof-woosh*—the sound in her ears reminded her of Father when he got out of breath from his climbs up from the river. She rolled her head and saw a hominid, its back to her, working an apparatus that opened and closed like a dragon's mouth, complete with folding *griff* at its sides.

A crackling and a glowing came from the huge egg's mouth. She smelled burning charcoal. The heat increased, and she basked in it before she slept again.

She woke to a salubrious greasy smell, like the road-dwarf's sausages, only more powerful.

A steaming double-handled iron pan appeared before her, filled with a greasy broth. She glanced around, saw a roof above held up by thick rounded beams. Doors wide enough to fit a full-grown dragon had been flung open to the summer air and light.

The faint smells of horse and goats interested her, but not half so much as the broth. She found enough strength to take two tonguefuls.

The hominid, standing so still, he might have been one of the timbers holding up the roof, watched her from a good dragon-dash away. Probably a male: he had prominent, angular features, a lean, narrow-hipped body, and a clean-shaven head covered with a thick film that reminded her of the high mountain rocks with winter lichens she and Auron had climbed.

An elf.

Father's stories about the killing prowess of the elves came back to her in a rush of imagery. . . .

He stayed away. There were windows and the wide doors closer to her than he—though with her body feeling limp and drained, she wondered if she could even manage to right herself for a dash—

A mist-colored horse at the other end of the interior regarded her warily. This place was divided into a number of smaller chambers along a central alley.

Another sip of the hot liquid, and she felt newly hatched, despite the strange surroundings full of disconcertingly straight lines.

Wistala examined her wounds. Cracked scales and any number of brown-stained injuries marked every limb. The brown stains puzzled her. They didn't smell of dried blood, but a sharper smell. But stained or no, the wounds were certainly healing up nicely. She rolled onto her other side and saw that a terrible rend in her *saa* interior had been sewn like a hominid garment.

Perhaps the elf was healing her to make better sport of her later.

She rested a few minutes, then had a little more broth, rested and then lapped, until finally by midday, the pan had been licked clean. Then she slept, deep and dreamless.

After sundown, she dragged herself—standing hurt her wounded limbs too much—to a central stone cistern, where she smelled water fed by an outlet coming down from the roof beams. She drank deep. Then she slept against the stone.

A gentle cough woke her. The elf stood there, perhaps twice the length of her body away. He squatted, toadlike with his gentle eyes and long, folded limbs.

This time she didn't tremble. Whoever he was, whatever his aim, she read in his eyes that he meant her no harm. He rocked on his haunches. It took her a moment to realize he was inching forward, putting one or the other leather-strap-bound foot after another an almost imperceptible length.

The horse didn't seem to like her presence at the trough. He expelled an angry breath and stamped, chewed on a wooden rail in a sidelong manner. Wistala thought horses timid creatures, but this one seemed to be eager to get out of its alcove and at her.

The elf reached one long hand out, palm empty and toward her. He tickled her under the chin. She couldn't help her *griff* lowering a little or her fringe standing on end, not with her nostrils full of the terrible odors of elf and horse from that day she lost Auron.

She watched his eyes. They never seemed to be the same color. Brown when they looked at one of the beams holding up the roof, a dull red color when they glanced down at the bricks paving the floor, green when they briefly rested on her. Now, looking at the water in the trough, they became dark and reflective.

The elf pulled up a handful of water, let it trickle

through his fingers. "*Anua*," a voice like a soft fall of rain said. "*Anua.*"

She tried making the sound in her throat. "Ennuh," she managed.

The elf brought a handful of water to her mouth. "*Anu sah.*" He put his lips to his palm and sucked up the water.

"Ehnu-ssa," Wistala repeated, and lapped up some water.

His mouth crinkled. "Anu sah!" he said, pushing a wave of water to her. She took another tongueful.

"Ahnu-ssa," she said, and nosed a wave at him. She splashed him a little by accident, but he didn't seem to mind. Next he taught her his name: Rainfall.

After that, Rainfall drank with his mouth turned up at the corners.

In the following days, as her strength returned, they made slow progress with her Elvish. He learned her name, though he preferred to call her by the familiar Tala, as it was easier for him to pronounce. Dragon traditions weighted lightly on her. She took her lessons in turn, naming things around the *stable*.

Shortly, she dragged herself outside. The mountaintops to the east were just visible through a part in the trees. She must have come some length down the river, perhaps as far west as Tumbledown, though the hills here were covered with grass and rock, and trees seemed to grow thickly only out of the wind.

That she'd come so far without drowning was as miraculous as if she'd sprouted her wings. Yet she had not the tiniest memory of being in the water beyond the leap off the cliff with the dogs dragging at her.

The elf's behavior surprised her as much as her survival. According to Mother and Father, elves were soft-stepping hunters of spear and bow who blew horns and sang swanlike warbles over the corpses of dead dragons as they danced, holding hands sticky with dragon blood.

The only part of that legend that rang true was the elf's quiet nature. Whether passing over brick, wood planking, or soft grass, he hardly made a sound, save for the whispers of the wind moving around him. The rest of his manner was as gentle and tender as a mother dragon's over still-wet hatchlings.

Thoughts of Mother and Jizara left her cold and sleepy and miserable. Why didn't memories heal and fade like wounds?

That evening he cooked her a platter full of organs and entrails in a sharp-smelling herb she'd learned to call *garloque,* or dragonbuds, as the smell of the white clusters when crushed was faintly dragonish.

The meal filled her gorge but did little for her anguished mind.

To divert her thoughts, the next day Wistala ventured out of the stable and viewed Rainfall's home.

It was a vast home and garden for a single hominid and a few animals. Treble vast when she learned that the wild orchards, melons, and wheat- and tuber-fields around were also his. He made no effort to farm as she understood the word, though he threw the horse's manure on two beds of flowers surrounding the trees on his threshold.

They were the oddest trees Wistala had ever seen. They became positively animated when Rainfall worked in their vicinity. Their leaves rattled, and their branches scraped against each other, and now and then he looked up and spoke to the limbs, or plucked a bloom and left it to rest in one of the trees.

Then there were the goats.

They came in a variety of colors, sizes, and temperaments; the only attribute they shared was a fear of dragon smell. The goats wandered away whenever they saw or smelled her, horned billies keeping a watchful eye as their charges paced away with tails flicking. They climbed to the highest peak of the house—

And such a house!

Wistala had never seen anything like it.

The house stood on, or rather comprised, a hill and the trees that grew on it. The main door stood between those two vast and arching oaks Rainfall attended, beneath a sort of webbing that had any number of brambles and berries stretching from the oaks to the hillside entrance. Several of the tree limbs supported a sort of stone-and-wood balcony that offered shelter to anyone at the door below.

There were smaller balconies of stone, not shaped but cleverly laid together, windows you couldn't see unless the sun hit them just right, and chimneys rising up through old stumps.

The inside had narrow passageways and stairs that opened up on wood-paneled rooms with skylights carrying down birdsong from the outside. It was like a cave with surprises at every turn, including a lower room that held a small waterfall that ran warm after its passage around the chimneys, or so Rainfall explained.

Some of the rooms echoed every claw-click of her *saa* on the wooden floors, others—the sleeping rooms—absorbed sound with moss-covered walls and ceilings thick with roots. At the uttermost top there stood a room filled with paper bound up in leather wrappers or enclosed in tubes, lit by a cupola of crystal that, when slightly opened to air the room, carried in the bleatings of the nimble-footed goats.

Wistala passed a chamber that made her wonder if it was an armory, with many big-doored cases in between, perhaps for armor and shields.

But the weapons seemed frail and lacking in edges.

Rainfall took down one of the devices, vaguely like a small bow, and ran his long fingers along it. A sharp, clear sound unlike anything Wistala had ever heard came from a series of strings that hummed until they quit vibrating. Wistala's nostrils opened in surprise—was the odd bow alive?

"*Senisote*," Rainfall said.

Apparently one could create *senisote* by blowing into tubes and tapping on clay cylinders topped with leather, as Rainfall demonstrated. She enjoyed it all.

He pulled out a wooden construct so he could squat

without folding his legs and played on the instrument she liked best of all, a long wooden tube with a hollow chamber on the end like a hulled melon. It created a sound as pure as birdsong, sweet as a sigh a mother dragon might make over her hatchlings, and as varied as a waterfall.

Wistala gave her first *prrum* in what seemed like an age. Her neck stiffened, and she began to bob her head. Strange magic. Her head rose and fell with the tune.

Rainfall stood and stepped crabwise, his eyes so merry that Wistala couldn't help but move opposite him so she could keep him in view. He turned a circle, and so did she, and the next thing she knew, they were moving this way and that across the floor. He capered as he played, and she imitated; the slight pain in her joints couldn't keep up with the pleasure the music brought.

The tune ended, and her host attempted to strike a pose that involved entwining his legs and spreading his arms, but he must have misstepped, for he collapsed to the floor with a bit of a bump.

And then he began to laugh.

She'd never heard the like. The sound was as pleasing as his music, and infectious besides, for she found her *griff* fluttering and scraping against her scales.

The elf sat back and wiped his eyes, face split by his mouth that now seemed to stretch from cheekbone to cheekbone. He reached out with his foot and tickled her under the chin, and she couldn't object.

"A rare delight," he said, and she took perfect understanding, for his words came out with such a wave of happiness, it was almost mind-speech.

"Very good," she said back. He used the expression whenever she pronounced an Elvish word particularly well. It must have suited him, for he gave a little bow.

Wistala saw a smaller version of the stool the elf sat on as he played. She ambled over to the seat, thinking she saw a cat-size creature sitting there, but she realized it was only a bit of craft bearing hair and painted-on eyes. She sniffed at the rather dirty thing—it smelled of elf, but differently from her host.

"How this played?" she asked, not seeing strings or blowholes in its design.

At this, the elf stood. "I . . . you . . ." He fled from the room, leaving Wistala to sniff and wonder.

The gray-white horse was another puzzle, for he did no work. Wistala knew little about the doings of the hominid world, but in the home cave she'd heard stories enough about horses—usually while dining over a piece of one—to know that hominids had them pull or carry or bear them.

Indeed, he appeared to own Rainfall rather than the reverse, for the elf labored long in keeping his berth clean and the horse properly brushed.

Wistala, while exploring the stable one morning in pursuit of mice, came close to his stall. The horse snorted and reared and kicked. His simple beast-speech was easy enough to understand. "Away! Stomp you! Kick you!"

"You mistake me for a dragon. I'm but a hatchling."

It occurred to her that she was no longer fresh out of the egg; she'd survived aboveground and breathed her first fire. *I'm a drakka!*

The horse seemed in no mood to make zoological distinctions. He danced in his stall. "Away! Beast! Sharptooth! Away!"

Wistala left him stomping and raging and hopped out the window. She examined the roof and felt up to a climb, using a wide-bellied wheeled contraption—*cart,* she corrected herself—to gain the roof. She sniffed at the clay-lined holes that guided the rain to the central cistern and gained the peak.

From here, even with some of the treetops, she could see more of the lane leading west away from the hill house and barn. She saw stone walls disappearing into overgrown fields, and a few roofless constructs at the base of two massive, partially bald hills to the north.

She could see nothing of other hominid habitation, unless the ruined houses counted, but she doubted elves, men, or dwarves would live in homes with shrubs growing in the doorways and young trees poking through the roof.

The only breathing creatures who seemed to be thriving in the vicinity were the goats.

"Rah-ya! Rah-ya! Rah-ya!" came a joyous cry. The sound traveled from window to chimney to door of the house. Rainfall danced out the door and into the overgrown yard separating home from barn, dressed only in a cross-tied wrap of thin white material. He let out a whoop and ran to the weed-choked pool surrounding a statue of three figures.

Rainfall tipped, plunged his head into the water, looking just like a duck on a dive, save for the long kicking legs.

Wistala couldn't imagine the causes and consequences of such action, so she jumped down from the roof. The impact pained her, but only a little.

By the time she crossed the courtyard, he was head-side-up again.

"Rah-ya, Tala! Rah-ya!" Rainfall said. He pointed to his head.

At his temples a pair of fuzzy growths, like clover heads, hung rather limply from the rest of the lichen growth, and she detected a few patches of fuzz. "See? See?"

"I see—yes. I understand—no."

"You wouldn't, would you?" Rainfall said. "I've been . . . down. Ill. Wounded."

Wistala saw no scars. "Wounded?"

"Not as you think. I'm old, but still a long way from my final *haspadalanesh*—age."

"The . . . greenstuff . . . means healing?"

"Yes. Means healing. Thanks to you."

Wistala couldn't imagine what she'd done. He'd stuffed her with hearty kid stews, swabbed her wounds. How would that improve his health?

"You know a little of our language, but nothing of our souls," Rainfall said. "In time . . ."

"In time . . . ," Wistala repeated.

"Very good."

Time passed, and it was very good.

The elf presented her with books, and she began to

learn to read by associating sounds with the simple illustrations within.

Once she began to read, her ability with Rainfall's language took wing. Though she still made him laugh now and then with her pronunciations, they learned each other's minds better through unfettered words.

Now and then men, hairy, oily, and smelly, rode in to visit the estate Wistala learned was called Mossbell. Rainfall received them in his hall with as much food and drink as he could quickly prepare while she hid her body and odor in a masking grove of pines or up a yew tree. These visits always left Rainfall dispirited, and clumps of his bark-colored hair, now sometimes bearing tiny white flowers and red berries, would drop out.

"Just formalities," he apologized upon her return as he fed her in the stable on their leavings, which were ample, as they ate only the choicest goat loin.

"Where are they from?"

"His Rodship Hammar, the Thane of Nure and the Illembrian Foothills."

"Is that like a king?" Wistala asked, using the only human title she knew other than Dragonblade.

"It may as well be, for Hypatia has no more knights to send to keep his ambitions in check in these dark days.

"I must teach you Parl, the Hypatian vernacular, so that you might climb up one of my chimneys and listen. Though you'd fall asleep at their discourse and drop down the chimney like Old King Yule himself. And your appearance would bring no Solstice merrymaking."

"Correct me if I err. Hypatia is all the lands between the Inland Ocean and the mountains?"

"Once it was much more. It ringed all the Inland Ocean like a necklace. But the necklace's caretakers let it fragment, and others have grasped at the loosened jewels. Most are gone now, and even the chain is breaking. Once you were a Citizen of Hypatia first, and only a man, elf, or dwarf second. But tribalism has taken over since then, between the conniving Wheel of Fire and that madman Praskall howling up his humanist mobs in the Varvar lands. I fear I'll live to see the last few jewels of Hypatia torn and stolen."

"Is Mossbell a jewel?"

"Nothing so grand. But Mossbell does have charge of a link in that precious chain. Tomorrow I'll show you."

The next day Rainfall put a light sort of woven saddle on the irascible horse—Avalanche was his name, and a stallion still, she learned as Rainfall spoke to him—and rode out with Wistala trailing along. First he cantered the horse a few times around the buildings to warm him and take the edge off. Only after this would Avalanche walk down the cobblestones to the Road.

The Road impressed Wistala, once it had been explained to her. Fully wide enough for two carts to pass and space for outriders beside, it was raised up and paved with fine stones, smashed so as to give them teeth that allowed wheels and horseshoes to grip, keeping mud down and dry surface against wheel, boot, or sandal. Or so Rainfall said.

"In my grandfather's time, fully six hundred and forty years ago, he'd done his duty to waxing Hypatia in the Battle of the Swordgrass to the south. His skill in battle won him much renown. As a reward, the Imperial Directory awarded him this estate and charged him with keeping the roads and the bridge. He named it Mossbell for an ancient gong he found at the site of the old ferry. A light duty, one would think."

"Bridge?"

"We're coming to it shortly. Happily, it's the cause of our meeting."

The trees grew close about the road here, and it seemed little traveled. Rainfall continually watched and listened to the west side of the road. "If you hear a crashing, or deep and whistling breathing from these woods, hide yourself as best you can."

"Is there something to fear?"

"Rarely in the daylight. There's a pestilence dwelling on the banks of the river south of here in the form of a troll."

Wistala wasn't sure what a troll was, other than that they were more ravenous than a brood of hungry hatchlings.

Rainfall continued: "None dare settle flock or cot here. Much of my grandfather's estate is now the troll's stomping ground. Once many sheep and cattle, even horses, were raised here, along with the best four-season trail oxen in the northlands, if you'll forgive my pride."

"Is there no way to be rid of the troll?"

At this, her host blinked and set his mouth, as if barring a gate to keep the words in. "It's been tried."

They arrived at the bridge, and Wistala stood still in wonder until her eyes could comprehend it.

The gorge here yawned far wider if a bit less high than around Father's retreat, still so steep-sided that a hominid could climb it only with a careful choice of path and much use of hands. Naked rocks and broken timber filled the river, flowing hard but without the bank-to-bank froth.

The bridge crossed the river in four arching leaps, columns of shaped and angled stone like towers bearing the road. There had once been a fifth arch in the center, but it had fallen and been replaced by wooden planking under an arch of its own. A stout stone bridge house stood at the Mossbell end. Wistala would hardly have noticed it, except that Rainfall slipped from the horse and went to the door.

"I was attending to the lock here when I saw you. Oddest thing I ever saw, a condor was circling close over you, but not stopping to eat. You were just there," he said, pointing to a black length of shattered timber sticking out into the river, "lying atop that grandfather bole. Even at the end of your strength, you managed to pull yourself out of the river. I had to pry your tail from one of the knots."

"What did the condor do?"

"Flew off mountainways."

"You climbed all the way down there to inspect a half-drowned drakka?"

"And more. I used my *balagan* to get you up."

"What is a *balagan*?"

"A device for lifting things, using ropes and blocks. Another word for it is *crane*. It allows one to lift the weight of three."

"Whyever would you trouble yourself?"

"Curiosity. Dragons are seen only rarely nowadays."

"And if it weren't for you, they'd be rarer."

Chapter 12

R ainfall was a fountain of information about everything but his own misfortunes. Only through numerous questions could she piece together his story.

She tried asking Avalanche, but he was a simple, literal fellow, and at the slightest head-bob, *griff*-rattle, or harsh syllable would become enraged and threaten her with a stomping. And most of what Avalanche did know related to the quality of the hay, or displeasure at not being put out to pasture with the chance of meeting females.

So she spent most of her time with Rainfall, his diverting conversation limited to lighter topics.

Other than his grandsire, the only time he talked about his family was in the portrait gallery. Elves, evidently, had a "study" done of themselves once they reached maturity.

A study didn't use paints or inks, but instead bits and pieces found outdoors—tree bark and colored sands being the two most common media. Done in life size, the "portraits" were remarkable once you got away from the odd textures. Rainfall's certainly captured his gentle expression, warm eyes depicted with carefully polished and carved stones.

"And at the end we have my wife, son, and granddaughter," her host said.

Did elves not keep their family about? "I'd like to see

them in person to compare with these likenesses," Wistala finally said. "Will I meet them?"

"An impossibility with Nyesta and Eyen, my wife and son. They are dead."

His wife had a softness to her features, done in colored sand and painted shell. "I hope she had a peaceful passing," Wistala said.

"Age and infirmity took her too soon, as it does all humans. But we had many years of comfort together. I met her when she passed through with Old Nightingale's Circus, now under Ragwrist—though, like everything else these days, much reduced in scope and splendor. She left me comfort in my son, transitory though it was; he had something of his mother's temperament and my father's courage."

She looked at his portrait. Some manner of sash was woven about the harness that held his sword. His eyes challenged, as if daring the portraiteer to capture him.

All that served to remember his granddaughter was a sketch. A simple charcoal depicted her; Rainfall apologized that he had no skill with formal portraiture. The girl-child had overlarge eyes compared with the others, but perhaps hominid youth accounted for that, for if the sketch was life-size, she was a good deal younger when drawn than the others. The elf blood came through strong in her cheekbones and delicate ears.

"She still lives?" Wistala asked. Curiosity about her host made her stop in front of the drawing.

"Yes, but Lada's been away from me these eight years."

"With her mother?"

"We never knew her mother. Or I should say, I never knew her. Some sport of her father in one of the taverns of Quarryness or Sack Harbor, I expect. She arrived on my doorstep as an infant, bearing a note my son burned rather than show to me. She was my comfort after her father's death. Since—since—please excuse me."

Rainfall turned his face to the wall, and after a last look at the charcoal portrait, Wistala crept out of the room.

*   *   *

As the leaves turned color and dropped, Wistala explored the broken houses at the base of the two hills, pulling nails and hinges from the ruins to satisfy her hunger for metal. She'd come terribly close to stealing a small silver candle-holder from a side table on one of her passes through the house and decided to hunt metal on her own.

When she returned, all her claws counted thrice worth of horses were standing in the field beyond the barn under the care of two boys who occupied themselves by throwing rotten apples at each other from opposite sides of a stone wall that held the saddles.

She circled the house to get downwind of it and found a yew tree to climb, where she spent an uncomfortable night. The riders left in haste the next morning—she saw only the backs of cloaks and a few gamboling dogs of the ordinary sort, not the huge savage brutes she'd pulled over the ledge.

Somewhat stiffly she climbed down from the tree to hear Rainfall calling:

"Tala Tala Comeoutfree! They're gone, and it is safe."

He hurried to meet her as soon as she extended her neck above the bushes.

"More of the thane's men?" she asked.

"Better and yet worse, at least for you. It was the Dragonblade and a party of hunters."

Breath and death, the Dragonblade! Wistala couldn't help but crouch at the name.

"He said a young dragon had escaped him, blamed the miss over the loss of his beloved pack in the summer. He has to go back to training pups for a while."

"You fed him and his horses, then?"

"What could I do? He carries a Hypatian Knight-Seal. I'm old-fashioned enough to bow to any who carries it, even if he hunts a friend. Though I felt no need to disclose your presence, especially as his line of questioning allowed me to keep my honor and your friendship."

"What do you mean?"

"The description he gave was laughable. He got your size right, but had the color wrong—lots of talk of wolves' hides and such. I could honestly say I'd not seen anything like that about the road."

"Why the road?" she wondered. *Of course, they first came upon my scent on the same road near Tumbledown.*

"I gave his dogs as vast a meal as I could manage so they'd sleep rather than sniff around the barn. Same with the men. I fear our dinner tonight will be their leavings, little though there are."

Wistala was grateful for a moment that she hadn't been hidden in the barn or somewhere closer. There would be danger, yes, but temptation. Men were vulnerable when they took off their armor to sleep. She'd learned the knack of walking silently through the home without letting her claws touch the flooring to save Rainfall's woodwork.

"Have they gone for good, or will they be back?"

"They're hurrying south. They believe you to be heading in that direction, but on what evidence, I can't imagine."

"I may have left southbound marks crossing it from the old hovels beneath the twin hills."

"Or perhaps the Dragonblade makes guesses to impress his men. A right guess is long remembered, and there's always an excuse for a wrong one."

Wistala spent another cold night in the yew tree that evening, just in case the Dragonblade doubled back.

Rainfall had her observe him carrying out his duties on the road, more as a mental diversion for her than anything else. For two active weeks as the temperature dropped, he and a dozen men went along the road, filling in holes; then they applied pitch to the timbers of the bridge to proof them against ice and snow. This part of the north saw frequent freezes and thaws and snow, thanks to the air currents of the Inland Ocean a few horizons to the west. Even once the labor was done, he bargained with the men a little extra to dig up vegetables and bring in hay and slaughter and salt some goats.

Payment was a problem, for Rainfall had little money. He gave away odds and ends from the vast house in return for their work, anything from candlesticks to cooking skillets. Wistala understood now why the place seemed so bare, save for his high room of books and basement of wine.

Then they settled in for the winter.

Wistala had been installed in what had once been what Rainfall called a "health-room," a wooden enclosure of fragrant cedar wood, where stones heated in the furnace would be brought so that water might be dripped on them. It had a gutter in the center that made for easy cleaning, and she was happy to find hatchling scales on the floor each morning, with new ones coming in fast and thick owing to a supply of tarnished brass plates and drinking vessels she smelled out buried in the dirt floor of one of the abandoned houses.

Wistala asked about hominid commerce one night over dinner, and Rainfall did his best to explain it. "A dwarf would make it simple, I'm sure. I've not much of a head for additions and subtractions and excises and taxes."

The last in the list seemed to be his chief worry. As she understood it, twice a year he owed his thane an amount of money that had been set at a time when the estate was prosperous, and though Mossbell had the misfortune of having a troll appear and pillage the lands, he was still expected to produce the same sum. No amount of pleading with the thane could alter it.

"What do you get in return for these taxes?" Wistala asked.

"The thane's protection."

"But not from trolls."

Rainfall poured himself a little more wine. "He has posted a reward, in the form of a small sum and relief from all taxes and excises for five years. But few are willing to take the challenge. What happened to Eyen is still fresh in many minds."

"Your son tried to kill the troll?"

"His death is my fault. The bundle containing Lada had just arrived, and I'd engaged a wet nurse. He and I argued about his scattering bastards around the thanedom. Elf blood passes down an alliance of aspect and tongue that human females find pleasing, and he took advantage of manner and countenance. I ... I challenged him to perform some useful duty. I meant that he seek gainful employment to defer the cost of his daughter, but he rode out on Avalanche, the last of his grandsire's line of mighty warhorses, to solve all our difficulties on the point of his lance." Rainfall struck the table with his elbows so hard, the plates and goblets jumped. Then he concealed his face with his long-fingered hands.

Wistala stood still, never having seen a violent move from her host before.

"I beg your pardon," he said when he collected himself. "You've finished your salmon already. Would you care to dispose of mine? Having a drakka about so simplifies the clearing up."

Wistala learned the cloudsign for snow, sleet, and rain that winter—what weather Mossbell saw depended on the direction of the wind. It blew mostly from the west, and if it veered farther south for a while, it grew warmer, but when it came out of the north, it became bitterly cold and made her alternately ravenous and torpid.

Father had hunted in this winter wind a year ago to feed his hatchlings?

Being indoors frustrated her, and on the first sunny day after the sun turned south again, she set out to walk the grounds of Mossbell.

It wasn't an accident that she walked west, crossed the road, and plunged into the broken forests covering old grazing land. The ground was still snow-covered where the afternoon sun couldn't reach, and what wasn't snowy was wet. She found sign for wild pigs and roaming goats.

Finding troll tracks took a little time.

She found several troll-*traps* easily enough. It took a good deal of ear, nose, and eye-work to establish what they were. The troll would dig holes in the ground, perhaps her full body-length deep, and then cover them with a lattice of slight branches and growth, with fragrant berries in the center. It lined the bottom with flat rocks chipped and broken in the hope that a sheep or pig would blunder in and injure or trap itself.

She found bones at the bottom of one.

Then she cut across its tracks. The troll had huge three-toed feet, though the toes didn't point in the same direction as they did with elves and dragons. Something like the mark of a horse hoof stood in the center, with the digits stretching out not quite in opposite directions, like widely spread bird toes. Here and there, similar, smaller versions of the tracks could be seen that she guessed were its hands.

She found a heap of droppings close to the river-cliff edge. They were like a rotten melon filled with little white worms left on a hillock. Her nostrils closed in disgust.

The ground here had a trodden-on look like a cattle wade, with a profusion of tracks and divots, and grubby prints on the rocks at the edge of the cliff.

Wistala couldn't see her host's bridge from this part of the river, and the twin hills near his estate were just bluish lumps. The river canyon stood so wide here that objects on the far side couldn't be distinguished from each other.

White birds crisscrossed the river, looking for food. Another variety, gray with yellow beaks, poked around the rocks at the base of the cliff under all the marks.

Wistala craned her neck out as far as she dared, digging her tail into the crevice between two sturdy rocks like one of Rainfall's fishhooks buried in a trout's jaw.

A cave marred the fluted sides of the canyon wall, closer to the top edge than the base.

She could imagine what the birds at the base of the cliff were feeding on.

Instincts older than she took over as she evaluated the troll's home. Fresh water would never be a problem. Enemies couldn't reach it without a good deal of difficulty, it would take a huge climbing pole or ladder to reach the cave mouth from the river, and anything that walked on two feet would risk its neck climbing down from above. A dragon might like it even better: you could fly in through the river canyon at night, skimming the surface, and escape observation. She imagined there was usually food of one sort or another to be had near a big body of water as the Inland Ocean, just a horizon downriver.

Wistala examined the cliff until she found a ledge thick with mosses and ferns, downwind from the cave. She wanted to get a look at this troll. She climbed down and settled between the branches. It was cool, with the wind whipping up the river valley, but she'd spend nights in worse spots.

Tired but not exhausted from her trip into the troll's lands, she tried not to sleep, but rather to rest with one eye upon the cave from a perch upriver. Softened by her regular meals at Mossbell, she regretted her missed dinner as the moon rose.

She heard the troll breathing before she saw it. A *snerk-snerk-snerk* sounded from the cave, startling her into full awareness.

A face emerged in profile from the cave, if it could be called a face. A fleshy orb at the end of a long snakelike body no thicker than Wistala's tail emerged and waved around. Whether the head smelled, heard, or saw the approaches to the cave mouth, Wistala could not say.

Wistala was just congratulating herself on not being afraid of the wormlike body when two giant limbs unfolded themselves from the cave mouth, gripping the rocks above with three-toed hands. They pulled out a stumpy body split by a wide mouth that reminded her of a frog, especially since its skin seemed wet with some kind of oily extrude. At the tail end, a pair of smaller, but still spindly, limbs steadied the body as long forelimbs did the work of climbing.

Wistala realized she'd been mistaken in her analysis of the tracks. The troll was almost all forelimbs—thick near the body and digits but bone-thin through the long middle part and joint. Its hind legs ended in the smaller graspers she'd mistaken for hands.

The troll's body seemed featureless save for warts establishing a striped pattern back from the edges of its wide mouth. A snorting sound came from the troll. It shifted and stiffened, opened the huge mouth, and spat out a mass about the size of a large pumpkin. It splattered on the rocks below, and Wistala recognized the foul smell of troll waste even at that distance.

Wistala watched in wonder as the long arms folded against the stars; then it sent its snakelike sensing-and-breathing (she assumed) organ over the edge of the cliff to examine the ground. The *snerk-snerk-snerk* sounded again, and it reached up with those tree-length arms and pulled itself up and over the ledge. As it breathed, its body expanded and contracted at the pale belly.

Then it was gone.

She argued with herself over exploring the troll's cave. For all she knew, it was full of hungry young trollings or a she-troll, if such even existed. Then there was the danger of the troll coming back and squashing her the way she might burst a tick under her *sii*.

In the end, caution won. She trembled at the thought of an encounter with the thing. Her nerve wasn't what it was when she explored the ruins of Tumbledown or outwitted bears with Auron. She crept back in the direction of Mossbell.

Rainfall's eyes went agog: "Poison a troll? You might as well poison a stone," Rainfall said. "They thrive on a month's-rotten corpse."

Wistala looked across the wide book table at him. Most of his library shelves held nothing but cobwebs, but a few volumes remained behind glass, and it seemed natural history was a favorite subject of his. If they could somehow get the troll to eat of a poisonous plant—

"He's temporary," Rainfall said. "The troll's ruining the estate, but he won't live forever. Mossbell was standing before he came; it'll still stand after he dies."

Gentle was a fine quality, but this, this, *passivity* vexed her. "It's not a storm. There's got to be some way to rid a land of a troll."

"Yes. Starve it. But the wild pigs and goats have moved

west of the road, and even if we hunted them down to the last piglet, the troll would just feed from the riverbottom. Or worse, come after my goats or Avalanche."

"Apply to your thane—"

Rainfall grew so agitated that he interrupted her. "Tried and tried again."

Wistala hated even to mention her final idea. "This Dragonblade fellow. If he's able to kill dragons, I'm sure he could handle a troll."

"An excellent idea, but I've no money to hire him. The only thing I have of value is the title to Mossbell. The Dragonblade can't expect to profit from the small reward. And then a troll's skin and bones yield little compared with—I beg your pardon."

Yes, the odds and ends of a dead dragon bring a great deal of money. Neither here nor there.

"You must have some weapons. Arm your crew that helps you maintain the roads."

"What are we to do, snare it with the crane? Shovel gravel at it? While it's been long since I've engaged in an argument, I'd wish we could engage over the merits of Swanfellow's songs, or Alfwheat's dramas. The troll! The troll! As if he doesn't hang over this estate like a cloud, you have to bring the gloom into my library."

Spring came.

Wistala feasted on the sun each day as she would on a slaughtered sheep. A wooded copse stood at the base of one of the twin hills, and there was an old half-blown-over walnut still fighting for life, judging from the buds upon the upper branches. Wistala liked to nap on the incline or watch the clouds go by, idly taking up bark beetles with her tongue as they explored the rotting underside of the walnut.

Sometimes she ventured up the easterly of the twin hills and watched the road that ran between, crossing a stream at two short stout bridges. There was little traffic, and as far as she could tell, her host derived no benefit from it. Carts, wagons, and passengers on foot hurried through Rainfall's lands as though the ground were accursed—which it was, in a sense.

Traffic on the road went so far as to time their travel through Rainfall's land. If headed north, the proper hour to step on the bridge seemed to be about two hours after sunrise. If heading south, one wanted to be on the road between the twin hills at about the same time. Each side would take some rest and water their animals at the walls and gates of Mossbell as the sun reached its zenith, but they'd admire its curious lines only from a distance as they ate preserved food out of bags and jars.

As far as Wistala could tell, Rainfall had all the duties of keeping a road open and drew none of the benefits. She explored just outside his lands along the road in the morning light and near dark and saw marketplaces and inns to either end of his lands, but thanks to the troll, no one dared set up so much as an applecart near the bridge.

Of course, need or ignorance or foolishness sometimes had messengers riding across the bridge at night. Rainfall showed her the effects of some combination of the three one morning—a pair of neatly bitten-off horse hooves and a dropped hat lying on the road with the stain and smell of blood on the gravel.

"Probably some young buck from Newcrossing trying to see his girl in Glenn Eoiye," Rainfall said, picking up the hat. "That's a new red feather in his hat, quill cut to write her love notes or a Letter of Intent. In a year, it'll be a sad song, and in ten, they'll have new names in the old tune."

His Elvish fell effortlessly onto her ear with six months of practice. She responded easily: "I don't suppose a company will be formed to kill the troll and avenge him."

"Thane Hammar isn't that energetic. Let's see if we can learn more of the sad tale."

They followed the tracks back to the bridge, and Rainfall gaped at what he saw. One whole side of the bridge's superstructure had been torn away from the wooden repair in the center.

"Oh! I'd have an earthquake come if it would just seal

that wretched troll in his cave. This is a month's labor. I'll
have to hire timberers and see about chain and staples."

Wistala checked the road for traffic before she ventured out onto the bridge. She crossed the arches, the high-
running river filling both banks below, to closer inspect the
damage.

"A rider comes," Rainfall said, but Wistala already
heard the hoofbeats and scuttled over the edge of the
bridge on the downwind side. There was the briefest of
ledges there so men might anchor themselves and inspect
the stones at the bottom, and she could easily grip it with
sii and *saa*.

She heard Rainfall call a greeting and recognized the
Hypatian tongue used by men in these parts. The rider
trotted on without reply. Wistala waited some moments
as the elves reckoned time before climbing back up and
employing her nostrils.

"Not so much as a wave of his hand," Rainfall said.
"And he wore the garb of a high tradesman. A man with
an eye toward commerce is usually better mannered."

"I found something under the bridge," Wistala said. "I
think it tells the tale of the young man with the red feather.
The troll lurked under the bridge for some time, and had
been there much before. Smears of droppings are all along
the pilings."

"It's been a hard winter. Maybe it had trouble finding
enough pigs and goats for its appetite. Ah well, the waterfowl return, and it'll get its fill of them. I must get the
bridge repaired. A bad storm now could blow the wooden
span to bits."

Birds and words! Wistala thought, with her tail as stiff
as an icicle. *He's got the advantage of the troll, and he
doesn't even consider how to use it.*

Wistala watched the labor for the next few days, from
the felling of two great trees for lumber to the sawing, the
ironmongery both in the barn and at the bridge, and then
placing the new beams with the crane. The last fascinated
her, and Rainfall attempted to explain it over dinner with
a great deal of talk about fulcrum points and levers and

counterweights and blocks, but as soon as she learned one working of the crane, it seemed to force the previous one out of her head.

It wasn't until she watched it at work the next day that some of his discourse made sense. After the workmen had gone—few dared labor long past noon, as they had to travel home on foot, save for a blacksmith or two who lodged with Rainfall at Mossbell—she stayed up and asked a few more questions about the crane.

"Ah, you're getting it. You've no mind for theory, but when you see it in practice, you learn like lightning. I've noticed that with your Elvish, as well. Just when I thought you'd never get the hang of the extrafamilial oratory, you—"

"Bother oratory forms for now," Wistala said. "The crane looks like it can go to a great height, above most treetops. Could it lift a tree upright?"

"Easily. Vertical, horizontal. Vertical is actually easier to maneuver; you don't have to have stabilizing cables, as the shape of the tree works for you."

"I've got an idea for your crane. But it would have to happen soon. And I expect you'd have to get a group of men willing to brave a shot at the troll."

"Whatever can you mean, Wistala?"

"Get a piece of paper. You shall draw as I speak."

Four nights later, with the bridge still unfinished in its repairs, so excited was Rainfall by her idea, Wistala walked Avalanche back and forth across the bridge.

Nerve, Wistala, where is your dragon courage? A drakka should be firebellied on the night of such a hunt, such a challenge.

The crane stood at the north end, hidden in the trees by the hard climb of stairs leading up the side of the cliff. It held a long, thin, straight pine, shorn of many but not all of its limbs. The wider bottom end had been sharpened, and ax-heads, saw edges, spear-points, and knife-blades stuck out from the bottom in a ring, like porcupine quills, though all had been blackened by soot so as not to catch the light.

If it weren't for the intermittent drizzle, she'd be able to see Rainfall atop the crane. But she wanted bad weather for this job to help mask sounds and smells.

Avalanche wore a thick blanket of quilted leather folded and tied across his back and neck, and grumbled a good deal about being out in the wet and not being near the mares of some of the men—only a handful had been willing to take up with Rainfall, mostly friends and relatives of the snatched young man. Not that Wistala had met any of them; her role in all this would hopefully remain secret.

Wistala walked again to the south side of the river, and thought she saw a bulge in the river, but it was hard to tell. She pulled on Avalanche's reins—

"Careful!" Avalanche objected.

—and walked him to the side.

Yes. A dripping arm clung to the side of one of the stone arches. It moved, pulling up a sodden shape.

Her hearts pounded.

Father always said this was the worst moment. The moment before action was inevitable, that there would be no further delay, and from the next beat of your wings you were committed. The moment of choice.

She stood frozen. *So big. It will be fast if it can run.*

If she could commit herself with words first, maybe the rest would come easier: "It's time, Avalanche."

There. I've said it.

"Now for battle?" His tail flicked up, a white battle banner.

"Now for battle. All you have to do is run from the troll."

"Brave Master Eyen rode battle. Troll came. Brave Master Eyen fell. I ran then." His ears drooped a little, but maybe it was because of the wet.

"This time I want you to run," she said, jumping as lightly as she could onto Avalanche's broad back. Even with her scales, she couldn't weigh as much as a young elf warrior arrayed for battle. "The best thing you can do is run. Faster you're out of its sight, the better. Now walk on."

Avalanche walked, but she could feel him holding himself back at every step. According to Rainfall, the stallion had spent his colthood and youth in training, learning to run at other horses and enemies, and the old instincts were coming back with action in the air, though there were wiry gray hairs mixed in with his softer ones on his mane and tail these days.

Wistala was grateful to ride Avalanche. She wasn't certain her feet would be as sure as the stallion's, walking along a bridge toward the spot—just across from the repaired timbers—where she knew the troll lurked.

But she was committed. Avalanche would walk her into peril whether her feet were willing to go or not. She felt her *griff* extending and contracting nervously, she tried to hold them tight against her neck hearts to stop the rattle.

They clomped across the wooden timbers, a dragon-length expanse covering the fallen arch. She felt certain her hearts were on the verge of quitting.

The snake-head orb at the end of its tendril lay on the side of the bridge, motionless, looking like a forgotten drinking gourd left by some traveler. Though she could smell the troll now, as could Avalanche. But he moved on, stepping faster if at all, with sure-footed courage.

Wistala's claws set themselves into the leather quilting.

She heard the troll shift weight.

"Now, Avalanche!" she squeaked, in Drakine, but she slapped his muscular rump with her tail.

Avalanche let out a cry and leaped forward onto the stonework, hooves slipping just a little in the wet. Wistala hung on for all she was worth, but far better than the excitement of the run was the absence of fear.

The troll's dreadfully huge three-digit hand just brushed Avalanche's tail as it came down, and she felt no fear. The body, all gaping mouth and terrible stench, heaved itself onto the bridge behind them, and she only looked with amazement at the length of its forelimbs illustrated against the familiar width of the bridge.

She urged Avalanche on with another tail-slap.

The troll began to run after them. It used its long front

legs and short back limbs in pairs long-then-short, long-then-short, in a strange unbalanced sort of run that made her think of a goose taking flight across a still lake, with wings beating strong and feet frantically working.

Avalanche was almost at the far end of the bridge when Wistala jumped off, giving him a last flick of her tail. She skidded to a stop on the wet bridge stones.

The troll came, Wistala thought its gait ungainly compared with that of a horse—even a dragon-dash was a thing of beauty compared with the troll's careen.

She jumped to the east rail of the bridge, where her rope was tied. This wasn't part of her original plan, but an addition of Rainfall's, who didn't like the idea of her belly-flopping into the river, even with the banks in spring flood.

Now to attract a troll!

She stood on her hind legs and extended her neck as far as she could. Her *griff* bristled, and she rattled them against her scales for all they were worth.

Tchk-tchk-tchk-tchk-tchk-tchk-TCHK!

Her ears rang with the sound. The troll pulled up, confused by the sound, its waving orb-topped tentacle turning her way, backside expanding and contracting as it breathed.

Avalanche disappeared into the distant rain.

The troll set its arms and legs, ready for anything, battle or flight.

"Here's a mouthful for you!" she shouted. She gripped the leather wrap on the line and dropped over the edge.

She felt the heat of her passage even through the protective grip—again, no fear in her hearts but the odd words *friction heat* crossing her mind, even with the troll gaping over as she dropped away.

It reached for her and missed, but caught up the line. By the time its slow brain made the connection and it began to draw up the line, Wistala was almost at the river.

She dropped into the water.

A hominid wouldn't have been able to make it to the cut stairs, but drakka were strong swimmers; they could clasp their limbs to their side and put their whole body into the effort, sucking air through the nostrils. Wistala was bothered by the cold more than by the current—it brought back awful half-memories that took the courage out of her.

She reached the landing and pulled herself up, weary as though from a long dragon-dash.

The troll marked her movement, and it reached out with one long arm for the stairs and swung itself down.

"That's right," Wistala croaked, a puny vocalization that didn't even disturb a stalking bird three rocks away. She drew breath and roared her best battle cry.

The orb turned down on her, and the troll hurried its climb. When the troll filled the view between her landing and the suspended pine trunk above, she called on her flame.

She didn't aim her sole effectual weapon at the troll. She loosed it out, as far out into the river as she could. It struck the water and formed a pool there, floating downstream with the current.

She could never be sure what happened next, save that Rainfall saw her orange-red signal and cut the tree trunk free.

Perhaps it was the number of camouflaging branches left on the trunk that made a sound. Perhaps the tightly stretched cable's parting at Rainfall's ax-blow—it made a crack like a nearby lightning strike according to her host, who was in a position to know. Or perhaps the troll's sense-orb could see in all directions, rather than only one—no one had ever lived long enough in the company of a troll to conduct any studies.

Wistala's brain had no time for perhapses—as soon as she gave the signal, she jumped into the river.

The troll shifted as the tree-trunk fell. Rather than hitting it squarely, the projectile opened a gash in its side. This just enraged the troll rather than skewering it. Luckily for Wistala, it took its temper out on the tree, which had lodged itself in the shallow water of the riverbank. The troll picked it up and cracked it against the cliff side, again and again until only a shard remained in its grip.

Only then did it notice the arrows and spears from above.

Brave or foolish, Rainfall's gang flung spears and fired hunting arrows down at the troll as Wistala made it to the first pillar of the bridge. She saw a spear lodge in the troll's back. The sense-stalk stood straight up, and it began to climb.

The next thing Wistala knew, she was climbing. Using the deep crevices between the joined stones, a skilled man could make the long climb, but it would take him ten times the effort it took Wistala, with her four shorter limbs and thick muscles. She crawled up the bridge's support like an ant hurrying up a grass stalk, her pace not greatly reduced from what she could achieve on flat ground.

But she was only halfway up when the troll reached the men.

One, a lumberman, judging by his broad leather girdle, tried his axe on the troll's hand as it came to the cliff top. She heard the sharp *thwack* of the blade as it bit into the troll's fountain-size hand even from her distance. The troll's other hand came up and struck the lumberman such a blow, he exploded into pieces.

She passed over the bridge-rail to find the troll standing on the cliff top, searching the tree line for the fleeing men. It flushed a man and ran him down on the road, where it smashed and then swallowed him. A group of horses fled screaming from the woods, one or two pulling men along.

Wistala wasn't sure what she could do, but she hurried toward the north end of the bridge anyway. She had one good gout of flame left in her fire bladder, if not two; she'd eaten heartily for months, and there was still an angry liquid ball inside her, waiting to get out. She'd diverted the troll before; perhaps she could again, long enough for it to lose track of the men. . . .

A white flash on the road ahead. Wistala, gulping air as she ran, recognized the shape.

Avalanche!

The stallion—with blood in the air, even on a rainy

night, and the frightened calls of mares behind him—had given in to instinct and stood his ground, eagerly pawing at the road.

The troll rounded on the stallion.

"Come on! Beast!" Avalanche neighed. Then he screamed and reared up, front hooves cutting the air before him. "Try to take of mine. I'll kick your teeth out!"

Wistala dragon-dashed, her vision red with lost breath. The troll's air sacs bulged from its behind; she could see flaps of raised skin like a pinecone opening and shutting as it tried to catch its breath—or was it damaged in some way? No matter—she homed in on the deep whooshing sound.

Then the troll lunged forward, its gait even stranger because of cradling its wounded hand. . . .

The troll reared up and reached for the horse as Avalanche charged. But the stallion danced sideways, and lashed out with a hind leg, kicking one of the thin forearms. Avalanche reared up and struck the troll in the mouth-without-a-face that constituted the front of its body.

The troll backed up and lifted itself.

The sense-orb hung over all like a watchful bird. As the troll's mouth dropped open, seemingly with the idea of swallowing Avalanche whole, Wistala slid to a stop and spat her fire, as though trying to get an extra few tail-lengths of distance into it by letting momentum carry the contents of her fire bladder up her throat, accelerated by ring after ring of throat muscles.

The sense-orb whipped around, and Wistala caught one glimpse of a wide-open eye? nostril? ear? in the center of a wormy fringe—

The fire struck the troll in its breathing sac.

It spun, tucking its hindquarters and covering the breathing spicules with its rear legs. An elbow knocked Avalanche aside, and the stallion crashed down, as though tripped. The troll jumped awkwardly away like a spastic frog, stomping on Avalanche in its flight, beating at its hindquarters with its rear feet where Wistala's flame clung and dripped and burned.

It made for the river, by plan or blind flight of instinctive pain. The troll hurled itself into the trees along the roadway and fell in ruin, its limbs no longer capable of supporting the mouth-body. The sense-orb looked this way and that at the twitching limbs before it, too, collapsed.

Wistala couldn't stand and gape—she hurried to Avalanche.

Avalanche fought for breath, his tongue extended and bloody foam on his lips and the roadway. At her approach, the stallion raised his head a little.

"Beast?"

She realized it wasn't an epithet, but a query. "It's dead. You killed it."

"Kicked its head in. Warned it."

"Yes, you did. I heard."

The head fell back to the ground. "The mares. Hear them?"

Wistala couldn't hear anything but the soft rainfall.

Avalanche let out a friendly nicker, sightless eyes rolling this way and that. Then his struggling body ceased to move, and the horribly lolling tongue went still.

Wistala flung herself across her old stablemate, determined to fight off wild pigs, crows, bears, and set Bartleghaff himself ablaze if any but Rainfall came to claim the body.

Chapter 13

Rainfall took her to a quiet corner of the estate, a long-sloped hill overlooking the river gorge. It was a scenic spot, but too rocky to be of much use.

Trees thrived there. Well spaced, with thickets of wildflowers all around, bursting with the blues and yellows of spring.

With them was a windburned lumberman named Jessup driving a team of timber-horses pulling a haywain bearing Avalanche. He had been introduced to her as the younger brother of Lessup, the brave lumberman who'd taken his ax to the troll's hand.

Jessup also served as a foreman on his bridge crew and had seen the whole fight from a hiding spot in a muddy ditch beside the road. He was a man of trim beard with the close-cropped head hair married humans in this part of the land wore, and liked to whistle through his teeth, though he didn't do so today out of respect for their duty.

"This is his spot," Rainfall said.

Wistala stood up a bit from the wain. The trees crowned the hill in a half-circle, and within the arms stood a pile of quarried rock, placed so as to make a wide pair of stairs in mirror image facing each other.

"This is the cairn of my son. He loved Avalanche, and

Avalanche loved him. It's only right that Avalanche rest at his feet."

Jessup said something to Rainfall. One of the words might have been *rocks*.

"We should get to work," Rainfall said. A month ago, Wistala would have been happy to dispose of the horse-flesh in the most efficient and belly-filling manner possible, but her omnipresent appetite vanished when she looked at the dead horse.

The humans had gathered to do service to their own killed at sunset. Wistala had seen it only from a distance—torches flamed at the spots of their deaths and some kind of priest had passed out powders that the families threw into the torch flame. Puffs of colorful smoke came up, and they marked their faces with fallen ash. Rainfall walked among them, embracing many, but took no other part in the ceremony.

They'd burned the troll's body.

All that was left was Avalanche. Rainfall showed Wistala where to dig, and she began to work.

Wistala enjoyed the labor. It felt good to score up soil under one's claws, pull up rocks, tear through thin tree roots. Her body had recovered from the encounter with the Dragonblade's dogs; even if her spirit was happy at Mossbell, her body craved effort.

She smelled metals under the cairn rocks nearby, and rust bleeding into the soil, a fact she tried to take little notice of. Imagine Rainfall's reaction to her prying up the cairn-stones of his son and gobbling down a few buckles and buttons! But civilization requires ignoring one's instincts, as Rainfall liked to tell her in their fireside chats.

Perverse to have such thoughts about a man who'd saved her life.

Earth . . . rock . . . rock . . . more earth. She smelled a mole and extracted it with her tongue.

Rainfall maneuvered the wain so they could roll Avalanche out from the uphill side. He was a wonder with the horses, who didn't like her smell one bit and shifted nervously whenever Rainfall didn't stand at their noses to calm them. Once the wagon was in place, Rainfall led the horses into the trees so they could rest and eat with dragon out of scent, out of mind.

Jessup helped by widening the channels she dug. Eventually they had a shallow grave and a pile of earth and rock to go atop it.

Wistala rested after they pushed Avalanche out of the wagon. Rainfall and Jessup placed earth and rocks over him.

With that done, Jessup ate and drank from a meal he'd packed in a bag. Rainfall led Wistala up to the crest of the hill and the ring of trees. The canyon wind took up his willow-leaf-like hair, and he tied it together with a bit of red-colored silk.

"How do you like this spot, Wistala?"

She looked across the gorge. A series of small waterfalls ran down the opposite side, though the wind caught much of the spray and turned it into a white mist.

"There must be good fishing under those falls. Look at the birds."

"We're going to have to work on aesthetic appreciation this summer. You're all gastronomy, my child.

"I've ancestors in this ring of trees," he continued. "One day I'll come up here and never return, and learn stories older than any book from my fellow trees."

Wistala didn't understand much of elvish mysticism. Whether they actually became trees or simply lay down at the foot of one and waited to die depended on whose story you listened to.

"Who'll take care of the bridge?"

"There's more to it than just the bridge," Rainfall said. "The whole Hypatian Order is breaking up. Of course, Starfall, the poet-philosopher, tells us all things must pass, even the mountains and oceans, in time. But I love the Hypatian Civilization: the laws I once upheld, the high and low priestdoms, the ceremonies and the titles that brought out the best in us and held the worst at bay.

"Take the thane. Hammar keeps the Hypatian Law,

but twists its intent so that he can live in the manner of a Varvar Despot or an Overking of the Ghioz Golden Circle. Half the people of this land are indentured to him, thanks to civil debts—slaves in all but title, myself included."

Wistala was pretty sure a badger had made a home at the hilltop somewhere. And there were birds' nests to raid in the cliff side—

"Can't you petition elsewhere about him?" she asked, realizing Rainfall was waiting for a question or comment.

"That's been tried."

"You can't be the only dissatisfied one. Go burn his house down."

"I'm no firebrand. A new, worse thane would rise from the ashes, perhaps one who wouldn't even make a pretense of adhering to Hypatian Justice. Besides, my Lada is in that very hall."

"Your granddaughter?"

"Yes. He took her as a ward when she was a child. I've been in default on my taxes for some years, you understand, and that gives the thane certain powers. He was able to seize her as thanedroit, thanks to his corruption of the high judge and high priest. Thanedroit! Again, a polite name for a terrible usurpation. She's a hostage to my debts. If I die or quit the estate she inherits, and as she's untitled and of questionable parentage besides, Mossbell would revert to Hypatia—meaning Hammar would get Mossbell."

Wistala's head hurt from trying to see through the hedge of words, but she could see the pain in Rainfall's eyes.

"You should have quit it while the troll still lived," Wistala said. "Let the thane inherit troll-blighted lands."

"Oh, he would have rid himself of the troll quick enough if—" Rainfall stopped, looked anew at Wistala. "You don't think— Oh, the infamy! Black infamy!"

Rainfall was silent and bitter all the ride back to Mossbell. She stretched out in the back of the wain. Jessup kept looking at Wistala in a sidelong manner.

Wistala, more to break Rainfall from his mood than

because the human annoyed her, asked her host to inquire after the purpose of Jessup's stares.

After some words, Rainfall handed the horse reins to Jessup and turned around. "He didn't know it bothered you. He said you're beautiful, and he was trying to memorize your proportions."

"Beautiful?" She was her same thick-bodied self, with nothing like Jizara's elegant neck and tail.

"Interested in aesthetics now?" Rainfall asked.

"Has he been in your awful bramble-wines?"

"I agree. I told him he should wait some years, when you have wings. Then he'd behold one of the most perfect creatures in creation. The running horse, the flying frigate bird, the peacock, the fabled Tigers of Ghioz—none of them compare to a dragon with wings held high."

A messenger waited under the somber figures of the silent fountain turnaround of Mossbell, a down-cheeked boy with a sweated mount. At Rainfall's order, Jessup kept the wain at a discreet distance so as not to alarm the horse.

Rainfall jumped lightly down from his seat and welcomed the messenger. After inspecting the seal, he read the contents. He stared at the boy, then hurried into the house, where he remained for only a few moments before he returned the paper to the messenger, resealed, along with a silver coin.

Wistala suspected some sort of crisis; Rainfall had very little coin in his hall, unless he kept a secret noseproofed supply.

Rainfall invited Jessup to stay for dinner, but the timberman had to get back to his family and his brother's widow and children.

As soon as they sat alone, waiting for his bread to cook and drop off the clay-sided oven as a joint sputtered inside, she asked about the message.

"Another of the thane's humiliations, under a masquerade of civility," Rainfall said. "He summons me, ta-hum ta-hally to his hall, so that I might fully tell the story of the death of the troll and claim my reward. Of course, it'll go toward back taxes. The accounting will be announced to all present."

Wistala turned the handle of the spit, rotating the joint. The turn brought a fresh fall of juices into the gravy pan and mouthwatering smells. "Refuse him."

"I cannot. There'll be many a jape about elves not being able to keep two pennies proximate."

"Let them talk. No one ever lost an eye to a joke."

"I'll have to beg some part of the reward that should rightfully go to my crew. Imagine: pleading so that the widows and orphans might see some monies, and the men be rewarded for their courage, when the thane should be bowing to each and opening his purse wide to the survivors!"

"I thought being rid of the troll would solve your problems."

"It will take time to assemble decent tenants for the land, and they'll need roof and stock. I shall have to go beg of the dwarves. The Wheel of Fire will give me more upfront, but at ruinous rates. The Dwarves of the Diadem are fairer, but only lend a small sum at a time."

"Wheel of Fire?" Wistala asked.

"Your eyes have gone all hot and tight, Wistala. Have you had dealings with them? Oh—the joint burns! Quick, get it out."

They extracted the haunch of mutton and took the baking tubers from their metal case. When dinner was laid out—Wistala had learned to eat neatly from the table, but she still had to lift her head to let the food slide down her throat, a gesture that always made Rainfall shake his head—they continued the conversation in what had been the food-servers' nook, a smaller room off the big, dark, and drafty dining hall, warmed by the heat of the oven.

Rainfall moved on to happier subjects, mostly the chance of seeing his granddaughter at Hammar's hall, and Wistala put the dwarves out of her mind. The mention awoke dark thoughts and set her *griff* twitching. She'd promised her father to forget the past and live for another generation of dragons.

*   *   *

Wistala kept herself deep inside Mossbell House all while Rainfall visited the thane. Visitors were traipsing across the grounds to see where the troll had fallen.

Rainfall returned in the company of a small ill-favored horse. Its shaggy coat and hooves were thick with layers of dirt. He put it in the stall opposite what had been Avalanche's, and when Wistala made sure there was no one around, she approached Rainfall.

"How passed the audience?"

"As predicted. I bowed and begged. He gave me half the reward to distribute to the men, then sent a low priest along to see the money distributed. As though my word wasn't enough."

Rainfall brightened. "However, he is keeping his pledge as to taxation. I shall have five years breathing space to turn Mossbell around, thanks to you."

Wistala bowed; elves took great pleasure in the giving and receiving of bows.

"The only cloud was that he refused me a visit with my granddaughter. She's living in a room in the fast tower. I should have gone out and shouted for her, but he pulls up the bridge at night."

Wistala saw an opportunity, and questioned him about this curious feature. She learned much about the thane's hall, from its almost windowless first level to the small herb garden on the roof. The thane's hall sounded impressive and extensive.

"Galahall should be fine, for the excises and land tax," Rainfall said.

That night she made friends with the horse—or mule rather, as the beast was quick to correct her—as Rainfall saw to its hooves. The mule was either too stupid or too sick to mind her smell, and seemed ill-disposed to talk.

"There's a spot of hoof-sprout in the cracks," Rainfall grumbled as the mule stamped and swore. "I'll have to make a paste and bag his feet. What kind of stablemen is the thane keeping?"

"How did you come by this unfortunate?" she asked.

"Yet another of the thane's jokes. He frowned when

I told him of the death of Avalanche, my last source of steady income, thanks to stud-price, and offered a replacement. Stog here was the most wretched specimen in his stables, so the hostler presented me with him."

The black ears of the mule perked up at the mention of the name.

"Hello, Stog," Wistala said in the beast-tongue the mule had used in his calumnies. "Welcome to Mossbell."

"Drop all the two-leggeds," Stog said to no one in particular. "Left to rot again."

Rainfall worked long into the night on the mule's hooves, gathering plants and then mixing them with a white powder he kept in a clay jar. Then he filled four leather-bottomed canvas bags with the sharp-smelling mix and tied them to the mule's hooves, after fixing a wooden gate around his neck that kept him from lowering his head to chew the poultices free.

"Bug me! That stings," Stog said, and tried to bite Rainfall as he worked.

Too stupid to recognize a kind turn, Wistala thought, and settled down in her old spot to sleep.

Rainfall was still at work when she awoke. He'd cleaned, brushed, and clipped every inch of the mule, who looked immeasurably better but still angry.

"Ah, there you are," Rainfall said as she drank from the central cistern. "Could you watch him for a few hours? He's trying to kick the bags off. I hobbled him"—he pointed at a line between stable and the horse's rear leg— "but I wonder if he's out of tricks."

"I'd be happy to."

Rainfall extended a hand to Stog's nose, but he just tried to bite again.

"As you like," Rainfall said. He left, shoulders sagging.

"You should be grateful," Wistala said from a high perch in the almost-empty loft.

"Gut-kick gratitude," Stog said. "Torturing two-leg. He's burning my hooves right off, I'll signify."

Stog spoke the beast-tongue better than Avalanche. Perhaps he was a well-traveled mule.

"He's kind beyond my ability to tell. It may hurt now, but your feet will feel better soon, I'm sure."

"So speaks the drakka with her claws all clean and cool."

This was strange. Not only had the mule identified her as a female, but he'd correctly guessed that she was no longer a hatchling.

"You know about dragons," she said.

"I know about killing them. I was in the Dragonblade's mule train." The long brown face told her nothing, but the ears twitching this way and that suggested that Stog would welcome a fight.

"The last time I saw the Dragonblade, it was just him and his dogs. No mules."

"You saw the Dragonblade and lived?"

Wistala tried to remain as calm as the mule. His ears were forward with interest. "Big broad man? Black armor like dragonscale?"

"Not like, it is. I've borne many a dragon-hoof or hide-scraping on my back."

"Then why aren't you still carrying pieces of slaughtered dragon?"

Stog tried to stamp, but the hobble prevented his moving. "The Dragonblade was hurrying north, and I came up lame. I was traded for a shaggy-faced pony and left in the blackest hole of an old stable.

"I waited days and days for him to return. How could he forget his stoutest mule?"

Wistala saw the mule's ears droop at the memory. Finally his tail swished, and he looked at her afresh as he spoke: "I pulled a trash-sled in snow up to my fetlocks now and then. The stablehands beat me like a muddy rug. Until the hooves started to go. The hostler tried to sell me off, but the clodclutters took one look at my hooves and wised up."

"So you know the lay of the land around the thane's hold?"

"Some of it."

"Tell me more."

"Why should I do that?"

"To take your mind off your hooves," Wistala said. "Besides, there might be a way for you to give them a bite back for their mistreatment."

"I wouldn't mind catching the hostler bending over with his back turned. I'd send him through the wall. But even a good stomp would fix me. If you hit hominids on the inside of their hoof just right, they hop about shouting. Most gratifying."

The moon changed all the way round once, and then to half so fast Wistala hardly knew time passed, save for the changes for the better to Stog's hooves, healing under Rainfall's constant attention.

She took to exploring outside Mossbell's grounds, particularly to a high ridge to the northeast. From the trees on its top, she could see an even higher ridge with a single line of trees and an old broken watchtower that marked the edge of Galahall's lands, according to Stog. The ground between was little used, as it was poor in soil and water.

She worked on her Parl by asking Jessup about the woods, ostensibly with an eye toward the hunting prospects of the Thickets, as that part of the thanedom was known.

Jessup was working the roadside near the river, sinking a well. He'd laid out a few stones in what Rainfall's study-books called a *rectangle* on a flat, firm piece of land. Every now and then he would fell a few trees and place them on the rocks so they could dry without touching the ground, whistling more loudly through his teeth as the pile of lumber grew.

He quit working as she nosed around, and took off his ear-flapped cap to scratch his head. "Hunting? Some pheasant, a gobbler or two. No wild boar or deer left—the thane has hunted them all."

"I'd like to avoid notice."

"Then keep to the thorn hollows. Not a problem for you. Your skin should keep them out." He looked doubtful, then took a step closer. "May I touch?"

Wistala raised her head and turned sideways. "The ones on my back are the thickest."

He ran his hand over her scales. "Like . . . like cast iron, only rougher."

Wistala used a *saa* to scritch at the back of her shoulder, where a few of her hatchling scales still clung. One dropped off, and she flipped it to him with her nose. "One of your own."

"I may keep this?"

"You may."

He bowed in gratitude.

"Could I ask a favor of you?" Wistala asked.

"I've more wealth than my father saw in his lifetime, thanks to you. I'd do my best."

"I'd like to start bringing home game to Mossbell. Rainfall has been feeding me for so long, I'd like to do the same for him."

"The master gives too much. He's . . . he's noble that way. Go on."

"I need a sort of harness that will allow me to carry a few birds or a quartered deer. Can you manage it?"

"I'll see the hidesman and blacksmith a-morrow." He scratched his close-cropped head again, circling her and cocking his head this way and that in thought.

Wistala bowed. "Thank you. Anything I can do to help—"

"Stand still."

He took a ball of string from his pocket and measured her, along the back, around her neck, across her shoulders, making little marks on the string with a bit of charcoal. "I expect I'll have it done by blueberry day."

"Which is?" The profusion of hominid holidays were all jumbled in Wistala's head; they celebrated everything from turns of the stars and moon to hop-picking to the ripening of the first plum.

"Eight days."

"Thank you."

"I'm the one obliged, Wisssakle."

"Wistala."

Jessup did better on the second try. When Wistala nuzzled him and gave a bit of a *prrum* to congratulate him, his face broke into a grin. "Me conversing with a dragon in its own tongue. Like something out of a bedtime story."

With the air warm and spring in full bloom, Stog came outdoors. His hooves had been turned flaky and white by Rainfall's applications, but strong and healthy hoof lived beneath, revealed as the diseased parts fell away.

Wistala took Stog to see Avalanche's grave, as a final proof of Rainfall's goodness and the turn of his fortune marked by the mule's arrival at Mossbell.

Stog snorted. According to the mule, horses got all the glory, and mules did all the work. "We can go twice as far, carrying twice the load, on half the feed as a horse. Up hills they'd break a leg on and down valleys that would mean their necks, too. But where's the poetry, the statuary?"

"Just wait. I'll give you a chance to show a pack of horses a trick or two."

Jessup came through on his harness. It was a clever bit of craft, looping around her neck, tail, and forelimbs. There were eyes here and there in the leather straps, where she could hook game nets (*or bags, or waterskins,* she thought). She had room in the buckles for her to almost double in size. He took it away almost as soon as she tried it on, insisting on improvements, and returned it with twin linked straps running ladderlike down her back. She found some game nets in Mossbell's dry attic and learned to fix them on herself.

With that, she told Rainfall she'd be gone a few days and plunged into the Thickets. She did hunt, but her real purpose was a trek to Galahall.

Know your hunting ground, Mother always used to say. As hatchlings, Auron had always ignored that advice and plunged straight into the center of the home cave as if expecting a slug to pop up and ask to be eaten. Hunting took patience, knowledge of game trails and habits, and above all, a feel for terrain, weather, and wind.

She waited for an evening that promised rain to approach Galahall. She sneaked onto its lands, circled wide of its herds and flocks, trotted through ditches bordering its fields, and eventually came upon the Thane's Hall.

It had grown over the years, ever larger, she guessed by the quality of the stonework. The oldest, blockiest, and worst-laid stones were in a tall square tower that stood at its corner. The tower, higher than an oak, had narrow windows and an overhanging platform at the top. A building had grown up around it, extending first north and then west and then south again so it turned back on itself, with the tower watching a wide courtyard. The north and west buildings were rough-hewn as the tower on their first level, almost windowless, but the level above was fancier and decorated with flourishes that Wistala thought looked like leaves and faces of woodland creatures.

The south part of Galahall had a huge door facing the tower with a grand balcony above, and windows filled with tinted glass bigger than any door in Mossbell. Smaller supports helped hold up the high, smooth walls of that part of the hall, and there were beds of flowers and shrubs in between under the windows.

If Wistala didn't know better, she would think that a truly splendid fellow lived inside.

The whole of Galahall was surrounded by a wide ditch filled with water, bridged under the tower. She approached the moat and sniffed at the water. It smelled faintly of sewage, but the bottom-feeding fish living in it didn't seem to mind.

She paid close attention to the windows of the tower. Unless the rooms were very small, each level of the tower would probably have only one room. The stairs must be on the inside.

With that, she left, angling for the ridge marked by its single line of trees.

She came home to Mossbell with her bags full of pheasants and rabbits, and her mind full of paths and stream-crossings, thorny runs and thick stands. Crows followed her intermittently on her way home, as if hoping that she'd drop a tidbit, but she arrived at Mossbell with a week's worth of dinners and stews to receive hearty words of welcome and praise from Rainfall.

Even Stog seemed pleased to have her back in the stable. He trotted up to her on healthy hooves. "The mice and rats ran wild while you were hunting," Stog grumbled.

"Next time you'll come along. We'll see if you're a match for the thane's horses."

Chapter 14

W istala planned her venture all the next week, as the pheasants and rabbits made the transition from the cool room to stews and pies and soups. She brought up the subject to Rainfall as he worked in his garden, mentioning that she'd seen deer tracks in the thickets and had a mind to bring back a tender young yearling.

She explained her plans for the next day to him, all the while hugging her real intent to her breast.

"I've found some hollows even the hunters avoid. Stog seems willing to carry a deer home."

"I'm sure he'd enjoy the exercise."

"I'll need a harness for Stog, of course, and a bag of meal."

"I'll rise early and put the harness on," Rainfall said. "If that suits you."

"You're too kind," Wistala said. Her host's pleasant manner inspired frilly language in return. Though she stifled a *prrum* only with difficulty, imaging Lada's arrival at Mossbell atop Stog's back, and Rainfall's delight at having her returned to him.

She stayed in the house that night, too excited to sleep, and studied Lada's sketched portrait by candlelight long after Rainfall had turned in. Finally she sniffed the doll from the little chair under the musical instruments until she knew the odor, then wrapped it in a clean cloth from the larder.

On her way out, she noted that the house looked even more bare, if that were possible. The cloak room was bulging with a last few treasures Rainfall doted on: everything from furniture to rolls of heavy draperies to a jeweled belt his grandfather had been awarded for a victory to a silver music box that played a tune his mate had been fond of. Rainfall was sacrificing yet more of the home's interior to raise funds to bring tenants and livestock to his lands. Perhaps matters had gone ill with the dwarves.

The doll was hidden in with a few game bags by the time Rainfall entered the stable the next morning. He wished them both farewell and a fortunate hunt.

"All the spits will be cleaned in expectation of a successful return," Rainfall said as he waved them off. "Rah-ya! for an increase to your summer's tally!"

Wistala capered around Stog as soon as they were out of sight of Mossbell, trickery and adventure in her blood. "We're finally off for Galahall."

"Where I get to show up those oat-stuffed horses."

"Yes. When we get to the ridge, you'll have to show me what you can manage. That's the only path I couldn't pick for you."

They passed through the Thickets easily enough. Stog was both strong and sure-footed, following her in and out of the network of thorny hollows with nothing more than a few bitter oaths when a thorn got him. It was a bad place for flies, too, as it turned out. They ignored Wistala, but they clustered around Stog's eyes, ears, and tailvent.

They paused for grain and water at a muddy hole. The flies grew thicker than ever as Stog pawed up mud to gather drinkable water.

"I was bit by a centipede the size of a snake once," Stog said, his teeth working in their strange sideways fashion. "Burned like dragonflame. I've never much minded flies since then."

They rested for an afternoon in the shadow of the ridge with its strange line of sentinel trees. It promised to be a fine night, but they couldn't wait forever. Stog found a path up as the sun set. The other side was steeper still.

"We'll be crossing this again in a hurry, and at night, so keep that in mind when you pick your trail," Wistala said.

The soil was summer-dry and tended to slide as they went down and entered the grounds of Galahall. They cut through fields, watched only by scarecrows.

"I remember the smell of this grass," Stog said as they came within sight of the hall. They stood in a mass of oaks hugging a stream, immature acorns in the boughs above. They rested again until the lights began to go out in the hall's second-floor windows.

She poured out more grain for Stog. "Wait here. I may be coming back in a hurry," Wistala said, checking the fitting of her game-harness. "Wish me luck."

Stog didn't wish her luck. He was chewing.

Wistala kept low as she approached Galahall, making for the old tower that came close to closing the near circle of buildings. She passed through the foul-smelling moat and emerged slimy with duckweed.

Then she began to climb.

She peeked in the first window, open to the warm night, perhaps three lengths up off the ground. Here Wistala had her first doubt: the window was barred, though not reinforced with crosspieces. Oh, why hadn't she climbed the tower before!

Through the bars she could see that this floor of the tower looked to be one big room, with a stairway running up the side and a stout door set into the ceiling—or the next room's floor, depending on how you looked at it. Laundry hung off lines everywhere, and she smelled an odor like boiled cabbage.

The floor above looked more promising from the window: two beds with drawn-back curtains held sleeping figures. She peered carefully inside until her eye adjusted to the gloom. Both had similar reddish curly hair—not Lada, who according to her portrait had straight hair.

There was no connecting door between the two levels;

the lower's stairs just ran into the upper. She climbed up the outside to the next level. This one had a single bed, with a miniature bed beside that Wistala recognized as a place for hominids to lay their freshly hatched— No, they didn't hatch; they popped out live in considerable pain and confusion, she corrected herself. There were numerous windows on this floor, all ancient and narrow, perhaps for the firing of arrows. The woman sleeping here was round-faced. She and her infant had fallen asleep together, the child attached to her like a suckling pig. Something about the set of her eyes and nose made Wistala discount this one as a possibility.

She tried to guess if there were two floors above or just one as she climbed.

The next floor marked the end of the stairs. It was cramped and low, with a short ladder propped up at the wall near another hatch. The windows here were round, with one on each side of the tower, and the glass pivoted on a central column to admit the breeze. Wheels edged with gears and pegs stood in a cobwebbed pile on one side of the room, taking up much of the space.

There wasn't a bed such as she'd seen at Mossbell or the floors below, just a fabric mass on the floor with bits of straw coming out at the seams. Someone slept there under a wool blanket, with an oily-smelling dip beside the bed upon a pile of books. The sleeping figure had drawn the thin covering up to her nose.

Wistala examined the fixture in the window. It would break easily enough; nothing but wooden pegs held it in place. Hooks at either side of the round would help hold it against a wind.

She guessed there to be nothing but a watch-platform above, though one of Galahall's owners had added a wooden roof. If another one of this Hammar's wards slept up there, it would be quite cold in winter. The girl in the bed was the most likely candidate, as the others had been eliminated.

She just got her hips through the window, at the cost of a slight scraping sound and a whisper of a creak.

The figure stirred a little.

Wistala took the doll out of its bag and unwrapped it, mindful of the ears at the bottom of the stairs.

Wistala came still closer, feeling her way across rough, dry wood. A washbasin bowl with a little water, a bit glass with a number of dried wildflowers in it, a half-finished woven basket, and a few odd and ends of clothing hanging from some pegs were all the room contained.

A foot with the five ridiculous, almost-useless hominid toes stuck out of the blanket. Wistala gave it an experimental lick.

The figure stirred again.

"Hsssst," said Wistala, as quietly as she could.

A wide green eye opened.

"Don't be afraid," Wistala said in Parl.

The human figure sat bolt upright even as she scooted up against the wall, drawing the covers up with her and bunching them under her eyes. But there was no question, the eyes, forehead, and hair belonged to Rainfall's grand-daughter.

Wistala smiled and bowed. "I bring tidings—"

"*Aaaaaaaaagh!*" Lada shrieked.

"You don't—," Wistala tried, backing away. She held up the doll.

"*Heeeeeeelp!* Monster! Esithephe, your baby!"

A clunk and a bawling sounded from downstairs. Wistala advanced, tipping the doll right side up and upside down to prove that it was just a bit of craft, but Lada snatched up the waterbasin, and liquid flew.

"Aiiieeee!" the girl—no, young woman, Wistala could see the smallish protrusions wherewith mammals suckled their broods—shouted, throwing the basin. Wistala lowered her head, and it crashed into the pile of pegged and geared wheels, sprinkling her with water as it passed.

Wistala tried again: "No! Your name is—"

A mouthful of pillow cut off that sentence. Lada rammed it home as she fled in a jumble of knees, elbows, and white nightshirt toward the stairs down, still screaming her head off.

The pillow came out of her mouth with a tear, and feathers flew.

Now screams echoed up from the lower levels.

"Lada!" Wistala shouted, spitting feathers.

The girl screamed as she fled down the stairs.

Wistala heard footsteps, shouts from below caught up in a babble of voices and a screaming baby. She considered going after Lada, but a male voice bellowing questions made her turn back to the window.

A heavy tread on the stairs decided her. She squeezed back out the circular window.

Something gripped at her tail, and she pulled it away hard and climbed up the tower.

Up?

She checked herself. She'd instinctively headed toward the safety of the sky. If only she could will her wings into appearing.

She turned around, testing her digits against the rough stones for the climb down. She watched pillow feathers drift, gently turning and rocking as they fell, and realized some of them had stuck in her scales.

A hairy face, pale in the dim moon, looked out the window. The man must have heard her, for he looked up.

She swung her tail down and poked him back inside with its point. He let out a howl.

I must give them an urgency beyond hunting me, if I'm to escape.

She gulped and squeezed her fire bladder, spat a thin jet of flame up into the wooden roof above. She looked across the narrow gap between tower and the south-facing leg of Galahall.

All interior-facing windows were open in the summer air.

She hurried over to the west side of the tower and, clinging rather precariously, extended her neck and spat. Missed—she'd judged the fall of flame badly.

Shouts from the courtyard—she tried again.

This time the flame passed through the window. Orange light glowed within.

She looked into the courtyard. Shirtless, barefoot men were emerging from doors while female faces, holding gowns closed at their throats, peered cautiously from the windows. She caught the gleam of a sword blade and a pike point. A spike-haired boy pointed up the tower—at her or the growing flame, she didn't know—and screamed a warning.

Wistala saw a faster route down. She moved around to the south side of the tower and jumped to the roof of the east-running building, and from that leaped down the wooden roof of an exposed stable by the entrance. She jumped once more and hit the ground running, with men shouting and giving orders behind and a growing clamor of excited dogs.

"Horses! To horse!" the booming voice she'd heard in the tower bellowed.

Wistala hurried off into the night. Her muscles began to burn as her dragon-dash gave out. The tree-crowned ridge seemed very far away.

Stog had vanished. All that remained of him were some tracks and a little of his feed scattered on the ground.

"Stog!" she called, panting. The run had been a night-mare of breathless rushes from hiding spot to hiding spot, with dogs barking and crying behind when the horsemen weren't blowing horns at each other. "Stog," she shouted when she had her wind.

She snuffled around and found the trace of a scent. He'd gone off in the direction of Galahall. Had he seen the flames—the top of the tower still burned like a beacon— and gone off to give assistance? They'd missed each other in the dark, and no wonder: she'd splashed through every ditch she could find to confuse the pursuit. Or had he be-come frightened at the hunting horns, even now sounding across the wide lands south of Galahall?

Looking for him would be suicide.

She looked up the tall ridge and started up. The slow, steady climb suited her short limbs so much better than the

run across the fields. By the time she reached the line of
trees, she felt almost herself again. Hunger gnawed at her,
but she was nothing like starved. She body-slid down the
other side, flying down on chest and tail.

The hunters, if they didn't give up upon reaching the
edge of Galahall's grounds, would either have to go round
either side of the ridge or lead their horses up a very
treacherous climb and then down again. By the time daylight came, she'd be deep in the Thickets.

Stog would have to find his own way home.

Will they never give up?

The question hardly left her mind as she made her best
speed through the Thickets, a sort of sore-footed trot.
Winded, thirsty, hungry, scratched at nostril and earhole,
under-limb and tween-toe by the endless thorns, even her
left eye had been poked, and it hurt abominably.

She plunged into yet another strand of bramble as she
heard the clattering noise of the men behind.

The men signaled each other by rapping pairs of hollow wooden pegs, setting up a clatter that might have been
designed to drive her insane, as though the Thickets were
full of maddened woodpeckers. Her mouth was so dry,
nothing but cottony saliva covered her teeth, and all it did
was catch dust and dirt kicked up by the horses thundering
past her hiding spots.

Her one solace was the thought that she'd probably
burned Galahall to the ground. What else could cause the
thane to summon every man with a horse and boy who
could whack two sticks together to this wild and uncomfortable corner?

Wistala listened and then crept up another dry ravine.
The soil in this part of the Thickets kicked up a chalky
dust, and even the thorn-vines and succulents looked
sickly and undersize. Nothing took root at the hilltops, or
anywhere the wind could reach. She stayed just below the
empty crest of it—no need to create a silhouette for one of
the hundreds of pairs of eyes looking for her to see—and

took a bite out of a green segmented plant. Its buds were bitter-tasting but juicy enough to at least give the illusion of moisture.

She could see the twin hills of Mossbell in the distance, green and alluring, but she didn't dare make for them. Who knew what the thane might do to Rainfall if he thought her host had sent her on purposes of possible assassination or proven arson?

Instead she headed for the river, carefully cresting yet another slope. They wouldn't—couldn't—get their horses easily into the gorge, and it would be a brave rider who'd swim his horse into the rocks of the fast-flowing river.

The beaters must have spotted her tracks, for the noise level rose and several came together *clack-tchick-clack-clack-tok-clack,* no rhythm at all, just a crescendo of sound driving her on.

A man negotiated the precarious rim of the finger of land she had to cross. He bore a horn of metal, a long tube wound about itself like a sleeping snake. Obscenely close-set eyes surveyed the thorny runs from above a scarf wrapped round to keep out the dust. He bore a short spear with a long, sharp head and tapered tail.

He'd chosen his spot well. She couldn't cross behind him, not without a climb in the open, though a brief one, perhaps exposing her to the noisemakers in the Thickets.

But a good deal of thornbush filled a gentler slope leading up to his vantage. He amused himself by relieving himself into it.

Wistala was downwind, and the odor struck her nose like a challenge, the clattering in her ears a rattle of an enemy drake's *griff.* She crept slowly through the densest brambles, sliding around the clusters of branch with their pitiful clumps of earth held tight by roots, until his shadow practically fell on her through the thorny lattice.

She took two steps closer, marked the route she'd use in the final dash—

He saw her approach too late and extended his hand, not the one holding a weapon, but rather to show some kind of talisman.

Wistala exploded out of the thorns, touching rock once as she leaped onto the hunter. She struck high, throwing her weight into his chest to knock him off the narrow crest of the hill.

They tumbled off the hill and down the other side—the direction she needed to go anyway. She dug in with her claws and shut her eyes to keep out the dust. Down—they both broke against a rock, its impact harder on her lighter body but bloodying the unprotected skin on his arm—and she went for his neck.

Vertebrate prey were most vulnerable there. If you got a good grip, you opened windpipes and blood vessels, and they couldn't bite or gore you back. Her teeth closed, and she tasted blood and heard a strange high wheeze. The man's hands raked at her face but found a nostril instead of her more vulnerable eye or ear holes.

He went limp.

She dropped the crushed neck, the man's eyes dry and empty. She opened his gut with her *saa* to make sure of him, and his body gave a reactive twitch. . . .

The corpse twitched again as she found his liver.

Tearing the oblong organ loose, she raised her head and let it slide down her throat in two big gulps. She sucked blood from the wound, and saw something in his hand shining in the sun. Tarnished gold or brass—either would be welcome. She nibbled it free from the leather thong fixed to it that the man had wrapped about his wrist.

It was a thin round device of hammered heavy metal, a hominid figure in a circle. Hominids had strange superstitions and believed in invisible forces that attracted or repelled evil or good. Was this some kind of proof against dragons?

She licked it. No sharp taste of poison, just the thick metal-saliva. Satisfied, she sent it down her gullet to join the liver, where it would gravitate to the pocket of her innards that absorbed metals.

Smelling, listening, she picked her way south.

All the way across the next flat, the terrified, dead eyes of the man stayed with her. She'd killed a hominid from ambush. Rainfall might call it murder. While hungry, she wasn't starving, and attacking him had been a foolish risk.

The fact of the matter was, she'd let her temper get the better of her and killed to spite the beaters behind.

She heard a faint, wailing horn. The beaters had probably come across the body. Two more blasts, some kind of signal?

The wind out of the southwest whistled as it cut through the thick thornbushes all around her. The gorge must be near; she couldn't see any more hills to the south.

A faint and rising sound of hoofbeats came across the wind. Wistala found a rock and climbed near the top, keeping to the shadow side so light wouldn't reflect off her scales.

Riders! A dozen at least, traveling in pairs, their horses and legs garbed in some sort of leather tenting, perhaps to keep out the thorns, trotted through the brambles, lance-tips sparkling in the sun.

All moved to cut her off from the south. She heard howling; they had dogs with them. Even if the riding men blundered past, the dogs would smell her out.

The thane's men no doubt wanted her hide in return for some burned shingles and draperies! From Rainfall's description, Hammar wasn't the sort to leave an account unsettled.

Wistala gulped, the blood she'd wetted her throat with long since caked over by the dry dust she breathed. Her thoughts felt slow and thick as her blood. The men would probably . . .

Dry!

She came off the rock, spat one jet of flame into the tangle right, then trotted a few steps and started another fire left.

The thin branches supporting the thorns caught fire easily, and the wind pushed the flame northwest.

She'd set up a signal to every beater in sight.

But the men would keep from downwind if they knew what was good for them.

Wistala walked along between her two columns of conflagration, nostrils held low to keep out the smoke. At new thickets, she helped spread the flame with another *torf* or two.

Horns, more confused signals from beyond the smoke. But most of the noise was well behind her.

Now the fire raged so she couldn't hear anything but its crackling. Her scales reflected the worst of its heat, but she still panted, trying to see through the smoke. A stand of pine, a little above the flat, was burning, and she made for it.

The flame had already consumed the dropped needles; only the tops of the trees burned now. The tough old pines would be green again next spring, but if she wished to be breathing in a year's time—

Wistala took a deep, lung-filling breath from below the smoke layer, picked a gap, and dashed. She felt flames licking at her flanks. The betweens of *sii* and *saa* burned in the hot soil, and she instinctively closed her digits, and she was through, coated with nothing but a thick layer of soot.

And suddenly she breathed cool, dry air, the inferno behind eating its way northwest under a mountain of smoke. From far to the west, she heard more calls as the hunters searched in smoke and confusion.

Wistala got her bearings, noted happily that the sun had fallen almost to the horizon, and moved toward the river.

She negotiated the gorge and swam downriver to the bridge and the landing where they'd tried to smash the troll. The river refreshed after the heat, ash, and dust.

The burns between her digits were painful, made more so once she climbed up the rough stairs from the landing when the blisters burst, but she'd learned a valuable lesson that would outlast the pain about her body's resistance to fire. Next time she'd close up her toes, she thought as she passed over Mossbell's road wall.

A dim light glimmered from the stone-flanked skylight to the library. Perhaps he was still up, reading. She smelled horses in the turnaround by the old fountain.

Wistala decided that the stable might not be the best

place for her to sleep. She climbed up her yew tree and made herself as comfortable as possible in the branches.

Exhaustion allowed her to sleep.

She found Rainfall out the next day, gathering blueberries into a satchel that smelled of strawberries, acorns, hickory nuts, and onions.

"How went the hunting expedition, Wistala?" he asked with his back to her. Perhaps he smelled her approach—he had a sensitive nose.

"I . . ." She groped for the right Elvish word. "I've misspent your trust and lost Stog."

He turned, his countenance a foggy morning. "I heard a most curious story from one of the thane's riders. Two nights ago, the most astonishing creature crept into Galahall."

"Yes—"

"According to the eyewitnesses, it was bluish, had two heads on long necks, one at either end, feathers all about the face, and shot flame from its glowing eyes. Half the country is rooming with their sheep as men stand guard with fire buckets. I don't know what to think. Should I be on my guard that a two-headed featherface come to burn down my hall?"

Wistala's mouth opened and then shut again.

Rainfall suddenly laughed. "Rah-ya! I'm sorry, Wistala—I shouldn't torment you. Come inside and have a little soup and what's left of those rabbits. I wish to hear this story."

Wistala fought the urge to nuzzle his cheek against hers—she could just reach if she stood on her hind legs—and instead turned a quick, happy circle.

"What?" he asked as they walked. "You thought I'd be cross with you? Ever since I dragged you out of the river, there's been excitement. Save for the awful loss of Lessup, and, of course, our Avalanche, I'd say those old tales out of the East about dragons being omens of good fortune have been proved. And don't worry about the mule; Stog will turn up. He's smart enough to find his way home."

They went into the house, and he passed her a platter that held the remains of his stew and grease-fried entrails.

As she ate, she told the whole story—save for the death of the hunter. She didn't feel a bit sorry for the damages to the thane's Galahall, but relating the loss of Stog made her miserable, as well as her confession that she'd failed to return with his granddaughter.

"I wish you'd have discussed this adventure with me before you'd set out. I would have saved your claws the burns and wear."

"But it's not right."

Rainfall poured himself a little more wine and juice squeezings. "Had you come back with her, I would have taken her in both hands. But then I'd have escorted her straight back to Galahall."

"But you could conceal her, as you did me—"

"Tala, how can I make it plain to you? The thane misuses the law, certainly, whether he breaks it in his misuse is not for me to say. But that doesn't relieve me of my obligation to live by it. Laws stand only by common consent; enforcement can do only so much."

He paused and waited until she nodded, then went on: "The thane at least keeps most of the Hypatian traditions, which are just as important as laws in their way. In other provinces, there are thanes who rule like the despots of old. I've heard of thanes who force their landholders to will their estates over to him, lest they be labeled traitors and executed, then find an excuse to execute anyway once everything is set down in writing. All quite legal on the face of it, but appallingly against the Hypatian tradition. Hammar will die or go into his dotage eventually, and Hypat will appoint a new thane."

"Someone like you should be thane, then. An elf is better than any man."

"Oh, that racial rubbish. Have you been listening to the soldiery? There was a time when Hypatian citizenship was what counted, not the shape of your legs and angle of your shoulders."

Wistala took a last mouthful of fried entrail. "So you're content to let those blighters in Galahall rut about your granddaughter, and not see her again?"

"What's that? Rut?"

"That tower. There were babies in it. Well, a baby."

Her host's face writhed. "How young? Perhaps he's warded a child. . . ."

"I'm not sure. Still suckling at his youngish mother, anyway."

Rainfall passed his hand through his hair, dropping a long, thin willowlike leaf or two. "He wouldn't. Not wards of the thane! Oh, if only I'd been more provident with my gold plate, I could sell it or melt it."

A thought struck Wistala. "The form of the wealth doesn't matter?"

It took a moment for her words to register. "Well, the thane is entitled to assess the value of anything that isn't Hypatian coin. What do you have in mind?"

"Another expedition."

Chapter 15

A moon and a blustery week of storms later—five weeks as the hominids reckoned things—Rainfall and a group of local men and boys stood on one of the wall-crossed hills of Tumbledown, speaking with the local shepherds and farmers.

And Stog, incredibly.

Stog stood in this distant field with some other working beasts, all muddy, thin, and miserable.

The expedition had come to fruition easily enough. Wistala, after looking at a map and taking a trip to the nearest hilltop with a good view south of the bridge, decided that the same road Rainfall had in his charge cut through near Tumbledown—or Hesstur, as Rainfall insisted on calling it.

"One of the eight sister cities from the founding of Hypat," Rainfall explained after Wistala described the three hills and wet ground in between. "It was burned in one of the barbarian wars."

A good deal more history followed this, but without being able to see the battles and kings and generals and so on Rainfall spoke of, the names and dates left Wistala's head almost as soon as they entered it. If only hominids could pass mind-pictures down!

Rainfall had no difficulty pulling together some men

and their sons for the trip. The killing of the troll had given Rainfall something of a local reputation, Wistala guessed, and it even attracted one of the thanedom's low priests. She seemed a sturdy woman, in her black robe and tassled hat, white hair at her temples making the rest of her black hair, cut so evenly at the bottom, it might be mistaken as a helmet, look darker.

Wistala had to watch it all from a distance. Her presence had to be kept hidden for her—and Rainfall's—safety.

They made quite a procession. Thick-shouldered farmers and their thicker-shouldered horses, Jessup with a smart new leather work apron driving his cart loaded with feed for hominid and animal, the low priest with boys in tow, showing them strange roadside mushrooms, flowers, and berries. Rainfall walked at the head, wearing layers of heavy traveling clothes, leather-fringed sandals, a cloak, and even a short, slightly curved sword with a guard at the hilt.

She traveled ahead of the group on the overnight journey south, moving before dawn and after dusk and sleeping out the day while the others caught up. Now and then she met with Rainfall on the road a little ahead of the party. The journey was uneventful, save for some boys throwing dung-balls from cover as they passed through a muddy village. One clod hit Rainfall in the thigh.

"Wish I'd seen that," Wistala said.

"Boys being boys. Their parents should soap their tongues until they learn civil expression, though," Rainfall said. " 'Elvish maggot.' Right in the heart of the village, too. An old woman bowed and apologized for the insult. Perhaps it was the star."

Wistala had not seen the golden device before. It had eight short points around the edge and a blue jewel at the center. Some mark of his status as the bridge-keeper and road-warden, she guessed.

So, led by Rainfall's star, they came to Tumbledown and saw the field with Stog.

The low priest—her name was Feeney—and Rainfall conducted the negotiations with the locals of Tumbledown. Then both sides withdrew, the newcomers to their tents with a purchased sheep, the shepherds and small-holders to their cottages and ricks and cots.

Rainfall wandered the woods until Wistala caught up to him. They sat together on an old wall dividing one part of identical forest from another.

"I let Mod Feeney do the talking. We will split whatever we find exactly in half with the locals. They claim that the ruins have been explored a dozen times a generation, and that they've been stripped to the last *lumik*."

"*Lumik*?"

"A bit of art that throws off light when you rub it."

"Then they're doubly wrong. I'll show you one when we enter. I saw Stog in with the other animals."

"What other—? Oh, the farmers and so on?"

"Yes," Wistala said. "I didn't dare approach. There were horses, and I was afraid they'd scream their heads off."

"You are certain? Many mules look alike."

"Yes. Though he looked thin and dirty."

"I'll try to buy him back tomorrow."

The stupid beast didn't deserve Rainfall's kindness. "I'll see if I can talk to him during the day tomorrow," Wistala said. "Assuming they don't have him pulling loads of rocks or whatever work these humans do."

"The night is wasting."

Rainfall never seemed to need sleep, though his face was less animated at night than at other times.

They walked into Tumbledown. A dog barked in the distance, and they stood close to a wall, but they met no further challenge. Soon they were at the triple broken arches that marked the way down to the rats' underground realm.

"I smell bats," Rainfall said. "I should hate to get bitten—they carry sickness."

Rainfall opened his satchel. He fiddled with a brass bowl that smelled of oil. Then he poured some powder that smelled faintly of rotten eggs into a rough stone channel, and drew a piece of wood all splintered at one end across it. The powder and the wood burst into flame. He touched it to the closed top of the bowl, and a flame glowed.

"All that effort for a bit of fire?" Wistala asked. "You should have just asked me."

"I couldn't impose on your great gift for something so mundane as a little light," Rainfall said. "Doesn't a wise dragon keep her fire bladder ready?"

"I don't see a battle breaking out between your construction gang and the sheepherders. There'd be plenty left to torch some rats if they swarm."

"Show me the way, my shining friend."

"Fair warning: you'll get dirty."

She led him down. When they reached the passage that had the glow bulb, Wistala showed it to him.

"It is a *lumik,*" Rainfall said, rubbing it so it glowed. "This alone will pay for feasts all the way back to Mossbell, and buy Stog besides." He pried it loose and worked it with a bit of cloth until it shone like a slice of moon brought underground.

The underground still smelled of bits of worms and rats. Rainfall just squeezed down the dug passage to the sewer. It was drier than Wistala remembered. Rats *yeek*ed at them from the corners as they fled the light.

Had she really been here? Fought a channel-back? The sewers felt like some mind-picture from a distant ancestor.

Rainfall followed, scratching marks onto the walls here and there with a piece of soft stone that left white traces. "I don't have your tunnel sense, my dear."

She led him into the room where she and Yari-Tab had fought the rats and spoken to the old milk-eyed specimen. Rainfall didn't mind the smell or the filth thick on his sandals. He spoke of false walls fallen away as his eyes wandered ever upward, to old writings and chipped drawings running the edge of the chamber's ceiling. He stepped over to an old doorway, rusting hinges still projected out into a space where the wood had long since rotted away. He reached up and marked the lintel with an *X*.

"It's down these stairs," Wistala said, standing at the gap to a circular passage. Rat eyes glinted in the shadows.

"There's a high crypt this way— No, I shan't disturb any bodies."

Wistala wouldn't have cared if he wanted to juggle the skulls of kings. But Rainfall continued: "Sets of edicts can sometimes be found with a thane's remains, or biographies. Both are fascinating reading."

She caught a whiff of precious metals on the stairs. "I don't dare go any farther."

Rainfall's hand dropped to the hilt of his sword. "Ho! Is there danger?"

"Only from me. A dragon's heart can grow fierce at the sight of gold. The last time I came down these steps—it could have ended badly for my friend."

He raised the crystal, and sharp shadows sprang up on the stairs. As he went down, the shadows retreated and advanced as though terrified of the light. His footsteps were so light, she could only just hear them.

"Rah-ya, Wistala, here's a hoard worthy of a dragon," he called up. "Silver and gold and baser coins."

"Will you be able to find it again?"

"I'm sure of it. I return. Close your eyes, for I've a handful of gold."

She shut her nostrils, too. Her mouth went wet, and her stomach growled at the faint smell.

Rainfall spoke in her ear. "Now open your mouth."

She complied, and felt a hard fall on her tongue.

Rainfall spoke: "Just a mouthful of the best silver I could find."

The coins slipped easily down her throat, greased by the thick saliva the smell of metals brought to her mouth.

"But you need the coin," she objected. (Once the coins were safe in her stomach!)

"I matched need against deserve, and deserve won. I have some proofs of the money resting there still in my bag." He pulled on the strap of his satchel so the coins within jingled.

Wistala napped out the morning light under a cool slab in a quiet corner of Tumbledown, concealed by a cascade of runners dropped by the ferns clinging above. She'd gone to the pasture to look for Stog, but only a mare and her colt remained. The men must have put him to work.

She felt a soft nuzzle under her chin. "*Tchatlassat?*" came a familiar purr.

Wistala came wide awake in a flash. "Yari-Tab?"

She'd grown wide-bodied feasting on rats, or had a bellyful of young, perhaps. "I smelled you as I was finishing my night's prowl and followed the trail. Such doings in the Tumbledown. Digging by my entrance to the Deep Run. What's the hunt?"

Wistala had to think for a moment—she was so used to speaking in Elvish. "Hominids come for the gold."

"Will there be fighting? The rats would like that."

"No, my host has arranged a diversion."

"Serves them right, savage beasts. But when mice can't be found, I'm glad to have them."

Wistala raised her head and stretched. "Sister! I've a wonderful idea!"

"Yes!" Yari-Tab said, settling down in the warm spot left by her throat. "A good nap till noontime. Then perhaps a sunbath."

"No. I know of a catless barn that has the mice running wild. Come along to it, and I can promise you all the hunting you like. Perhaps a little goat milk now and then. The owner is a kindly sort."

Yari-Tab fixed eyes on her. "Warm and dry?"

"Yes."

"Oh, *tchatlassat!* I would like that."

"You deserve it. I'll explain things to Rainfall. Once he knows that you're the spring from where this new stream of wealth flows, he'll take you in. I'm sure of it."

With Yari-Tab running scout, Wistala made it to a hillside downwind from the sheep and watched events beneath the triple arch from an overhanging slab. Shirtless men brought the coin out in small buckets, to be laid on a clean white sheet spread out on the ground in front of the hole that had been widened. Feeney and another man dressed in similar robes and tassled hat passed the coins back and forth before moving them to a chest—in the case of the visitors—or a low trough.

Stog made an appearance, dragging a sledge piled with firewood. The man leading the mule struck him about the flanks to drive him on, and Wistala felt her fire bladder pulse. Poor Stog—he was an extraordinarily strong beast.

Yari-Tab grew bored with events and fell asleep in the sun.

By evening they'd brought out the last of the small hoard of coins. Rainfall emerged from the tunnel dirtier than ever, holding what looked like a platter of considerable weight wrapped in a piece of leather. He showed it to the pair of priests.

Wistala couldn't see much from her vantage. It looked like a piece of pinkish stone, but the low priests both touched it as they spoke. After they nodded, Rainfall took it away to Jessup's wagon, spoke to him, and placed it on the high driving seat.

As the sun set, the gathered hominids set up a feast. A bonfire was lighted with the pile of wood Stog dragged. Some of the shepherds took out pipes and drums and small hand harps as others roasted a pig.

"That's a mouthwatering smell," Wistala said.

"Aye, but I must hunt," Yari-Tab said. "I've kittens growing fast within, and they're hungry, too."

Wistala marked Rainfall wandering the opposite hill outside the bonfire light, taking a small bite now and then from a joint of the remaining mutton from last night's meal. He probably meant to find her and offer it. "Wait. I might return with something tastier than a sewer rat."

The moonlight-washed ruins frowned down on the figures moving about the bonfire, as though waiting for the merrymakers to disperse so they could return to their gradual collapse.

Wistala saw Rainfall, smelled the mutton, and rattled her *griff* against her scales to attract his attention.

Rainfall turned and opened his mouth to speak, but a thundering sound rolled through the night. Hoofbeats!

Two lines of riders crested the southernmost hill and rode down toward the bonfire.

Wistala counted seven . . . eight. One carried a high standard, a banner suspended from a crossbar the length of an ax-handle. Wistala's night-sharp eyes distinguished a thin-legged, long-necked bird standing out white on the material of the standard.

"Dis!" Rainfall said. "Bandits, you think? Go and keep hidden, Wistala. Oh, there can't be fighting!"

He tossed the mutton shank in her direction and ran toward the bonfire, his hair making a sound like leaves hitting a wall on a windy night.

Wistala wouldn't leave the mutton to prowling rats and dogs. She returned it to Yari-Tab at the angled overhang.

Yari-Tab sniffed the greasy, ragged joint. "*Tchatlassat*, you're a wonder!"

"Please stay here," Wistala said, an eye toward the center of the three hills. "There's a new group arrived in Tumbledown. I don't like the look of it."

Wistala circled around through the ruins and found all a-tumult. Shepherd boys guided their flocks off the grassy hills, dogs barked everywhere, and around the bonfire, the celebrants had divided into two huddled groups.

At the edge of the fire, the men stood their horses, the banner in the center and another man, rather shorter but above the rest thanks to the size of his horse, speaking with Rainfall.

The riders had thrown back their cloaks to reveal metal plates fixed about their chests, hands on sword hilts, save for the tall one with the bird standard. She let the wind carry the words, along with the aroma of roast pig, humans, and the horses, to her.

"I'm thane here, elf. All your legalisms and tricky word-play won't change that."

"You claim to be thane here, Vog. The maps say differently. The ruins of Hesstur belong to the Directory. You interfere with one of its agents."

Vog, the short man on the tall horse, laughed. He snapped his fingers in the air. "That's for the Directory. All sound and no presence. Those doddards couldn't muster an Imperial Host if Hypat itself had barbarians climbing the First Walls."

"They could if their thanes attended to their duties instead of wine and hunts."

"Do you mean to insult me?" Vog sputtered.

Wistala crept around toward the newcomers' horses.

"I beg your pardon for not making myself understood. If I meant to insult *you*, I would point out that your roads are so overgrown that a wagon can hardly pass without being tangled in branches, that there are a dozen washouts to a *vesk* at least, or that I cannot distinguish the difference between a pig-chasing dog's collar and your men's livery, or that you act and speak in the manner of a barbarian warlord rather than a Hypatian Thane, who would dismount to address a fellow citizen."

Vog put his hand on his sword hilt. "How dare you—"

"How dare you, sir," Rainfall roared. Wistala wouldn't have thought him capable of making such a sound; she froze in her tracks where she crept behind the horses. "How dare you touch your sword when addressing a Knight of the Directory, a Temple Star, and a former Judge Imperial."

Vog's mount danced backwards from Rainfall's fury, unsettling the other horses. Wistala heard a rattle, saw one of the men take a handle with a chain leading back to some metal objects that looked like small metal balls set with dragon teeth.

When Vog had his mount under control again, he leaned forward. "I dare because old titles don't frighten me any more than old moss-backed elves. You're badly in need of a hiding, prissfall. I've a mind to give you one."

"Your having a mind to do anything beyond drawing breath comes as a shock to me," Rainfall said.

"Insult! Bind him!" Vog shouted.

Wistala, at last upwind of the horses, rattled her *griff* as loudly as she could and loosed her urine. Once before, in her journey with Auron, she'd used her urine to scare off a prowling bear. This time the trick worked to spectacular effect. The horses jumped and plunged as though ghost-ridden. Four riders fell, Vog jumped off, and the rest held on to mane and rein for life and limb as their mounts bolted.

The men of the wading-bird standard must have blamed Rainfall for the madness of their horses. They picked themselves up and, following Vog's example, drew their swords, or swung the whirling metal ball in the case of the man with the chain weapon. It made a sound as it cut the air that reminded Wistala of eagle cries.

The two camps scattered, plucking up their children in the case of the shepherds, while the visitors retreated to Jessup's wagon and Mod Feeney.

Rainfall sniffed the air and chuckled. "Put away your weapons, Vog. A pile of old coins isn't worth blood being spilled."

Vog snorted. "See, men of Lossend! Just like that Praskallian said: 'Elvish insolence ends at the sight of steel.' "

"Sight of steel," repeated the man with the whirling chain.

Vog and his men took a step closer. "Stop!" Mod Feeney shouted. "This is hallowed ground, of temples old and proud. The gods weep."

Rainfall drew his thin saber with one hand, detached his cloak, and whipped it about his arm. "Vog! Remember yourself!"

"You've breathed your last insult, elf," Vog said. "At him, now."

In later years, Wistala only remembered Rainfall's lower limbs. He fought as though performing one of the little jigs he did when happy, as on the morning his hair began to grow back in. The power of blocks and strikes came out of his legs and hips, not his arm, extended as stiffly as though it and the blade made one long weapon.

In a flash, Rainfall punched a hole through Vog's ear. He sidestepped, knelt, and sent his next thrust into the kneecap of the man with the whirling chain. As the second man fell to the side of his injured limb, Rainfall got out of the way of the whirling balls, which wrapped around the man's helm and went home all about the head and neck.

He fell and did not move again.

Rainfall threw his cloak-wrapped arm around the sword of the next man coming in—Wistala heard a *krak!* and as Rainfall stepped away, the sword fell and the man clutched his injured limb.

Rainfall rewrapped his cloak about his arm as he put his sword-point before the final pair.

The last two stood shoulder-to-shoulder as they advanced on Rainfall, swords held in both hands in front of them, each urging the other to close and occupy the blood-tipped point while the second finished the job.

Finally one worked up the nerve to raise the sword above his head. With a brave cry he came forward, struck a blow that cleaved the figure before him—

But the figure was Rainfall's cloak, falling to the ground anyway. Rainfall's sword penetrated the thick muscle at the attacker's backside. The second man, seeing his lone ally hop about cursing, thought it best to drop his sword and run.

Vog rejoined the fight with a cry, the side of his head red with blood.

Rainfall parried, parried, ducked out of the way, parried again. Wistala heard the pants of both opponents, but Vog's was the more labored.

Rainfall spoke next: "Blood has washed away whatever quarrels, old and new, we've had. Let us cry 'settled' and remember the example of those who built Hesstur's walls and columns."

Hooves sounded from the darkness, and two of Vog's men trotted up, one with the bird-standard muddied. The thane looked around at his wounded, grunting men.

"I've been a fool," Vog said. "I'll beg your pardon and bury the sword-point." He plunged his weapon into the dirt.

The riders relaxed atop their horses.

Rainfall nodded and turned. "Mod Feeney, let's look to the injured." He wiped his sword on his cloak and resheathed it.

Wistala didn't like the look of the man Vog, the way he

turned to his side and glanced around. So when he sprang forward, a dagger aimed at Rainfall's back, she was already in motion.

Just before the blade went home, Rainfall twisted—too late. The dagger still plunged in.

Wistala's dragon-dash had carried her only a third of the way—

Rainfall let out the softest of tired sighs like a man hanging up his hat at the end of a long day. He fell to the earth as Feeney screamed, perhaps at the infamy, or perhaps at the sight of a drakka shooting across the ruins like an arrow.

Vog twirled his dagger. "You forget, star-polisher, that victory's all that matters in the end. And tonight the victory's—"

As victory was so important to him, Wistala felt it only right that it should be the last intelligible word to pass his lips. Her spring cut off the rest.

Terror took the horses of the mounted men yet again.

She landed hard atop Vog's back, *sii* and *saa* extended and digging. Vog squeaked, rabbitlike, as she opened him up under the rib cage. She took out a mouthful of neck to be sure of him.

She hurried to Rainfall's side. "Oh, Fa— Rainfall. Speak!"

His eyes still lived, anyway. They fixed on her. "Dragon-daughter."

Footsteps. Mod Feeny rushed forward, a pickax held high.

"I'm helping him, you fool," Wistala said in her best Parl.

She pulled up, still with the point raised, and Wistala made ready to jump out of the way.

But here was Jessup, chasing her down. He put a hand on Feeney's. "Hold. She's friendly."

Rainfall managed to raise his hand. "I still breathe," he whispered.

"We need to leave," Wistala said. "Get him on the cart. Don't forget the coin." To Jessup: "I'll meet you back at Mossbell. If there's a hunt, I'll confuse them." A strange clarity had seized her; she had no idea where the words came from, but they flowed steadily. "Gather those horses and that mule there so more may ride. And weapons, that you might overawe any in the village. Vog's a blackheart and deserves to lose all."

"I'm not leaving the injured lying in the mud," Feeney said.

"Then stay and see how your kindness is rewarded."

Next Stog was there, the bonfire revealing the mud on his sides and the filth about his hooves, a broken rope dangling. "Wistala. Strange fortune brings us together again. Forgive—"

Feeney and Jessup just stared in wonder at the mule, nickering and tossing his head at the drakka.

"No time for words, Stog. Do you wish to return to Mossbell?"

"Is clover sweet? Of course."

"Then you can do me a favor, and bear a burden back."

"I'll carry the master to the icy tundra if I must, and stomp any—"

"No," Wistala said. "He's riding in the cart. I want you to carry a cat."

Stog ended up carrying two cats, Yari-Tab and a night-black female named Jalu-Coke, who had a litter of rambunctious kittens.

"She's a good friend and a stalking good huntress," Yari-Tab said. "She hears like a bat. Speaking of which, I've seen her leap and bring one down—"

"Fascinating," Wistala said, forestalling more anecdotes. Once cats got talking about themselves, they'd go on about whisker length or tail-balancing until the sun came up, and she didn't have that kind of time. Or Rainfall didn't.

Jessup fixed a thick knit blanket and a bread box on Stog's back. The cats and kittens rode easily enough.

Rainfall, his shirt bound about his waist, rested in the back of the cart, gripping his leather-wrapped treasures to his chest. He begged them to leave the shepherds' share of coin.

Mod Feeney was the last to leave the ruins. She bandaged the foemen and spoke many words about how lucky they were to come away with only two dead, and any pursuit would just call up another vengeful fury of red tooth and claw, for the treasure was cursed and only she held the ward-key. Then she hurried down the road after the receding creak of the wagon-wheel.

Wistala watched it all from the ruin-haunted hillside nearest the road. The wounded were helped off to the hovels of the shepherds, leaving the bodies of the two slain men to the rats.

The old milk-eyed rat's prophecy had come true.

Vog's men made a pursuit of it that night after all. As Wistala trotted up the side of the road, she heard them a long way off, a faint but growing sound of hooves. If they'd walked or trotted their mounts, they probably would have caught up to the plodding cart anyway, but perhaps the sight of two bodies, one belonging to their thane, had inflamed them into recklessness. Besides, they were armed and arrayed, and their foes humble.

As to the stories of a scaled beast, confused accounts by injured men and shepherd boys watching from afar might make a freak encounter with a channel-back more than it seemed, and as for the warning of the priestess, trumped-up midwives are always making dire predictions.

How the coin figured into their reckoning of risks, vengeance, and rewards Wistala could guess.

She had to delay them. But how?

Improvise, Mother's voice said to her. She couldn't outfight the men, or outrun the horses. Horses . . .

Rainfall was right about one thing: the road here was in terrible shape. On the north side of the river, it was trim, dry, and even. Here it was sunken, rutted, and holed, with either side of the verge thick with plants.

Rainfall was right about the washes—a veritable stream cut through the road a little ahead. It had eroded until it was as deep as her neck, almost as treacherous as a troll trap.

Slowing up the men and slowing up their horses were one and the same. Would a troll trap do that?

Wistala went to the wash and placed branches in a grid. Next she tore up twigs and leaves and covered the wash as best as she could. She felt bad for the poor heedless brutes—and the four-legged beasts under them—but they would bring battle.

There was a chance that the men would just leap their horses across the wash. But with a long chase behind and possibly ahead . . .

Wistala concealed herself a little behind the trap, by the side of the road in the thick undergrowth, listening to the growing noise and wondering how many riders this thane might have seeking vengeance.

She should have made it deeper. She cleaned the moss off a flat stone and sharpened her claws against it as she tried to count the growing hoofbeats.

At last they came, emerging as a solid mass out of the night, filling the tree-circled road like a rush of dirty water coming down a drainspout. Perhaps six or eight. No, ten, counting a last few with that bird-banner at the back. Too many for her to fight, then.

The men urged lather-soaked horses on with bits of rope or sword hilt. They passed her in a solid wall of hair, leather, steel, and thunder.

Then they hit her trap.

A horse went flat on its face, throwing its rider. The next behind was agile enough to leap out of the way, but the third beast skidded on its hooves as it tried to stop, and went into the wash sideways. Another behind jumped into the woods, dismounting its rider on a branch, and yet another rider went over his horse's head as it skidded to a stop.

The banner hung almost above her, where the back three had stopped in safety to laugh at the chaos ahead.

Wistala hated that stitched-up bird. She aimed and spat a thin stream of fire up into it. It burst into flames immediately, and in the subsequent alarm, she quietly backed down the road to cross ahead.

"Elvish magic!" a man shouted, stomping on the flames.

Wistala's nostrils flared. *Superstitious hominids. Imagine my tricks taken for spellcraft!* She stifled a self-satisfied *prrum*.

"That old leaf-head is a sorcerer!" another agreed.

"Our horses have grown treacherous. He whispers to them on the wind, I'll set my hand on it!"

Wistala slunk across the road once all eyes turned to the ring of men in argument.

The second rider, the one whose mount managed to dodge the first fall, stayed on his horse. He wore an odd double cloak, one hanging from each shoulder.

"Someone help Plov," he said. "How many are hurt?"

"Two cannot ride," a gruff voice from the group said.

More mumbling. "And three more will not," a shriller voice added. "That elf isn't the only one stabbed from behind by Vog. His landsmen have felt their purse strings cut more than once. Gold is not enough of a lure for us to face sorcery to get it back."

"That leaves four to ride with me!" the two-cloak man said. "Hurry, before they're back to the bridge. The cowardly can tend to the injured horses, as that's all they're fit for."

"A man who promises murder to a priestess on the Old Road at night should be careful about that word," the gruff voice said. "You're down to three, Vorl; I ride no farther with you."

"More gold for us, then. Take up the banner!"

Wistala was having a hard time picking out the words as the argument continued. She found an oak with heavy branches stretching above the road and swarmed up it. She tested how far her tail could drop. Then she searched the underbranches and cracked off a drooping limb almost bereft of leaves. She tested her tail's grip on it.

The hoofbeats came again, and she just had time to press her belly to the limb overhanging the road, watching the riders through the gaps in the leaves. They came on this time at something more than a trot and less than a gallop, the two-cloaked rider the others called Vorl at the lead.

The third man in line held what was left of the scorched bird-banner.

"Let's have a song, men," Vorl shouted. "Some airs of wine and women, and all the diversions that gold may buy!"

"How about—?" the last man said, but screamed when he saw the branch swing down from above, striking the rider with the banner full in the face.

Wistala felt the impact run up her tail with some satisfaction.

The banner bearer flipped backwards across his horse's rump, his heels high and his cloak fluttering. He hit hard and the horse behind jumped to avoid hitting him.

Wistala flattened herself into the branch, barely daring to peep at events with one eye.

All the horses snorted and danced, probably smelling Wistala above.

"What now?" Vorl rasped.

"The tree hit him," the fourth man shouted, getting his horse out from under the oak. "A limb full of twigs reached down and struck Gleshick full in the face. It was the tree!"

"Vorl," the other rider said, searching the dark overhang of branches. "Perhaps it's time to leave reins and take up bedcups."

"My horse cannot be controlled!" the last in line said, spurring his mount away. The beast galloped southward, its rider's hindquarters lifted high as he hung on. "An evil magic drives it! Good luck!"

"Brothel spawn!" Vorl shouted at the receding figure. "Come. We're a short way from House Gamkley. He'll remember the thane and mount his household."

"What about Gleshick?"

"A bloody nose and a night on the gravel will teach him not to sleep in the saddle. Let's hurry! Perhaps we can catch up to that fool and talk some sense into him."

They galloped off south, and the empty-saddled horse moved to follow them in a halfhearted manner. Wistala dropped from the tree onto its back.

She clung as best as she could, digging her claws into the mane as the men did with their fingers.

The horse bucked and screamed. Wistala hung on with all four sets of claws.

"I'm not here to hurt you," Wistala said. "Bear me but short run the other way, and I'll release you."

"No!"

"Otherwise you'll not live another minute," Wistala said. "I haven't had horse since I was a hatchling, and your quivering makes me long for the taste."

The horse tore off up the road north. They hurried through the village where Rainfall had been abused and were out of it again before any but the barking dogs woke.

As their racket faded behind and they reentered the woods, the horse tried to knock Wistala off its back by passing under branches, a difficult proposition as she could flatten herself on the horse's back better than any man and still keep her grip. Wistala struck its rump with her tail. "Keep to the center."

"Pity! Exhausted—"

They left the thicker woods and came to open, rocky ground that smelled of sheep and yellow late-summer wildflowers. Wistala saw distant shepherd fires to both sides of the road. Quartz veins in the protruding rocks caught the moonlight. The river ridge broke the horizon in the distance, notched where the road cut through it. She knew that notch. The river ran just beyond.

"Up this far rise, and you'll be done," Wistala said.

The horse quickened his step but breathed more heavily than ever, snorting and gasping as though each labored breath might be his last. Wistala made out the wagon cresting the notch.

"Well enough," Wistala said, hopping off. "Go where you like, but on the other side of the river—"

The horse tore off down the road, away from the fearful dragon-smell.

"Stupid brute," Wistala muttered. *Ah well, of such mentalities meals are made.* She trotted at her best pace after the wagon. As the sky grew pink and then orange, she breached the rise.

She couldn't help but think that the notch would make

another fine ambush site. Its steep sides meant that with a little work they could block the bend ahead, and she could rain fire upon anyone at their heels. . . .

And here was the wagon. She scrambled up the ridge—her hearts beat fast and hard at the sight of the river and the bridge—then got ahead of it.

She counted heads. Each face was drawn and exhausted from the long flight. One was missing: that priestess, Mod Feeney. Had she gone off the road?

"Jessup!" she called when they came within the sound of her voice. "Jessup! Does Rainfall still live?"

"The avenger calls!" Jessup said.

What has that man been telling the others? He halted the wagon and set the brake.

"Rainfall asks for you," Jessup shouted. "He begs you to join him."

Wistala came forward.

"That's a dragon?" one of the men said. "I've yearling pigs that weigh more."

The horses didn't like her smell, and only Stog stood quietly next to the wagon, cat-filled breadbox on his back as the other brutes stamped and danced.

Wistala jumped into the wagon, and some of the men gasped at the quick move.

Rainfall's skin had darkened, like fresh game-meat exposed to air. He sat propped up on a sort of cushion of bags of horse feed. A piece of marbled stonecraft, with letters deeply cut and coated with time-tarnished metal, sat at his side. He rubbed it absently as a man might pet a dog while conversing.

"Wistala, daughter," Rainfall said. "You are here."

"And glad to see you still alive."

"Jessup, drive on," he said with some energy. "The sooner we're through Mossbell's gates—" He winced at some inner pain as the wagon lurched into motion.

"How is it?" Wistala asked. Oh, the inadequacy of words, even tuneful Elvish! If he were a dragon, she could let him feel her concern. Let him know . . .

"I can't move my legs, Wistala. The pain isn't bad at

all—if anything I'm cloudheaded. But such wounds . . . if I should succumb, you must bring Lada to Mossbell, look out for her until she is of age to run the place. I've told Mod Feeney, and I've told Jessup—" He sank back into the cushions again.

"What happened to that priestess?" Wistala asked.

"She rode ahead," Jessup said from his seat. "Hammar has a healer more skilled than she."

It would be hard to say who heard the pursuing hooves first, the horses or Wistala. Both startled.

"Jessup, try to get a little more out of the horses," Rainfall said. "Whip them if you must."

He turned his gaze on the drakka. "Wistala, if they catch up to the wagon, jump on Stog and take that bag of gold to Mod Feeney. She'll see that a judge and a high priest come before the thane and restore Lada to her home."

As dawn came up, some of the men began to run toward the bridge. Home stood just on the other side of the canyon. A more clearheaded one jumped on the lead wagon horse and urged it on.

As they came down the road—the incline helped speed the wagon—Wistala saw the first rider appear behind. Others, ten or eleven in all, came down in a long straggling line. She saw no sign of the bird-banner.

She looked ahead. A group of people stood on the bridge. She recognized Mod Feeney by her odd hat.

Behind, Vorl drew his sword and waved it forward, calling to his men.

Rainfall looked at the coming riders, moving at a pace to catch the wagon before it even crossed the bridge.

"Wistala, on Stog, now!" he gasped.

"No. Wait," Wistala said, seeing the group ahead. What sort of warriors had Mod Feeney gathered at the thane's borders? They seemed dreadfully undersized.

The wagon rattled past Feeney's gathering, the horses' hooves thundering on the wooden planks that bridged the central arch in the ancient masonry. The apron- and tunic-clad assortment were mostly women and children. Wistala guessed them to be families of those in Rainfall's ill-fated expedition, from the way they waved and called to each other.

Jessup halted the column well across the bridge.

The men dismounted and embraced their wives and children. Many of the latter shrieked as they circled the cart with streamers tied to sticks. Curly-tailed dogs barked, adding to the happy chaos.

Wistala peeped at it all through gaps in the wagon-boards. Some of the dogs barked at her.

"For the last time, Wistala, take Stog and go!" Rainfall said. "Look, Vog's armsmen come."

"Your Feeney's building a wall to stop them," Wistala said, watching the activity behind.

Rainfall lifted himself a little higher. "What's this?"

A strange sort of barrier was stretched across the bridge, mostly the women and children holding hands. Their men ran to their families, and Mod Feeney pointed them into place.

"Don't let go of each other. Even if they ride straight for you," Mod Feeney said over the clatter of the approaching hooves.

The riders slowed their horses, pulled up.

"What's this supposed to be," Vorl snarled.

"You'll do no murder in our thanedom," Mod Feeney shouted back.

"Then we'll retrieve that elf and hang him from thane Vog's high lintel," Vorl said. "He stabbed my lord in the back."

"I was there—it was Vog who did the backstabbing," Mod Feeney said.

"Ha! Out of my way, or we'll ride you down," Vorl said. "Stirrup to stirrup now, my men."

"Is it come to this?" Mod Feeney said back, her voice a little more high-pitched. "One Hypatian Thanedom riding down the children of another? High honors to carry home, the blood of babes on your horse's hooves."

"Enough, Vorl," said the compatriot Wistala recognized from her oak-limb perch above the road. "Buy your way into the thane's hall with different coin."

"And Thane Vog not cold yet!" Vorl said. "How dare you—"

"How dare you lie to the men of House Gamkley. Beware, men. He lied to you about Vog's death. He died a scoundrel. I should have spoken then, but I've been a fool. A fool drawn by promises and unearthed gold."

Vorl brought his horse around, pointed it straight at Mod Feeney. His heels went out, and his spurs turned inward.

Wistala nerved herself to jump from the wagon. If Vorl rode through the line of people, she'd turn him into a pyre of burning cloak and horsehair. Nothing would reach the wagon but the stench of charred flesh—

The man who at last spoke the truth to Vorl's company rode up and seized his horse by the throat latch. "Enough, Vorl. Remember the battles of our boyhood. Thanedom against thanedom at Ciril and Starkhollow. Would you see that repeated? Hammar has the friendship of barbarians and more besides, and he's rich enough to hire mercenaries. Let us put away sword, bury Vog, and take counsel."

"Elvish bewitchment, taking the heart out of you!" Vorl shouted, turning his horse south. "You're all under it! I'll call none of you my friends again."

The others gave short head-bows to Mod Feeney and turned for the south end of the bridge.

The man who had grabbed Vorl's horse looked at the linked-arm assembly and smiled. "My compliments on your battlements, Mod," he said. He rode off.

Mod Feeney sank to her knees. "I should have turned to candle-selling and book-copying long ago," she sighed.

"I'll see her a high priestess if it's my last act," Rainfall said, falling back into his feedsack chair. A long brown leaf dropped from his hair. "Jessup," he called. "Take me to Mossbell, that I might die clean in my bed."

Chapter 16

Rainfall did not die.

As he recovered from the blood loss, it became clear to all that he would never walk again, barring some kind of miraculous healing. At first Wistala wondered if it was best that he had lived beyond his wounding (though she later looked back on that sentiment with shame). He could not walk, and he made a rather pitiable sight being hauled around like an arrowed deer over the shoulders of Forstrel, Jessup's nephew.

The only time he moved as she remembered him was upon Stog, for he rode the mule about Mossbell's lands, offering advice—that's how it sounded to Wistala. He was far too polite to issue anything that sounded like an order to the new tenants. And at table, he presided from his chair with his former charm.

To help him in the house and on the grounds, the Widow Lessup and her whole family moved into Mossbell. With Rainfall unable to so much as work the handle of his well-pump, he needed a good deal of assistance.

Wistala helped him up and down stairs. She regularly wore her game harness, and Rainfall sat atop her back gripping it as she negotiated the tight, winding stairs of Mossbell.

"I should flood the place and pole about, as they do in

Wetside," Rainfall said. She'd heard stories of its famous water gardens before.

Mossbell's old ferry-call rang thrice for dinner, forestalling another tale of spiced shrimp and tuna. The Jessup and Lessup clans trooped in from the fields in answer.

Yari-Tab had her litter of kittens in an old laundry basket upstairs, and Jalu-Coke followed with a fresh litter of her own in the barn. Thanks to Mossbell's odd hole-and-corner architecture and rich gardens, the kittens had no end of places to explore, and the older cats feasted upon the mouse and rat population. The inside cats took to following the Widow Lessup about, for she was constantly moving the remaining pieces of furniture and ordering her daughters and sons to clean, polish, and organize, and the curious kittens had learned that explosions of startled insects or mice could result every time a wardrobe was pulled out.

"A hundred years of dust in this house, if it's a day," the widow said. "Len-boy, fetch fresh rags from the washroom and tell your sister she's falling behind on the laundry again!"

Rainfall could only spread his hands and apologize when the widow found a pile of ancient crockery under a chair in the morning-room, or spider-sacs thick as peas in a pod under his bed, until Wistala wondered who was truly the master of Mossbell now.

"Carpentry and cooking are the only indoor work I've ever been able to manage," he said, after another astonished outburst when she awoke a family of raccoons napping out the day in the upstairs linen armoire.

Wistala had become something of a public figure on the estate. The Lessup boys brought their friends, and they'd watch her napping in the sun, not knowing that dragons often cracked an eye as they slept, nerving themselves for an approach. Eventually they'd come up to her in tight little groups of two or three, and one would reach out his grubby hand and run a fingernail across her scales. She'd lift her fringe and drop her *griff* and bring round her head with a piping dragon cry, and they'd run away shrieking as though expecting to be roasted.

Little girls clapped their hands over their eyes when they first saw her, but once they got over their initial shyness stepped across the line into overfamiliarity, even outrage, for they liked nothing better than to set wildflowers in her scales and fringe until she looked as though she was sprouting like a young elf.

"That's women for you," Rainfall said, plucking a red blossom from the fold in her skin where she tucked up her *griff.* "Always improving on nature."

And then it was time for Rainfall's granddaughter to return.

Because of the elf's wounds, the high judge attended Rainfall personally. He came with a dozen attendants and counted out the coin Rainfall owed in back taxes, then sealed Rainfall's petition to have his granddaughter restored to him with a great deal of melted wax and ribbon. Wistala thought the high judge an odd-looking fellow made mostly of wrinkles and sags, with a dismal attire all of black deep as cave-dark, though it made the polished gold star on his collar flap and the golden tips of his boots look all the brighter.

The judge and his men ate vast meals before they left, leaving the Widow Lessup clucking that the whole household would be eating roots and apples for the next week.

The next day music woke her.

She stretched and followed the lilting tune until she found Rainfall in the music room playing his bell-pipe. This time she couldn't dance with him, but she could chase her tail and caper until Widow Lessup stormed in with shrieks about what Wistala's claws were doing to the polished floors.

"I admire your good humor," Wistala said as she left. "You look fully recovered."

"Fully?"

"Your eyes sparkle, and your hair is thickly leaved. Such colors!" The willow-leaf locks in his hair had gone red and gold and orange.

"I am happy. I've had a letter. Lada comes home today."

"Do you mind if I ask a question?"

Rainfall's eyes sparkled. "You've chosen a good day to crave a handful of silver to eat. I'm in no mood to deny anything."

"I should like that. But those tablets with the engraved writing. You held them close all the way back to Mossbell. I'm curious, did you find an old family relic in the ruins?"

Rainfall sat straight upright. "Our legends say dragons sniff out a weak spot the way dogs find bones. There must be some truth in it."

"If it's painful to you—"

"Oh, no, nothing like that. Closer to shame, perhaps. I think I told you that Hesstur was one of Eight Sister Cities who founded Hypatia, yes?"

"Yes," Wistala said.

"Let me sit on you, and you can take us into my library."

Rainfall put away his bell-pipe and got on Wistala. When he patted her side, she stalked off toward the library, and they soon arrived. The lectern that had once stood under the window was gone, probably sold, but a pair of old chairs filled its place with a velvet-covered object like a small tabletop upon one.

Rainfall seated himself beside it. "Such humble accommodations for history so important.

"When it became evident that the city would fall to the barbarians, those inside did their best to hide their valuables. I'm sure some priest had charge of these tablets and sealed them in one of the lower crypts before all entrances were sealed. She—I say she, for the clues were voiced in the feminine—made some signs in the old law-tongue, the father of the Hypatian high-tongue and the grandfather of Parl, though only judges and librarians read it much now. If the fires and collapses left the chamber intact, earthquake or grave-robbers later opened it again, though I expect the only ones to benefit were the rats."

"This doesn't tell me what the object is."

"An idea, more than anything," Rainfall said, removing the velvet. "When the eight sisters joined, they formed the King's Council. The tyrant Masmodon did away with the

King's Council when he broke the Imperial Staves, but after the Reformation, the Directory modeled itself—"

You could never get a simple answer out of Rainfall when he fell into history. "What does that have to do with the tablets?"

"These tablets are laws that applied to the Kings on the original Council. It was quite a remarkable idea, kings subject to law. Each of the sister cities was afraid of bad rule, or the assumption of a tyrant like Masmodon, so as a condition of their confederation—"

Wistala wasn't sure what that last word was but dreaded interrupting now that he was getting to the point.

"—made eight laws, one for each city, that the Kings on the Council would have to obey. The idea that laws applied to kings was the work of the dwarf-philosopher Doomzeg, though some say he was inspired by the practice of Royal Responsibilities in the ancient Blighter Uldam Empire. It doesn't do to mention those sorts of theories, especially around the priesthood."

"Naturally," Wistala said, lost again.

"Not that Blighter Civilization is established. It's still much debated in the—" Rainfall cocked his head, and his hair-leaves rustled. "You jest with me. But let me illustrate from the tablets: 'No ruler shall kill, maim, imprison, or exile without trial by judge.' That's an important one. 'No ruler shall make law that applies but to all.' Oh, I fear I've translated that badly, but in essence it prevents a king from issuing an edict preventing, say, one shipmaster from transporting wine if other shipmasters are allowed to. Specific laws were the ruination of many in the days of the despots. 'No ruler shall accept or give divination'—another old practice that might be used to get around the other laws, declaring yourself or a family member a god so that one's word becomes religion rather than law. 'No ruler shall confiscate—' "

Wistala stopped him before he could read through all eight and closely examined the tablets. "Why does the ownership distress you, then?"

"When I found them, I swore to myself that I would make the journey to the Imperial Library at Thallia. Oh, I could lose myself there like a drunkard in a brewery! But I find I can't bear to part with them, even if I had the use of my legs. I've spent much time cleaning the inlay. Now they shine like a mariner's guiding star in these dark times. Is it wrong for me to keep them here?"

"Why in the Two Worlds would you ask me?"

"While your judgment is not yet developed, your heart is usually in the right place."

Wistala didn't correct him that a dragon had several hearts. He continued: "You tell me you are not yet two years of age, yet your mind is so far developed."

"We learn from our parents while still in the egg."

"Fascinating. But what surprises me—"

The tolling of Mossbell's signal interrupted his thought. "It must be Lada," he said. "I asked Forstrel to ring as soon as any riders appeared. Wistala, bear me to the front gallery window!"

The front stairwell had a landing with an arched window in it looking out on the balcony between the two trees, made of glass so fine, there were hardly any distortions when peering through. He worked the latches and forced open the frame.

"Odd that she does not ride," Rainfall said. "She used to love ponies. Yet—it was cool this morning, good of the thane to provide her with more comfortable transport."

A two-wheeled cart—very like but a little more elaborate than that of the wandering dwarf with the ponies Wistala had met on the road—moved up the lane with a rider behind.

"Perhaps you should remain inside, Wistala." Forstrel, all hair and limbs, was still ringing the bell as though the barn was going up in flames.

"Young Lessup!" Rainfall called. "Yes, Forstrel, up here, please. I should like to meet my granddaughter on my steps."

One of the Widow Lessup's daughters had the sense to put out a chair for Rainfall, and Wistala saw that he was installed before the rig had even turned around in front of the house.

The escort, only a little mud-splattered in the blue livery of Thane Hammar, didn't descend from his horse. Wistala could tell from Rainfall's stiff manner that he didn't care for this discourtesy.

"Here's your spawn back, and more besides!" the escort said as the rig-driver stepped down and lowered a support for the cart. When that was locked in place, he opened the doors at the back of the cart, and Lada stepped down.

"Phew, she's tossed all over the inside," the driver said.

Lada, a little stained about the neck, was helped out of the cart. Her eyes were wide and wet, and she shot an accusing look at Rainfall.

"Rah-ya, Lada, my moppet," he said, extending his hands. Wistala saw a little skirt behind and decided that some of the Lessup household were standing behind their master. "I'm sorry for the rough journey."

"Monster! Demon! You've ruined everything! Everything!" she said in so loud a voice, her words cracked. She fled into the house, dodging around Rainfall as he reached for her.

"And you're welcome to her," the thane's liveryman laughed. He reached into a bag on his saddle and drew out the doll Wistala had brought. "Here's her mystery doll, Rainfall. You should be more careful in your plotting than to leave such tokens lying about."

Rainfall put his arm about Forstrel's shoulders, and the youth took him inside as the house went into uproar. She heard doors closed, shouting, crying, and quick steps as the Lessup clan gathered to discuss events.

Wistala could do nothing. She watched the rider and rig disappear, then went to Rainfall's library. If he were greatly troubled, he'd probably go there. She curled up about his tablets and waited, unable to simply fall asleep.

He appeared as the juicy smells of dinner being cooked began to fill the house, brought in by Forstrel in a wheeled basket used for gathering fruit.

"I really must have one of those sick-benches built,"

he said as he settled into his reading chair. "Thank you, Young Lessup. Ah, Tala, you appear again when you're most needed. You can see about getting some dinner, Lessup. I won't eat tonight."

The boy placed a blanket over Rainfall's legs and left, shutting the door behind.

"So much for homecoming joy. But she's beautiful, do you not agree?"

"I'm just getting so I can tell hominids apart," Wistala said.

"Perhaps not in a way that can be captured by portraits or sculpture, you have to look into her living eyes to appreciate her. Wild and open, like my son's. I wonder what her mother was like."

"Why was she angry to you?"

"I need a glass of wine," Rainfall said. He moved for his bell—

"I'll bring it," Wistala said, glad of an excuse to make the trip to the cellar and back. "Which kind?"

"The blueberry, I think. Something sweet to wash the bitter words from my mouth."

Wistala crept past the room that had been prepared for Lada and heard sobbing from the crack beneath. Her *griff* extended a little, and she descended to the wine cellar and searched the tags on the month's table wine for the blueberry picture.

She carried it back up in her mouth, startling one of the younger Lessup girls as she emerged from the cellar. The child let out a squeak and ran off toward the kitchen. It was the one who liked to tie her hair up in ribbons, Wistala noted absently; all the others in the family simply watched her as she went about Mossbell.

Rainfall opened the cork-and-wax top and poured himself a generous glass. "Once I had thirty of these," he mused as he rolled around the purple liquid. "And I didn't have to make my own wines. Though if the estate prospers now, I'll continue the practice. There's a satisfaction in enjoying the fruits of one's own labors. That's the one thing

I've learned all these wretched years since the troll came. Oh, and about dragons. Forgive me, Tala."

"You ask my forgiveness? Since you saved me from the river, you've lost the use of your legs and your granddaughter's love."

"If you'll indulge me in applying a correction: Don't be so quick to mark fate and toss it into baskets marked 'fortune' and 'misfortune' as though you're sorting apples. It was an illness that forced me to cease traveling as a judge—a heavy misfortune—yet that same illness kept me in Tysander, where I diverted myself at the circus and lost my heart to the most skilled rider that ever sat atop a horse. My wife could stand on a horse's bare back with reins tied to her hair all day and still beat me with her strategy at Advantages when we played at night. I imagine if her father or grandfather had spoken against me, she would have cried out, too. I should never have shouted at her. Unforgivable."

"What is the quarrel?" Wistala asked.

Rainfall looked out the library skylight—still cobwebbed and dusty, the Widow Lessup hadn't climbed a ladder in the library yet—and blinked.

"She's convinced herself she loves Hammar."

"A man who stuck her in a cold attic?"

"Apparently she blossomed up there like a solstice succulent shut in the Yule dark. Hammar is young and wild. Nature and instinct took its course."

"So they are mat—married?" Wistala asked.

"They can't be, not under Hypatian law, because of her age. But sadly, she's not too young to bear his child." Rainfall's fingers tightened on the glass stem, and it broke.

Her host blotted up the wine and his own blood with blotting paper. "And the last of the thirty are gone. Oh, what shall I do, Tala? I've suspected he wanted to add Mossbell to his lands, but to resort to this?"

"Wait, this is about land?" Wistala said.

"'I've no doubt of it. With the land—soon to be prosperous again now that the troll is gone—goes responsibility for the road and bridge. He should like to make all who cross pay a toll."

"How does he stand to get the land?"

"He won't have any difficulty getting me declared an invalid, with the judge in his pocket. It would devolve to Lada, save that she is not of age to run an estate. Lada's child would naturally inherit—I'm pierced from my own quiver, insisting Eyen to confirm his parentage with the priests and courts. And she's only too happy to name Hammar as the father. He would become master of Mossbell."

Wistala's head hurt from trying to follow the convoluted circumstances. "I'm not sure I follow the law, but in all your talk of courts and powers—I thought it was to ensure justice and fairness. This strikes me as quite the opposite."

Rainfall admired the glass one more time before discarding it.

"The law and fairness often dance together, but they are not married," he said. "Lately I've grown too fond of engineering, for one can trust calculation and breaking strengths. No thane may change the weight of a stone, no matter how much he wishes. But! I am still master of Mossbell. Perhaps I shall sell it to the dwarves and move south."

He sniffed the air. "But I'm keeping you from your dinner."

She wasn't hungry; perhaps Rainfall's upset and sour mood had transferred itself to her by something like mind-speech.

Mossbell's problems were like a tar pit, the more she struggled to help her host, the worse his plight became!

She went out to the stable barn and found Stog licking at the remains of his evening grain. Jalu-Coke's kittens, all ears and tails, were chasing each other about on clumsy paws. This was the sort of law she understood: the mice ate Stog's grain, and the cats ate the mice.

"Does the master need me?" Stog asked her.

"Oh, no," Wistala said. "I wanted to think. The house was closing in on me. You're looking well."

"Good grain and clean water," Stog said. "I am lucky. It is a blessing to know how lucky one is."

"What happened that night we parted? Did the men find you?"

"Not the way you think," Stog said, shifting on his hooves. Wistala nipped his bristly tail—the donkey in him showed most at the mane and tail.

"Tell me. I need a diversion. Treks and tracks, I shan't be mad."

"Silly, really. I took my chance to get back to the Dragonblade."

Wistala was so astonished, she couldn't speak.

"What?" she finally said.

"You hate me now," Stog said. "But I've been wanting to tell you since our return. I'm grateful to you, unlike these fool kittens, I know what you've done for me. Let's have honesty between us."

"Was he such a fine master as all that?"

"Not as kind as our good elf. But that didn't signify. It wasn't the treatment; it was the excitement of the hunts. I, a pack mule at column-back, used to have flowers thrown on me as we passed through towns, mouth stuffed with carrots and sugar beets. Cheering. You must know that a dragon can wreck whole lands."

Wistala tried to keep her tail still. "I've heard of dragons being blamed for storms and earthquakes."

"You may well glare, but that doesn't signify. Hominids fear your kind."

"Conceded. So you thought you'd make a try for his hall?"

"Yes, I know the look of the mountains; it's not far south of here. But I stopped in a field to avail myself of some corn . . . and the next thing I knew I had a rope around my neck and another bad master. Then you appeared again. In the Dragonblade's mule train, I learned not to fear the dragon-smell, but I've never liked it until you."

"So the Dragonblade lives not far south in the mountains? He must be close to the Wheel of Fire dwarves, then?"

Stog's ears went up and forward. "Close? Of course. He lives in their city."

For the second time since entering the barn, Wistala was startled into astonishment. But of course he would live with dwarves, as they helped him kill dragons.

"The Wheel of Fire?" Wistala asked.

"The dwarves build fastnesses like no others, and he must be guarded sky and tunnel. It must signify to you that the Dragonblade's line has made enemies, very powerful enemies, of your kind."

He's made an enemy of me, small, stumpy, and misfortunate. But she'd promised Father nests of hatchlings.

She was making herself miserable and hungry for metals, so much so that the tools hung by the hearth looked tempting. Rainfall had written a letter to the metalsmith's guild in the coastal town of Sack Harbor asking for a quantity of brass and copper meant for the melting pot but so far only an answer had arrived naming a price. Wait, that Jessup fellow said something about spare shingles. . . .

"Stog, thank you for an honest tale," she said.

As the night deepened, she wandered the grounds, prowling, really, for the vegetable garden's fall planting was coming up, and if she was sharp, she might get a raiding rabbit if wind and shadow favored her.

Were she Father, she'd take Stog's knowledge, every memory, every path, and learn about the Wheel of Fire dwarves and the Dragonblade. There were headless, clawless corpses of her own blood with only her left to mourn. What had those men shouted? "The Avenger"?

But she was alone and small. Even Father in full fury hadn't been a match for the dwarves, and she had nothing like his experience in battle.

Then there was her promise.

Even the worst cave has a best spot, Mother would say. She'd found a good spot here at Mossbell. But if the thane claimed Mossbell, there'd be no more clean, quiet cellars and hearth-roasted goats or Widow Lessup's mutton stew and gravies. Hammar would certainly turn her out—or worse—and if Rainfall sold his estate, would he be able to find a new home with a growing dragon in tow? They'd make a sight on the road: an invalid elf riding muleback, a pregnant girl hardly out of childhood, and a stumpy-legged drakka. Of course, Mother would tell her to improvise.

Curse Hypatia and its laws and courts and judges, robbing a kindly elf of his all. Hammar shaped the law into an ax to cut down a better citizen than he.

Couldn't the law be used to strike back at Hammar? No. Rainfall understood it better than she; he'd called it hopeless and would sell.

Of course. She hurried back to Mossbell, dragon-dashing when she saw the door and flushing a rabbit.

The household had gone to bed, and she had to draw back his bed curtains and wake him. The room smelled like the hot stones in their grate that warmed the metal plate that supported his bedding.

"Rainfall, I've got it," she said when he left off blinking and rubbing his eyes.

She was disappointed to see the number of leaves left on his pillow as he drew himself up with his new bedrail. "Let's have a light and hear it, then. For—"

"Never mind." She spat into the iron plate that caught the wax from his bedcandle. He lit his candle from the flame. "Some great lord would probably give you employ just to do that," he mused.

"I've had an idea about the estate."

"Let's hear it, then."

If she had the right muscles for it, she would be smiling. She tried pulling her *griff* as high as she could, and felt the corners of her mouth go up. "Sell Mossbell to me! I'd let you live here until the end of your days, without asking for anything. My way of repaying the debt I owe you for saving me."

Rainfall's face fell. "Ah. An excellent idea, but it wouldn't work, I'm afraid."

"Why not?"

"Wouldn't be legal. There are actually two objections.

You must be a Hypatian Citizen to own Hypatian land. The estate also controls the bridge and road, and only a titled Hypatian may own that."

"So to own the estate entire, I must be a Hypatian citizen and titled. No other objection?"

"No. I'd once hoped Lada would marry well, but she's been dishonored beyond any man with a title taking her."

"Why can't I become a Hypatian citizen, and titled, then?"

At that Rainfall's hand gripped the bedrail so hard, his knuckles went bloodless. "By the Guide Divine, you're right! Why not? Rah-ya, Tala. Rah-ya! I know just how to do it. Rah-yah! What a joke! To my library, I'm sure there's a precedent of use."

Chapter 17

Rainfall sat in his reception hall with the tablets on his lap.

"It's a sacrifice, but one I'm prepared to make for our sake. Look on the words with me one last time, Wistala."

The words may have been illustrious, but the reception hall wasn't much. According to Rainfall, there'd once been a grand set of chairs and trophies in the form of helms, scabbards, and weapons belonging to his grandfather—all long since sold. Only his azure battle sash remained, draped behind the very ordinary chair that sat against the wall opposite the arched door, bereft of the gilding that had once adorned it.

But good light came in through the narrow windows. Yari-Tab protested as she was removed from the sunny ledge in preparation.

"Perhaps you should step into the attendant room, Wistala, until the dwarves have gone. I don't want to startle our guests."

Wistala hooked her *sii* claw in a wall knothole and pulled open the paneled door with a squeak. She closed it again, and found she could see much of the room admirably through the knothole.

"You may show them in now, Yeo Lessup," Rainfall said.

The lanky boy, in a new suit of clothes and his first pair of attending slippers, raised his eyebrows in surprise at the use of his household title. He gave a little bow as he turned.

"Forstrel," Rainfall said. "When at court, always finish your bow and then go about your business."

"Sorry," he said.

"No need for apologies. Please go about it properly, Yeo Lessup."

This time the youth bowed and came fully upright before leaving.

Within moments, two dwarves entered the room. They wore riding apparel with long scarves woven into diamond patterns. Their faces were masked behind stiffened leather, with gauze covering their beards. They removed their hats and bowed. The foremost was a little taller and heavier than the one behind, and had golden coins set into his belt.

"Ah, couriers of Chartered Company," Rainfall said from the humble chair. "I trust the funds sent were adequate for your appearance?"

"Yes, sir," the foremost answered in easy Parl.

"Well, here's a Hypatian Silver for each of you anyway for being so prompt. Whom do I have the honor of addressing?"

The masks turned toward each other.

"The signs of the Diadem are not enough?" the foremost said. "We'll show you our seals, if you like."

"No need. It's simply that I wish to be social."

"Elgee and my nephew Embee, sir, and honored."

"May I address you as such?" Rainfall asked.

"Of course, sir."

"Elgee and Embee, this package and the accompanying letter must arrive at the Imperial Library at Thallia intact. Have you been there?"

"I know Thallia well, sir," Elgee said.

"It is inherently of no great value, but impossible to replace. There should be no danger beyond the usual minor difficulties that go with travel. I would prefer that you go by land rather than water, for the winter winds are coming, and I should hate to lose it to shipwreck."

"Some thanedoms welcome dwarves better than—," the smaller one behind said.

Elgee stamped. "No need for that, lad. Sir, you have the word of couriers of the Diadem that it will arrive."

"Give it to Heloise. If she no longer lives, give it to whoever holds the Hypatian Archive Table-Head. I expect some tokens in return, and would wish you to convey them back here with the same care."

"Barring delays in Thallia, you should see our masks again before the moon comes about again. Will you write your price and terms?"

The younger dwarf drew a small case from his cloak. Wistala thought it looked like it held paper. The dwarf worked the box, and a fresh length appeared at the top. He offered a quill and ink to his elder, who wrote upon it. He knelt and presented it to Rainfall.

Rainfall read it. "Prices have gone up since I last used your services."

"The roads have become treacherous," Elgee countered.

"This covers all expenses?"

"It does. And the bonding: our coin belts shall be yours if aught is lost."

"Ah, you no longer negotiate each separately. It is acceptable, then. Shall I sign and seal?"

"A signature is all that is necessary from a Knight of the Hypatian Directory, sir," Elgee said with a short bow.

Rainfall signed the paper revealed at the top of the box. "Ah, how courtly the tongues of the Diadem remain. You should give lessons to your cousins of the Wheel of Fire."

"They'd rather burn their beards than listen to—," the younger said with a hiccupping cough that Wistala guessed to be dwarf laughter.

"Keep your tongue behind mask," Elgee said. "Forgive my nephew, he's but—"

Rainfall held up his hand. "No, a jest is not out of place after business is concluded. Will you stay and bed this night?"

"Diadem couriers lose not an hour, once commissioned," Elgee said. "It is written on our cloak-latch. We ride at once. Thank you for your business—and the hot sup. There remains only the portion to be paid."

"Beneath my chair there is a chest. Would you be so good as to retrieve it?"

The dwarves turned toward each other again; then the younger stepped forward and lifted the small iron box. He passed it to Rainfall, who opened it.

When the accounting was settled, both dwarves bowed low, with more grace than Wistala would have credited them, and Rainfall bowed in return. After his head came back up, the dwarves raised theirs.

"A good journey," Rainfall said.

"If we are not back by the Winter Solstice, write the Chartered Company and claim your bond. Thank you again."

With that they left, escorted by Yeo Lessup.

"Wistala, come back. I think there's one more bit of business, and I want you for this."

She nosed open the passageway. "Gracious dwarves."

Rainfall locked his chest with a tiny key, which he returned to a small bag he kept about his neck. "You can't always trust appearances with dwarves. They mask more than their faces. But the Chartered Company will keep its bargain. Now all there is to do is hope there's still friendship, or at least honor, at the Imperial Library."

"What do you wish me to do?"

"Sit and be amused, dragon-daughter. Yeo Lessup, send in your uncle."

This time the youth bowed properly. Jessup came in, apologizing for the muddiness of his boots and carrying an oilskin-wrapped object the size of one of Mossbell's larger windows.

"How goes the inn, Jessup?" Rainfall said as he set down his burden in front of him.

"Well enough, sir, but I'll beg you to help me with my figures again. I thought running an inn meant tapping kegs and keeping the bedding aired, but I never dreamt of all the counting!" Jessup was looking at Wistala again in that funny way of his.

Rainfall said: "I admire a full-grown man who is so attentive to lessons. Is it done?"

"Just about," Jessup said. "You were right about the paints at Sack Harbor. Such colors! Who knew there were so many."

"Then let us see."

He untied a string around the oilskins and removed them.

Wistala blinked and looked at the wooden panel again. There were eyebolts in the top and fretwork to let the air pass through. Was it some kind of miniature door? Wait, it had a design on it, a painted figure. She recognized a long figure, depicted in profile, mostly upright, green and black-clawed.

"It's you, Wistala," Rainfall said as the meaning dawned on her.

"I'm calling the inn The Green Dragon," Jessup said. "And a good inn needs a good sign that travelers remember."

"If you've got no objection," Rainfall said. "He does this as a form of compliment."

Wistala understood, but understanding didn't bring a surcease of confusion. "But the troll, my plan, your brother died . . ."

"All the land round Mossbell and the twin hills honors his bravery and is happier for it," Jessup said. "I can't blame you for the troll's doing."

"So, do we have your agreement?" Rainfall asked.

"Why do you need it? The man may name his inn as he wishes."

"I'd be happier to have you touch the sign," Jessup said.

Wistala didn't answer, but stepped up to the sign. She extended her sharpest *sii* claw and dug a chunk of wood out at the eye. "You made the eyeblack round, like a hominid's eye or a tailvent. Dragons have eyes like a cat."

"Another story," Jessup said. *"The dragon herself marked the south-side eye, to look in the direction of the fight with the troll.* A good story to tell over honey-mead."

"When do you open?"

Jessup swiped his nose with a *sii*—fingertip, Wistala corrected herself. "All is in place. I've been brewing all summer since I bought out Old Golpramp's entire supply of clover-honey. You have advised me on wine. My wife is ready to do the baking, and my son the butchery. There is still much sewing needing to be done, but I can make do. I was going to hang the sign tomorrow."

"Delay another week or two. My old friend Ragwrist leads his troupe south even now, and this is his year to go the north roads. He should stop any day. The presence of his circus would make for a grand door-opening."

"As my landlord wishes," Jessup said.

Lada kept to her room. The only time Wistala saw her speak to her grandfather was when a messenger arrived. Forstrel took the letter to his master despite the outcry from Lada.

So great was the fracas that Wistala couldn't help but attend her host. She found two of the Lessup girls listening outside his library door, whispering to each other.

"What has happened?" Wistala asked.

Both jumped, for Wistala's steps were light on the rag rugs Widow Lessup had made to save the hall floors from dragonclaw and tailscale.

"The moony girl's got a thane-letter," the older of the girls said. "The master insists on reading it before giving it to her."

Lada exploded out of the library like Auron leaping up onto the egg shelf, and all three listeners instinctively flattened themselves against the wall to get out of her way.

"Beast!" she said to Wistala, clutching the open letter to her breast as she fled to her room.

Wistala went into the library, found Forstrel standing behind Rainfall in his chair.

"I think that last was intended for me, my dear," Rainfall said.

Wistala had once seen Jessup turn his younger son over on his lap and strike him for starting a fire out of some scrap wood where the inn was being constructed, and couldn't help but think Lada would benefit from a similar treatment, for she had no snout to tail-snap in Mother's fashion.

Widow Lessup's voice intruded through the door as she sent her girls off to work. Forstrel made himself look busy at the bookshelves.

"Can I get you anything, sir?" Widow Lessup asked, her dark eyes hard and angry.

"A little wine, thank you, ye'en," Rainfall said.

"Perhaps the letter held an offer for her to return to Galahall, that we might have some peace?" Wistala said.

"A brief mention that she was often in his thoughts and that he yearned to see her again," Rainfall said.

"He's well consoled by his other wards," Forstrel said.

"Rumormongering improves nothing, Yeo Lessup," Rainfall said. "He's still the thane, and I won't have that kind of talk. Go save your mother a trip back upstairs, if you please."

"Why doesn't the thane just marry her?" Wistala asked after Forstrel left. "Wouldn't that make his path to ownership that much shorter?"

"Ahh, but Hypatian tradition allows only one wife, so he must choose carefully. Poor Lada is small fry from our river. Hammar has cast his net far at sea looking for a greater catch."

Wistala digested this. "Have these circumstances been explained to Lada?"

"She will not listen. She's like a sleepwalker who will not awaken till she falls off a cliff. Let us survey the road and bridge. I won't have Ragwrist hurling jests as he once did daggers about the state of the roads under my care."

The dwarven couriers returned before Ragwrist arrived, and rather than another formal session in the reception hall, Rainfall invited them to a quiet dinner at the Green Dragon Inn.

While the dwarves saw to their mounts and packhorse in the barn, Rainfall and Jessup together hatched a plan to give the dwarves a fine tale to carry back to their delvings.

Rainfall and Jessup took her into the great common

room of the inn, showed her the wide river-stone chimney dividing the kitchen and storerooms from the common room and two of the sleeping rooms upstairs. Rainfall told her what to do when he snapped his fingers once, and then the second time.

She smelled that one of Yari-Tab's kittens had already installed itself as the inn feline. Ah, there it was, sleeping on the mantel of the smaller fireplace on the outer wall of the common room.

Wistala found the inn rough-hewn and bare compared with the careful workmanship of the interiors of Mossbell, but something about the thickness of the logs and stone-and-masonry walls Jessup had used suggested safety and comfort as much as the carven doorframes and window seats of Mossbell. She recognized a mug, a favorite of Rainfall's, on a special shelf all its own behind the counter of the common room.

"The landlord's mug, may it be refilled many times," said Jessup, taking it down and pouring a sweet-smelling liquid from a tapped keg resting on one side of the bar.

"I see you've copied the old style," Rainfall said, reclining on a lounge next to the big fireplace. A blanket covered his legs. "The first Hypatian posthouses were built much like this, when there were barbarians of doubtful behavior to consider." He sampled the mead. "Delicious. My compliments to the innkeeper and Old Golpramp for his clover-honey."

Jessup smiled at being called an innkeeper. He poured himself a pewter mug. "To better days between the Apple and the Whitewater, thanks to troll-killings and dragon hoards."

Wistala felt she should point out that the coin from Tumbledown would be more appropriately called a "rat hoard," but she let the hominids talk. Jessup's family watched her from the doorway to the kitchen. They'd seen Wistala only at a distance until now and stood as still as the painted dragon on the wood panel leaning next to the door.

"Father, the dwarves come," the youngest of Jessup's boys shouted as he came in through the door.

"Very well, Wistala, up the chimney."

Though it was wide, she had a little difficulty backing up it. Her tail end found purchase, and she braced herself with her legs.

"As you bid, we've returned with a response from the scroll-sorters," Elgee said upon entering and after words of introduction. "And a whole host of seals and ribbons their baton contains. Caps are intact, you'll see, Sir Elf."

"Thank you. I've prepared a purse with the balance of your fee. Would you care for it now?"

"Only if you'll deduct the cost of a pouring of this fine-smelling mead!"

Rainfall again: "That's quite impossible, my good dwarf. I rounded up, and there are no pennies within."

"Then the round and sup besides will be paid by our expense purse. A feast, good Innkeeper, and don't skimp on the side dishes!"

Wistala shifted her weight in the chimney, wishing Rainfall would play his trick.

More drinking, lip-smacking, and beard-wiping followed. "This is one dragon I'll be glad to see anytime I'm on the Old North Road," Embee said.

"Would you like to hear the tale of how the inn came to be named?" Rainfall said.

"Stories always make the food come faster," Elgee said.

"Then put that kindling on the fire, would you, Embee."

Wistala saw a short-fingered hand appear, placing the splinters in a stack with plenty of air space between. "Shall I call for the innkeeper's fire?" Embee asked.

"This inn has all the modern conveniences," Rainfall said, and snapped his fingers.

Wistala let loose her *foua* on the stack of wood, which promptly burst into flame. She heard gasps of astonishment from the dwarves. Then she heard a sizzle like fresh meat thrown on a hot stove, and green smoke boiled up the chimney. Wistala hadn't been expecting that, and as she held her breath, Rainfall snapped his fingers a second time.

She dropped down the chimney and jumped to avoid

the small fire. She was a bit clumsy with her tail, knocking the burning wood to the side, but landed credibly.

The dwarves fell backwards off their hearthside bench and did amazing backrolls, coming up with hands at sheath hilt.

"What in the Lavadome?" Elgee sputtered. Embee moved to draw his weapon, but his uncle held his arm.

"Rah-ya," Rainfall said. "I'm sorry, good dwarves, I couldn't resist. Please, laugh with me at this little trick. This is the Green Dragon herself."

"What, have you conjured her?" Embee said.

"Ach, she was hiding up the chimney, blockhead," Elgee said. "Sorry for the violence of our reaction, sir. Robbers may be found round the keg-tap as well as on the road, and we're accustomed to being always on our guard when outside the Delvings. Let me replace the spilled drinks."

When everyone was settled, Wistala told her tale. It came haltingly at first; then the words flowed more smoothly. She found herself imitating the strange, loping, two-by-two run of the troll and mimicking its roars.

The dwarves' eyes were white behind their masks, and they hardly looked away save to take another mouthful from their mugs until she was finished.

"Well told, good drakka," Rainfall said. "You have a talent for pleasing an audience."

Wistala bowed, hoping the dwarves didn't hear her *prrum*.

"Will she dine with us?" Elgee said.

"You'll find your expense purse lighter than you might like when you pay the tally," Rainfall warned. "I've been feeding her these eight months."

"What's the price on being able to say you dined with a dragon?" Elgee said.

"Though my grandfather said many's the time he feared being dined on," Embee added.

"Keep your—," Elgee warned.

"Oh, I'm sure he meant it as a joke," Wistala said. "You dwarves tweak your beards when you jest, and I saw Embee pull at his."

"So we do," Elgee said. "Mark! I look forward to telling

this tale to my directing partner when I return to the Delvings. A courtly dragon!"

Wistala ate, even tasted a little of the honeymead on her tongue, but found it too sweet. But even a drakka's appetite, somewhat guarded by Mother's repeated warnings against gluttony, couldn't compare to the amount of food the dwarves ate.

When farewells were said and the dwarves installed in their room upstairs, weighted by the vast meal, mead, and Rainfall's coin purse, Rainfall sat beside the fire with the bit of craft from the Library at Thallia on his lap.

"Aren't you curious to see this opened, Wistala?"

"Honestly, I am," she admitted. The "baton" was made of black shining leather, stiffened in some manner, and capped at one end.

"Then open Heloise's seal, and let us see their answer."

The wax—it featured what looked like two sets of identical steps rising to a peak—yielded to Wistala's *sii*-claw with no trouble at all. The seal held a leather thong closed over a tiny metal nub, which in turn secured the leather cap in place, as tight fitting as a hominid's footwear covered the feet. Both a rattle and a rustle came from inside, as she turned the tube.

She looked within. Rolled paper, and something glinting. She extracted the thick paper.

"Fine cotton paper, Wistala," Rainfall said. "I expect good news."

"I can't read it."

"May I?" Rainfall asked.

"Of course." Wistala handed it to him.

"Ah, it's in the priestly tongue, the oldest script of Cloud-temple of Thellasa and therefore Hypat, and only used these days for ritual. I shall translate:

"Be it known within and without the . . . *ahem* . . . civilized land that Wistala of Hesstur, having been of service to scholarship and common enlightenment, is recorded among the ancient and exalted order of Librarians, Keepers, and Archivists; is entitled to call herself an Agent in and of the Librarians; is admitted to the commons of all Hypatian Libraries; and is presented with insignia of rank and station in the Hypatian Order, all of which are to be recognized and held for the remainder of her natural life."

A thin hammered disk of gold had been set into wax and pressed hard into the paper. Wistala inspected the device, another triangular shape with a star at the top.

Rainfall smiled at her. "The old phraseology sounds a little ignorant these days. It was used before Hypatia knew of aught but barbarians beyond its borders. How do you like being an Agent-Librarian, *Nuum* Wistala?"

"*Nuum*? Oh, for an expression easier on dragon-tongues." Wistala sniffed the paper: ink and a dry sandlike smell were overlaid by the gold and the wax. "I can't say yet. What must I do?"

"Avoid swaggering your entitlement about, unless you wish to be laughed at. Even a Surveyor-Mapper will receive more bows, for on his lines are fields and pastures divided. Should you want to take pupils, it is useful, I suppose. Now let us admire your badge of title."

The badge was a triangular gemstone, about the size of Yari-Tab's nose, set in silver and fitted on the top with an eyehook for a chain.

"Golden topaz," Rainfall said. "It matches your eyes nicely. Symbolic of a clear head and clear vision, and enlightenment. The motto on the back reads *lun-byedon,* 'light-giver,' in the old priestly tongue."

The polish of the stone made the baubles Father used to give Jizara and her seem like dull quartz. "I would like to wear it."

"It would look well set into one of your scales, I suppose, and all elves would smile, for our victory garlands are of wound green and gold—but you shed them, don't you? Chain about your neck? But you'll outgrow anything we can find around here."

"How do the others at the library wear them?" Wistala asked.

"Some fit them into their hair so they hang just above and between the eyes, an old tradition dating back to the priestly scrollkeepers. Or they will puncture the earlobe and dangle them there by a sort of hook."

Wistala looked at her reflection in a polished piece of copper near the door. Hominids made a little ritual of gazing at themselves before stepping outside.

"Then I shall fix it in my fringe, at the fore, as I don't have a hominid head with that grotesque plate of greasy skin above my eyes. You may have to help with your blacksmithing tools. A drakka's fringe is nerveless, but tough."

Jessup returned, and he and Rainfall pointed out different features of the public room to Wistala, and Rainfall suggested the addition of a notice-post outside the door. "I fear I'm becoming in danger of being entirely too pleased with myself," Rainfall said. "Making Wistala a librarian and getting you the rank of postman."

"Postman? I'm hardly able to read, sir," Jessup said.

"Oh, I'll improve you. Without being able to work my gardens, I need more mental diversions, and if I stay within my library all hours, I'll be thought a hermit. A reliable post will bring visitors to the inn. But before making you postman, I must give Tala her oath of citizenship."

Jessup dropped his mug, sending mead across the assembly. "A . . . a dragon. A citizen?"

"And why not?" Rainfall said, wiping away the stray mead on his hand with a small cloth he kept in his pocket. "There are precedents, albeit ancient ones. She can understand our laws and take the oath."

Jessup chuckled. "The teeth will drop out of his skull."

"But we must hurry. I can administer the citizenship oath, and you shall witness it, Jessup, and then we will have a bill of sale, and it will be done. What say you?"

"I fear."

"What do you fear?" Wistala asked.

"The course of these events. I don't want to be the one whose witness frustrated the thane."

"He'll count me as an enemy if he does anything to you and yours," Wistala said coldly.

Rainfall turned. "I must ask you, Wistala, for something of an imposition."

"Nothing would be too great to my savior and host," Wistala said.

"I'll adopt you as my daughter. That confers on you full citizenship after you reside in Hypatia for six years. A simple oath gives you citizenship for now."

Wistala had been practicing the words daily.

"I'd hoped to hear the words in the Hypatian Hall at Quarryness, but Jessup's Inn won't be hurt for having one more story to tell about its sign."

Jessup looked out the windows, as if fearing hostile eyes in the night.

Rainfall pointed to the floor before him. "It's customary to touch the hem of the officiant's robe of state before taking the oath, but I'm afraid this mead-spattered bit of blanket will have to do; it's the words that matter in the end."

Wistala laid her *sii* on his blanket.

"The oath-taker usually kneels before the officiant. But having four legs—"

Wistala folded her *sii* under her. In consequence her *saa* and tailvent were raised, but as they were facing in the direction of Galahall, it seemed befitting.

"Do you understand the difference between a truth and a lie, and the seriousness of an oath, Nuum Wistala?"

"I do," Wistala said.

"Then take the oath."

"I, Wistala, promise to take up the responsibilities of a Hypatian Citizen. I will obey the Hypatian laws, keep the Hypatian peace, and maintain the Hypatian lands and seas against all enemies. May my strength and honor sustain this oath and Hypatia's glory from now until the end of days."

"Rise, Citizen, and never kneel again," Rainfall said.

"Walls fresh up and already hallowed," Jessup said. "That reminds me: I should have Mod Feeney in to bless the post and lintels."

"Jessup, I must beg for a delay in the rites. Wistala and

I must go into Quarryness. Wake up Forstrel and tell him to put my saddle on Stog. Oh, and could I trouble you for a pennysworth for Tala?"

"Of course, sir, but she needs no pennies here. As long as I've got a bit of bone in back, her meals shall be free under this roof."

"Not for food, Jessup. She must purchase Mossbell, and while I'd accept her loosest dragonscale, a land sale's not legal unless it's in Hypatian coin. And it's just bad form for me to lend it to her."

Stog could keep a punishing pace when he put his will into his hooves. Wistala loped along the road northward in the evening dark as best as she could, and finally begged him for a ride behind Rainfall's special strapped saddle.

"Fine," Stog said. "But sheathe your claws."

Wistala climbed up, and Stog broke into his buck-trot again.

The night was foggy and turning cold, the moisture thick enough to collect at the branch-tips and drop with soft, wet taps into the fallen leaves. There would be a thick frost by morning, she expected.

"You dragons are supposed to be able to sing," Stog said. "I'd like to hear a song of the merits of mules. What horse could carry this burden at this pace?"

"Is he complaining about the weight?" Rainfall asked. "My beast-tongue is not that of my forefathers—I've been too long in tamer lands."

"He wants a song," Wistala said.

"Perhaps it would help pass the time," Rainfall said. "Beside, I don't think I've ever heard you sing."

Wistala cleared her throat. "Drakes and dragons are more fond of these kind of displays, and more skilled, but I'll do my best:

> While a horse will carry any fool
> If the going's hard you'll want a mule!
> Twice the load on half the feed,
> A mule is tougher than any steed!

But treat him well when put to task
Or he'll knock you on your—

"Ask no more verses of me, I'm out," Wistala finished.

"Prettier than any nightingale," Rainfall said. "And a good deal louder."

"Let's have it again," Stog said. *"While a horse will carry any fool . . ."* he brayed in time to his hoofbeats.

And so, with Stog repeating the verses until dogs whined in complaint, they came into the Quarryness around the midnight hour.

The town was bordered by Rainfall's road to the east and a great hill to the west. The hillside facing the town was one long cliff, with some wooden scaffolding up the side where men took building stone. A small watercourse cut through the town, bridged in two places by stone. There were several constructs of two or three levels at the center of town around a rather muddy common and a few leafless trees, but the rest of the town was a small warren of narrow, twisting streets.

"The thane allows for division and subdivision of the town parcels," Rainfall said. "He forgets that the old Hypatian engineering, while somewhat wasteful of space, also prevents fires."

There were still a few lights in some of the upper windows and galleries of the town, but none strode the streets save for a pair of men Rainfall identified as firewardens—also charged with keeping the peace. Downstream Wistala heard faint notes of music and song.

Rainfall turned Stog into the center of town, just off the main road. He stopped Stog before a stout, triangle-topped building with a silver banner-staff at the peak. "High temple," Rainfall said, pointing to a grand, round-topped building. "Low temple," he said, referring to a long, flat-roofed stone-walled building opposite. "Court-house and muster-hall."

Ranks of carved men carrying spears and shields decorated the sides. "Bring me right up the steps to the door," Rainfall said, in beast-tongue, to Stog.

The doors were metal-covered and fitted in such a way that the hinges were concealed.

"There will be a low judge or two within," Rainfall said. "*The law never sleeps,* as old Arfold, my law-teacher used to say. Strike the door with your tail, Wistala, and wake them."

Her scales rang on the metal surface, and the pounding echoed within.

The pair of firewardens watched from the common, talking to each other quietly. One hurried away toward the road.

"Again, please," Rainfall said.

Wistala pounded on the door again.

A decorative panel in the door suddenly opened. "I rise, I rise. What have you to say that can't wait until a daylight hour? Is there a murderer to be celled?"

"Good evening, Sobyor," Rainfall said.

The man's rather small eyes widened. "Your Honor!"

"Oh, that title's long since washed to the sea. What are you doing manning the door-minder's garret, Sobyor? You were once the best low judge in the three north thanedoms."

"And high judge for three whole days, thanks to you. What in the worlds is that?" he asked, staring at Wistala.

"She's my legs, if you'll let me through this door. We've some small matters of business to attend, and I'm afraid they cannot wait. Admit us, and help me mind the mule, would you?"

"I'm . . . I'm not to recognize you," Sobyor said. "Orders from High Judge Kal himself."

"What authority does Judge Kal have to give you such an order? This is a Hypatian Hall, and I require admittance."

"I am . . . I am not alone in here," Sobyor said with a glance to his right.

"Who is in there with you?" Rainfall asked.

"A pair of firewardens."

"Tell them—," Wistala started to say.

"Hold your temper," Rainfall cut in. "Sobyor, how is your practice in Thellass-tongue?"

"*Mus mis palandam,*" Sobyor responded.

"Rah-ya!" Rainfall said. He rattled off a string of speech Wistala didn't understand, but it meant something to Sobyor.

"*Opt,*" Sobyor replied, shutting the panel.

"What are you about?" Wistala heard a gruff voice inside say. There was a brief rattle inside, perhaps a hand checking the lock on the door.

"My duty," Sobyor's voice replied.

Quieter now: "What was all that grotting about?"

The voices faded.

"Wistala, how would you like to perform your first duty in defense of the Hypatian Order?"

"Sir?" Wistala asked, lowering and raising her head.

"There are airing windows up under the overhang of the roof on the side walls of this building. Climb up and see if you can get through one, and open the door."

Wistala didn't like leaving Rainfall perched on Stog at the big doorway; it seemed the whole town was laid out to look at the stairs leading up to the Hypatian Hall. She couldn't imagine what danger to expect, surrounded by paved streets and rain-collectors in the quiet of the night, but she didn't like it.

The columns were fluted, which served her claws admirably, and alternating grips between *sii* and *saa,* she gained the roof despite the slick mist-wet. The roof tiles were long and thicker than her *sii,* chevron-shapes interlocking as they descended from the peak, and spotted with generations' worth of bird droppings.

She lowered her head to look under the cornice at the side of the building and saw the gaps Rainfall had mentioned. They were recessed so that it would be hard to see them, let alone shoot arrows or other projectiles into them from the street. Wooden shutters filled the intermittent gaps.

Gripping the roof with one *saa* and her tail, she managed to poke one open. It gave way on a horizontal pivot-point with a loud—to her—squeak. Flattening herself, she crept in under the shutter.

An entrance gallery yawned below her. She looked down on a row of frozen head tops—larger-than-life busts were on display on the inner side of the walls, and there was little to see beneath but a few benches. The back two-thirds of the building was blocked off by a wide staircase leading up to a semicircular forum, with banners on display above wooden doors.

Wistala heard voices from a smaller half-door set beneath the great stairs.

She lowered her tail and managed to test one of the busts below. It seemed solid enough. She jumped down to it and perched for a moment atop the great man's head—he had a heavy brow and a nose of a size to equal the fame he must have gained in life to be so immortalized—and from there leaped down to the floor.

The floor was smooth but a little dirty, and had a series of strange divots and channels carved into its surface, not deep at all and useful only in collecting dirt, as far as she could tell. But the object of this exploration was the door.

Or door within a door, rather. There was a smaller portal set in the mighty wooden doors, barred by simple iron bolts set into tubes. She drew back the bolt on the smaller door and opened it.

"Daughter, you are a wonder," Rainfall said in his elf-tongue.

Wistala took pleasure in hearing the familiar, but wondered if she could ever call Rainfall *father*—even in elf-tongue.

"I do not think you can ride Stog within unless I open the larger doors," Wistala said.

"I'll have to ask you to bear me inside." He slid off Stog, using a leather strap to lower himself by the hands in the manner of a laborer she'd once seen come down from Jessup's roof by taking a rope hand-under-hand. Then he switched to his rough beast tongue: "Stog, this shall only take a moment. Don't befoul the steps, please."

Once he was seated upon her and holding on to her fringe, she took him through the door.

"Take me to the ingress under the stairs—that's the attendant-judge's office."

Wistala bore him into the hall.

"Locks on a Hypatian hall door. Where are late-riding couriers supposed to shelter, or impoverished travelers? And what's this . . . the design on the floor's been taken up!" Rainfall said as they passed the channels in the floor. "Where had the poor gold gone, I wonder . . . gilding the cornices at Galahall, no doubt."

Flickering light and voices came from beneath the stairs.

Rainfall sighed. "This hall has become a tomb to old ideals. In my grandfather's time, at this hour there were travelers sleeping beneath the gaze of Iceandler, or Torus the Elder, the smell of pine knots burning in the braziers. I suppose the only crowds nowadays come on Taxing Day."

Wistala saw at the base of the ingress another door, half wood and half bars, with a sort of cut-off table in the middle and a space just big enough for a man to put his fist through above the table. On the other side, Wistala caught a glimpse of shelving, divided and subdivided into cubbyholes filled with tied scrolls.

Voices and moving shadows came from the other side of the door.

"Careful with that light, there. You'll burn my ear off. Oh, now I can't see anything," Sobyor's voice echoed out into the hall.

"Take me to the grate," Rainfall said.

Wistala went down the eight steps to the area before the barred door. Some old, dirty quill-feathers lay on the floor.

"Ahem," Rainfall said.

Wistala heard quick startled steps inside, but kept her head down and out of sight.

"How did you get in?" a rough voice barked.

"The more interesting question, firewarden, would be by what power you kept me out of a Hypatian Hall."

Rainfall's voice returned to its usual soothing melody: "I just need the court's seal on the two small matters we spoke of earlier, Sobyor," Rainfall said.

"Prepared, and here's the logbook, as well," Sobyor said. "Just as well to have all neat and proper."

"We're not to have any business with him," a shriller voice cut in.

Wistala heard a heavy tread step up to the grate, and smelled *gar-locque* and onion. The light from inside the room was almost shut off entirely. From seemingly atop her, Sobyor's voice said: "Best sign it fast, sir. The wardens are restless tonight."

"Judge Kal will hear every particular!" the shrill voice warned.

"Certain particulars will catch up to the high judge, one of these days," Rainfall said. She heard him writing. "Wistala, your penny, please."

She passed it up to Rainfall. "The transaction is witnessed by the court," Sobyor said. "Make a record of Nuum Wistala's credentials."

Sobyor again, quieter: "Is that the—?"

"I must make do as best as I can," Rainfall said.

"What are you doing, there?" the rough voice said.

"Completing a little court business," Sobyor said. "You could read it yourself. If you could read." Wistala smelled a candle and hot wax. "There. Signed, sealed, and seconded in the log."

"Thank you, Sobyor," Rainfall said. "You always were the best of men. I'll leave you to this gloom and the barred doors." He tapped Wistala.

"This will really get up the thane's nose," Sobyor cackled.

As she climbed the stairs bearing Rainfall, Wistala glanced back and got her first look at Sobyor. He was an enormous man, both tall and fat, with thick curly hair. No wonder the firewardens protested his behavior with words only. Sobyor closed one eye at her; then they were back in the entrance hall under the statues.

"That went better than expected," Rainfall said. "Had there been a hostile low judge on duty, I would have had to submit petitions and so on, which could have slowed us up."

It seemed a slow enough business to Wistala, who was beginning to wish she'd burned Galahall down with Thane Hammar in it, saving trouble all around. Except that would have brought a frown to Rainfall's face. He set such a store in his legal niceties.

They walked the road a good deal slower on the trip home. Wistala trudged along ahead of Stog to keep the pace comfortable, but even Stog seemed tired. Rainfall passed the time by explaining to Wistala about the importance of the Thanes to the Hypatian Order: they could more effectively lead troops from their thanedom when gathered under a general than strangers and were supposed to be the shield and sword of the other elements of the Hypatian Order, the priesthood and the judges. But military power, pomp, and panoply went to some men's heads like wine.

Wistala was happy to see the twin hills at the edge of Mossbell's lands pop out against a suddenly pink sky. The far-off chain of snowy mountaintops to the east glowed orange as the dawn crept up.

Then she heard a frighteningly familiar sound from ahead.

"I hear hoofbeats," Wistala said. "Many riders."

"What's that?" Rainfall asked, waking. Stog halted.

"Riders ahead," Wistala repeated.

Rainfall looked down at her. "Get off the road, Wistala. I'll handle them."

"I hope there's a few horses from the Galahall stables," Stog said. "I'll give them—"

"I'm not leaving you alone," Wistala said.

"Oh, I suppose your existence is public now. I'd hoped to wait until you were a little older and stronger."

Wistala sat in front of Stog and waited.

There were seven riders, two riding close to the edge of the road on either side, and the rest in back in a bunch that expanded and contracted as the horses trotted close to each other and then veered away.

The riding party spotted Stog, and the five in back formed into a line, blocking the road.

"Rah-ho," Rainfall said quietly to himself. "The thane himself rides. This should be an interesting interview."

Wistala tried to guess which one was the thane. There was a tall powerful man all the way over to the left side in the group of five. He kept looking at the others.

She couldn't tell if they were arrayed for war, for they wore cloaks against the chill. The two in front had short horse-bows, and all wore helms of silver color—no sign of spears or lances.

The men slowed, walking their horses up, the front two falling in a little closer to the others. One dropped back a little, as well. He was shorter than the others, perhaps some kind of servant to the warriors.

Rainfall bowed from his tied-on seat. "Thane Hammar. How nice to meet you on a chilly morning. Your countenance always warms me."

Astonishingly, the one farthest to the rear spoke. "Greetings! Rainfall of Mossbell. I won't say I was surprised, for I rode looking for you. Your thane recognizes you."

Rainfall bowed again.

Wistala examined him more closely. He was a youth, as far as she could judge men, perhaps Forstrel's age, but more slightly framed. Tiny wisps of facial hair at either side of his mouth made his upper lip look as though it had sprouted wings, and his cheeks were spotted. His red horse, though bigger than the ones the others rode, didn't bring him close to their head-height, and his helm, shinier than the others', swept up to a forward point like a hawk's beak, though it seemed overlarge and heavy for so small a head, for its brim came down almost to the bridge of his nose. He kept looking at Wistala from beneath it.

"News!" Hammar said. "I'm sorry to hear of your injury. I had no idea it was so severe, and word has just reached me. I wish to provide comfort."

"As usual, the thane is all kindness," Rainfall said. "But there is no need for you to exert yourself in my behalf, or add to your cares. I am managing."

"I'll not be dissuaded. Your burdens must be lightened.

Especially now that your granddaughter is happily returned to you—"

"Bearing your progeny," Rainfall said in a sterner tone.

"Please! Pay no attention to rumor," Hammar said. "The brat might be anyman's. I've heard it was my stableboy. Or possibly one of the gamekeepers."

Wistala suddenly hated this half-grown bit of tailventing. Like Rainfall's history lectures or talks on leverage, nothing cleared and settled her mind like seeing, smelling, and hearing.

"I'm shocked to see a girl not yet sixteen so insulted, in so many despicable ways," Rainfall said.

"Watch your tongue, elf," the tall man on the left said. "Notch!" He turned his head toward the thane. "I don't like the look of that creature in front of the mule. It seems ready to jump."

The two riders with bows put arrows to their strings, but did not draw.

"Wistala, stay still," Rainfall said.

She tried to keep her tail from moving, but it seemed possessed of a mind of its own.

"The road seems an uncouth place to trade words," Rainfall said. "Perhaps you can return to Mossbell with us and we may talk over breakfast, once weapons are properly hung up."

"Goat-milk yogurt is not to my taste," Hammar said. "I bear a warrant which must be answered in court. You shall appear before Judge Kal to answer. You're no longer fit to be the master of an imperial estate."

"Our opinions are alike, then," Rainfall said.

The thane's eyes widened. "You are wise to acknowledge your limitations."

"Advice that might be taken as well as given. Our opinions are alike, but I've made my own arrangements. I've sold Mossbell."

The red spots on the thane's face suddenly seemed darker against his skin. "To whom?"

"*Nuum* Wistala, who you see before you."

"No! *Nuum?* This . . . creature?" Hammar said.

"The creature before you is a titled Hypatian," Wistala said.

"It speaks," one of the men with the bows said.

"She's an Agent of the Librarians at Thellasa," Rainfall said. "And my legal adopted daughter. Daughter, mind you, which takes precedence over granddaughter, should I meet with some unfortunate accident on this highway. The bill of sale is recorded."

"Ho! You are undone!" Hammar said. "This creature attacked Galahall not three months ago, intent on arson and assassination. I'll have you hanged for treason next to her hide!"

"Please! Pay no attention to rumor," Rainfall said in a rather squeaky tone that mimicked Hammar's. "I heard a two-headed, feathered lizard attacked Galahall. She has but one, and as for feathers, it's plain to see she bears none."

"Kill that creature!" Hammar shrieked.

"Pull and loose!" the tall man ordered.

Wistala hugged the road as the archers fired. The sharp strikes hurt, but the arrows bounded off down the road. The men couldn't have chosen a worse angle to fire upon dragonscale.

Stog screamed piteously, as though mortally wounded, though no arrows came anywhere near him.

She loosed her bladder, and the horses, already unnerved by Stog's bellows, began to dance at the smell. She shot forward, still piddling, a road-hugging green javelin moving straight for the thane. The thane's big red horse reared, its front hooves awhirl, and Hammar, perhaps overbalanced by the enormous helm on too slight a body, went backwards out of his seat.

Wistala pounced upon him, pinned his arms with her *sii* and left one *saa* pressed against his belly, ready to pierce and gut.

Hammar screamed, almost as loudly as Stog.

"Anyone draws a blade, and I open him," Wistala said to the men, who were fighting to control their horses.

"Hold, hold everyone!" Rainfall shouted in his deep

and commanding tone. Then in beast-tongue: "Quiet, Stog."

Stog left off his bellows.

"Murder will only make things worse," Rainfall said. "Hammar, you would spill blood on a road like some common brigand? You bring shame on your title. Let him up, Wistala."

Wistala, hot anger still in her veins, replied: "Let me at least bite off a finger or two as a reminder not to—"

Hammar squeaked like a rabbit.

"Oh, very well," she said, releasing him. Rainfall knew the best course of action in this odd little world the hominids called civilization.

Hammar wiped his nose as he rose. "Mark! You think you're so clever, elf. There are those who know how to deal with dragons. I've an acquaintance—"

"Killing a Hypatian Citizen of any line is murder, good thane. Come, let us forget this ever happened. I won't have Lada's child growing up fatherless. I will write to you."

"You are a famous correspondent," Hammar said, re-settling the helm on his head. The tall man retrieved the thane's horse. "Some might use the word *informer*. Know! I will write you, and if you do not agree to my terms, you'll find yourself in court again and again until you turn to wood like your forefathers. Then I'll have you made into chamberpot-coals."

His men chuckled. Rainfall came forward with Stog, and they parted. One put hand to hilt, but the thane barked at him and Rainfall passed through.

Wistala watched them until they were out of bowshot, then hurried to catch up with the mule.

Chapter 18

They returned to Mossbell to find the household under frosted enchantment.

The house looked beautiful beyond words to Wistala, with the greenery silvered. From the ferns clinging to the wide chimney to the grass from the fountain to the wall along the road—a little despoiled by goat tracks—the house looked fairy-dusted in the early dawn light.

The new owner of Mossbell and her steward left Stog to wander on the lawn.

But the enchantment ended as soon as Wistala carried Rainfall into the house.

"Sir, you've returned," Widow Lessup said. "We're agog here. The thane! His Honor came looking for you in the night."

"We saw him on the road. I'm sorry I was out—he didn't threaten anyone, I hope?"

"Oh, no, sir! It's—Lada's room, you must go up to her. She ran out to him, barefoot as a nymph. I'm not sure what was said, but she came back into the house in tears. She's barred her door somehow, and I'm afraid for her. I sent Forstrel for Mod Feeney. I was afraid she'd hurt herself!"

Wistala bore him upstairs. Lada was still in her room, sobbing, with two of the Lessup girls outside, tapping on her door and trying to bring her a morning infusion.

"Anja, tell my granddaughter that I saw the thane on the road. I'd like to see her in my library. And if she doesn't want that infusion, I will be happy to have it. Tala?"

"The library?"

"Yes."

Wistala brought him up to the top floor—the skylight admitted the diffuse morning light through a melting frost pattern. He moved from her back into his desk chair.

Rainfall sighed. "I've not used them, but my legs feel terribly tired."

Anja brought in the infusion, and Rainfall drank it gratefully. "I'm forgetting you, my noble steed. Anja, can you—?"

"I can find food in the kitchen myself," Wistala said. She didn't like people waiting on her; not hunting for her meals seemed dissolute enough.

Lada appeared at the door, a housecoat over her night-dress, though she had on day-slippers and footwrap. Her nose was as red as the spots on the thane's cheeks. The part of her hair not bound up fell in loose curls that reminded Wistala of flowering vines, though unlike her grandfather's locks, her hair took after that of men or dwarves.

"Grandfather, I didn't dress but came at once."

Wistala made for the kitchen, but Rainfall halted her with a word. "Tala, I want you here so you may bear witness to the truth of what I say.

"Lada, I hope you know you have my love, as does the child you are carrying."

Wistala's chin dropped at this.

Rainfall continued: "You must listen to me now. You'll come to the truth of this fixation now or later, and you can spare yourself much pain by accepting it now: Thane Hammar does not love you, does not care for you, and has no intention of taking you into Galahall as his wife or anything else."

"Elves lie so—"

"Let's have none of that," Rainfall thundered. "You're a fair token of elvish blood—"

He spoke no further, for Lada shrieked and threw herself against the bookcase with a wail. She began to cry, and push whole rows of books onto the floor.

Rainfall sighed.

Wistala stood frozen, paralyzed at the emotional display.

"Lada, stop that," Rainfall said.

She threw another set of books on the floor.

Widow Lessup appeared at the library door. "Sir, may I—!" Her mouth clamped shut when she saw Lada knock down a map hung between bookshelves and a scroll-case, and her lips pursed so tightly Wistala would have sworn she was about to spit *foua*.

"Sir," Widow Lessup said. "May I take her in hand?"

"Perhaps you can bring her to her room. An infusion might do her good."

"As you wish," Widow Lessup said. She marched over to the sobbing girl and grabbed her by the ear, twisting it the way she did her daughter's.

"Now come along. . . ."

Lada shrieked even more loudly as Widow Lessup dragged her out of the room by the ear.

Rainfall sighed. "Wistala, follow and see that no harm comes to my granddaughter." He moved from his chair to a lounge just behind his desk. "I'm so very tired."

Wistala caught up to the pair just as they disappeared into the upstairs washing room. Lada was still in hysterics, sobbing until Widow Lessup overturned a pitcher of water on her head. That stopped the crying for a moment, and the matron shut the door in Wistala's face.

"Now let's hear your side of the story," Widow Lessup said. "For I know my master's."

No harm seemed likely to come to Lada in the washing room. She was too big to fit down the drain, and a wooden scrub-stick couldn't hurt any worse than the tip of Mother's tail—so Wistala went downstairs and assuaged her appetite in the cool room. She sneaked a pair of brass buttons out of the sewing room, the stress of the fight in the road having left her famished for metal, and immediately felt guilty and went back upstairs to confess to Widow Lessup, but she was still washing-closeted. Her voice could still be heard through the floor crack.

"Men and love! Ho! but that brings back memories. Sonnets and sour cabbage. Let me tell you about men and love, my dear. . . ."

She checked on Rainfall and found him sleeping on his lounge, and diverted herself by reshelving the thrown-down books as best as she could. Rainfall's system wasn't pleasing to the eye at all; she preferred to shelve the books so that they made rising wings, with the shortest at the center of the shelf and the tallest at the edges.

But for some reason, she could only think of Auron and Father.

Mod Feeney arrived at Mossbell, worried that there were deaths and hangings within the walls at the very least. Within moments she, Lada, and Widow Lessup were all sitting in Lada's room with the two oldest Lessup girls.

The house was considerably calmer when Feeney left, but she had a short interview with Rainfall before returning to her other duties.

"I offered her a position as my acolyte in the Priesthood, after the baby comes," Mod Feeney said. "But she seems bound to have it and wait for Hammar to claim fatherhood."

"He has little reason to, now that the estate is Wistala's."

"I fear for what may be tried next to wrest it from you," Mod Feeney said. "By the rites, I owe my congratulations to our four-legged friend. *Nuum* Wistala, you have my duty."

Rainfall looked at the splash of sunlight on the floor as Yari-Tab, licking milk from her whiskers, plopped down in it. The feline had more or less adopted the library as hers, as it was the highest, sunniest, and warmest of Mossbell's rooms, and frequently claimed Rainfall's lap against some of her rangy kittens. "Speaking of which, as the crisis seems to have passed, you might be about your rounds. Will you stay for lunch?"

"I will wrap something from your kitchens, if it's not asking overmuch," Feeney replied.

"No, of course not."

The priestess bowed and left.

"She reminds me of my lack of manners. I should congratulate you, as well, Wistala. You're a well-propertied drakka now. Have you any thoughts? I've reason to believe there might be copper in the twin hills, if you wish to look into mines."

Copper. My sole surviving brother. Is there anything of Father and Auron in him?

"All I care to do with these grounds is see that they help preserve you, and our friendship," Wistala said. "And your granddaughter, even if she doesn't deserve you."

"For such a young dragon, you have already an old heart. Have some sympathy for such as her. It's the rare hominid that has much wisdom before a score of years pass."

The weather grew colder in the next few days, and little changed at Mossbell save for fewer harsh words and exasperated sighs from Lada, who seemed sick and moody and had trouble keeping food down. Mod Feeney and the Widow Lessup made a trip to a herbalist in Quarryness for medicines.

They returned following the strangest procession Wistala had ever seen upon the road, or anywhere her travels had taken her.

Three great hairy beasts, almost the size of a dragon though taller, with tusks and flexible snouts that reached the ground and beyond, each pulled a one-and-a-half-level house on iron-rimmed wheels, with ox wagons and horse carts and dwarf-bearers besides.

"Ah, it's Ragwrist's Circus," Rainfall said. "Later this year than usual; perhaps bad weather delayed him."

Forstrel made ready to put him on Stog's back, when summoned to the gates of Mossbell.

Wistala gaped at the long-haired creatures, for fully half the beasts were visible above Mossbell's road wall. Dwarves rode them just behind the head.

"Those are gargants, out of the glacier dells." Wistala

just saw the head-tip of another, perhaps a young one, following behind one of the houses.

"What is a circus?" Wistala asked.

"Entertainments, diversions, and wonders," Rainfall said.

An elf on a snow-white horse in a colorful striped coat turned into the gates of Mossbell. "Come, if you please, Mistress Wistala, I think you'll like Ragwrist and he'll like you. At least I hope so."

Wistala couldn't imagine why it would matter if a traveling elf liked her or not, but she pulled her *sii* down her *griff* and smoothed her fringe. *Mistress Wistala must look her part for greeting guests on her lands.*

Rainfall had been calling Wistala by that title whenever in the presence of any of the estate's people, to impress upon them the change in ownership, though Wistala left all decisions in the care of her—*what was the position again? Oh yes, steward.*

Ragwrist dismounted. He did have a colorful twist of twine about his wrist, but it was the coat that really caught her imagination. It was red and yellow and green and brown and several other colors, pleasantly arranged in panels and pleats, making him look like an aggregation of colorful bird feathers. His riding boots were of the deepest black and matched his hair, which reminded her of tree roots.

"Our homeleaf is graced," Rainfall called in Elvish.

"This traveler is comforted," Ragwrist answered. His voice had a heartiness to it and came from deep within his frame, and though he spoke normally his words carried from the road wall to the stable.

The elves embraced.

"Is that char-oil I smell in your hair?" Rainfall said. "Honorable frost is nothing to make one shamed."

"I'm not here the time it takes a drop to fall from a low cloud, and already I'm undone and reproached," Ragwrist said, though he kept glancing at Wistala.

"Neither," Rainfall said. "How were the barbarian lands?"

Ragwrist straightened his coat's lapels and collars. "Tiresome. In some villages they hid their children from us, and without their glad cries, a circus is a joyless place. We've come away with only enough to sustain us, and the wagons need new axles. There are improvements around here I see, and new faces."

Rainfall marked his pointed stare at Wistala. "Poor manners, so glad was I to see your face and get the news. This drakka is Wistala, the rarest gem I've ever met on four feet. She's brought me back into the world, from hair-tip to foot-pad, and saved much more than my lands."

Wistala preferred that Rainfall's effusive manners remain directed at courtesy, as she felt little liking for praise that to her mind she hadn't earned. "If you're old friends with Rainfall, you must know that he does go on sometimes," Wistala said.

Ragwrist danced in an elegant sort of balancing bow that put Wistala in mind of a goose drinking. "Such Elvish!"

"She's gifted with tongues. Her Parl is intelligible, though the palatals sound a bit loud.

"I was hoping you'd set up about the new inn near the bridge," Rainfall suggested. "The owner is our good friend, and if you'd send your criers about, he'd welcome the chance to serve visitors."

Ragwrist sniffed the air about Wistala, looked as though he was going to say something, but turned back to Rainfall. "Of course. Assuming the troll stays west of the road, that is."

"The troll is dead. Wistala's doing."

"This is news! Oh, we must have some wine and hear about this."

"Shall we meet inside in a dwar-hour?"

"Let me say but a word to my lead gargant-dwarf, and then we shall drink. But quick! If we are to perform, I must attend as we encamp."

"May I see the show?" Wistala asked.

"Nothing would please me better," Ragwrist replied. "Provided you stay downwind, if I may abjectly beg your pardon. We have horses, and they are not used to a dragon's airs."

*   *   *

Wistala did watch from downwind, and enjoyed herself immensely.

They placed the three wagons in a line in the fields next to the inn, with tenting flanking wagons to somewhat conceal the behind.

The wagons themselves unfolded on one side so as to make a linked stage, with poles that Rainfall told her were as tall as ship-masts set at either end with a cable between. Balancing acts, exhibitions of swordfighting, and even a comical dwarf negotiated the line from one pole to the other with some skill in the case of the former, and a great many shrieks of fear and expostulations from the latter.

The dwarf wavered midway, trying to prove that he could do anything an elf could and now apparently regretting it, for he kissed his hand and then slapped his behind with a ribald oath in preparation. At the next step he fell to the joined screams of the crowd and disappeared for one eyeblink into the stage with a crash that struck Wistala as coming an instant too soon. But the dwarf bounced back up, high in the air, then came down on the stage with a loud thud.

"Dwarves always bounce back!" he roared to the crowd.

On the stages men threw axes in such a way that they cut plums from branches, which they then threw to the children; hominid females in clothing so scanty that Wistala wondered how they avoided lung infections danced or sang or jumped and turned and tumbled so high, it seemed they were made of air and sunshine.

In between the shows the dwarves brought a gargant out for the amazement of all, and one of the dwarf handlers let the gargants rear up and put an enormous foot on each shoulder as he knelt, then with shaking legs he came to his feet.

The underdressed hominids came out again, riding horses around the crowd as those at the back suddenly had the best view and others fought for position. They stood on their horses' backs, or leaped between mounts, or dropped off the sides of the horses and vaulted from one side to the other, and finished by rearing their horses up and having them turn circles.

Wistala wondered if Rainfall's mate had once performed such tricks from under a few wisps of thin cloth.

With the shows ended, Ragwrist came out and announced that any in the crowd could have their fortune read—"If you dare!"—in the blue tent by the famous Intanta, possessor of a shard of the seeing-star, which fell to earth in the days of the dragons and had been the object of no less than six wars.

Others could visit the green tent, where the finest crafts from around the Hypatian Empire and beyond even the Golden Road in Wa'ah could be found—"Happy is the wife possessed of even the smallest bauble bought or traded from our display!"—at bargains merchant-houses couldn't afford to give thanks to the need to keep a roof overhead.

"So what do you think of the circus, Wistala?" Rainfall asked from Stog's back as Stog's ears followed the pounding hooves around the audience.

"Delightful! I've never seen happier people," Wistala said. "They all perform as though driven by joy, rather than the coins flung at them."

Rainfall leaned down. "Some of the coins are thrown by the circus men themselves, to give others in the audience the example. They are more often paid in eggs and cheese. But I am pleased you enjoyed yourself. Ragwrist is one of my oldest and dearest friends—though a sharp rascal, as you will learn."

Wistala wondered what the last portended. Rainfall sometimes preceded action with an assortment of exploratory statements to judge reaction, like a cook tasting broth as the ingredients went in.

Many of the performers continued their exhibitions, informally of course, in Jessup's tavern that evening. Rainfall held a dinner in his long dining room for Ragwrist and a few of his "Old Guard"—the expression in Parl was one of Rainfall's, but Ragwrist seemed to know who he meant. They gathered around two mismatched tables covered by a single ill-fitting cloth, sitting on chairs that had been brought in from other rooms—Rainfall's better dining furniture had been sold off in his years of want, and there were candelabras under the fitting for the missing chandelier.

Other than Ragwrist, who had cast off his colorful coat for a plain black long-shirt, were Intanta the fortune-teller—a toothless old woman who turned her food into mash, the dwarf Brok, the long-bearded lead gargant-driver, who stuck his facial hair in a special sleeve to keep the food off it, and a horse trainer named Dsossa, whose tight-bound white hair seemed brittle as ice, though otherwise she looked human.

Dsossa and Rainfall seemed to share some special understanding, for they clasped warmly on her entry and touched hands frequently throughout dinner.

Wistala, who had eaten earlier, sat at the far end of the table and crunched the others' fishheads and tails— smoked fish from the fall's salmon run up the Whitewater River had been served—as they finished their meals and started on their wines. As they reminisced, she learned that Brok, in his wild youth, had been judged by Rainfall after he was caught breaking into a bakery to steal food. Rainfall offered him one year of quarrying stone or two years indentured to Ragwrist.

Of Intanta she learned nothing, for the old woman kept silent save for a polite comment or two. But as the conversation echoed events she'd never seen and faces she'd never known, she began to doze.

She awoke to a rattle before her. Someone had rolled a coin down the table so that it dropped off the edge before her nose.

"Yes?" Wistala asked, as wide awake as she'd been deep asleep a moment before.

"A coin for a good story, green daughter of the skies and the earth's deepest flame," Ragwrist said. "I want to hear how you disposed of the troll!"

"I hardly did it alone," Wistala said. "And I'll tell without asking for payment. I might as well ask for money to look at me."

Ragwrist laughed, and Wistala liked the easy sound of it. "Ho! Our ears are quite closed to that line of argument. Rainfall says coin aids your digestion or somesuch. There'll be another if I'm well entertained."

Wistala told it again, imitating the noises as she had with the courier dwarves. She found she took less pleasure from remembering the events and more from her audience's reaction. She was rewarded with a coin from Ragwrist and another from Brok, and they soon joined the others within, leaving Wistala in a contented mood.

"I have a suggestion, Wistala," Rainfall said. "Will you hear it?"

"I'll hear anything from you," Wistala said.

Rainfall looked around the table and got nods from everyone save Intanta, who dozed. "I'm of the opinion you should travel for a while with Ragwrist's circus."

She didn't have to think about it. "I can neither ride nor clown. I can't imagine what use I'd be."

"Will you hear my reasons?" Rainfall said.

She tired of having her head raised above table edge—she became light-headed if she went nose-up too long—and approached the party and wound herself into a circle next to the table. "Of course."

Rainfall brought two fingers together under his chin. "First: Hammar now has a grudge against you. Your life is all that stands between him and possession of Mossbell, its lands, and the bridge. He's not above hiring even the Dragonblade. He fears no murder charge."

Two more fingers came together. "Second: in happier days it was the custom, as part of a High Hypatian's education, to tour the cities of the Empire, the Inland Ocean, and such lands on the borders as are of interest. I've begun your education with the few poor volumes left in my library, but I want you to become worldly in the best sense of the word, and love the greater Order as I do. You cannot travel in the normal manner—once I'd thought of taking you on a few brief journeys myself, but since—well, I won't repeat the obvious."

He brought the rest of his fingertips together. "Lastly:

our rate of sheep and goat, lamb and kid consumption is alarming, and will only grow with you. A prosperous circus should be able to afford your upkeep."

"Prosperous?" Ragwrist objected. "You haven't seen my accounting recently. Bled by—"

Rainfall ignored the interruption. "And consider this: You will eventually sprout your wings, perhaps wish to find a mate. You'll have more knowledge of the lands, though I should like you to return now and again—in fact, the law will require it."

"Why is that?" Wistala asked.

"The thane will have you declared legally dead if you do not show yourself at least every five years. Of course, there are provisions, were you to be serving in the Hypatian forces, for your existence to be verified, but I mention it more in hopes of receiving visits from you than as a legal matter."

"We come up the Old North Road every two or three years, in any case," Ragwrist said.

"What would I do? Stand like an exhibited animal?"

"That would hardly pay for your food," Ragwrist said. "Wistala, I will offer you the same terms all other entertainers get. You pay me each new moon for your food and sheltering—"

"He only adds the smallest of surcharges," Dsossa said.

"Ho!" Ragwrist said. "I take great trouble managing the supplies; I've yet to receive thanks for procuring palatable wine among the Vang Barbarians or those Pellatrian ascetics! But back to the deal: I receive a tenth-part of such coin as you acquire in your displays—"

"Fair warning," Brok said. "If you keep three coins in ten out of his clutches after upkeep and surcharges, you're doing very well!"

"If I'm such a scoundrel, I wonder why you've been with me these threescore years, my good dwarf?" Ragwrist asked.

"There are skimmers in all walks of life, but few do it with such pleasant smiles and compliments," Brok replied.

"And I've a soft heart and softer head for honeyed

words," Dsossa added. "Being cheated by Ragwrist is painless."

Ragwrist extended his arm and pointed to a patch at the elbow of his shirt. "Cheated! Do I look like a rich man? My teeth are worn down from biting off the ends of pencils to keep accurate track of expenses, and my voice grows hoarse haggling over quality of flour, all so my beautiful riders may keep flesh on breast and hip."

"They would happily be spared your frequent evaluations of same," Dsossa said.

"I will sympathize after I see the accounting books of the Diadem dwarves, who you yearly visit with chest-laden pony," Brok said.

"This is the reward for generosity, Wistala!" Ragwrist said, turning to the young drakka. "Wild tales! Accusations."

"How would I earn?" Wistala asked.

"A dragon is an attraction, certainly," Ragwrist said, pulling his hair behind his elegantly shaped ears. "One so well-spoken even more so. But while your aspect inspires admiration, and later awe as you grow, we must marry that quality to a reliable moneymaker for you and the Circus at large."

"I'm all interest," Rainfall said. "I thought she might just do fireworks."

"Any competent chemist can make better," Ragwrist said before turning back to Wistala. "I mean for you to be my new fortune-teller. Intanta all this year has begged to return to her family, now stretching four generations beyond her, but I've hesitated, for her protégés have been disappointments."

"I've tol' ye manys," Intanta said with a yawn. "A fair smile's fine, but sen' a girl of wits. Lev' her know when to keep those teeth hi' and be silent, for the signs are best read in silence."

Some of Wistala's warmth for Ragwrist left her. "I've no gift at that sort of thing. I can hardly foretell the afternoon weather on a fine morning."

"It's part skill, part showmanship," Ragwrist said. "You can better both with practice."

"To tell folk what they wish to hear takes no skill a'tall," Intanta said. "The trick is the know of which wor' their ears long for. Aye, there's the magic."

"That seems like . . . lying," Wistala said.

"Not lying," Ragwrist said. "Offering—guidance. Insight. Your opinion. People bring their dreams and fears into Intanta's tent, and come out happier and better prepared for meeting both. Is that so bad?"

Wistala felt confused and crunched some fish bones to hide the fact.

"Ragwrist can talk a falcon out of his talons," Brok said.

"I should decline," Wistala said. "Kind as your offer is."

"Don't be so hasty!" Ragwrist said. "Talk to some of the other performers. Join the circus and see the world! See the fishing boats come in across an Antodean sunset, or the Grand Arena of Hypat, the crystal waters of Badrink under the mountain towers of the Wheel of Fire, the red pennants flying from the walls of Kark—"

"Rainfall! Save us from this travelogue!" Brok said. But Wistala didn't hear him. She'd stopped listening as soon as Ragwrist mentioned the Wheel of Fire.

"How often do you visit these places?"

"We have regular routes," Ragwrist said.

"And you'll return to this good elf and enjoy his gentle talk that washes all road-weariness away," Dsossa said. Wistala marked warmth in her gaze and new softness in her voice.

"When does the circus leave?"

"We'll perform again tomorrow, and then pack up," Ragwrist said. "The winter is rather ahead of us."

"You will have my answer before you leave."

Wistala spent a sleepless night thinking of dwarves and the Dragonblade, promises and parentage. Unable to sleep, she walked around and around Mossbell and the barn, until one of Widow Lessup's daughters tossed the cold ashes from last night's fire on others in the dustpile.

The next day Hammar and a party from Galahall rode in to see the circus and sample the wine and drink of the inn. Rainfall, at the urging of his granddaughter, offered him the use of Mossbell's stables. Fortunately his party arrived early, before Lada was properly dressed and coiffed.

Hammar paid only the briefest call on Rainfall, and Wistala watched from her former nook. After barely perceptible bows and cold pleasantries Rainfall invited Hammar to dinner after the show.

"I will decline," Hammar said, refusing a chair brought by Forstrel with a wave. When he didn't have the oversize helmet on his head, he was a more pleasing youth, especially when clad in a dark riding cloak and festive winter neck-cloth.

"Have you read my letter?"

"Unless you have any proof beyond the words of a girl of dubious parentage, I wondered why you bothered."

Rainfall leaned forward. "Both of us are guilty of hard words to each other in the past. I fought your assumption of the thane-title on your father's death, and you have coveted my property as more suitable ground for the thane-seat than Galahall. The coming child gives us a chance at alliance in Hypatia's interest, if for no other reason. I offer you this chance before we become enemies."

"Open enmity?" Hammar asked. "That's not like you. As to chances, I've higher title, better men, and enough good yew bows to feather the creature better than that torn pillow. You took too great a gamble when you put so much hope into one scaly beast. Its head will adorn my trophy room."

Rainfall cocked an ear toward her panel door, perhaps fearing a telltale creek.

"She's a Hypatian Citizen, and I hear murder being threatened against her in my own receiving hall. Hypatian law is greater than any man, yea even a thane."

"Law is only as strong as the men to enforce it," Hammar said. "And here, I'm the law. I'll wish no good day to you, elf." Hammar turned on his heel and strode out the door.

"I sometimes wonder if it would be easier to just give him Mossbell," Rainfall said to her when she emerged.

"How can I ease your cares?" Wistala asked.

"You're careworn enough, stomping around the grounds last night. Go watch the circus and forget all worries."

So Wistala watched the antics again from a discreet corner of the inn's roof, sheltered from the wind by a warm chimney. The audience, prosperous farmers and tradesmen, were better dressed today, and had ridden from farther away to attend, answering the calls of Ragwrist's announcement-riders. Jessup's Inn—she couldn't call it the Green Dragon, the name seemed silly to her—had a number of parties staying.

Numerous bills and messages were tacked to the notice-post in front of the inn, surrounded by those literate enough to read and discuss the news as they passed, but the local talk of villains wanted for hanging and auctions left off when Lada walked across the road from Mossbell, intent on seeing the circus and attended by Forstrel.

She looked lovely, Wistala guessed, judging from the stares of the locals, in her heavy fur-trimmed coat, which hid the small increase at her midsection, hair under its cap curled and tucked so it resembled a bouquet of flowers. Her eyes and cheeks, brightened by the cold of the day, glowed.

All eyes were on her but the ones she sought. When Hammar rose from his chair before the stage and took his party of huntsmen to the inn for a new cask to tap, he walked out of his way to avoid her at the edge of the crowd. She fought her way through, tripped and muddied herself, but managed to come up on the men at last.

Wistala didn't catch what she said, but she did hear her call out to him.

Thane Hammar stared at her for a moment and then turned his back. The tall man who'd given orders on the road stepped forward. Two of the men at the tail-end of Hammar's party slapped each other, pointed to her, and laughed.

Lada broke into tears and fled the circus.

Wistala didn't overly care for Lada, whatever Rainfall's

regard for his granddaughter, but even if she was an un-
grateful whelp, she didn't deserve contempt.

Wistala decided.

She missed the rest of the circus to hurry back and
speak with Rainfall, once he emerged from Lada's room in
the small barrow-chair Forstrel moved him about in.

"I want to stay at Mossbell," Wistala told him as Widow
Lessup sighed at the dirty dragon-tracks on the stairs. "If
things go hard with the thane, I want to be at your side,
Father."

"It will fade. Hammar will put an arrow through a winter wolf or a mountain bear and forget all in boasting,"
Rainfall said. "But your presence here might tempt him
into rashness."

"I'm set."

"Oh, my poor floors. I wish she would go away," Widow
Lessup said to herself—loudly enough for all in the upstairs to hear—as she bent with a rag.

"Nevertheless," Wistala said.

Rainfall sighed and scratched her between the ears. "I
shan't be sorry for your company. You are a far smoother
ride up these bumpy stairs than this barrow-chair. I suppose next spring I can teach you how to properly tend the
garden, even if vegetables aren't to your taste."

Chapter 19

Wistala heard feet hurrying up and down stairs the next morning—more than the usual morning noises. There'd been another raucous celebration with the circus folk, but Wistala had kept to her low room. When Anja threw open the door of Wistala's basement refuge, she knew something had put the household in disarray.

"Is Lada down here?" Anja asked.

"Why should she be?" Wistala asked.

"She's not in her room, and sir's asked for her," she explained, hurrying off.

Wistala wondered at her absence. She might have gone for a walk—save that nothing tempted Lada from a warm bed in the morning until a steaming infusion roused her. She yawned, stretched, and went upstairs to the lively sounds of running feet and doors slamming.

She heard Rainfall in his dressing room. As she walked through his bedroom, she smelled fresh ink by the bed—it was very unlike Rainfall to work in his bedroom. He might stay up all night in his library but believed in leaving any cares elsewhere when it came time to go to the dreamworld.

Forstrel was pulling Rainfall's riding boots on, an easy operation, thanks to the somewhat withered state of the elf's legs.

"She was in a mood last night," Rainfall said. "I should have talked to her."

"What has passed?" Wistala asked.

Forstrel finished with the boots and handed Rainfall a woolen vest.

"Lada has run away, I fear. She took her new winter boots, her hairbrush and comb, her favorite book of Tenessal's poems, and riding habit. Anja said there was a wet quill on her desk, but we found no note."

"Note? Have you checked your bed?"

Forstrell didn't wait to be told but hurried over to the bed and overturned pillows and heavy winter blankets. He came up with a folded piece of paper.

"Wistala, you're a wonder," Rainfall said, accepting the paper. "How—? Oh, I suppose you smelled the ink, or paper, or her footsteps. You'll all excuse me for a moment while I read this?"

Wistala and Forstrel stepped out of his dressing room and eyed each other.

"Fried fish for breakfast, I suppose?" Wistala asked.

"I hope," Forstrel said. "With tart applesauce. But we'll miss it, I'll fear."

Wistala heard a sigh from the dressing room, followed by a chuckle. "The joke's on me, Wistala. Rah-Ya. Forstrel, my cloak and hat!"

"What does she say?"

Rainfall held the letter at arm's length and squinted. "After the usual summation of my crimes against youth, including entailing away Mossbell, which she quite regards as hers, she informs me that she's joining Ragwrist's circus so that the local shepherds no longer snicker at her. So by the circus I gained a bride and lost a grandchild. I must go after her, but I suspect it will be futile."

"Why futile?"

"She's old enough to be apprenticed on her own word. If she's earning her keep, the law gives me no recourse, and I'm not up to dragging her back by her hair."

"I will be happy to pull my share of the locks."

"Then you can come along. It'll give Ragwrist one more

chance to talk you into joining. I hope Stog is in the mood for a quick trot. The sun is up, and they'll be across the bridge by now. I don't want to pursue too far into the next thanedom."

Rainfall rode Wistala down to the yard, and Forstrel helped him up on Stog. Stog stamped his foot when he saw Wistala.

"Drakka! Didn't you hear me call out last night?"

Wistala watched Forstrel secure Rainfall on his special saddle. "I heard you bellowing, but I thought it was just another fight with Jalu-Coke about using her claws to get up on your back."

"I saw an old not-friend in the party of the thane's horses. A mountain horse named Hob. Let me tell you what it signifies: Hob is a courier horse for the Dragon-blade. One of the Dragonblade's men was in the thane's party yesterday. He poked around the grounds all day. You're in danger."

"I didn't catch all that, Wistala. What's he worried about?"

"Nothing of importance," Wistala said.

"He most definitely said *danger,* didn't you, Stog?" Rainfall said as he set the mule toward Mossbell's gate.

"Danger to Wistala!" Stog brayed.

"Let's have it!" Rainfall said. "I don't want to play score-question with you."

"One of the Dragonblade's men was here yesterday, riding with the thane."

"Hammar wastes no time. Wistala, all I know of this fellow makes me fear for you. Certainly he won't kick down Mossbell's door to get you—at least I hope he won't—but we must have some thought on the matter together."

They found the circus still packing up, with dwarves frantically fastening harnesses on their gargants, whose appetites added to the cleared meadow behind the inn. Many of Ragwrist's circus folk were red about the eyes—perhaps the empty mead barrels stacked on the south side of the Green Dragon Inn, being cleansed by winter cold and sun, had something to do with it.

Ragwrist, again in his colorful coat and walking his horse about, left off shouting orders and greeted them. He waved Dsossa over, who looked perkier than most in her riding gear with lead lines hanging over her shoulders like a frilled cloak.

"I won't ask why you're here," Ragwrist said with his elegant, balancing bow. "Do you wish to speak to her?"

"Indeed," Rainfall said. "Thank you, old friend."

"Just as well we were delayed in our departure," Ragwrist said.

"Only because you've not issued orders with your usual vigor," Dsossa put in.

"Dsossa, bring your new horsehand forward." She trotted her horse toward the last of the gargant houses-on-wheels.

Wistala watched the gargants being brought into line, along with laden wagons drawn by more brutes. The smell of all the horseflesh reminded her of her missed breakfast.

I've been too long indoors if I'm regretting my third meal in the sun's track, Wistala thought.

Dsossa brought forth Lada. There was some reluctance on the younger's part, but Dsossa kept a firm grip and so brought her to her grandfather.

"I thought your story of the farewell kiss a bit overripe," Ragwrist said to Lada. "Here is your grandfather. Say farewell properly."

"Lada, what are you doing, pray tell?" Rainfall asked.

"I want to leave this place!" she said. "I'll make my own way in the world."

"Sixteen years of experience and already so worldly?" Rainfall asked.

Lada raised her chin. "It is too late, Grandfather. I've signed a contract and been apprenticed."

"Ragwrist!" Rainfall said, and seemed to run out of words after that.

"Ho!" Ragwrist said. "There's always use for a pretty face and figure in a circus. She knows something of horses."

"She used never to leave Avalanche's stall," Rainfall said, leaning forward on Stog's neck for support. "As horses are one of the nobler passions I indulged her. Oh, me!"

"Come, come," Ragwrist said, winking broadly at Rainfall in a manner Lada could not see. "I will not break the contract. It's only a four-year apprenticeship. I intend to teach her much of value. You'll see her when we next go north, perhaps in as little as a year and a season, and she may be better disposed to your roof after an absence."

"Did she tell you she is with child?"

"Don't worry, my friend," Ragwrist said. "She's young and strong, and old Intanta has seen a hundred babes into the world. We've even got a priest in the caravan, so the child will be properly named under her stars and the Hypatian gods."

"I shall still—Wistala!" Rainfall said.

"Yes, Father?" Wistala said, though she suspected what was coming.

"I asked you once before to travel with Ragwrist. Now I beg you, beg you as I've never begged in my life. I'll feel better knowing you are with her."

Wistala looked at the familiar stretch of road, the new inn, the twin hills to the north . . . Just land. It was the old elf she'd miss, his little readings from books and his lessons—

"I will. But I still say I can tell no fortunes."

"Must she come!" Lada didn't so much ask as shout.

"Watch that tongue, girl. It's for Ragwrist to say," Dsossa said.

"We have no enemies in the circus, Lada," Ragwrist said.

"Sir!" Wistala blurted. "I should tell you—I'm being hunted—maybe—by a man called the Dragonblade."

"She's done him no wrong," Rainfall put in. "She's marked by her breed and by the events I told you of the other night."

"Ho! You've found the soft spot in my heart, Wistala. Lost causes and refugees. No circus is complete without them. Have no fear, we are capable of guarding our own. But I see the gargants are in line and all is ready. Everyone must say their promises and farewells quickly. Rainfall! I look forward to my next visit and Mossbell's table—and the Green Dragon's mead, sir." He extracted a silver tube from his coat; it rattled as though a pea were inside, and he blew into it. A piercing, whistling call like a kingbird song, only amplified, seemed to travel right through Wistala's skull.

The gargants creaked into motion.

Ragwrist led his horse to the head of the column, where some ragged-looking horsemen awaited.

"The place will smell more wholesome with you gone," Stog said quietly.

Wistala couldn't jest with him. "Take care of our master," she said in the beast tongue, and gave the same caution to Forstrel at the lead line in Parl. He bowed.

Rainfall said to her: "You must write often, and let no opportunity for learning pass. Keep an eye out in the bookstalls for the paired volumes of Alantine's moral-plays, would you? I've had no luck buying my copies back. Lada, will you take my hand and go with my blessing?"

She took it, but held it at a distance. "As long as I may go and forget this place and everyone in it."

"Back to the wagon with you, girl," Dsossa said.

Dsossa lingered. "Can I trust you to think of yourself for a change?" she asked Rainfall.

"You're too kind," Rainfall said.

"I grow tired of the road. Are you still thinking of raising horses at Mossbell?"

"That was before my son . . . ," Rainfall said.

"May I write you with my plans?"

"Ahh, I'm too old to be of any use to you."

"That's not an answer."

Rainfall took her hand. "I delight in letters. Send me as many details as you care to. But any substantial improvements in the place will need the owner's approval."

"Mossbell is yours as it always was," Wistala said.

Dsossa backed away. "I will write. Good-bye, sir."

"It's hard to leave, at the last," Wistala said.

"I fear Mossbell is too small to be much longer a real home to you," Rainfall said. "But hold it in your heart as such."

The gargants were already on the road, and the wagon wheels struck up a chorus of ground gravel.

"Don't eat all the coins you earn," Rainfall said.

Ragwrist trotted up on his horse. "Well, sir, as usual, I wish I could stay with you through the full course of a moon and then some, but duty to my poor fellowship—"

"You may spare me the act, you old rascal," Rainfall said.

"Wistala, you will ride in the second car, second gargant, inside or up top as is your choice. That's Intanta's spot. She shares with a pair of jewel smiths and the laundry pots, but there will be ample room."

Wistala looked at the column, already a dragon-dash away. She must run to catch up.

"Until we meet again, elf-father," she said.

"That will be a happy day, dragon-daughter."

"Go on!" Ragwrist shouted. "Or do you have another list of books your library lacks?"

Wistala hurried away, leaving Ragwrist and Rainfall talking in the road.

She ran as best as she could to catch up, and heard horse hooves behind.

"Don't look so sad, Wistala," Ragwrist called from the saddle. "What dragon heart doesn't yearn for adventures in other lands?"

"One that knew happiness where she was," Wistala said.

"Mossbell keeps a little piece of an older and better world. But our good elf wants you to see what else civilization holds. Believe me, you'll value him all the more after a few months in the heart of Hypat. See the ladder to the roof of the car? Jump to it and knock on the door in back and they will accept you. They know you are coming."

* * *

Second Moon of the Winter Solstice, Res 471

Beloved Father,

You will recognize the hand as Lada's, though the words are mine. I write you from the Salt Road west of Hypat, with the sound of the ocean near in the great estuary of the Falnges. All in the circus are in good health. (Grandfather, that's not true, I'm sick day and night, but Intanta says it's the babe's doing!—L)

It turns out we are not the only ones who joined at Jessup's Inn. One of Jalu-Coke's young toms made himself likable to Brok, perhaps an affinity for one almost as dark, big-eyed, and hairy, and now they are inseparable.

Lada, after a few days with the horses and draft animals (They worked me like a pigfarmer's own hand, Grandfather!) was put to work caring for me (scooping dragon—-t, she means) and under the tutelage of Intanta and the other older women of the circus. Though Intanta has no teeth, I think her tongue has grown overlarge and sharp to replace them, and she keeps your granddaughter busy. (Slaving! At laundry and sewing if there's not filthier duties at hand.)

We have enough to eat, just, and are only beginning to know our work well during the "open" and "close" that comes with every relocation. They have me climbing up and down poles with lines—I've learned something of knots—I see looking over Lada's shoulder that she is adding commentary. (And why not? I've a right to address my own grandfather!)

As to fortune-telling, I have observed Intanta and her mysterious crystal through a veiled tent-hole several times. Intanta tries to point out how she makes guesses at the contents of her "seekers' " lives and hearts by dress, or jewelry, or grooming, or even the rough spots on their hands, but I can't keep such details. I can tell elf from dwarf, and that is about all.

Lada helps with the costumes of the riders during the performances. (She means the girls throw their sweaty rags at me and yell for the next piece of flimsy all at once, eight hands would not be enough!)

In happier news, I have seen some of the towns and cities of the Falnges and I never imagined such crowds of people. I am brought out to set a straw-stuffed man on fire at shows, and sometimes I am pelted with fruit (which she makes me pick out of her scales!) though Ragwrist overdramatizes the danger of such acts. Fruit is better than arrows or the deadly looking crossbow bolts our dwarven gargant-drivers carry.

I imagine Ragwrist is regretting the expense of our food rations! I cannot see that I am earning him much money. (So he makes me do twice as much work! He is quite cruel, Grandfather.) I fear your granddaughter has not seen any real cruelty in her life to put that in—and I hope she never will. (I have been treated cruelly by those who I thought loved me!) I fear this letter is dissolving into nonsense.

We are now at two-moon's camp on the estate of Director Emeritus Pondus, and many of the circus have left to see family or spend their earnings in the spirit houses. The dwarves are busy patching, mending, and building, and Brok is at work on some kind of harness for me. If you write soon, a letter is sure to reach us here. Rainfall has made up the itinerary for our summer in the southlands, and I enclose it so that you may know our schedule.

I (we) remain your grateful family,
Wistala (and Lada, who would like to know if Thane
Hammar has spoken of regretting me?)

When the two-moon rest ended, the circus took to
the roads south and visited Shryesta, with air fragrant of
honey and dates, home of the Amber Palace, where the
Hypatian Directors held their spring and fall meetings.
They saw Vinde, with its waterfalls and famous jeweled
bridges, and the sea-elf city of Krakenoor, thick with water gardens and the lively trade of its boardwalks. They
played at Fount Brass, home of a thick-limbed race of
men who counted dwarves in their ancestry, who rode
on even thicker horned-and-hided mounts, and finally the
riverside city of Adipose, whose skilled papermakers and
glassblowers brought coin for even the lowliest apprentice
and slave.

Wistala grew slowly that summer on her meals of
stewed offal mixed with a few choice tidbits saved "for
the dragon" by Brok and Dsossa. She found she enjoyed
the chaos behind the line of wagons during performances
more than the shows themselves—performers painting
their faces with dyes and powders, adorning hair and body,
readying their props. She bounced on the stretched canvas the clown-dwarf used for his drop from the tightrope,
and some of the performers took to rapping her scales or
touching the Agent Librarian medallion. She now wore
the emblem between her eyes on a double-strand of chain
the jeweler-women created for it.

She grew to love them all.

The one personality she still wondered about was Intanta. Fortune-telling seemed like a cheat to Wistala,
though the "seekers" left her tent happier than when they
entered, and sometimes gave her extra money beyond
the fee she asked. She'd met the "family" Intanta wished
to return to at the two-moon camp; they seemed a curious bunch, heavy with metal amulets, necklaces, and hair
wrapped in seashells, pipes both musical and for smoking
tucked into overlarge pockets on the two or three layers

of coats many wore. One tried to steal a loose scale from Wistala's tail.

They dined only among themselves, with Lada cooking and cleaning.

If there was any magic to it, it came from the oddly shaped crystal Intanta used. It looked a little like the estuary crabs they sometimes ate boiled.

"A shard from the great crystal of the lost city of Kraglad, enchanted by Dread Anklamere himself!" Intanta said, whenever she removed the rune-woven silk that hid it until her seekers had paid for the telling.

They worked her into the fortune-telling gradually, fixed in a collar and chain harness at the end of pegs hammered into the ground. Wistala could release all by pressing her claw into the keyhole at the collar-join; Brok had built it that way. Intanta became a "medium" between the dragon-seer and her seekers. At first, Wistala kept so still that some of the seekers thought her a statue, so she learned to rock back and forth a little.

Intanta, after consulting with a drunken, disheveled, one-eyed elf who visited the circus to see the dragon—"So it is a drakka. Usually it's just a painted sandrunner," the elf said—suggested mosses and herbs that would make her fire bladder more gassy and smoke appear, but Wistala feared a poisoning of her *foua* or other harmful effects. The one-eyed elf looked rather disreputable.

Close association with Lada brought little improvement in their opinion of each other. Wistala suspected the girl of spitting in her water as she fetched it, and Lada said dragon reek was making her nauseated day and night and harming the baby.

Once a week, Intanta downed a bottle or two of wine and played dice games with her cronies. Afterwards Intanta was well disposed to all and sundry, and sometimes let Lada hold her magic crystal, which relaxed the girl and soothed her nausea. Intanta often looked into the crystal as it sat on Lada's swelling belly and cackled, or sang or whispered to the growing baby to quiet its movements.

Wistala learned the rhythms of the circus. The shaggy-looking riders who went ahead of the column were scout-outs. If they learned a town had been struck by disease, or recently visited by tax agents, or had suffered some other disaster to commerce like a fish die-off or a mine closing, Ragwrist bypassed it. Otherwise they found a hospitable landlord who would sell them fodder, well-use, and shelter for a few days while the circus encamped. They only ever performed for a day or two and then moved on, usually with all the land's children watching the gargants from fence rails.

They lightened Lada's duties as she entered her final moon of expectation and they traveled at the borders of the southlands. Dark-skinned hominids in silk headwraps visited the circus, and Wistala learned other accents of Parl. Birds that reminded her of Bartleghaff soared above the sunny grasslands, home to vast herds of cattle and horses, and Ragwrist bought beef for all.

Wistala did no better at learning how to read the seekers.

"That one was a prince. Had you but bowed to him when I winked and foretold his rivals in power one day bowing to him, he would have given us his golden bracers, so pleased was he with the telling!" Intanta groused as they went over the afternoon's events.

"But he wasn't showing his teeth," Wistala said.

"People in this land don't show their teeth to any but family! If they're pleased, they purse their lips thus—" Intanta lifted her lips so they almost touched her nose, an expression Wistala found revolting.

"I heard him take in breath and hold it as you spoke of his rivals. He seemed excited. His heart was pounding."

"You could hear his heart?" Intanta said.

"Louder than yours," Wistala said. "Yours makes a faint slooshing sound when you are aggravated, by the way."

"You give me apoplexy, young dragon. But this is of interest. Perhaps instead of reading faces and hands, you should listen to their air and hearts. That'll let you know when you're on the right track."

* 　 * 　 *

Moon of the Summer Solstice, Res 471

Beloved Father,

I write you from the Lumbriar Heights in the city of Thallia. How right you were about travel, though we see almost nothing of the cities we visit, for we are too busy either opening, closing, or performing.

I am happy to let you know Lada and her child are well. He is a healthy boy of sparse hair but merry eyes, and his name is Raygnar, a name Lada took a liking to when we visited the Barbarian Passes, for it sounds a bit like good Ragwrist's moniker, and it is the custom in this circus to have babies given names that are some tribute in sound. He came quickly and vigorously into the world, an easy birth according to Intanta (Easy for her to say!—L) but it seems a messy process compared to eggs. Your granddaughter clasped Intanta's odd crystal tight all through the birth, staring into it. (The images summoned within did bring some relief.) We have put his handprint in the margin, though now he mouths the ink—

I will keep this letter short, for Lada tires easily. (True!)

I visited the Library at Thallia, and the librarians were somewhat surprised at my appearance. I met your Heloise, who they told me is nearly a hundred, though still keeping busy with her duties. She questioned me closely about you and the tablets restored to them—I think they suspected an arson attempt—but they allowed me into the common room, where I found myself answering questions long into the night.

Ragwrist and Dsossa, who says she has written separately (Thank the holy soulkeepers!) send their

regards. I shall end this now. Ragwrist says next summer we are to go north again.

Wistala, Lada, and Rayg

"Behold, Wistala, the vale of the Wheel of Fire," Brok
said at the end of a long summer day the next year. His
black cat, whom he called Chunnel, slept neatly balanced
on the gargant's hairy dome.

Wistala, though now the weight of a large pony or a
small horse, was borne on the back of the gargant as easily as its fleas. She sat perched atop its spine, a little above
Brok at the neck-saddle.

By special request, she was riding gargant-back on the
lead animal, offering her the best view of a vista many artists traveled far to depict.

Until they reached the plateau, it seemed another
mountain pass, easier than some, along a good road bordering a rushing river of white. But then you passed between two long mountain arms, with a low stone wall
running the spine and shorn-off towers at the roads with a
catwalk between. According to Brok, the old fortifications
were supposed to look deceptively ill-kept.

Once beyond them, the ground rose a little and you
came to the Ba-drink.

The Ba-drink was a mountain lake, dammed at the west
beneath the towers, surrounded by steep mountainsides
and cliffs. Shaped somewhat like a crescent moon, with
horns facing north, its southmost rim was usually enclosed
in a thick mist where the colder glacier-fed waters ran into
hot springs. Between the horns on the other side were
three short, sharp inlets reminiscent of a dragon's foot-
print, though the digits were somewhat foreshortened. The
mountains between the two outer inlets were almost sheer-
sided where they met the lake and faced each other.

"They say that rive was formed by the fire god's ax,"
Brok said. "Though, of course, the best view is from the
lake. You can just see one side of the Titan bridge at Tall
Rock. The sides of Thul's Hardhold and Tall Rock are

both much cut with galleries and balconies, though those towers to the south are where the greater dwarves of the Wheel of Fire live, among their terraced gardens of soil brought all the way up from the lowlands. We shall camp here at Whitewater Landing, for the dwarves let few across the lake to their doorsteps."

"Do they have mines in these mountains? It seems an inhospitable spot, and cold!"

"I imagine so. I've visited only a tower or two, and the Titan-bridge. They're descended of warrior-dwarves settled in here to guard the three passes through the Red Mountains, enjoying the patronage and protection of the Hypatian Empire in Masmodon's time, but it doesn't do to mention that now, for now they tell stories of the prophet Thul who led them here."

"Why are they called the Wheel of Fire?"

"Let us hope you never learn this the hard way! Oh, don't look at me like that; I don't mean to be mysterious. It comes from their banners and war formations. I can't explain it—I'm no tactician." He lowered his voice. "To be honest, other dwarves call them the Appeal of Gold, for they fight not for defense or honor or justice, but sell their axes and bolts for money. Shameful."

"Is it?"

"Death is too serious a matter to be a subject of commerce, don't you think?"

They set up camp as they always did, though under the direction of Wheel of Fire road guides. The dwarves dyed their leathers and face-masks a dull red, and black were their flared helms—how ugly the memories associated with that shape!—and cloaks. Wistala found Intanta playing with Rayg, showing him her glowing crystal, and asked for a favor.

"What's that, me scaly student?"

"I would like to handle the dwarves by myself."

The toothless lips formed a perfect *o*. "Now ye have the courage to do so, but skill lackin'. Still, I've no love for t' dwar beggars and would be happy to have my ease. Let's see to t' tentin'."

Wistala begged a few extra candles from Ragwrist, who sighed about expenses. Lada installed them around and behind the spot where she was "chained" so their shadows played across her face and body in an intimidating manner. Lada did many of her tasks with a happier, more confident air these days, and anything that didn't involve the routine of cleaning, feeding, or sleeping her baby made Lada break into quiet song. She had an eye for artistry, and costume, and pleasing arrangements of even the most mundane candlestick.

Though she still stuck her tongue out at Wistala when she thought she wasn't being watched. Hominids underestimated the sweep of a dragon's gaze.

The first day she had many visitors to her tent, but few of the dwarves asked to have their fortunes read. Wistala wished for Intanta's crystal . . . perhaps that would invite the dwarves to have a peek and ask a question. Instead they peered from their heavy masks into her eyes, or muttered to each other in the dwarf tongue about she knew not what. They left as soon as she invited them to have their fortunes read.

At last a young dwarf—or one who had lost his beard, for he had but a grassy fringe on his chin—came into the tent and flung himself on his stomach before her, a gesture she wasn't sure how to interpret.

"Oh great daughter of dragonkind," he said in rather glottal Parl. "I crave your advice. What do you ask?"

She used the speech she'd long rehearsed, a variation of Intanta's invocation when she sat in the tent. "Rise and place a coin upon my tongue; the quality of the metal brings quality of insight." She extended her tongue a short distance.

"I'm poor . . . but I have a ring of my granddame," the dwarf said, coming up to bended knee. He reached into a pocket in his leather vest and extracted a short chain with a few pierced coins and a ring with a shining green crystal at the end. He placed it on her extended tongue—she took the opportunity to smell his hands—and she brought it to her mouth and pretended to swallow. The ring she tucked into her gumline.

"You are troubled. Desperate," Wistala said, which was evident enough.

"Yes!" the dwarf bubbled.

What would a short-bearded dwarf be troubled about? Love or his position, she expected. Perhaps both. The other dwarves smelled of goose grease or salted pork and beer, but this one's hands only had a faint floury smell to them. His eyes looked tired.

"You labor hard. Something to do with wheat." *A miller? In the mountains? No!* "A baker."

"Truly!" the dwarf said, his mouth dropping open.

"You love what you do?"

"Nothing is better than the smell of rising dough, or the steam from a freshly baked bun just opened."

She shut her eyes. Did his family not want him to be a baker, or was it someone else? "I see a problem. You fear you are not loved and respected by those you wish to keep close to your heart. It is hard to put your images and impressions into words."

"Oh yes! She jests with me almost every day when she comes for her order, and will speak not with the owner but only with me. But she's from a house with a chair at the council table! And who am I?"

So that is it. She jests with him.

"But she smiles at you, good dwarf, every day that you meet?"

"Oh yes, but she's famous for her disposition. She's kindness itself! She laughs when I juggle buns and always buys extra for the poor."

Wistala found herself liking this young dwarf. She'd been prepared to make him miserable, as a member of a clan who'd done murder to those dearest to her . . . but this fellow seemed so troubled, her heart pitied him. Then, of course, he was a baker, who would probably not be foremost in a charge into a dragon's cave.

She spat the ring out. "The stars and winds, waters and stones weep for your unrequited love, and will not have your offering. Take it back. Present the ring to her family, as a pledge of your love for her. Ask that you may borrow gold against the value of the ring and open a bakery of your own. If you prove yourself worthy of her hand, you shall have it."

"How is—?"

Wistala bowed her head. "Do not question the workings of the Great Spirits. Ah, they've gone. I can see no more."

The dwarf sniffled. "Thank you, thank you, great dragon!"

Ragwrist and Intanta were aghast. "You did *what*?"

They spoke to her in the wheeled cabin of the washerwomen and Intanta's cronies that night by the light of a single candle.

"I couldn't take the ring from one so earnest and desperate. Besides, he needed it as a pledge against borrowed money." The last wasn't quite true, since she'd suggested that the dwarf borrow.

" 'Tis the most desperate that needs their fortunes told most," Intanta said.

"Wistala, I cannot deny that you are a draw," Ragwrist said. "Mostly to children who spend not a penny. I cannot pay for your upkeep, or take a percentage, on *nothing*. You see the position this puts me in? Why, Lada is worth more to the circus than you."

Wistala didn't give a dropped scale for Lada's worth, though her hand had improved somewhat in the letters to Rainfall. "I will try again tomorrow."

"No, Intanta will do the fortune-telling tomorrow. You may sit like a stone statue and keep silent."

"Let her try again," Intanta said. "I'm glad of the chance to mingle. She hurts none."

"And helps none," Ragwrist said. "But this is not the first time I've carried deadweight. Curse my soft heart! Sit in the fortune-telling tent again tomorrow, Wistala, and try not to give away my wagons."

Her supper that night was a poor thin jelly of cooked-down horse hooves—remains such as these were sometimes used as waterproofing or to grease the wagon axles.

Short of giving her dirt, she could not see how her rations could get worse.

After nightfall she gathered every particle of information from Brok and the other dwarves about the Wheel of Fire and their habits, then prowled the rocky slopes and managed to get a sick carrion bird. Then she sat and stared at the distant lights glimmering in the tall rocks that faced each other, mirrored in the surface of the Ba-drink. There were towers at the tops of the cliffs. No wonder Father had broken himself against them. Where was the Dragonblade now? In those rocks, or did he hunt her?

The next morning Ragwrist himself woke her, not through noise or touch but by the smell of a thick joint still sizzling on the platter he bore.

"Wistala, up and get to your tent and prepare yourself! There's already a line outside the fortune-tent!"

She rushed her breakfast—meaning it took her three eyeblinks to eat—and hurried through the show preparations for the back flap of the fortune-telling tent. Lada was already inside arranging the candles; Brok stood ready with her chains and collar.

Brok spoke in her ear as he helped fix her in the false collar. "The dwarves all say an ambitious young dwarf named Stava demanded entrance to House Steelforge last night. He was so insistent, so fair-spoken, and so complimentary about their eldest daughter and plans for his betterment that Dwar Steelforge himself put their hands together, and the engagement party will last a week. There's some talk of Stava being an unchaired member of the Wheel of Fire Council. A few say Dwara Steelforge just wanted her over-ripe eldest out of the way so the younger ones could marry, but there's a sour belly at every feast. But all say it was our dragon's doing, and that you bring fortune."

Much of the morning passed in a blur.

Ragwrist himself helped usher dwarves in and out of the tent. Most offered her silver or gold coin in return for advice with their problems and plans, though a few grumbled when the "Spirits" failed to return the coin as she had the ring. If Wistala seemed stuck, Ragwrist announced that the reading was over. They had to take two breaks to extract the coins from her gums.

"I'm hardly able to speak without rattling or shooting silver into their faces," she said as Lada put new candles in the holders and fresh incense in the brazier Ragwrist had confiscated from the luxury trade-tent.

The afternoon went much like the morning, only more so.

As the sun fell, there was some murmur outside, and the sound of dwarf bodies dropping to the ground.

Ragwrist bowed as he opened the tent flap and a dwarf strode in, a thin red cape of silk hanging down from a light ornamental helm that reminded Wistala of a spiderweb or the loose-knit caps of the librarians in Thallia, for it was more holes than plate save for a line of what looked like dragon teeth at the top, descending in size from large at the front to small at the base of the skull, rather like her own fringe. His faceplate was golden, and had flames at the edge like those used on some sun signs of the astrologers in Hypat. He carried a staff fully as tall as he was in his left hand, and atop it was a reddish crystal the size of his fist.

"Hmpf," the dwarf said. "You're not four years out of the egg."

"Her egg drifted down the Holy River of Mherr," Ragwrist said, still in his odd balancing bow, "and was plucked from the bullrushes by a daughter of—"

The dwarf tapped his staff on the ground. "Spare me the biography. A fortune-telling drakka?"

"I hide nothing from your greatness," Wistala said. Ragwrist bobbed a bit, and Wistala bowed.

"How much am I to give you?" the dwarf said.

Ragwrist raised his thumb three times.

"I can ask nothing from one who has a chair at the Council Table of the Wheel of Fire," Wistala said, and Ragwrist turned his thumb into a fist and shook it at her. "But if you care for my oracle, you may reward me as you wish."

The fist stopped shaking.

The dwarf gave a nod that bent his waist just far enough

that a charitably inclined person might take it for a bow.
Wistala concentrated every iota of her attention on him;
were her perceptions claws, they would be dug into his
eyes. "My name is Fangbreaker. That's all I'll tell you,
drakka."

"No, it's not," Wistala said, having heard his heart miss
a beat as he spoke the name. Ragwrist toppled out of his
bow but came to his feet again quietly.

The staff came down hard enough for Wistala to feel it
through the packed mountain dirt. "Gnaw! It is!"

"Were you born with that name?"

She saw eyewhites inside the mask. "I am titled Fangbreaker, but you speak the truth. I was born to a common
name. Gobold was I on the day of my birth."

"Let us call the score even." She studied his hands.
There was a white scar across one set of fingers, those of
his right hand. He was wide, even for a dwarf, and still
puffed from his walk into the tent. Perhaps wheezed a
little.

"I'm not the first dragon you've matched yourself
against," Wistala said, feeling her *foua* pulse. "You're a
warrior at heart, now relegated to the table and dusty pa-
pers that make you sneeze."

"True. But I wish to speak of the future, not the past."

"You are often opposed at the council table."

"Any rower on the icewater could tell you this. I would
know the future."

Wistala wondered what kind of seeds she could plant
behind that fiery golden mask. "You will put your armor
on again. You will lead your dwarves into battle. You will
take an act other generals will call rash, but it will bring
you victory and accolades. Complete victory and high
accolades."

"Can I trust a dragon?"

"Yes."

"Because I have before, a mated pair who cheated me."

Wistala had trouble forming the words. "If I cross you,
I will die as they did."

"Hmpf," Fangbreaker said. "You take the chance that I

will not chase you down the mountain road. But I will cross the Inland Ocean and carry vengeance even into the earthquakes of the fire coast beyond if you prove a charlatan."

Wistala took a deep breath. She might as well be skinned for a bull as a calf. *How would Prymelete put it?* "Then hear my oracle and judge: You must and you will master the council table. You must and will throw away the ways of politic and traditon that hold you back. You must and will master yourself, go down the mountains again, burning off the girdle of fat and replacing it with one of leather and iron. You must and you will master your people, as once Thul did, be firm and they will love you for it. Be hard and they will worship you." She half-heard his lips form a familiar word out of Rainfall's histories. "Forge them into one weapon, and I see no power on the Upper World or Lower that can stand against you—yes, even the ten-jewel crown will be yours—"

"The crown of Masmodon," Fangbreaker whispered. "Such an oracle. Oh, dreams! Oh, dreams!"

Wistala collapsed, knocking over some of the candles. Ragwrist stopped one before it could set the tent alight.

"No more, I beg you, great dwarf," Ragwrist said, falling to his knees. "You'll be the death of my poor dragon."

Wistala watched the dwarf out of a rolling, water-lidded eye. He shook himself from his reverie. "Hmpf. The story's worth some coin, though the pratfall at the end is a bit much." He reached into his purse and flung a handful of golden coin at her. It rattled off her scales like hail. "Spend it quickly if you lied."

"You're too generous!" Ragwrist said, gathering the gold, though he didn't offer any back to make Fangbreaker's payment more equitable. Wistala again heard dwarves dropping on their bellies as the staff tapped its way off.

Ragwrist added to the drama by telling the prone dwarves outside that the fortune-telling was over for the day, but by special engagement, the circus would stay one more day before moving off.

That night Wistala ate at Ragwrist's table.

"Keep up performances like that, and at next two-moon's break this winter, I shall have a new wagon built special for you, drawn by a tusked-and-silvered gargant. Yes."

"Aren't you afraid he'll come after us if my prophecy doesn't pan out?" Wistala asked.

Ragwrist wiped grease from his chin with his multicolored sleeve. "They never do. Most hominids spare themselves the embarrassment of admitting they were cheated. Ah, Wistala, this is the beginning of a profitable friendship."

The circus packed up, though no dwarf children were brought across the lake to see the gargants go, and only a few dwarf-helms showed at the broken towers.

One odd group of humans did come across to watch the circus go, however. A tall, handsome woman in a blue cloak, a young girl, and a towhead boy watched the train pack up. The woman knelt beside the boy and continually pointed to Wistala and spoke to the youngest child, and soon the child was pointing, too, but the wind carried her words away.

Wistala wondered if this was the Dragonblade's family, and for one awful moment was tempted to run up the hill and burn them down to charred bones, so that the Dragonblade might come home to destruction and grief, but she suppressed the evil thought.

She was a dragon, after all, and better than the assassins.

A month later, the circus stopped at the prosperous Green Dragon Inn. Wistala couldn't say how she felt about the homecoming: happy that she was again seeing familiar faces, or saddened that she would leave with the next "close."

She appeared at the Quarryness Hypatian Hall and confirmed that she still lived, much to the delight of the children who gathered on the common and stairs to watch.

Rainfall was his same courteous self, and Widow Lessup still despaired at the damage Wistala's scales did to the doorframe and stair walls, though Wistala walked about the house with claws retracted, trying to pad as lightly as Yari-Tab, who now had a velvet cushion under the sky-lights in the library.

"And the thane? Still angry with you?" Wistala asked at dinner. The same Old Guard sat around the table, with the addition of Lada and the subtraction of Intanta, who was watching over Rayg.

"We correspond but little," Rainfall said, Lada hanging on his arm, as she had from the moment of their arrival. "He has more barbarian emissaries out of the north visiting him than agents of the Hypatian Order."

Rainfall tickled Lada under the chin, and she beamed.

"Circus life agrees with Wistala, who's grown to twice her former size," Rainfall said. "How do you like it, Granddaughter? You seem a little thinner, and not just at the waist."

"They work me from sunpeep to the last red cloud," she said.

Ragwrist refilled his wine goblet. It was not such fine crystal as the glass Rainfall had broken in his library, but it still sparkled, due to Anja's applications of rag and ash. "Such thanks! You've received an education that will last the rest of your life. And I've two more years on my contract."

"Perhaps I can buy her out of the rest."

"I'll ask a heavy price of affection from Lada, before I let her go," Ragwrist said, raising an eyebrow.

Lada frowned suspiciously. "How dare—!"

"Hear him out!" Dsossa said.

"I want but two concessions. I demand first that you mind your grandfather in matters of education and deportment, for both you and your son," Ragwrist said. He winked at Dsossa, and Wistala noticed that she and Rainfall were holding hands under the table. "Secondly, I demand that you accept Dsossa as your grandmother, for she has said she also wishes to quit my circus. Much thanks that I get!"

"I promise," Lada said, kissing her grandfather's hand and then Dsossa's cheek.

"Oh, how will I make up two such losses?" Ragwrist asked.

"Marlil's as good a rider as I, and her bosoms are still high and full," Dsossa said. "I'm sick of the stench of gargant-vents, and would rather smell hay and horse feed."

"Fallen bosoms or no, count yourself lucky that you've not employed with the long-scrub under that point," Lada said. "Gargants have a sense of humor about when they answer nature's call. I would rather shovel up after the dragon."

Chapter 20

Second Moon of the Winter Solstice, Res 480

Beloved Father,

I hope you can read the hand of my apprentice. She has a lovely voice, and I often think she should be singing rather than learning to be a fortune-teller, but what the Air Spirit gave her in voice—I know as a good Hypatian you tut-tut dragon cosmology, but it is the belief of my sires and it abides with me—dutiful Earth forgot to place in her hand.

I pray you, Dsossa, Lada, and Rayg are well. I hope the volume of the history of Ghorghars did not go astray. The bookbinders should cover the gilding on the page edges somehow. Does Dsossa still risk her neck at the road wall on her hunter? How is the new Mod Lada handling her duties?

I am now too big to ride in a house cart without folding myself in halves. Brok tried building one of greater length but the axles wore so on the turns, they were continually breaking off wheels. He believes craftsmen of the Diadem could supply us with a flatbed, but Ragwrist moans at the expense, and besides

I am large enough to hang a banner on, so I go down the road ahead of the gargants announcing the circus in words and pictures.

Speaking of Ragwrist, the dwarves of the Wheel of Fire have written him again asking for my services to be "sold" to their council, as though I am a slave to be bid for in a market square. He shows me the letters, laughs, and then politely declines, though he keeps threatening to accept the Hypat Arena guild's offer whenever I complain about the quality of the fowl and fish he buys.

I have little news to tell you save that which you've already no doubt heard: your old friend Heloise of the Imperial Library is dead. They asked me to attend a special ceremony for her (as a curiosity, I supposed) at the small Library Hall in Vinde, and as we had only just left it, Ragwrist gave me leave to go with only a few words of regret. I earn his purse and my stomach enough coin each year. After the ceremonies, some of the Librarians warned me about the fortune-telling. They think it reflects badly on my title. I promised them to give up the name "Oracle" soon . . . for reasons I'll explain below. I caught up to the circus with some deal of bother with the river dwarves and took the first opportunity to write.

I am weary of fortune-telling. My heart was never really in it; I dispensed more advice such as I saw things rather than prophesy. Sometimes my heart would be so grieved by the stories I heard, I gave away my own small store of coin, but that led to every beggar in Hypatia showing up outside the tent, or so it seemed to the circus. Odd that I should be talented in guessing other races' minds, but there you have it. One improvises to survive. How else could a dragon see the cities of Hypat in such celebration and safety? For this I thank your foresight, in knowing that eventually I'd want mental diversions and new experiences. I love every road, river, and shore of Hypat, but I fear I must leave it within a year or two.

There are tiny bulges running my back now, elf-father, and they will swell and I shall have my wings and the ability to go wherever there is wind. I have promises to keep and I will go when they come despite the mawkish lamentations of Ragwrist, who, having heard my dictation, has just popped his head in and offered his regards. But don't worry, I shall still fly back to Mossbell every three or four years at least and prove that I am alive. I hope to sell the place back to dear Rayg (is he still raiding Jessup's honeycombs?) one day if his wit continues to so impress you.

We are readying to go back on the Old North Road again, so you should expect us in springtime.

Traveling in hope,
Tala

The Old Guard assembled again in that easy spring, and for the last time, as they had other years under similarly disposed stars.

The party dined in the receiving hall so that Wistala might fit, and the youngest Lessup girl who once so feared Wistala darted back and forth with trays beneath her neck with giggles to her sister. Rainfall, who scooted about the house on a wheeled chair made by a journeyman dwarvish artisan, worked the big back wheels with his arms as he circled the table, pouring wine for all despite the gentle imprecations of Yeo Forstrel, who was trying to out-Rainfall Rainfall in courtesy and decorum.

The party adjourned for the Green Dragon Inn, now at one end of a semicircle of a full dozen homes and establishments, from whose narrow windows song carried up and down the road. The post had expanded into a full news-case, with glass, and a special window had been added to the front of the inn to handle letters for Mossbell's tenants, artisans, and a handful of professionals owning houses along the road who liked Rainfall's manners and easy terms.

Wistala, as was the custom, called out the inn's evening company and then stood under the sign and raised herself up a little so that she could touch nose to the weathered board, and all put lips to glass after a glad cry.

Jessup kept his son at the tap and his daughters with the mugs. He now wore a coat with gold buttons, thanks to the sales of his brewery-mead to taverns in Quarryness and Sack Harbor and beyond.

The next day the circus moved on to the common at Quarryness. Wistala promised to return to the quiet of Mossbell in the evening across the twin hills, home to Dsossa's two herds of horses, though as the day progressed, she wondered if the throngs who'd descended on the town to see the show would keep all performing late. After her customary appearance to old Sobyor, who'd grown fatter than she knew humans could achieve, she spent the day letting her apprentice "interpret" the dragon's impressions of the seekers.

Many of the seekers asked their questions in Parl with a barbarous northern accent.

But eventually the crowds trickled off.

As she passed up the road on the way to Mossbell, sniffing the early-summer countryside on a fitful wind, she noticed a blue firework burning atop the eastern of the twin hills. Did Mossbell's shepherds and horseherds signal to each other in some manner? Fireworks, as she knew well from Ragwrist's moanings, even blue signal flares, cost a good deal of money, for only specialists, usually dwarves, could accurately mix the ingredients—

Signal flares?

Hearts hammering, she left the road and cut cross-country to more quickly reach the house, troubled by the strange lights against the night sky. When she finally broke through the last line of the back woods and looked out over the garden—full of beanpoles and tomato vines and fragrant with basil and peppermint—and saw the house at peace, she ceased her headlong, bush-tearing charge.

Worried for nothing. Were you expecting flames from the library skylight?

She still slipped cautiously around to the front, smelling and listening, and pulled on the bell.

Dsossa herself, with Forstrel behind, answered the door. She wore an ordinary housecoat; he still had on a button shirt and polished shoes even at the late hour.

"Our fortunate dragon! We'd given you up."

"It was a rare day at the circus," Wistala said. "Is all well here?"

"I'm sorry, but we've dined already. We did save scraps, and Rainfall is still up. We're having a digestive gruel and infusions—would you join us in that?"

"You mistake my meaning. There aren't strangers or barbarians or anyone dining tonight?" Wistala asked.

Dsossa and Forstrel exchanged glances and shrugs. "What are you fearful of? Don't tell me you've had a premonition."

"The only auspices I read glowed upon the twin hills. Someone burns fireworks on your property."

Dsossa came out from the door and walked around the side of the house. "I see nothing now. Why would shepherds do something like that?"

Forstrel disappeared into the house with a quick step, and the wind died down. There was a vague murmur to the east.

"Hoofbeats?" Wistala asked.

"I hear nothing," Dsossa said.

"You should return to the house," Wistala said.

"No. I hear them," she said, her hand at her throat. "There are no roads to the east—that land is nothing but thickets and gullies."

"I know."

"Rah-ya! Wistala, what passes?" Rainfall called from the tree-flanked balcony above the door. Now the hooves could be heard even when the wind blew.

"Lock the doors and shutters!" Dsossa called as she

raced across the lawn toward the stable, the ends of her housecoat flapping.

"Forstrel, the doors! The windows!" Rainfall shouted as he turned his seat on the balcony. He spun around again, completing the circle.

"Wistala, get in here!"

"But the main door—"

"Climb up here. The front gallery is wide enough, and I don't care if the paintwork and floors get scale-chipped. Hurry!"

She could see lights in the tree line to the east, along the little path Jessup had driven the wagon the day they buried Avalanche. "Name of Masmodon!" Rainfall said, his arms falling limp. "What's this?"

"Invasion," Wistala said.

Wistala heard alarmed cries from within the house, both male and female, and Forstrel's echoed voice bellowing orders: "Drop that, girl, and get all the shutters on the top floor. Latch and bolt! Hurry!"

Wistala climbed the tree trunk nearest her easily enough, despite the light-headedness she felt at the thought of a battle, and as she put *sii* on the balcony rail, the hoofbeats grew thunderous with alarming suddenness.

A clump of torch-bearing horsemen with no more formation than a broken egg emerged from the wood path. They spread as they came, one part riding for the garden, the other for the front turnaround.

"Inside, Wistala," Rainfall said, his voice so deep and hard for a moment, she thought she heard Ragwrist beside.

Her shoulders and hips made it through the double doors. It occurred to her that she'd fit on the grand staircase down, but she might not make the tight squeeze to the third floor, should it become necessary.

Wistala turned—with some difficulty, and stuck her head out of the gallery door next to Rainfall.

Forstrel came down the hall, squeezing past Wistala. "I've seen to the lower level myself, Master," Forstrel said.

"Douse the lights—let's not give archers a mark," Rainfall said. Then he whispered to Forstrel.

Wailing battle horns sounded from the riders, now individually distinguishable. Most were hairy and bearded; they rode blanket-back on shaggy mounts, handles of weapons sticking up from their back and belts like quills on a porcupine. But at the center of the group riding hard for Mossbell's door was a better-arrayed company. Wistala marked a man in dark plate with a white sash about him atop a black-armored horse, followed closely behind by a boy-man in black leather with a red sash draped across his shoulder.

Behind that pair rode another score of warriors, and more men at the back with packhorses and strings of those sharp-faced dogs with the twin lightning bolt runes emblazoned on their side.

Wistala remembered the dogs as being bigger and fiercer looking. Now they just appeared to be like any other pack of tongue-lolling hunting hounds, albeit matching in size and color and odd marking.

"How can this be? The thane rides at their head," Rainfall said.

Wistala looked out. Near the man in the black armor rode Thane Hammar, clad in chain armor and blue-and-yellow cloaks and subcloaks trailing down across the horse's back to its hocks.

"Mark! What does she do?" Rainfall said.

Dsossa exploded out of the barn in a knot of horse-flesh, her bare toes clutching at the saddle stirrups and fingers holding both reins and mane of her mottle-gray horse. Backside raised and head close beside the neck of her horse, she galloped across the lawn toward the road wall, similar horses flanking and behind her, running for no other reason than that the lead had taken flight. At the rear was Stog, gray all around the nose, eyes, and hooves, who gave up the chase at the fountain and turned to watch the intruders with interest.

The black-leather-clad youth, fair hair showing under his cap, said a word to the men behind him. A group of six rode to the other side of the turnaround, taking great recurved bows off their backs and arrows from saddle quivers.

Thane Hammar pointed and cried out, and three of his saddled retinue charged after Dsossa.

"Let the archers bring her down," the armored rider said, pointing with a long crossbarred spear. Wistala's heart went cold; she knew that armor and spear of old.

The archers nocked their arrows and edged their horses so they could fire clean.

"Stog," Wistala shouted in the beast tongue, and the giant black helm on the armored rider turned toward the balcony. "Cry out, as you did that night on the road!"

But Stog was already running, tail up. "Better!" the old mule cried, and threw himself at the heads of the line of horses. As Stog tore through, kicking at the bigger horses left and right, the archers lifted their bows. One arrow shot almost straight up into the sky. Stog plowed into the horse bearing the young man in black leather, knocked it and the rider over, and jumped clear.

"Kill that beast!" the bright-haired youth called.

Stog wheeled and ran so that he'd be a crossing target. The archers fired, and as the arrows hit, Wistala felt their impact in her heart. She no longer feared a fight, but longed to plunge into the array in the courtyard, to rend and tear with claw-tips wet and hot— Rainfall took a breath.

Stog collapsed, falling forward. Wistala lunged, but Rainfall grabbed her by the rattling *griff*.

"No, Wistala. They want that. There's the Dragonblade out there, with his spear!"

The archers put new arrows in their strings and turned toward the receding figure of Dsossa, heading for the road wall rather than the gate. The Dragonblade passed his spear point across a torch carried by one of his men, and it sparked and sputtered as though it were a firework.

Stog moved and rolled, snapping arrow shafts, then rose, blood running from the piercings. The young man, dusting disgustedly at the dirt on his leather suit, gaped.

Froth dripped from his mouth, Stog stared fixedly at the archers, now drawing against Dsossa. He began to stagger toward them, braying:

While a horse will carry any fool—

"Shoot that wretched animal!" the youth said. The archers turned.

"Eliam! She's getting away," Thane Hammar shouted. He turned his head to the man heating the spear. "Drakossozh, your son's a fool."

The arrows flew again, striking Stog all about the shoulder point, neck, and withers. Stog stumbled but did not fall. Wistala saw his ribs against his skin as he took a deep gasping breath.

"If the going's hard, you'll want a mule . . . ," Stog brayed, oblivious of the arrows. He staggered forward toward the archers.

"Again!" the man-boy shrieked, his voice breaking. "Will no one find that horse's heart?"

Stog, still lumbering forward, may have understood the words, or at least that he'd been called a horse, for he turned toward the voice, eyes white and staring. The arrows cut air again and struck with wet smacks, and this time Stog's front legs collapsed. The back pair pushed the body forward another nose-length or two, then sagged.

But Dsossa was at the wall, gathered self and horse, and went over a slight sag in its length in a flash of gray-white. Wistala heard hooves pounding up the road toward Quarryness.

The three riders after her aimed for the spot, as well, but the first horse balked. It tried to turn, sliding on its hooves, and went over sideways, back crashing into the wall with rider pinned between. The second horse half-sat down as it skidded forward, and the rider, carried by momentum, slid forward up its neck and hit the wall at the knees. He spun feet-up as he went over. The third managed to turn his horse to run along the wall but got tangled in the legs of the mount who'd gone back-first into the bricks, and horse and rider tumbled.

"Get back, Wistala," Rainfall said. "I have to delay them so Dsossa has time."

To do what? Wistala wondered, staring wretchedly at Stog's body, trying to will the old mule back to life. Warn the Inn—no, she'd turned north. Get to the circus? She shifted backwards into the hall.

Wistala counted heads. There were over a hundred riders to the front of the house, and she could hear others in back, probably a like number, though there were still no sounds of destruction to the house. What could anything but an army—?

"Who do I have the dubious pleasure of addressing?" Rainfall shouted from his balcony.

"Into the old wood dry-room behind the chimney," she heard Forstrel saying as light feet ran down the stairs. "Then down. Quickly now." Forstrel approached, the azure blue battle sash of Rainfall's grandfather held as carefully as though it were woven from a morning mist.

The barbarians, who'd been poking around at the stable door and looking into rain barrels, moved to look at the tree-flanked balcony. Thane Hammar turned his horse, but kept to the other side of the fountain, perhaps fearing arrows. "Your Lord Hammar is paying a final call on Mossbell!" he shouted.

Wistala, her fire bladder pulsing, noted that he hadn't had success with his beard, which was still thin and scraggly, for all he tried to shape it into a point below his chin. "It's time for us to finally settle accounts, in a single night-of-blades."

"Night-of-blades—tsk," Rainfall said. "Barbaric phrases, from a Thane of the Hypatian Empire."

The Dragonblade raised his spear; its tip glowed faintly red, like cooling metal from the furnace, but the steel couldn't have been more than torch-hot.

Forstrel knelt beside Rainfall's wheeled chair and tied the sash about his waist, as calmly as though ten-score armed barbarians didn't surround the house. Rainfall raised his arms a little so Forstrel could work the knot after wrapping the silk twice about his waist.

"I appreciate the call, though not the companions. You keep strange and lowly company these days, Hammar."

"Ha!" Hammar shouted. "This from an elf with a pet dragon!"

"You come bearing arms to this estate, do violence to my animals, and attempt to murder my wife," Rainfall said. "I suppose you know your thaneship is now utterly forfeit."

"Glad I am to be free of the title," Hammar said. "You will wish, before the moon reaches its zenith, that you'd shown more loyalty to me. The barbarians have admirable methods for dealing with those who show disloyalty to their lords."

"I've never claimed loyalty to Hammar, only to the office of thane," Rainfall said. "If you had a jot of your father's wisdom, you'd know that way is better."

A rider with a knotted beard and heavy tattooing above his eyes grunted something at Hammar.

As they spoke, Rainfall turned to Forstrel. "Good work, Yeo Lessup," he said quietly. "Now get to the tunnel with the others."

"My mother stands in the hall with her laundry ladle, swearing to brain the first barbarian through the door," Forstrel said.

"Drag her down by the ear if you must," Rainfall said out of the side of his mouth. "I want you in the escape tunnel forthwith. Don't stand there rooted—obey!"

"Master," Forstrel said, bowing, and there were tears in his eyes.

"Watch out for him," Forstrel whispered as he squeezed by Wistala.

Outside, the barbarian finished his speech.

"And you shall have it!" Hammar shouted. "Warriors of Kark, Blacklake, and Turi Fell, all that you may carry off between the Whitewater and the twin hills is yours. Beast, coin, garment, bag, and babe, take what you will."

Rainfall lifted himself out of the chair, gripped the balcony railing in white knuckles. "You know not what you do, Hammar," he shouted, but the barbarians were cheering so loudly, Wistala wondered if he was heard.

The barbarians divided, and Wistala, peering over his shoulder, saw a contingent ride off in the direction of the Green Dragon Inn and the homes around it.

"I know exactly what I do, enemy. I've got men in every town of the Minelands and the Quarterings. Loyal men, and I'm declaring myself Lord. My alliances are set, and my plans are just begun. But there's one small irritant, no more of consequence than a road pebble in my horse's hoof, and that's this estate. I now take what is rightfully mine."

"You and your barbarian wife are welcome to it," Rainfall said. "I will go in peace. Take Mossbell lock and window intact."

Hammar turned to the Dragonblade. "Have you ever heard the like? As though he's doing us a favor! No, that is water long since under your precious bridge. I'll have my justice for the years of insult and hang you by the boughs of your grandfathers!" Hammar turned to the remaining barbarians. "Search this wart of a hill from top to bottom, and bring out that elf and his riches!"

Four of the barbarians—it was hard to see where hair and beard ended and where the fur of their loincloths and vests began—drew war-picks and -axes and hurried for the door. Wistala heard crashes at the back of the house.

Rainfall backed his chair into the hallway.

"A good game while it lasted, Wistala. You should break toward Quarryness. The dogs and riders won't get over the wall, they'll have to go back to—"

A female shriek sounded from below. "Brutes!"

"Oh no," Rainfall said. "Don't tell me she wouldn't—"

Widow Lessup ran up the grand stairs with a speed that did her years credit, clutching an oarlike laundry ladle.

"Oh, sir, they're breaking in," she said. "I couldn't leave, I just couldn't, I tricked For and shut the—"

Rainfall ignored her. "Wistala!" he shouted.

Three barbarians ran up the grand staircase. Wistala extended her neck and spat her *foua,* its oily odor setting every fringe-tip down her spine aquiver.

The first two men dissolved in the hot spew; the third fell back down the stairs, his arms beating vainly as the liquid fire engulfed his head.

"Go now, Wistala, out the back gallery!"

The railing began to burn.

"No," Wistala said. "Not without you."

She whipped her neck up and crashed her head into the ceiling. A second smash—her vision went white for a moment—and she was through to the floor of the library.

Rearing up, she tore the hole wider with her *sii*. Rainfall pressed on a wooden panel, and a grid of steel dropped down behind them, closing off the balcony doors . . . though she imagined arrows could still be shot through.

"Up," she said. Both hominids stood there dumbly. "To the library!"

"I'm to climb your back?" Widow Lessup asked.

"No, go up the stairs," Wistala said, pointing at the nearby stairwell.

"But the master," Widow Lessup said.

Wistala closed her jaws on his seat back and, neck muscles straining, lifted him through the hole.

"Should have thought of this years ago," Rainfall said from the library.

Wistala climbed up and through the hole.

"If we're to die, I'm glad it's here, Wistala," Rainfall said. "Remember when I'd read to you from—"

"Always. But we're not dead yet," she said, looking down into the grand staircase, where smoldering barbarians were setting wood alight.

Widow Lessup ran through the door and shut it behind her. Below, they heard doors breaking, crockery smashing, and assorted calls in tongues perhaps only Rainfall understood.

"May For have the sense to keep them in the tunnel until this is all over," Widow Lessup said.

"I wish you'd gone along," Rainfall said.

"Me? Crawl through all those cobwebs? I'd rather be stripped and carried off by the Hordes of Hesstur out there than breathe spider sacs."

Wistala looked at the desk, nosed open a drawer.

"Whatever are you doing there, Tala?" Rainfall said.

"Your cord-and-seal cutter, there, the short sharp blade. Let's have it."

Widow Lessup ran for it. "Are we to slit each other's throats? This is just like that play . . . ummm, the one with the old tyrant king and the three children . . ."

"No. I need my wings. It's a bit early, but I can move them a little, even though they're still encased. I may be able to fly."

"How does a knife—?" Rainfall said. "Oh."

"Widow Lessup," Wistala said, pointing to the twin lines of raised scales on her back. "You'll have to do it. Hard and fast, parallel to my fringe, like you're dressing a goat."

Rainfall grasped her by the hand and pointed.

"Oh, I don't know—"

"Fast!" Wistala said. "But not too deep. Cut the skin along the stretch marks—that's probably the way it would open naturally."

Widow Lessup took a deep breath. . . .

The first one hurt. The second one hurt even more, because she still had the pain of the first lining her back. Wistala tried to ignore the pain, and concentrated on the crashing sounds on the floor below. She also smelled smoke.

She extended her bloody wings as far as she could in the library, marveling at their form. They seemed a bit undersize compared with her mother's, but then they weren't fully grown yet, as she was in the middle of her final drakka growth spurt.

"I take it you're going to go up and out?" Rainfall said, looking at the crystal cupola.

Wistala plunged her head through the hole in the library floor, as though she were going for a fish through an ice hole. She locked her jaws over the head of a barbarian running with an armful of stolen linens through the corridor below, pulled him up, and flung him skyward and through the glass, which mostly shattered outward from the force with which he was thrown.

Widow Lessup sighed. "It was such a pretty thing. Why must pretty things always be smashed?"

Wistala reared up on her *saa* and, using the scales on her *sii,* smashed away the remaining bits of glass. She took a deep breath and roared out her pain and anger into the night: "Let all who would burn these books know that there is an Agent of Librarians here. Enter to curses and peril!"

"You'll have to leave that wondrous chair behind," Wistala said. "I'm not sure I can carry you and it, as well."

"Take Widow Lessup first," Rainfall said.

"Sir!" Widow Lessup objected. "My heart will fail me anyway, carried aloft by a dragon."

He wiped his seal-cutter clean and placed it carefully on his desk next to his ink and quill box. "A Hypatian noble's first duty—and if necessary, his last duty—is to his servants. Carry her to safety, Wistala. I remain to defend my library and all it stands for."

He stared so levelly at her, she knew it was pointless to argue. She plucked Widow Lessup up by her apron and housecoat and lifted her up and out of the cupola. The grounds around Mossbell were bathed in light from the furiously flaming hay and meal of the barn.

"No! No! No!" Widow Lessup screamed as Wistala climbed out next to her and extended her wings, flapped them experimentally. The goats had either fled the smoke or blood and dragonsmell.

Wistala peeped over the roofline that was part hill crest, hoping the bush and wildflowers atop Mossbell hid her skull's outline.

There was chaos in the front by the fountain. The Dragonblade was shouting, pointing at her, and upbraiding one of his men with the back of his hand. The thane was riding in circles, trying to bring together barbarians, many with singed beards, who were running from Mossbell carrying everything from candlesticks to dining chairs.

Other barbarians, under the eye of their chief, stood their ground, waiting for action. Behind them were the Dragonblade's warriors and archers.

Save for one. The leather-clad youth called Eliam was chasing something around the courtyard. A blur of orange—Yari-Tab, running rather stiff-leggedly, for she had seen her share of winters since coming to Mossbell.

She yowled as the man-boy caught her and picked her up, but not a face turned toward the boy running with an old cat.

Wistala felt her fire bladder bulge as Yari-Tab clawed and bit vainly at the leather sleeve and gloves. He ran across the courtyard, laughing, swinging her by the scruff to pitch her into the fire—

Wistala launched herself, loosing her flame in a shower on the Dragonblade's warriors and dogs, who scattered or burned. As for the wretched boy, her mother's medicine would do for him.

She whipped her tail down and lashed him across the face with its scaly tip, knocking him off his feet. She beat her wings madly and gained altitude, a little more loopily than she would have liked, but she banked and turned back toward the roof of Mossbell, where Widow Lessup was running down a goat path with skirts held up.

She saw Yari-Tab dashing into the shadows of the side gardens, and the youth sitting upright in the courtyard, hands held to his face with blood running between his fingers, a sharp shadow thrown by the burning barn behind him.

"Teach you to wear your helmet," the Dragonblade laughed. "Even if it does spoil your hair and hide that handsome face."

She swooped in behind Widow Lessup, corrected—

Using her *sii* with claws tucked in, she grabbed the woman by the shoulders and pulled her into the sky, hearing late arrows fall through the air behind. . . .

Wistala, daughter of Irelia, lurched as she soared, thrown off by the struggling woman. It was a worse flight than even an aging sparrow or a sick bat could manage, but flying she was, better than in any dream.

BOOK THREE

Dragonelle

BEWARE BEGINNING A WAR. WAR TAKES MANY TURNS,
AND MOST OFTEN BACK ON THE INSTIGATOR.

—*Torus (the Elder)*

Chapter 21

Old muscles newly used tired quickly, and Wistala found herself panting as she circled over the Green Dragon Inn.

The scene below reminded her of a riot she'd once seen outside the Great Arena of Hypat after an underdog victory in a game of Flagstaff when bet payments ran out.

Two houses burned, and through the smoky air, Wistala marked the barbarians as they ran in and out of the other homes in no sort of order. A group of them stood looking sadly at a cart that had lost a wheel after being overloaded with tools and anvils from the smithy. Chickens ran everywhere, to be chased frequently, caught rarely, and then stuffed into sacks and baskets when they weren't dropped in order to pursue a loosed sow or piglet.

The inn had the most barbarians about it. A long low building in back had been torn almost into planking, and the barbarians dipped helms or hands into the mead vats, to guzzle and swill and then stagger off to find vessels to carry some off before others could drink the brewery dry.

Even if the spectacle below had comedic elements, it was a horrifying sort of comedy. Dead bodies, looking like dropped bundles of washing from the sky, lay in the streets and on the doorsteps. Only one or two of the bodies—in front of the inn's windows—were barbarian.

They'd had no luck getting through the narrow windows or stout door, and a flung torch or two smoldered on the tin roof. In the road before the inn, barbarians under the shouted commands of still-mounted leaders were piling tarry barrels and cut pine boughs on a wooden wagon, pointed so that it could be run toward the door of the inn. Others were busy chopping down the notice board before the inn stoop to give it a clear path.

Wistala's back burned like her fire bladder, and she longed to set the Widow Lessup down. The high roof of the inn seemed the safest spot, so she landed—the uncharitable would say crashed—on the Green Dragon's roof, striking first with her tail and then her hind legs, both from instinct and the desire to protect Widow Lessup.

"Cling to the chimney," she suggested, but the woman needed no prompting. She reached out, prostrate on the roof peak, and hugged brick, gasping for air.

Wistala folded her wings—such relief!—and licked at the blood running from the wounds from where her wings had come. According to Mother's tales, the emergence of one's wings was almost bloodless; just a clear, tangy fluid suppurated. She'd known she'd pay a price for cutting them free, and hoped it wouldn't be a lethal toll.

More hoofbeats sounded from the road, but Wistala could see little. Blowing smoke from flaming houses—four burned now—obscured all.

"I will try to return," Wistala said. "If they succeed in burning the inn, slide down to the roof of the well shed and keep clear of the brewery."

"Ohhhhh!" Widow Lessup wailed. "Don't forget the master!"

"I go for him now."

She extended her wings and launched herself off the roof. She left a trail of fire from the notice board to the wagon piled with brush and barrels, which promptly roared into flame and scattered the barbarians. As she flapped up into the sky, she noticed an arrow sticking into the inside of her *sii*—what difference would this blood loss make when so much ran off her back?

Every flap of her wings seemed like her last. She passed up the road, saw the Dragonblade and his horsemen in a tight formation riding for the inn, but they must have had their eyes to the sky, for they executed a neat turn, dispersing as she passed above them.

But she felt in no condition to face the Dragonblade. Besides, she had her mind bent on Rainfall.

She passed over the outer grounds of Mossbell and saw a throng of men in the courtyard around the statue fountain.

Oh, infamy! They had Rainfall there, hanging upside down from the statue, ropes looped about his ankles and the neck of the representation of law. The barbarians were hurling books—the one household item they saw no use for—at him.

Hammar and his men observed events from a little farther away.

Too tired to flap, she set her wings and glided in, spreading what was left of her fire right and left and scattering the barbarians.

She felt the arrows strike. She never remembered it as a painful feeling, more astonished that she didn't hear them whirl through the air or hit her, but hit they did. A lucky couple bounced off her sides but others plunged into her scaleless underside. The next thing she knew, she was on the ground, nostrils full of dirt and grass, a neck-length from the fountain.

She heard blood rushing in her ears—no, it was the barbarians hooting and cheering, sharp black shapes against Mossbell aflame.

Her breath came with difficulty, and her vision foreshortened. But Rainfall still breathed. She would die beside him. More arrows and a hand-ax bounced off her scale; she noted the strikes uninterestedly. She made one painful crawl toward him, got her nose on the edge of the fountain, smelled blood and water. One of the goldfish came to the surface and looked at her, mouth opening and shutting as it hoped for a tidbit.

Dully, she saw the column of the Dragonblade's men ride up. The Dragonblade pulled up, and the black helm waved this way and that as it took in the scene. The man-boy in leather, staggering and with the side of his face crudely bandaged and a medicine vial in his hand, pointed with the unsteady hand of a drunk at the fountain.

Wistala found she had a terrible thirst and drank, caus-ing the goldfish to flee to the other side of the pool. As she sucked water, she watched events in the courtyard with amazing calm. Even Rainfall's moans as he hung, upside down and red-faced, were just another component of the tableau.

The Dragonblade dismounted. He took off his helm, hung it on the pommel of his horse, and drew a gleaming blade. He strode forward, eyes burning.

This is the end. She wondered what would happen to her head and claws. Would they be sold together, as a set, or separately?

The Dragonblade swung, and she shut her eyes.

Amazingly she felt nothing, heard only a splash—her own head falling into the pool at the base of the statue?

She opened an eye. The Dragonblade had cut down Rainfall, pulled him out of the water and set him down on the ground, propped up so he sat against the fountain pool.

"Thank you," Rainfall gasped.

The Dragonblade glanced down at her, his broad, flat face frowning, gray wisps in his dark hair and thick at his temples, and he turned and walked toward Hammar, re-moving his thick gauntlets.

She felt Rainfall's hand on her snout. *So tired.* But the water was helping. She sucked a little more.

"The dragon's finished," the Dragonblade said.

Dragonelle, Wistala corrected rather absently. *I lived to fly and by rights must be called a dragonelle.*

"More by her own doing than any arrows," the Dragon-blade continued as he walked up to Hammar.

The Dragonblade moved so fast, Wistala wasn't sure what she saw, but Hammar fell backwards. Ah, the Drag-onblade held his gauntlets aloft; he'd lashed out and struck Hammar across the face. He threw the gloves into Ham-mar's face.

"I'm a slayer, and I quit whatever feud you have," the Dragonblade said.

"I'm takings her earsh," the man-boy slurred, drawing a blade and moving forward. "My idea to baitsh the creasure with—"

The Dragonblade reached out, caught him by the red shoulder sash and spun him around so hard that he dropped the medicine bottle and fell. The man-boy got to his hands and feet, and the Dragonblade kicked him at the tailvent, so hard that the youth went facedown in the dirt. "Get him on his horse," the Dragonblade said to the line of archers.

"Mount your horse, and let's be off," the Dragonblade said. "*Vagt kom trug mid suup-seep*," he said to the barbarians, who growled and fingered their weapons. He waited expectantly.

"I thought not," the Dragonblade said, turning.

One burst from the others, howling and waving a short ax in each hand. The Dragonblade whirled, lifted his scabbarded blade and used it to catch the pair of axes under the head. He lifted his arms so the squatty barbarian hung gripping the ax-handles with legs kicking, and head-butted him so that the barbarian dropped unconscious.

With the aid of one of his men, he remounted his armored horse. "I leave you the honor of finishing the beast off, brave and lordly men of Galahall— Ha!" He glanced back at the man-boy, who was sagging in the saddle he'd been hoisted into, and touched heels to horse flank. "Keep the rest of my fee, Thane. Gold from you could buy only wormy meat and ill-fitting shoes."

The thane's armsmen stirred and looked to their chief for orders.

Hammar held up a hand, and his men remained in their places. "You've made an enemy to remember—and regret!" Hammar shouted at the riders filing east. The Dragonblade tilted back his head and laughed. "Drakossozh!" Hammar screamed into the night. "You've insulted a king!" Only laughter answered.

Wistala found she had the energy to climb up into the

fountain. She settled into the water, rubbing her back and washing out her wounds but also washing out one of the goldfish, poor fellow. Pleasant warmth suffused her, and she curled in the pool about the statue so her head was near Rainfall.

Not only did the water feel good, but her underside was now protected by the pool's thick lip of masonry, as well. She rattled her *griff* in challenge and waited.

"Well. You heard him," Hammar said to his bodyguards. "Kill the creature!"

"We need spears for that, Lord Hammar," the closest said. "Longer spears than our allies carry," he added hastily, as Hammar pointed to the spears in dirty hands all around.

"You have your swords!"

A man with a deformed lip curled up to reveal brown teeth shook his head. "It's still moving. I'm not going near those jaws, whatever that dragon-hunter said."

"Then start at the back and work up!"

"The tail's just as dangerous. That boy lost his eye!"

Hammar opened his mouth as if to say something else but thought better of it. "Someone get me a bow!"

Barbarians began to ride across the yard, their horses laden with bags and tied barrels. Some carried off bound women and children.

The barbarians before Mossbell were conducting an informal market, swapping candlesticks for plate, furniture for spice boxes and kitchen implements. Hammar yelled something at one of the brow-tattooed leaders, who shrugged or glanced in any direction but the fountain or scratched their beards as if to say, *Dragon . . . I see no dragon!*

Part of Mossbell's sod roof collapsed with a roar.

One of Hammar's riders rode up with a hunting bow, fully as tall as a man. Hammar notched an arrow and drew.

Wistala saw him sight on her eye. She pressed herself flat into the water, which surged and washed over the rim.

At the last instant, Hammar shifted aim and fired an arrow into Rainfall's chest. The elf let out a weak cry.

"That was for practice," Hammar said.

Wistala lunged out of the water. It wasn't a dragon-dash, more of a desperate crawl, and Hammar backpedaled, dropping his arrow—

And Mossbell's south yard-wall exploded in orange and yellow.

Through the dust and falling bricks came three gargants, charging abreast, dwarves tied on their backs holding rein and weapon.

Behind the gargants rode others from the circus, men and women on the show horses who were used to confusion and noise and crowds, and behind them others on foot, carrying everything from mallets to clubs bristling with tent spikes.

Hammar gave them one openmouthed look and ran. Wistala did not have the strength to pursue him.

The barbarians instinctively drew together into a bunch to face the attack, linking wooden shields and raising warpick and ax, but the dwarves tightened their formation and let the iron-shod feet of their gargants crash through and stomp the barbarians as easily as they would a flower bed. All order left the barbarians, and they ran for their lives.

But the circus was not done yet. The dwarves situated highest on beast-back fired crossbows down into the rout, passing the empty bow back for others to load and taking up another with remorseless precision.

The riders harried the barbarians at the edges, throwing knives or small axes, or hooking men at neck or feet with ropes. Ragwrist himself sent Marlil and her women after the fleeing thane and his bodyguard. They lit red candle-fireworks and rode hard on the heels of the men, shrieking like loosed demons and throwing knives until the bodyguard plunged into the woods—save for the man who was dismounted by a branch.

The battle passed in fury. Dsossa appeared as though dropped from the sky, kneeling next to Rainfall. Those on foot were the last to leave the yard, clubbing their way through the lamed and the wounded barbarians.

Wistala tried to rise to her feet, failed. The front balcony on Mossbell fell in a shower of sparks.

Ragwrist returned, dismounted, ran to Rainfall, fell to his knees. Ragwrist used his thumbs and turned up Rainfall's eyelids. He detached the sobbing Dsossa, placed a hand on Rainfall's heart, then tore out the offending arrow.

"He is dead," Wistala said. She could hear no breathing.

Ragwrist blew his whistle, loudly, and again. He stopped only when he heard answering whistles from the thundering gargants.

"Quarryness is aflame," Ragwrist said. "It would appear the thane had enemies there, as well. That fat, low judge is hanging from the Hypatian Hall peak."

Wistala's light-headedness brought a strange sort of clarity. "You'd better move the circus south of the bridge." She would remain beside Rainfall, now and for eternity. . . .

Swinging, flying again—no, she was being hauled up onto gargant-back by dwarves with ropes all around.

Through a sticky eye she saw a golden summer dawn. Mossbell still flamed at the end of blackened beams. A door-pull glittered in the char-heap, and the wind was carrying off fine white ash—probably the remains of Rainfall's library.

They passed through the village, better than half the houses were burnt, and the others were emptied, but the inn still stood. The villagers had thrown the few dead barbarians on the burning cart before the inn, and added broken shutters and doors. Some joined the circus column, carrying bundles or pushing household goods in carts, and so passed over the bridge into the next thanedom.

Ragwrist arrayed his house carts to block the bridge, and the last memory Wistala had was of Widow Lessup consoling Mod Lada—Rayg had been at academy outside Quarryness, and none in the despoiled town could say what had become of him.

They buried Rainfall the next day on a cool summer morning of the sort that always saw him long at work in his garden.

Wistala, drinking like a horse fresh from a race, begged Ragwrist to drag a dead horse from the village and a team of dwarves with a gargant went and fetched two so that she might have one the next day. They hung one and she devoured the other despite the flies. With food and water in her, she felt up to a slow, stiff walk up the riverbank to a prominence overlooking Mossbell's grounds.

"He'd rather be rooted with the family across the gorge there," Ragwrist said. "But Hammar is a bitter man, I'd hate to have him take vengeance on a rooting elf."

Wistala watched the procedure. Under Ragwrist's direction they sat the body cross-legged, facing the river and bound up in canvas, then coated him with fresh clay, until he resembled a lumpy, three-sided pyramid. The crown of his head they left naked to the elements. His hair still sprouted there, if anything a little brighter green than before. "He'll like it better on the south bank anyway, the sun catches the river mist, and he'll have rainbows. And a better view of his bridge and lands."

She asked Ragwrist about the custom as Dsossa smoothed the clay sides with her hands.

"The being you knew is dead, certainly. The dormant comes to fore after death," Ragwrist said. "Some elf families bury their dead upright in a hole, others hollow out dead trees and place them in there. With us it is clay."

"Us?" Wistala asked.

"Yes, Rainfall is my brother."

She was shocked into speechlessness. "But you've only shown—"

"To elves family is an accident, Wistala. We are dutiful to our parents and try to pass on all we've gained from the world, in wisdom and wealth, to our children, but as to siblings or cousins or all that stuff humans and dwarves set such store by—" He shrugged. "Just as well, for I've seen feuds start between brothers over family obligation that make the Steppe Wars mild by comparison. It is sad to see another full-elf go. So few are born anymore these days."

"It is the same with dragons," Wistala said, as Dsossa kissed a new bud on Rainfall's head. She planted a handful of Mossbell's green lichen to keep him company. "Why is this? Are elves hunted, as well?"

"If I knew the cause, I'd be in a shell-house, looking out over the water gardens of Krakenoor. We have our enemies, true enough, but that is not the cause. They say the magic is being leeched out of the world. But what do poets know?"

Dsossa touched her at folded wing edge. "Wistala, I know Rainfall would want you to have this," she said, drawing the blue battle sash from beneath her weather coat. "It is a relic of Hypatian Generalhood and should go to his daughter."

The silk was so shiny and smooth, it was as though water had been woven into fabric. "I could not wear it. My scales would tear it to pieces."

"Carry it, then. What has become of your harness and satchels?"

"We lost much baggage in Quarryness," Ragwrist said.

"I will ask Brok to make you something more fitting," Dsossa said.

"Will you come with us south?" Ragwrist said. "If the circus is to continue, we must back to the winter camp and replace our losses. Would that they'd just taken money instead of lives! Money is so easily replaced."

Wistala almost snorted, never having heard *money* and *easy* so closely associated from Ragwrist. It took her a moment to answer the question, so conflicted were her thoughts.

Oh, the allure of familiar routine! Drained in body and brain, she could eat the wheel-size fish of the delta—

"I must think on this. I told you I would travel with you until I had my wings. But I must decide what purpose to put them to."

Wistala's wounds ceased bleeding whenever she moved the next day, though she suspected she still had an arrowhead in her, for if she struck her left *sii* out far forward it pained her.

Despite her fatigue she went across the bridge, and saw Jessup and some of his family rebuilding their brewery. She didn't pause to talk—though she did touch the sign for luck, which caused one aged man sitting on the doorstep to touch a phantom mug to his lips—but instead went to Mossbell. There she took Stog in mouth, holding him as tenderly as a gamesman's bird dog would carry a duck, and crossed Mossbell to the grove of Rainfall's ancestry.

She had to keep her eyes averted from the ruin. Remarkably enough the two trees flanking the front door still lived; though their smaller limbs had been burned, they were still green far above.

At the glade of Rainfall's ancestors, she found the remains of days-old campfires and a garbage pile, and noted that the barbarians had carved rude symbols in the tree bark with their blades and left their filth all about the roots. Whether it was chance or purpose, she could not say.

She laid Stog beside Avalanche and gathered rocks, and over the course of the day built such a cairn that not even the strongest badger would be able to dig his way through. When it was done, she sat atop it and looked across the gorge. She could just see a brown dot, Rainfall's cocoon, from which a tree would hopefully emerge.

Utterly sapped by the effort, she slept. She dreamed the trees were whispering to her, soft words made of wind and leaves.

Chapter 22

Even before the circus left, Wistala occupied the old troll cave overlooking the Whitewater River west of the bridge.

It wasn't a bad cave. The outer length stank of gulls; the cave mouth looked like a running sore, so thick were their droppings down the rocks below.

Farther inside, bats clung to the cave roof. They were oddly comforting, reminding her of the home cave. The more responsible part of her mind, which often spoke with Mother's voice and silenced those bits interested in old Elvish poems, Hypatian architecture, or the taste of sweetwater fish mixed with *gar-locque* or other herbs— and occasionally considered what composition of length, curvature, thickness, and number might make the most pleasing array of horns on a dragon, told her that the bat droppings would hide dragon odor. Not that the dog had yet been bred who could negotiate the cliff and stick his wet nose in her temporary lair.

At night she would visit burned Mossbell, which now belonged, as all ruins must, she supposed, to the cats. Jessup told her that Old Yari-Tab was sharing an upstairs room with Widow Lessup at the Green Dragon Inn until a house could have its roof and doors repaired.

Jessup also mentioned that the thane's men had already

set up a bridge toll and expected their mead and meals free as part of "guarding" the ruined village.

The younger cats ran wild in the ruins and gardens, hunting the birds and mice and rabbits that came for the beans and vegetables, but scuttled away whenever she approached one—as if a rangy cat would make more than a snack!

She climbed the burnt bark of the doorway trees and wrapped herself around the trunk at their height and tried to ignore the yowls of mating cats below. She looked off toward the ridge that shielded Galahall's rooftops from her vision, or the two hills, or the long lines of mountains disappearing north and south—she could just make out one of the peaks that bordered the Wheel of Fire dwarves to the north—and the Dragonblade, if he still lived among them.

"What dragon lives that doesn't count his enemies on more than one limb?" she said to the wind, wishing she had the strength to at least burn Galahall. But Lessup told her that some years ago Hammar had Galahall's roof recovered with slate and his cornices and towers shingled with dragonscale, bought at great expense from the Wheel of Fire dwarves.

Wistala knew, too well, how they acquired dragonscale. How much was Mother's green, or Father's bronze?

"I'm but one dragon, what can I do? Assemble an army of dragons? From where? I've not seen another of my kind since—"

She could keep neither the promise to her Father nor her private oath of vengeance—the scroll of the family slaughtered now included Rainfall and probably Rayg, for the barbarians could make cruel sport of captives—without knowing another dragon. A dozen would be better, but as far as she knew numbers like that had not gathered since the days of Silverhigh. Even Auron, scaleless and thin, would have been a comfort as an ally with his sparks of inspirational courage.

She would have to improvise.

She almost chuckled, she'd been so long among hominids. At least Auron wasn't keeping the rain off some grasping thane with delusions of kinghood. Did dragons naturally indulge in the humor of the funeral pyre, or had they developed it through dark years of murder and assassination? Poor Auron. She tried to imagine him curled around the tree opposite, probably complaining about his empty stomach or talking of the stars.

Where is his star again? Follow the Bowing Dragon. There. Susiron, always in your spot.

How sad that Auron never learned the joy of flight. She threw herself from the tree and opened her wings—she still wasn't strong enough to take off without a drop from some kind of height, and flapped up into the clouds.

She was still weak. To regain her strength, she'd go far away, and work herself until she was as strong and single-minded as the toughest barbarian. She would go north.

"It's as good a place as any for a dragon," Ragwrist said with a shrug.

She had heard the circus was going to leave the next morning and had sent a message through Jessup, and they met at Rainfall's grave on the eve of departure. The clay pyramid now sprouted at the peak like a four-head cluster of broccoli. "But . . . brrr. Not for me. And the tribes up there, they'll slit your throat out of pure meanness and take your skin for coat-shell."

"You won't find any libraries up there," Dsossa said. "Rainfall always appreciated the volumes you sent, you know."

Wistala hardly believed her eyes, but it seemed the growth atop the clay pyramid tilted ever so slightly in her direction. Had the broccoli *bowed* to her? No, it was simply responding to the moon above and behind her.

Maybe.

"I must go north. According to the librarians, there are others of my kind there," she said. "But I will come back to visit. Perhaps to your winter camp, so I don't get frozen solid up there when the sun runs south."

"Don't expect to lie around all day stuffing yourself

with veal at my expense," Ragwrist said. "You winter at my circus, and you'll be speaking to select seekers at a commanding price!"

"Oh, give it a rest. I'll buy her a bullock or two," Brok said. "If you'll give me a moment, I'll show you your new harness."

He'd made a leather neck pouch, easily expandable, that had stiffened cases all around the sides, about the size of the ones the dwarves used for their crossbow bolts.

"I put a couple *vesk*-stone of good softmetal in for you. Metal is rare up there. I understand they use bone fish-hooks and flint scrapers and such. Or at least that's what the traders bring back."

A transparent blister showed at the buckle on her breast, and a familiar blue sat within. "That's the old elf's battle sash. Safe from weather and wet in there, though honestly I wasn't expecting the cold of the icelands. If you open the latch," he showed her how, "you can unscrew the crystal if you'd like to take it out for some reason, but remember to seal it up again with good wax to make it airtight."

"You raided my ironmonger?" Ragwrist said. "Are you trying to ruin me, Brok? Am I to support the family of every blacksmith in Hypatia?"

Brok ignored the protestations and slipped it over Wistala's outstretched head.

Wistala thought it looked like an oversize gem, and wearing such a thing would make her feel flashier than a proper young dragonelle from her family should—*Your wings and scales should be advertisement enough,* Mother always said, *no need to adorn for Silverhigh aerials*—but had to admire the workmanship.

She put it on. It turned on her neck easily enough, and she could reach the cases, probably even while flying.

"Rub some fats into the leather now and again," Brok advised. "It's the finest hardened cowhide, but don't mistake it for steel. It needs care."

"Improvident—," Ragwrist sputtered. "He speaks of care. Care! Have care to my balance book!"

"I don't know how to thank you, Brok," Wistala said, ignoring the byplay. "You should have my coin savings."

"Ha!" Brok said. "I loaded two of these cases with it. Eat them sparingly, good dragon."

"What of you, Dsossa?" Wistala asked. "Will you live near the inn?"

"I will still breed my horses, though on this side of the river, and Hammar won't get one for any price. Old Avalanche left some colts on this side of the river, and I'll see if I can't better the bloodline."

"Stog might suggest a dose of donkey."

"Yes, I'll breed mules too. Less money in mules, but they are more easily sold in any market."

They looked at each other around Rainfall's rooting place.

"I shall be sorry to leave you all," Wistala said.

"That's circus. You've outgrown us," Ragwrist said.

"No. I've learned so much, and I could lear—"

"I don't mean that," Ragwrist said, waving away the dragon breath. "I mean the circus can't afford to feed you any more, or employ an army of shovelers to keep the air breathable."

Wistala slept out the next day in the old troll cave, half a horse inside her—she'd flown up to Galahall and snatched one from an outer pasture as it stood sleeping—and the other half hanging for breakfast, when she heard a faint shouting.

"Wistala! Wistala!"

It was a female voice. She sent the seagulls flying as she crawled out the entrance—from the noise they made anyone would think it was their cave—and cautiously peeped up the cliff.

Lada lay flat on her belly. She waved.

"I hate heights, you know," Lada said.

"You don't look well," Wistala said. "But I'm glad for a chance to say good-bye."

"I need to speak to you. Please!"

"I'd prefer if you'd come after dark. I don't want anyone to know where I am. Speaking of which, how did you find out?"

"Jessup told me. His oldest pointed out the cave from chalk hill. And tonight I must stay with a sick family."

Wistala sighed. It would be easy to fly up there, but any fishermen along the river and every shepherd on the hills would see her.

She climbed. Amazing how much stronger her fore-limbs felt with her wings out. In a moment she stood on the thick pasture grass.

"Let's try that little hollow over there, out of the wind," Wistala suggested. Also out of view.

Even without the hat Lada's priest's robes made her look older than she was. A summer ribbon bound her hair with the aid of a bean-stake. Her eyes were dark and worried.

"So this is more than just a good-bye, or a last moment of consolation over our father's death," Wistala said, once in the hollow.

Lada brushed some snails from a rock and sat down. "It's Rayg. His body was never found, you know."

"I saw several carried off," Wistala said. "He was taken at Quarryness?"

"Yes. Another low priest with experience in these mat-ters says he's most likely been made a slave. He's at the perfect age: old enough to work intelligently but still small enough to be overpowered by the least housewoman. Mod Daland believes him to be alive."

"But in barbarian hands."

"I went to see Hammar, you know," she said, her thin lips almost disappearing. "Just yesterday. Just—it took all my nerve."

"He claims to have influence with them."

"His hall is full of their banners, drums with claws and feathers on the heads, and that horrible reeking charcoal they use to toast their flesh. You can scarce see through the glass in the windows. But I threw myself down before him, on those stones full of dog hair and spit, and begged him. I told him that he could have anything—*anything*—if he'd help find my son. His son."

She hid her eyes under her hand. "He took my offer, took me. Took me and made a sport of my body . . . I can't describe more. But afterwards when I asked him to get Rayg back, he laughed and said he didn't need another bas—boy hanging about the place, counting on a position or thinking of the throne. He calls it a throne now. He said he'd make inquires so I could go north and seek him."

Wistala watched one of the brushed-aside snails go back up the rock. "I'm sorry to hear your troubles. But if you think I need more reason to hate Hammar—" She began to describe the scene before the fountain, but it so upset Lada that she stopped. "How can I help?" Wistala asked.

Lada wiped her eyes. "I'm supposed to be the priestess—oh, well, an inworld acolyte, I should say. This is so selfish, I've left the world behind but—he's my son! I'm supposed to be the one who helps people with their troubles. *The world is wheels within wheels, and each turn grinds* . . . but the words aren't helping me."

Wistala waited.

"I heard you were going north. I ask you to look for Rayg while you're there. If I learn anything about his location I'll try to get word—Copex knows how—but I'll try, and leave word with the circus. Then you can go in and get him and . . . and—"

"Burn anyone who gets in my way?" Wistala supplied.

"Yes," she said, hard and low and with eyes alight as though she relished the thought. Perhaps Lada had her heart no more in her role as priestess than as a circus performer.

"And if I retrieve him?"

"A temple built in your honor enclosing a statue of bronze and silver, if I have to work the rest of my life toward it."

Hominids and their strange vanities. How many times can you fill your gorge at a temple? "I'm not going to live in barbarian lands. I'm going beyond men, looking for my kind."

"I heard some sailors saw one of your kind. But it is a secondhand story, perhaps they got it wrong?"

"Where?"

"Oh, to the north, while crossing the Inland Ocean. They'd been blown off course by a storm and they saw a dragon aloft. They thought for certain they were doomed and made their last offerings, but the dragon only swooped low over them. They said a man in heavy fur rode its back, but sailors are always telling tales."

"Are they sure it was a dragon? Not feathered?"

"Yes, a dragon, and blue as the sky. Speaking of blue, I must admire that belt around your throat. Wait—if it goes around your throat is it a belt or no?"

"Harness, I call it, but I pity the man who holds on to it to ride my neck. He'll need something thicker than fur to save his skin."

Wistala pulled her *griff* up and back so the corners of her mouth could rise. Lada laughed.

"I used to hate you," Lada said.

"You were young," Wistala said.

"*Fair can be foul, and foul fair,*" Lada quoted. "*Proverbs of Experience* sixty-one. That means something to me. Now."

"I'll make no promises about Rayg, fair or foul," Wistala said. "But I will keep my eyes open. I intend to travel at night, though. Your best chance is through Hammar, distasteful as he is."

"He can be charming, as long as he's getting his way and his appetite is sated," she said. "I will dance to his tune, but as a viper does before it strikes the bird. A fair journey, Wistala, and peril only to your enemies."

"If I come south again, I will leave word at Jessup's Inn and the circus winter camp. I fly north tomorrow, but one of my hearts stays at Mossbell."

Chapter 23

Wistala flew north in easy stages, more from physical limitations than intent.

Even with her wounds healed over and her blood restored, she still tired easily and needed frequent rests, made all the more difficult by a thirst that seemed to start at her tail-tip and grow from there and a hunger that must have been worse than her hatchling pangs. (It wasn't, but lost memories are sometimes a kindness.)

She followed the road until it broke off into a series of trails or twin ruts, irregularly filled with increasingly crude bridgework. Even the distance posts of Ancient Hypat's short-lived Tribal Confederation, still in use to mark intervals of *vesk* even in lands where the word *Hypat* was a curse and *Hypatian* a synonym for "devil."

Flying mostly at night, but doing what she could to observe the villages and isolated hutments she passed in what felt like a hopeless search for Rayg, she avoided lights below.

Hearth lights and campfires grew less and less frequent as she ranged north, until she began to travel at dawn and dusk so that she had a better chance of dropping on a hoofed-and-horned meal. The snowcaps on the mountains, rich with all the dragon colors when the sun was level with them, marched lower and lower and glaciers hanging between became commonplace.

Then, over the course of a single night, she reached new air currents. The wind ceased blowing pleasantly warm from the southwest, and instead spun down the coast from the northeast, a cold, wet breeze that helped her to glide but she had to fight like an enemy for each hop north. She found that she traveled faster with less fatigue if her track crisscrossed the wind in the manner of a serpent.

Food was plentiful. Out on the coast there were shallows thick with crabs the size of a battle shield and great waddling tubes of flesh and fat that sunned themselves on sandbars and coastal rocks, the fattest often at the top where they could bark at the lesser, but the commanding height just meant they were easily plucked up by a hungry dragonelle.

The exhaustion of flying became too great.

She found a reef-sheltered isle, in seas she guessed were too rough for the boats of men, and spent a dozen or more days happily in the hardy bush and wind-racked pines atop sheer cliffs, taking various multilegged, pincer-armed crawlers from the sea during the day and plucking the occasional barker at night from the sleeping beaches.

While resting there, she saw not one, but three dragons. The sight shocked her, after spending much of her lifetime without so much as a glimpse of her kind. To see not just one, but three, all at once and together, froze her for a moment. They flew almost wing-tip to wing-tip, a slightly smaller silver leading two big reds.

Wistala threw herself into the air, fringe high and stiff with excitement, flapping madly to gain altitude.

Wing-tips rose in unison as they glided. They must have marked her. All turned gently for a better look.

That was when she noticed the riders.

It was so like horses, she glided for a moment, losing altitude, stunned. The dragons had reins, *reins!* running forward from the riders to the head and out to the leading wing bones.

Dragons fixed and ridden like horses had no appeal, and she didn't like the way they were coming around, spreading out a little.

She rolled on her back, dived, headed for the shoreline, where she wove around her plateau island and changed course a little southward so if they were moving to intercept, they might overshoot. She chanced a glance back and saw one of the riders was in difficulty; his dragon was circling oddly. The silver and its rider dived toward her, then came around in a great swoop, leading the other red, which could not match its turns. The pair headed to the aid of the other.

The last Wistala saw of them, as she plunged into the coastal forest, was the silver and undercommand red flanking the other as they turned back out to sea.

Summer days at the top of the world lasted forever.

Wistala saw patches of ground ice that must linger throughout the year, and inlets where glaciers flowed into the Inland Ocean. Heated by sun and perhaps current, the glaciers would groan and crack and send ice plunging into the water with a rumbling sound like a thousand thunderstorms.

Perhaps it was the rich sea diet, or all the exercise, but she found herself in the midst of another growth spurt and losing scales, despite her careful rationing of coin. But for all her loss of shining scale, her wings grew prodigiously, and she suspected that had she left them alone they would have uncased by themselves at this point.

She came to a marsh country, where the land looked like ocean, patterned into regular waves of higher ground mixed with wet patches below. Rabbits with oversize feet, herds of moss-antlered herbivores, packs of wolves, and little brush-tailed foxes thrived here, along with a few hardy humans who kept to the waterways in flat-bottomed boats.

The wind blew hard here, and Wistala used it. Every day she matched herself against the wind, once after the morning's hunt and again in the evening, every day fighting a little harder for speed, or height, or the length of time she could hang over one spot, gaining strength with each battle against the wind.

And met her second dragon here.

She spotted him while eating on one of the ridges—the wetter hollows were thick with mosquitoes, but the bugs couldn't cope with the wind on the hill humps—splashing through the wet, approaching her from land.

He looked wider than he was long, reminding her of a toad, and had rust-colored scales edged with white cracks and chips that struck her as unhealthy. He approached, nostrils sniffing her as if she were a dinner of venison, perhaps attracted by her smell or the blood.

"You are stranger, welcome," he said. It had been so long since she'd heard Drakine, it seemed more foreign a tongue than Elvish.

"UthBeeyan am I, dragon of the coldwinds. Which wind brought you?" He bobbed his head but kept his *sii* still. She guessed he meant no harm, but she left off eating so as not to be taken with a mouthful of bone.

His mind held nothing but hunger and an eager lust for her green flanks.

"Wistala am I, dragonelle of whatever winds may bear me. Are there many dragons in the coldwinds?"

"I drive away!" UthBeeyan said, which Wistala found easy to believe, as she was downwind of him. He let out sort of a croaking roar. "You hear my song, we mate now."

"We shall do no such thing," Wistala said.

He jumped at her and she backed up, putting her tail point in between his nose and her, ready to crack him across the soft spot between his eyes, but he settled onto her kill and took a mouthful. "You huntress worthy of spring wind. I take dragonshare. Find another."

Gladly, Wistala thought.

The weather turned cold, bitterly so, almost overnight, freezing the swampy areas and turning the soil on the hill hummocks hard. Snow blew some nights, but could only cling where the wind couldn't reach it, and Wistala returned to the rocky coastline. During the day everything turned a hard, uniform gray: water, shoreline, clouds, the sun at best a whitish circle behind mists.

She happened across a big boat, of all things, hugging the coast as it crept along south, a dwarf at the tiller and four men pulling the oars. All wore hides so thick, they looked like bears, save for the dwarf, who might be mistaken for one of the sausagelike barkers on the rocks, for his booted feet barely protruded from beneath his coat, looking like flippers.

More hides, entire bundles of them, were lined up in the center and bottom of the boat, along with strings of fox tails and what looked like wolf skins.

Swooping low, she saw the dwarf turn the boat for shore and lift a device that looked like an immense crossbow, wider of bow than she was high. She dropped into the water some distance away, upwind so her words might carry and any bolts fired would have to fight a stiff breeze. The cold, after its first shock, wasn't so bad.

"May I ask you a question?" she called across the water in Parl.

The dwarf startled, and the rowers bent over their oars and bowed and chanted and rattled strings of shells.

The dwarf lifted a speaking trumpet. "Question away, though I warn you, I've no coin."

"Do you know these lands, good dwarf?" she called.

"Know them? I love them, and will tell you why: Fools don't survive up here."

"I seek my kind. Are there dragons to be found?"

"None you wish to find," the dwarf said. "Wait! There are some decent dragons, though it is a long journey."

"Where?"

"East, over the Icespine and then across the plains a full two hundred *vesk* of journey. The Sadda-Vale. I've not been there in years, but once a goodly white dragon named Scabia ruled there with her kin and accepted some trade."

"What is the Icespine?"

"You may know them in the south as the Red Mountains. Cross them and from your heights you may just see the peaks beyond. The Sadda-Vale is pleasant, though rainy, but beware the trolls roaming outside it. They were thick there when last I visited."

"Thank you, good dwarf."

"Any news from the south?"

"Wars with barbarians, in Hypat's northern thane-doms," Wistala said.

"Ah. One's been building for a while. Luckily the Ya-yuit don't go in for such nonsense. Good day, dragon!" The dwarf thickened, and Wistala realized he had bowed. She dipped her head and swam for shore.

She went east with a serious storm, which forced her down to seek shelter in trees. It raged for two days, leaving her hungry and the land thick with snow. She followed a game trail down into a valley and found nothing to eat, save a dead bear frozen solid under a tree, which even her *foua* could achieve little against without burning the meat to uselessness. She picked at the bits of icy flesh, but it left her with sore teeth.

She flew east in the clear icy day, and came to a river. The local men—was there anywhere men did not go?—had chipped a hole in the ice and were smoking fish in a shack built next to the hole. They ran for a little cluster of huts standing in the shelter of a hill at the bank as she passed over, and so great was her hunger that she raided the smokehouse and gorged—even eating the poor iron fishhooks stored there. She broke the film of ice on the fishing hole and drank, then slept right on the ice, wrapped around the small fire keeping the smoke going, feeling as stuffed and pampered as though she were back in Rain-fall's steam-filled health room.

She awoke to chanting and the smell of burning fat.

Downwind on the iced-over river the locals were burn-ing a small fire, with a pot hung over it, and a tent pole stood next to it. When she raised her head, three contrap-tions went whizzing across the ice, pulled by dogs.

Wistala blinked the crusts of ice and snow out of her eyes and followed the smell, cold muscles only slowly warming to their work. There was no sign of a trap; indeed, if one could imagine a less likely place for a trap than a frozen river one had to put one's mind to it—but she still felt something was wrong. She probed the ice carefully before taking each step.

Back at the houses, the villagers were lined up along the river's edge, and she heard faint chanting.

Something moved at the pole, a little obscured by the waves of heat coming off the fire. She circled round, again carefully probing the ice.

A girl stood tied to the top of the pole, shivering in the wind. Pieces of dragonscale were fixed to its peak, in imitation of a flower. The stuff bubbling in the cauldron was hot fat, she could smell it clearly now. At the base of the pole were three dogs, old and scrawny looking, also chained to the pole. They were barking and trying to hide among each other at the same time.

Curious.

The girl was young, perhaps Lada's age when she was returned to Mossbell, and well coated with fragrant fats to keep the wind off her skin.

Or to make her more appetizing?

Wistala decided she was some sort of offering, perhaps a trade-off to keep the newly arrived dragon from raiding any more fish shacks. A dragon could destroy a village in other ways than eating the inhabitants or burning them out of their homes. What the dogs were for she couldn't imagine, unless they were meat to serve as an appetizer or dessert in the manner of the fancy tables Rainfall set.

The girl had her eyes closed, her face turned away, red hair—the only spot of color in the endless whites and grays in this land—whipping in the wind. Wistala reached up a claw and cut the bonds. She fell to her knees but made no attempt to escape.

"Go back to your people," Wistala said. The girl didn't move, probably not understanding Parl.

Wistala pushed her by the shoulder with her *sii*, and the girl finally came alive, struggling against her claws, pounding against her scales. Wistala knocked down the pole and stood on it with her other leg, as the dogs tried to run, still giving a whimpering bark now and then. Wistala put the girl's hand on the dog chains and broke them away from their fixture on the pole, and as she was pulled away in a shower of ice particles thrown up by the scrambling dogs, she looked at Wistala in wonder with bright green eyes.

After a quick taste to make sure it wasn't poisoned, Wistala tried the hot fat. Now *this* was a meal that readied one to face the winter winds again! She even ate the chains that suspended it over the fire before flying off, but sadly the kettle was too large to swallow.

One advantage of a cold wind is that it makes exercise a good deal more agreeable. Wistala managed to cross the line of mountains in a single day, thanks to a strong wind at her back shooting between the mountaintops. Then she was out over dry, treeless plains that she remembered from the day she and Auron had escaped up the chimney.

Only colder and more barren.

There was nothing to eat on the steppe-lands, as far as she could see. She saw some goats on the mountainside at a distance, but when she flew closer they disappeared, flowing into cracks and behind stones like water. No herds of sheep, no files of elk, just odd two-legged birds that could turn like a zephyr when she swooped in on them, running with bobbing heads and spiny feathers flying. She finally managed to brain one with her tail—by accident—as she pursued another, and got a thin, bony meal that was all skin, tendon, and feathers.

But she could see her objective in the distance, which gave her heart to go on through hunger.

She wondered what the trolls ate until she saw plots of torn-up earth around discreet holes in the turf.

The peaks weren't so high as the Red Mountains, and resembled dry rockpiles, with evenly layered lines stuck up this way and that, as though someone had broken up the upper world's crust. These mountains were thick with pine and littered with caves. She saw a few sheep with horns like helms and a huge wildcat or two, and smelled troll waste.

But she was now a match for a troll, unless one caught her unawares, and she had no intention of letting that happen. She watched the sides and floors of the canyon as she passed over trees, out of reach of even the longest troll arm from treetop below or concealing rock to the side.

Unfortunately, its attack came from above.

Later she visited the spot, and guessed where the troll had climbed when it saw her course. Perhaps it had been sitting on a high ledge, surveying the western slopes of the rock-strewn mountains, and climbed up a little farther when it saw her coming.

It was a good thing the sun was high when it jumped, for some piece of her noticed the shadow of its fall on the mountainside below, and she turned to avoid it before the rest of her figured out why. The hammer-blow of its arm therefore fell on her side rather than her wing or spine.

The troll grappled her with its awful rubbery fingers and she felt a tearing at her wing edge. She instinctively folded it down and out of the way, and her career through the mountains turned into a one-wing plunge into the stony slopes. She had just enough sense to roll over so the impact struck the troll—mostly—and her tail rather than more vital limbs.

The impact knocked the wind from her, and for a second she did not know where she was.

Fury took over when the troll's fingers locked around her neck, trying to twist, trying to throttle, and she clawed at it, but it moved with that horrible, rubbery mobility she remembered. She batted it about the body with her wings, and may have struck the sense organ cluster, for it backed off and swung up a rock, leaving smears of blood as it squeezed into a crack. She righted herself and spat her hunger-weak *foua* after it, but did not know if she hit it or not.

Fearing another sudden jump from above, or thrown boulders, she backed down the hillside, watching the black smoke of her fire disappear into the winter sky.

She flapped her wings experimentally. The right was sore but worked. She launched herself into the air and saw the troll wedging itself through a crack. It retreated beneath an overhang like a wary spider.

"Call it a new throw," Wistala said, using the slang of the Hypatian dice pits for when a bet is neither paid nor lost. She was breathing and unharmed, and wouldn't risk her wings going after a troll on a point of honor.

Her injuries allowed only a short flight before she had to stop and rest, but she made it to the other side of the mountains. From a prominence she looked out upon the Sadda-Vale.

The vale reminded her of a half-filled cauldron. Water filled the center of the valley, though unlike the Ba-drink, green flats and low hills surrounded the water. The water was calm and the color of polished steel, the grasses around a deep green that reminded her of seaweed. Forests grew in the spaces between the toes of the mountain.

Capping the cauldron were low-hanging clouds, made of mists rising from the water, or so it seemed from the sheets of moisture rising in slow spirals. The rock face on the inner ring of mountains was black with moisture. Wistala felt the cold wet on her face.

The temperature had risen considerably on this side of the mountain; Wistala no longer felt frozen and wind-struck, but simply chilled and damp. She didn't like this much wet in the air, it fed itchy growths that lived under your scales.

As she rested she counted waterfalls. It seemed every mountainside had a trickle or two running down, more easily spotted at a distance, as they cascaded between the thick fern growth—higher up they looked like faint veins against the rock face.

An orange flash caught her eye, a gout of flame that welled and slowly faded. The odd shape to it was evocative of a dragon's—no, there was a dragon there, on a ledge where the mountain was broken by a crack, like a smashed plate unevenly repaired.

So excited was she—hope died hard in Wistala—that

she immediately launched herself off the prominence, flying for the dragon as fast as sore wings would carry her.

The dragon—she saw it was a male by his distinctive coloring: a dull orange like a fading sunset that alternated with stripes of black. The pattern intrigued her; in her experience scaled dragons were usually uniform in color. Auron sometimes showed stripes like that against his gray, but he'd been born without scales.

She landed a little up the ledge from him—she folded her wings as she came in, absorbed the impact with her tail and settled with only a slight slip. She wanted the advantage of height just in case.

Though she thought it a well-done landing. But the dragon ignored her.

He nosed in a pile of broken rock, grasping pieces with his tongue and swallowing them. He had four horns, and two more buds, rising from his crest. Older than she, younger than Father, and there was a strange gold behind his *griff*: he had a ring threaded in the skin of his earhole.

He extended his long neck, took a big mouthful of water, then swung his neck to the other side, where the mountain face was broken. Wistala looked closely at the rock—there were threads of metal in the rock, like bits of ragged sewing.

The four-horn spat water into the broken rock. His head bobbed as he read distances, then he spat flame where he'd placed the water. The rock flamed and hissed, cracking, and with a suddenness that surprised her and made her edge back, he whipped up his tail and struck the flames. Pieces of broken rock slid down and hit the ledge, and he commenced nosing again, still ignoring her.

"I take it there's metal in that stone," Wistala said.

He swallowed a piece, and rolled an eye toward her as he sniffed over more shattered rock. "What is your name?"

"Wistala," she said.

"We don't know each other."

"No," she said. "May I have your name?"

"DharSii." He swallowed another stone.

The name struck her ear funny. If the word were rendered in the simplest form of Parl, a human would have called him "Sureclaw."

"Do you live here?" she asked.

He made a strange throat-clearing sound: *Ha-hem.* "As little as possible." He kept eyeing her leather carry-harness and the blue emblem at the base of her throat.

"How is the metal?"

"Adequate, though you have to eat a good deal for it to do any good. Cleansing, though."

He took another mouthful of water and spat it into the cracks in the rock face.

"I've come to find others of my—our kind." He said nothing in reply. "The water helps break the stone up, I take it."

"I doubt you'd understand."

Wistala felt her fringe rise a little. "I suppose when your *foua* strikes the water it vaporizes into steam. The sudden expansion in the confined space of the crack, combined with the heat, shatters the rock."

DharSii left off his mining and turned his head so he could fix her with both eyes. He seemed about to speak, his mouth opened anyway, shut again, and finally he said: "If your design is to meet the others, please follow." Then he launched himself off the mountainside and flapped away on wings long and thin that reminded Wistala of knife blades.

She couldn't say whether she'd been insulted or not, but she flew after him. He sailed off north, crossed the hills that Wistala noted held red, wide-horned, high-backed cattle, and was soon skimming the misty water of the vast lake. The lake was so wide, the trees upon the other side were an indistinct green smear; and so long to the south, the waters ate the horizon.

It felt distinctly warmer over the lake, and some of the mountains to the east smoldered from vents in their sides, adding to the overcast trapped between the mountains. The mist layer hanging above was tinged with green, gold, and even blue depending on the thickness of the murk and its nearness to the vents. Wistala saw more of the long-horned cattle with the mountainous humps projected up at the base of their necks. They grazed on the thick grass, stupidly oblivious of the dragons overhead.

Wistala caught up to DharSii, flying a little below—yes, he was scarred around the right pocket of his arm, and the outer toe was missing from his left *saa*. Not so scarred as Father, but not so old either. And his snout only showed the barest hints of white fangs—Father's had seemed permanently on display.

He rolled an eye toward her, and she felt embarrassed to be watching him, so she fixed her gaze ahead.

She marked a white construct of some kind on the northern shore, well above and back from the lake. Or was it some trick of geology? A spur of the mountain came down and divided, and from the divide on down the mountain was scored with white, far too regularly for the marks to be snow or ice.

The lake here steamed, tendrils of moisture danced across the smooth, clear water before dissipating into the chill. She saw a head rise from the water, dripping, and a golden dragon made a leisurely climb to a mushroom head of volcanic rock, where he scratched his belly on the stone and stretched out neck and tail with a bit of a yawn as his snout turned to the fliers.

Wistala dropped back a little, not knowing if there would be a battle between the dragons. Her striped companion paid the wet dragon no more attention than he did the fork-tailed birds zipping around the masses of rock. The stones here looked shaped, but to dragon proportions rather than hominid, progressing down into the water like irregular, broken steps.

Her guide continued on his way toward the point between the divided spur.

Closer now, Wistala could see a "garden" of thick thorn trees—she thought of it as a garden because it was, precisely edged both inside and out and regularly shaped, a great crescent with the points running up the outer edges of the divided mountain spur, thinning somewhat as they climbed the thin-soiled heights. The thorn trees were thick and intertwined, so it wouldn't be a matter of just cutting down trees, for they all supported and wound around each other; sever trunk from root and the rest would hang. She guessed a team of dwarves with axes could hack through it in a day or two—under a tasking leader—and it would be a remarkable thief who could negotiate that wall without becoming hopelessly lost or torn to pieces and waste much time backtracking out of blind alleys.

The thorn wall guarded a vast courtyard, almost as big as all of Mossbell's cultivated grounds, between the two mountain arms. Instead of wild cabbages and berry bushes, this plaza was paved with broken and irregular bits of masonry. Even the odd statue fragment of a hominid arm or face showed here and there, placed to fit between an old fountain rim or some unknown chunk of temple wall.

Two pairs of blighters walked here and there and swept up some long thin leaves fallen from the thorn trees. Judging from the size of the courtyard, when they finished they'd have to start all over again where they'd began.

She forgot the blighters as soon as she saw the arch.

The stone of the mountain had been formed and carved into a great gallery leading into the darkness between the spurs of the mountain, going up an interlacing like a woven basket of round reeds, meeting like snakes hooking at the neck. The stone had been carved so it evoked bones, or tree roots, or dragon tails, anything but dull and lifeless rock. It was supported both from the courtyard and the mountain ridge by pillars, all shaped to match the whole and etched with scale patterns. At the outer rim of the stony lattice there were holes big enough for a dragon to climb through, but the spacing grew tighter and tighter as it approached what looked to be a cave mouth, though the most regular and finished Wistala had ever seen.

It was wide enough for a dragon to fly into it and pick a comfortable, well-lit landing spot before the cave. DharSii glided in, widening and then slowly folding his wings as he alighted. Wistala tried to imitate him and made a clumsier landing, not expecting the smoothness of the courtyard paving. It wasn't a sprawl, but it could have been one if her tail didn't catch on a fortunately placed crack.

"Welcome to Vesshall," DharSii said, letting his *griff* give an elegant little flutter. "I will take you to the dragons within, but I shan't stay."

"Do you have enemies here?" she asked.

"You ask a lot of questions. Scabia will be delighted with you. Make your queries sound like praise, and you'll share endless hours of chatter."

A cave entrance, wide enough for two dragons to pass abreast, stood just above a ledge about the height of one human seated on another's shoulders. A ring of stones, chiseled and filled in with a black material like glass forming unfamiliar glyphs like thorns crossed and arranged, decorated the entrance.

"I don't know that script," Wistala said.

"It's the old iconography," DharSii said, rearing up to climb into the tunnel mouth. His tail gave a little twitch; perhaps he was pleased at her ignorance. "It reads 'Welcome is the dragon who alights in peace.' " They passed down a short passage, arched above to match the stone lattice outside, filled in with six-sided colored chips in all the colors of dragonhood, making patterns interlaced and winding above and beneath in such intricacy that Wistala wished she had an afternoon just to let her eyes travel the path.

But DharSii did not stop, but moved on into another cavern.

This one was vast and round, by far the biggest interior Wistala had ever been in. The far walls were so distant their old footfalls bounced back at them from the walls to join the fresh noises they made, waiting to take their turn to visit the other side of the cavern and return.

The convex ceiling curved high enough for Wistala to flap her wings and fly if she wished, and went up like an inverted bowl to a circular gap that admitted the outdoor light and aired the room. It wasn't big enough to fly out, she'd have to fold her wings to pass through it. A shallow pool of water stood under the skylight, and the floor under the light was much edged with bands of green copper, one of which the edge of splash of dim sunlight rode even now.

Around the walls of the cavern—or chamber, rather, for while there was mountain muscle to be seen there was no rock that was not shaped by artistry—long blocks of basalt stuck out of the wall, narrowing and rising to a softened point like an inverted dragon claw. At the far end, two scaly forms reclined.

Wistala saw more blighters at work beneath the smaller, scrubbing the tiled floor.

DharSii struck off straight across the floor toward the pair and Wistala followed, hearts hammering. The place smelled of dragons, rainwater, and fresh air; she relished every breath, took it in through her nostrils and clamped them so the homey smell might never escape.

There were still dragons in the world, not skulking and hiding but living in grandeur and peace!

At their approach the blighters carried off their implements, flattened and squeezed themselves through a thin gap at the base of the wall like escaping mice before a prowling tom.

They caught her eye only because of the motion. The two dragons on the jutting lofts of rock had her attention.

Both were dragonelles, one rather undersize, her green scales pale and almost translucent, well formed of limb though in a delicate way that suggested little in the way of gorge or exertion.

The other was a white dragonelle, formidably huge and perhaps a bit more massive than DharSii. Wistala had the odd sensation of knowing her without having ever been introduced, probably some vague echo of a mind-picture from Mother. But there was, yes, a half-familiar shape to her short, proudly curved snout, the challenging arc of her eye ridge . . . Her scales had thinned a bit around her jawline and above her eyes, the flesh sagged in a little where her *saa* met her spine; she was a dragonelle of long years but still formidable.

"I bring a visitor, Damesister." It took Wistala a moment to work out the relationship; she'd only heard the

word once before from her Father in one of his battle-
stories . . . a man or a dwarf would have said *aunt*. "I hum-
bly present Wistala, a dragonelle out of the south, who
seeks *ha-hem* succor and solace."

I never said that, Wistala thought.

The striped dragon turned to her. "Wistala, this is Scabia, Archelle of the Sadda-Vale, and her daughter Aethleethia, my *ha-hem* beautiful *uzhin*."

Both dragonelles fluttered their *griffs* at Wistala with
that same bird-wing delicacy. Wistala thought she should
fit in and tried to imitate it, but her *griff* rattled off her
scale, and the dragonelles glanced at each other.

The white dragon extended her nose just a little and
sniffed the air in Wistala's direction, her pink eyes as cold
as the glaciers Wistala had passed over.

"Will you not make her welcome?" DharSii said, and
Wistala liked him a little better.

"Who were your sire and dame?" Scabia asked.

"AuRel of the line of AuNor and his mate Irelia."
Wistala decided to make her introduction formal, and
spoke as Mother taught: "I was first daughter and fourth
out of the five eggs."

"Ah," Scabia said. "I thought I recognized your wing-
points. I knew your mother somewhat. You are how long
out of the egg?"

"These thirteen winters."

"And already wide-winged! I'm amazed."

Aethleethia extended her long neck and scratched herself under the chin with the claw tip on her loft, and Dhar-
Sii turned away to inspect a piece of iconography etched
on the floor in a manner similar to that ringing the entrance. He brushed away some dust with his tail so that the
black glass might shine.

A shadow darkened the splash of outside light and the
golden dragon dropped through with wings folded. He
opened them again with dramatic suddenness and alighted.
"Ah-ha! A visitor!" he trumpeted, folding his wings.

"*Ha-hem*," DharSii said, his eyes and nostrils half-
closed. "Wistala, you meet the dragonlord of Vesshall,

NaStirath." A certain airiness highlighted the words, but
what he meant to imply, if anything, Wistala couldn't
guess, not knowing him well.

"My daughter's mate," Scabia added.

NaStirath loosed a short but loud *prrum* in the general
direction of Aethleethia's place. The lord of Vesshall was
a finely formed fellow, long and well fed, not a scar on him
or a scale out of place, and he smelled of steam and hot
scale, being fresh out of the lake.

He spoke: "Just like you, DharSii, to guide a female
over me without an introduction. Don't tell me you're finally courting a mate."

"I hope not!" DharSii said. "Too wide of wing, and her
tail is so much longer than her neck."

The arrogant, two-colored—

"My dear *uzhin* always gives an honest opinion," Aethleethia put in. "It startles those who are not much used to
him."

"*Ha-hem.* I'll be about my business," DharSii said. He
fluttered his *griff,* but when Wistala met his eyes, fire bladder pulsing, he looked away. He turned and made for the
entrance.

The tap of his claws played off the walls as he crossed
the chamber.

"Two visits to the Vesshall from DharSii in one winter,"
NaStirath said. "I feel *so* honored, I'm having a hard time
not yawning."

"Tell us your troubles, dragonelle of AuNor, so that we
may comfort you," Scabia suggested.

"I'm the last of my family," Wistala said. *Was that quite
true? The copper still lives, for all you know.* "Dwarves of
the Wheel of Fire slaughtered them and took from their
bodies as trophies. Elves and men were also involved, but I
cannot say which for certain. One called the Dragonblade
was almost certainly aiding them in the assassination."

"We've heard this before," NaStirath said, in a bored
tone as if to indicate he was not much troubled at the news.

"We are sorry for your loss," Scabia said, though she
was the only dragon in the room that much looked it, for

nothing remained of DharSii unless he lurked still in the shadows of the entrance passage. "You may claim a loft here for as long as you like; there are ample to spare."

"I heard they got CuSanat and his mate, Virtuthia, in their cave as well," NaStirath said, stretching. "Such a shame we won't be seeing them again, even if they weren't exactly *uzhin.* The Red Mountains are being quite cleared of dragons. Is it bullock again for dinner, or fish?"

Wistala wasn't sure she was hearing right. Did these fools not realize—?

"We must take vengeance on these assassins!" Wistala blurted.

"I've no dead to avenge," NaStirath said. He climbed into a loft on the other side of Scabia. Odd that he didn't sit to the side of his mate—

"Be quiet, NaStirath," Scabia said, pronouncing his name in a way that labeled him still a wingless juvenile. "And have some feeling for our guest's sorrow."

"I shall achieve both through a nap, where I will dream awful, sorrowful dreams," NaStirath said, closing his eyes. "I rejoice in your survival and arrival, Wistala of the line of AuNor." He twitched his *griff* as he turned on his side.

Wistala remembered how Father had once caught Auron sleeping on his side, and though her brother was scaleless, punished him with a series of roars that left the hatchling quivering.

"Rest your wings," Scabia said. "Pick any loft, and wait for your nostrils to waken you."

Wistala crossed the room to be away from the others and climbed into one of the giant projections. One could arrange one's body so the head and tail were at almost any height for comfort. She hated Vesshall a little less, and slept.

Her nostrils did wake her, as the blighters brought out huge platters of pan-fried fish and dumped them before the three dragons, with much falling to the knees and arm-waving with palms held toward the dragons. Only the faintest light came down from the circle in the center of the ceiling.

Wistala felt horribly stiff from the troll fight even as she wondered why DharSii didn't join his relatives for dinner. Not that she cared to see him, of course, only that his absence struck her as odd.

She crossed over to the others.

More platters of fish arrived and Scabia pointed with her tail toward Wistala, shook it three times, and they made a mountain of cooked, blackened fish before her.

"It's quite safe," Scabia said. "The blighters look to us for protection from the trolls, and of course the other races of the world who have superceded them."

Wistala ate, but the charm of prepared food was nothing like that of Mossbell, with lively conversation and the friendly banter with Widow Lessup about the cooking. She felt like a pig at a trough.

"How many trolls have you killed, lord?" Wistala asked NaStirath.

"Hmmmmm. Killed? I set one aflame once and he made quite a spectacle rolling back to the mountains, but I don't care to close and kill. Awful, the stench of trolls. I'm not sure that burning improves the odor."

"I know DharSii has killed several," Aethleethia said. "Every time he does it, the blighters talk of nothing else for moons."

"Keen on sports, my good *uzhin* is," NaStirath said with a belch. "Shall we have molasses elixir tonight, to celebrate our happy arrival?"

"No," said Scabia firmly.

"Why do you care so little for the fates of other dragons?" Wistala asked.

The other three stared at her.

"Now see and hear, thirteen winters," Scabia said. "You're a guest, and welcome as long as you will be accommodating, but I don't want challenges or lectures and twaddle about what we must and must not do, or you'll find me a terrible enemy who'll drive you from this home cave with fire and tooth and claw. This vale is safe and distant, and those wise enough to stay here do well. As to other dragons' affairs, we keep out. It was a lesson dearly learned. My father? Dead. My brother? Dead. My mate? Dead. My sons? All dead. DharSii only just survived out there, was even a captive once, and it seems every time he crosses the mountain ring or goes down the river, he comes back with a new scar.

"We give no cause to the Ironriders or the wildhairs or the blighter bands on the steppe to feel aggrieved, and the trolls on the outer slopes of these mountains keep other hominids from the so-called civilized lands at bay. I don't look for trouble in the wider world, and the wider world comes for no trouble here. Am I making myself understood?"

"Perfectly," Wistala said. In different circumstances, would she have become Scabia?

"Oh, I don't care for this sort of talk," Aethleethia said. "Now let us have a pleasant game to aid the digestion. Wistala, how are you at add-a-couplet? We have a poem about dancing gems that is quite without a decent end."

Wistala woke to the sound of dragon claws on the floor below her loft. She came instantly awake, but it was only Scabia, with NaStirath fidgeting behind.

There was a little light, but just a little, coming in from the ceiling hole.

"Good morning, Wistala," Scabia said. "I came to say that I regret some of my words from last night—no, don't apologize."

Wistala wasn't about to. "You're most kind," she said, which was true, to a point. She'd been foolish to seek an alliance with other dragons.

"I'm really here to ask you if you wish to stay, to live with us," Scabia said.

"It is quite the most marvelous home cave," Wistala said, watching blighters clean up dragon waste about the pool.

"We would like you to be *uzhin*," NaStirath said.

"Wistala, I am like my *uzhin* DharSii in that I've no patience for disguise. My beloved daughter is the best of dragons but barren, and I would have hatchlings in this cave again."

Wistala stiffened.

"Don't look alarmed, I'm not asking for you to take wing on a mating flight now," Scabia said. "Nor even call any male here your lord. NaStirath is a fine dragon and would sire strong hatchlings. You would have a home and honor and, yes, even precious metals here for the rest of your moons if you would leave a few clutches for Aethleethia to sing over and raise as her own. Don't look so shocked—it was not an uncommon practice in ancient Silverhigh. You're obviously healthy; I've never seen such thick scale on a maiden before, more like that of your grandsire AuRye, who was always stuffing himself with well-armored dwarves and golden hilts from broken battleaxes. I will condescend to say that such a famous line will improve the blood around here."

Scabia cast a pointed glance back at NaStirath.

She'd always meant to keep her promise to Father; in fact, she'd dreamed of a clutch of restless eggs last night for some reason, but this, this— "Unnatural," she said. "It would be unnatural."

"No more unnatural than a dragon wearing hominid jewelry and a carrying harness," Scabia said. "Were you born with that icon on your fringe, perhaps? Or growing up among hominids, as I suspect you did. Tell me I guess wrongly."

"I . . . ," Wistala said, groping for words. "I didn't come here to find a mate."

"Is it a song you want?" NaStirath put in. "I know one or two:

> *"There once flew a maiden of AnFant*
> *Whose mind was as pure as her vent*
> *But when—"*

"You're not helping your cause, NaStirath," Scabia

said, again employing the juvenile—deservedly so, Wistala thought.

Scabia turned those faintly pink eyes back on her. "Now, dear, we shall have breakfast soon. Let's have you join us for a few more meals and we'll speak no more of this while you recover from your fatigues and hurts. Get to know my darling Aethleethia, and I'm sure you'll come to feel, as I do—"

"I must go," Wistala said, hopping from her loft and running for the exit. Grand, Vesshall was, but it was also hollow. Hollow of honor, hollow of feeling, hollow of—

She almost bowled DharSii over as she sprang out the tunnel mouth, leaped from the ledge, and spread her wings beneath the stone canopy that suddenly seemed as dreadful as the thorn garden below. He began to say something, but Wistala didn't hear the words in her eagerness to get away, flying south as fast as she could.

Chapter 24

I s this a joke?" Ragwrist said.

Wistala sat with him in the equestrian theater, a riding arena outside Hypat, where his riders practiced during winter camp.

She'd come south in easy stages, keeping to the west side of the Red Mountains and not raiding livestock. She slept only on the loneliest hilltops, and drank snow she melted with her *foua*, with an eye to avoiding the barbarians. In this way she made a long and ultimately fruitless search of the Red Mountains, even passing into the southlands and the borders of the Empire of the Ghioz, without meeting another of her kind, finding nothing but bats and bears and a horrid troll or two in likely caves. If any dragons did lurk there still, they were being quiet about it.

I am but one, and my enemies can't be numbered. I shall have to improvise. Perhaps the Dragonblade and the dwarves have a weakness only one familiar with their habits could exploit. Cunning is required, treachery even. What would Prymelete do?

"It would be a terrible risk," Ragwrist said after she outlined what she wanted him to do. They'd gone to some trouble to find a place where they could talk quietly. The new apprentice fortune-teller, Intanta's great-granddaughter Iatella, had been hanging about getting an eyeful of Wistala and peering at her through the crystal shard. Though she was a skinny little girl, Wistala didn't like being overheard, even by someone almost small enough to be gulped down in one swallow.

"I know. If the dwarves suspect me, they will kill me at once. And they know how to do it. I've seen the proof."

Ragwrist did not ask her to elaborate.

"No, I don't mean that. This Fangbreaker fellow is offering me so much money for you, I can retire to an estate and sell the circus to pay for the finest velvet cushions for my sore feet and sit-upon. I am afraid to trust myself. Especially since if your plot does not come off, I shall have made a powerful and implacable enemy."

"You may always plead ignorance and desperation brought by poverty," Wistala said. "You've had ample practice."

"You're getting as cynical as Brok. Where is the kindly green giant I once knew?"

"Still freezing her tailvent shut in the north, perhaps. Ah, I shall trust you. Perhaps my fate can balance out your desire to become a landlord like your brother."

"Canny of you to mention him. But remember, elves have no particular feeling for their siblings, and evoking his memory awakes in me no desire to help avenge him. All I want to do is forget that unpleasant night."

"Odd that you would send money to Lada to help her get Rayg back, then. Yes, I've been to the Green Dragon Inn and heard the latest from Forstrel. He's raising bees for Lessup's honey-mead now, near an old cave I sometimes use, and complained much of the share Hammar demands from all production. He also told me that you paid out of your pocket to fix some of the damaged houses. And that you raked the old ferry-bell out of the ruins and kept it."

"Rumor, rumor, rumor. I'm interested only in facts and expenses and how much I might get from the dwarves for you."

"I shall ask you to drive a harder bargain than you know. I want several conditions on the sale, all in the interest of my health, of course. Is Brok still with you?"

"Of course."

"I need him to forge a very stout collar for me, something that even a troll couldn't break."

"What, so that the dwarves may better chain you? Suppose you wish to break away and escape?"

"I didn't say that I wanted to break it. I just want to be able to open it."

Wistala stood in her new collar at the Ba-drink landing, a tiny escort of circus folk with her.

They'd set up a tent around her, specially sewn for the purpose, purple and patterned with powerful symbols, for she came to the Wheel of Fire dwarves not as an abject slave, but a great treasure, one to be guarded and protected and honored.

Wistala listened to the spring melt pouring over the dam spill and waited.

The collar itself was a thick ring of steel, leathered at the inside and edges, with two forged-steel loops, one at the top and one at the bottom, for the attachment of chains, though only the tiniest wisp of azure blue silk bound her to a silver peg in the floor. There was no latch or spot for a key, and if you ran your hands around the inside only hardened leather met your fingers. Only Wistala knew where, if you opened the stitching, you could insert a claw point and open the lock, which then left only a false weld to break before the collar fell away.

At last she heard the creak of oars in their locks, and shouts and orders and calls of dwarf voices.

"King Fangbreaker comes. Sound the trumpets! Beat the drums!"

If you're patient enough, and keep still out of sight and smell, the prey will feed itself right to you. . . .

Something took off with a whistling whoosh and exploded far overhead. Wistala guessed it to be a firework. A thundering tattoo broke out on the drums, it sounded like boulders coming down the mountains, and the trumpets pealed so high and clear, it was like sunshine had been turned to music.

Wistala, hearts hammering, waited for the audience.

The tent flap opened, letting in a little fresh air that Wistala welcomed, as Ragwrist was having incense burned to abate the dragon-smell for the honored guests.

"Winged, as you see. And a little grown, a little more appetite at mealtimes, but the same Oracle," Ragwrist said as he ushered three dwarves in. Wistala saw prostrate dwarves outside, who looked as though they'd been felled or struck by sleeping spells.

Wistala noted the changes in him even as the mighty dwarf looked her over.

Gobold Fangbreaker wore a silver mask now, emblazoned with a four-pointed star, two slits for his eyes and two more beneath flanking the ridges of the star, whose shining points extended beyond the dull plate of the mask. Below, his beard had swirling designs of gold and silver dust worked into it, and a golden cord bound it into a tuft at the bottom from which hung a piece of glass Wistala guessed to be a magnifier. He was somewhat thinner but still broadly built, in a cuirass of silver and leather cushioning, oddly like her own steel collar in its padding, only with more elaborate flourish down the centerline, evocative of spear heads. King Fangbreaker now wore purple caping at back and throat and sash.

The most obvious difference, though, was the absence of his right leg. An inverted half skull—Wistala guessed it to be a hominid's, though she knew not what branch had such strangely long fangs and a ridge at the temples that almost resembled horns—capped the missing limb at the knee. Projecting out of this and running to the floor was a rod of white crystal, like lightning frozen into immobility. A mundane steel-shod horse hoof at the base gave him some stability on the ground.

He still wore the helm capped with dragon fangs, only

now overlarge horn-tips projected from its sides, gilded and filigreed.

Evidently the crown of Masmodon still eluded him.

Behind King Fangbreaker stood two more dwarves, one bearing a tall banner he had to dip somewhat to fit in the tent. It was the old ruby-tipped staff Fangbreaker had carried before, only now grown and with a crossbar added at the top to support a small purple banner, and the ruby was the perch of a stern-looking brass eagle. The other dwarf lugged chests and bags tied on either side of a steel shoulder pole.

Wistala dipped her snout until it almost touched the ground. "I see changes in you, Gobold Fangbreaker. Did my oracle come true, or have you come for my head and claws?"

Why, why, why did you say that? It sounds like a challenge—

"Hmpf," King Fangbreaker said. "I come to do this, though there are many who will swear, when the tale is told, that it is an impossibility."

He approached her and threw his strong arms about her neck, and patted her three times with his right hand hard enough to make her scales clatter.

"Yes!" King Fangbreaker said. "So happy am I that I embrace you like a sister! For no sister ever gave brother such encouragement as you gave me. You set my heart afire as though you had spat flame into it! And look!" He cast his arms wide and lifted his purple robes. "Results speak louder than any words."

He spun on his horse hoof, then stepped over to Ragwrist. "Elf, let us settle the accounting. Name your price, and if it's her weight in silver, I'll melt every plate and goblet on both sides of the Titan bridge to meet it." He turned back to Wistala. "I do not come to buy you, Oracle, but to *free* you. I would not have one who has done such service choking in the wake of gargant flatus." He extracted a knife from his sleeve with such speed that it almost looked as though it had grown there and moved to cut the blue silken cord.

"No, I beg you, mighty king," Wistala said. "That twist could be broke at the slightest pull. I would keep it as a souvenir of happy journeys under the kindest of masters."

"I've never known a dwarf to begin negotiations at such a disadvantage as saying 'name your price,'" Ragwrist said. "I'm quite befuddled. But if that is the case, the negotiations shall be brief. I seek only assurances as to her treatment."

"Treatment!" King Fangbreaker said. "She may go where she likes. But if she will reside with the Wheel of Fire, she'll want for nothing as long as I have voice to call for it to be brought to her. I would ask only her counsel in return."

"Let us adjourn to my tent, if you will accept my hospitality, great king," Ragwrist said. "It would be unseemly to name a price before the object of the negotiations, methinks."

"Elves and their protocols. Of course, Circusmaster, of course, but I am tempted to simply behead all present and free the dragon."

"My king, no!" Wistala said.

King Fangbreaker laughed. "I joke, of course. Let's get this over with, Ragwrist. It's too nice a day for tents and incense."

The party left, and Wistala sagged. Her spine had been tightening, her body closing on itself like a telescope all through the audience, yet she could not account for her fear.

"Shall I read your fortune?" a tiny voice squeaked.

Wistala looked down to see Iatella crouching between brazier and piles of pillows, cradling Intanta's old, saucer-shaped crystal in her lap as though it were a very fat doll. The girl was on the fire-keeping staff and had come along to work the camp kitchen and get road experience.

"Certainly. Practice away," Wistala said.

The little girl stood before her gravely, then knelt, all seriousness as is the manner of hominid children when hard at play. She drew designs around the crystal, then found something wrong with its placement, and inclined it a little so it faced her better.

"I see tragedy in your life," Iatella said.

This was no great secret to anyone with knowledge of Ragwrist's circus, but it showed the girl had some skill, for you always wanted to start out on firm footing.

"Wonderful," Wistala said. "I'm most impressed."

"Elves, dwarves, men—you have seen a good part of the Hypatian Empire," Iatella went on, pulling at her lip in thought.

"Amazing," Wistala said.

"Birds, too," she added. "Birds and death."

How . . . Where was she going with this?

"I see you. Something in shadow, a dragon with a scarred face the color of an old soup-pot. And one of many colors, turned white as snow. You thought him dead when he turned white."

How was this possible. *Auron?* How on earth could she know about Auron, or that morning on the mountainside she thought him frozen to death?

"Oh," she said, and her voice was no longer that of a little girl, but something older and croakier than even Intanta. "A terrible reckoning. Three dragons, opposition, and the fate of worlds in the balance."

And then she screamed, such a scream that it seemed to shoot right through Wistala's body, the tent, the soil itself, and fainted.

A circus dwarf, one of Brok's staff, and a pair of the Wheel of Fire dwarves rushed into the tent.

"What happened?" the circus dwarf asked, after a dwarvish expostulation from the others.

"We were playing a game. I coughed," Wistala said. "I think it frightened her."

They patted Iatella on the cheek, and her eyes fluttered open. She claimed no memory of what caused her to faint, and picked up her crystal and fled.

Ragwrist entered next, and the same questions were asked and answered. The dwarves wandered back out, leaving her and Ragwrist alone. "No matter. The bargain was easily struck. You have been 'freed' by the generosity of King Fangbreaker, Wistala," he said, untying the azure band of silk.

"Dare I ask the price?"

"I kept it low, saying that his good opinion would one day be worth more to me than any gold, and he looked pleased, though I think sometimes dwarves wear those masks as much to hide their emotions when bargaining as to keep out the light. I or others may visit you at any time, though the dwarves, as always, hold the right to decide who will be admitted to their city, and you are free to fly as you will. But I wonder. He told me to strike off your collar, by the way. All that effort wasted."

"Ragwrist, you are good to run this risk," Wistala said, quietly.

"Ha!" he said, patting her shoulder, and her scales were happy to have a memory to replace the embrace of King Fangbreaker. "You still hold Mossbell's lands, should true Hypatian law ever be reestablished across Whitewater. It's the land I've got my eye on. So having let you know my true motive, will you take this last opportunity to turn back? This is no arguing council of dwarves. If Fangbreaker senses a threat, he will deal with you . . . harshly."

Wistala ran her tongue along her teeth. "Then I will share the fate of my family."

She crossed the Ba-drink in splendor, on the dwarves' largest cargo-barge, pushed and pulled by smaller barges filled with lines of rowers.

The blue silk stood in place of her collar, the long sash tied loosely so as not to grate on her scales more than was unavoidable. Her little triangular diadem of the librarians dangled at the front of her fringe, sparkling in the mountain sun.

King Fangbreaker stood beside her as they approached the Thul's Hardhold and Tall Rock. Tall Rock stood sheer-sided all around where it met the finger of water, but Thul's Hardhold climbed more gradually like some sort of fantastic staircase. Only to the east, where it faced

Tall Rock across the Titan bridge, was it as sheer as its companion.

Sheer or not, the sides of the rock were cut with galleries and balconies, precarious outer stairways, even gardens beneath jutting stonework houses holding still more balconies and galleries.

And every one was lined with cheering crowds of dwarves, dropping dried flowers (or bits of torn paper or waxen wrapping if they could not afford flowers) as they passed across the water between the Hardhold and the Rock.

"Not a dwarf lives that doesn't aspire to a balcony of his own so that he might take fresh air and skylight," King Fangbreaker said, waving vaguely to the crowds. "We value it more than the elves, since many of us see so little of it. Some add gold leaf to the railings, but I prefer the natural look of traditional sedimentary stonework, don't you?"

"I'm overcome," Wistala said, flowers and bits of paper catching all over her scales and gathering in the folds of her wings. The rock walls to either side seemed to be coming together at the top, closing like a pair of vast jaws. But it had to be a trick of eye and distance, she'd seen their shape from across the Ba-drink.

"Now, a tour of what your advice gave me the courage to break loose, like a gem in a mine wall," Fangbreaker said as the barge docked. They tied to a wharf next to a cave with water flowing out of it. "Had we taken the royal barge, we might have gone right in, but I fear all you would have to do is scratch your ear and you'd capsize it."

More dwarves threw themselves on their faces and another firework shot up between the sheer cliff faces as King Fangbreaker hopped onto the wharf. The cheering didn't stop until he took a short set of stairs up and entered a wide gallery. Court officials—at least, that was what Wistala guessed them to be, for they wore cockades of purple—met him on the stairs, approaching with a sort of permanent, cringing bow and rose only to speak quietly into his ear.

"Yes, yes, I'll attend to that later," he said, passing through the herd of bent dwarves. They clustered and swirled about him so that Wistala was reminded of bloodsucker bats in the hotforests around Adipose attempting to latch on to a fast-moving bullock.

Fangbreaker led the swarm around corners and came to a cavern bridge inside, where a narrow crack leading up to the top of the Hardhold inside had its walls thick with mosses and clinging ferns. Water ran down the sides of the rock in a thousand tiny trickles to a sea of ferns below.

"Thul's Garden," King Fangbreaker said, passing over a short wide bridge. Wistala tested it with a *sii*. "Oh, come now, Oracle," Fangbreaker said. "This is dwarf work of the highest order. We could stack dragons all the way to the sky above on this little bridge."

There were dwarves in blackened steel at the opposite end of the bridge, with tufts of purple-dyed fur at boot-top and helmet lining. King Fangbreaker used the guards to shake off the courtiers, the way a whale of the Inland Ocean's cold north might use a rock to scrape barnacles from its belly.

Wistala passed over the short bridge, her head already in the passage beyond before her tail-tip left the gap behind.

He went up another short, wide flight of stairs, luckily for Wistala, then turned a corner where dwarves in soft leather shoes opened a set of double wooden doors. Wistala just squeezed through into a room about the size of the presentation tent where she'd awaited the dwarf that morning.

A huge, polished black table that looked like it had been carved out of the mountain itself stood in an oval of curved marble walls. There was a great deal of writing chiseled into the walls, and more on columns that had evidently been added to the room. Wistala counted twenty oddly shaped chairs around the table, draped in black velvet so that their spikiness was softened and hidden.

"Oh, the years I sat at this table, arguing over nothings," King Fangbreaker said, gripping the table as though he wished to lift and overturn it. "Motions, countermotions, oppositions, reconciliations, none of them worth a pot of passed water. The war with the de-men was being lost on the darkroads, and all we could do was sputter at each other. Until—after your words—I took control.

"I said what was needed was a King with the Old Powers to forge our divided houses into a single spear." He pointed with a finger at a notch in the table. "That's where Barzo put down his fist in a Rock of Opposition. So I whipped up my sleeve-ax and cut it right off. Arterial blood all over the meeting notes. The others fell into line once I rolled his head down the table. Gnaw, what a day. Felt light as a feather after. Follow me."

As she bowed to let him pass back to the doors she lifted one of the velvet coverings to the chairs, wondering if they hid bloodstains, and was aghast to see green dragonscale. She suddenly realized what the unused velvet hid—dragon claws, opened and digits bent so the dwarves might lean in comfort against stiffened *sii* and *saa*.

She gulped down a sickening mixture of sadness, rage, and regret, and fixed her gaze on Fangbreaker's back. One short jump and—

But these chairs had stood around this table since long before Fangbreaker, most likely.

The king brushed more of the soft-shoed dwarves aside. "Oh, it's as if I've no staff at all," he grumbled, and led her to a tall, narrow hall, sort of an echo of the garden they'd bridged before.

There were paintings all over the smoothed wall, some old and flaking, some almost unrecognizable, but he led her to a new one, so broad it partially covered two others of dwarves linking arms, or shaking hands, or pointing in various directions and talking. The new painting depicted some sort of ghastly underground fight in hip-deep water, with canoes like hollowed-out trees filled with dwarves firing crossbows at blighters and other hominids with what Wistala took to be exaggerated evil features.

"The Battle of Domlod," King Fangbreaker said. "I wasn't actually riding the outside of one of the ramkaks, mind you, which is a fine way to get your head knocked off, but artists do insist on their frills and flourishes for dramatic effect. Lost my leg but won the war, and the de-men will be giving us no more trouble on the darkroads."

He let her admire it for a moment, and as they stood in silence one of the black-armored guards, this one with a purple half-cloak covering his shoulders, approached noisily and spoke in Fangbreaker's ear.

"Oh, I lost track of the time," King Fangbreaker said. "If the barge is already out, let's not keep the crowds waiting. Come, Oracle. By the way, do you have a name?"

"Those close to me call me Tala," Wistala said. "I would be glad to hear it from you, King." *For the best place to strike an enemy is close enough to gut,* as Father used to say.

"Very well, Tala, up the Hall of Invention and to the balcony over Thul's tomb."

They passed along another wide hall with many short antechambers, each filled with devices of metal and steel and cable, some even in motion, though whether it was to amuse or accomplish something Wistala could not say. She saw daylight ahead at the opening of a very finely wrought gallery atop a huge slab of solid red granite that read THUL in both Elvish and Hypatian scripts. There were other icons and scriptings, as well, though she did not know the tongues.

Curving stairs ran up the sides of the tomb to the gallery above. Dwarves in splendid cloaks and caps were already gathered there, and bowed low but did not throw themselves to the floor as King Fangbreaker climbed up to join them.

Not a few looked at her in wonder as she approached, but most of the others jostled for a place next to the king at the balcony rail, draped with purple velvet, Wistala noted.

She climbed atop Thul's coffin and some of the dwarves leaned their heads together at that, eyes heavily shaded, but most were still throwing elbows and hip-blocking to gain or keep a position near Fangbreaker at the rail.

Wistala looked out and down at the finger of water running between Thul's Hardhold and Tall Rock. A small barge looked to be fixed just downstream—if current flowed in the lake—from the Titan bridge where a crowd, but nothing like the crowd at the King's barge trip, had gathered to watch events.

"None at Vassa's balcony, you see, my mighty king," one of the dwarves said in Fangbreaker's ear.

Wistala didn't know which was Vassa's balcony, and didn't care. She looked down the sheer side of rock at the barge. A dwarf, shorn of his hair and beard and stripped to a loincloth, was staked out in the daylight, no mask on his face. It looked as though he had something wrapped around his head, but it was at the mouth level.

Five dwarves in black capes, with black great-axes, stood around him, at each limb and the head.

A dwarf on the Titan bridge was reading from a scroll box, but Wistala didn't understand the words.

"What is this?" she asked Fangbreaker. A long neck had its advantages for reaching over crowds.

"Justice. That fellow spoke against me in his guild hall. Dozens of ears heard it; there's no doubt as to his guilt. Oh, the poor fool. It's like a madness; it's struck some of the best families with balconies on the Ba-drink."

"He's gagged?" Wistala asked as the ax-men, at some signal, lifted their blades.

"We used to let them say last words, but it led to tedious and insulting speeches. Now we open their mouths and give them just enough time to scream."

The dwarf at the staked-out figure's head nodded at some signal from above, and bent to remove the gag. Wistala heard a shout in Dwarvish from the staked-out man, and Fangbreaker thumped the balcony rail.

In quick succession the ax-man at his right arm brought down his blade, severing the limb, and four regular strikes followed on the stained wooden deck of the barge. The assorted bits danced a little, like landed fish.

Some cheering broke out, loudest at the king's balcony, or so it seemed to Wistala's ears. She wondered what his limbs might be used for, but they were simply dumped in the Ba-drink.

"A traitor's burial," one of the lordly dwarves said in Parl, perhaps wanting to please the king by explaining.

"Hmpf," King Fangbreaker said. "Dismembered and dead in five tics. And with his last words he called me brutal!"

Chapter 25

The dwarves took her across the Titan bridge to the sloping top of Tall Rock and established her in the second-highest tower there. The only higher tower was that of the watch-guild, who kept the time of the hour-bells and looked for riders at each end of the pass through secret optics.

She found herself in the care of a blighter slave named Yellowteeth. Yellowteeth indeed possessed oversize incisors the color of dried hay, top and bottom. He kept them polished by dipping his finger in ash and rubbing his teeth, then rinsing his mouth out with water.

He grumbled a good deal in Parl, for the dwarves spoke their tongue only among themselves and taught few its secrets, save for a claw-count of pleasantries and greetings and oaths that were public knowledge anyway.

She soon learned that the dwarves used three different languages, and not surprisingly to anyone who has spent much time around dwarves, ranked them.

The lowest was Parl, the language of servants, slaves, and those who engaged in commerce. Above that was Dwarvish, "the golden letters that unite us all," according to a dwarf-philosopher Wistala had read somewhere or other. The dwarves of the guilds spoke specialized dialects—there seemed to be guilds for everything, from armor-making to woodworking. Wistala even heard whispers of a Guild of Assassins—she guessed the Dragonblade headed that one. The choicest and most talented dwarves studied the high language, that of mathematics, according to dwarvish legend the only remnant of the perfect world that existed before darkness filled the holes.

Her tower had once been an observatory. Like the council chamber she was trying to forget, writing covered the walls, at the top star charts, moon graphs and planet tracks, beneath them explanations in the cryptic styling of the dwarves.

The star-guild had left not only numerous charts and symbols painted on the floors but on her high perch, as well, a platform designed to be lifted right up and out of the tower.

She could just get her head out the hole in the roof, which could be shut by a sheet of reinforced tin by working a bezel running around the ring-hole. (The dwarves and Yellowteeth used a pole with a hook to work it. Wistala could reach it without rearing up on her hind legs.) There were eight windows with thick shutters and curtains set around the observation room. A fixture directly beneath for some sort of apparatus stuck up from the floor below the platformlike toadstools, but all had been disassembled before they moved her into the perch.

It was a high, lonely place and appealed to her—unless a storm worked up. The tin covering on the hole rattled like a drum when rain or hail hit it, which was frequent at that altitude.

She could not fly from her room, however, without descending the center of the tower on which the blighter sat, and then moving to the Titan Bridge or squeezing herself out through a tunnel which led to one of the workshop chimneys, rising hundreds of dragon-lengths up from the heart of the mountain. Whenever she did that she ended up with soot on her scales.

The dwarves of the star-guild, who were few in number as their only employment was making maps and charts for Wheel of Fire dwarves planning a long journey, attended to her needs. Soothseekers sometimes talked—or bribed, she imagined—their way up into the observation tower and got her advice, but those visits were but rare.

So she had a good deal of free time for thought.

Thought about the Wheel of Fire and the Dragonblade, Hammar and the barbarians, the Hypatian Empire and, sometimes, the dragons of the Sadda-Vale.

On days of clear weather and light wind she explored the mountain pass the dwarves had been occupying since Thul, a General of the Hypatian Empire at its height, had guarded its mountain borders. To the east, where the steppes of the Ironriders stretched farther than even an eye on dragonwing could see, a narrow road hugged the north side of the mountain. It saw so little traffic that when Wistala saw a pack train, a rider, or a file of walkers on it she stopped to guess at their mission. Herds of cattle or horses, so long that they filled the road from its origins at the foothills to the Ba-drink, were brought in from the east by the Ironriders to trade for trade-good-quality blades and shields and helms, and the butchers-guild would work days at a stretch slaughtering and smoking and the Ba-drink would see a scum of blood from their offal.

Hardy mountain fish with knobs like horn-buds all across their sides disposed of leftovers, and were in turn pulled up and eaten by the dwarves.

The track up the west side of the mountains was not as formidable, but there the dwarves had the low wall anywhere an army could possibly march, and watch-guild dwarves in other places. Just coming to the cusp of the Ba-drink would be a feat of generalship for any invading army.

But no army could reach Thul's Hardhold and Tall Rock without crossing the Ba-drink, and the dwarves kept all the barges in their inlets. Unless they could somehow fly over the steep, snowy mountaintops to the north, the attackers would not come within bowshot of the Wheel of Fire.

Father had been mad to attack this place.

She knew there were other roads, up from the Lower

World, but could find no guides willing to take her below some of the lower chambers, and any investigating she did on her own was inevitably stopped by narrow, one-dwarf ladders or passages she was too big to climb. The dwarves working underground chuckled and told her they were not fools, the lower way was shut to keep out blighters and dragons and the foul de-men Fangbreaker had dispersed.

The dwarves would never be destroyed by invasion. Only a long siege might humble them, but dwarves were legendary siege-breakers, and had been known to eat each other rather than relent, according to Yellowteeth.

He could talk, after a fashion, though his Parl was broken and thick.

"Father taken long ago in battle, became tunneler. Father die in collapse. I born water-bearer."

Bear water he did, up the long stairs, to arrive panting and empty his buckets into a barrel. But the dwarves hurried to install a clever system fed by a tank added to the roof; its pipes gave her clean, cold water in a brass cistern, as much as she liked, leaving Yellowteeth only food and coal to carry.

He had a platform in the tower hollow below hers, little more than an antechamber off the stairwell that had once held ropes and pulleys, and it struck Wistala as a dark and cold place. She let him bring his mat up by her fire, and he smiled as he settled in by its glow each night.

As he slept, she had ample time to study his physiognomy. There was something of each of the other hominid races in the blighter, though half-formed and rudely constructed, like an apprentice's clay imitation of a master's sculpture. He seemed to take three times as long to accomplish anything when compared with one of the accommodating dwarves, and burned himself once or twice in a stupid fashion on the coal furnace, which struck her as strange for one who'd been fetching and filling coal all his life, especially since he did most of his other duties intelligently. His intelligence might also account for the lack of scars on his hairy back; most of the other blighters Yellowteeth's age she'd seen elsewhere had bare patches on their shoulders and backs from the lash.

When alone she looked out the windows and dreamed as lazily as Yellowteeth shoveled waste. She kept thinking of the hacked-to-pieces dwarf, feeling somehow responsible for placing this dread monarch at the head of these dwarves, who she hated to begin with but now felt a little sorry for. After all, the whole nation of them didn't storm her home cave.

She knew what she wanted to do; she simply had no idea how to go about doing it.

In the end, as the summer sun reached its zenith, she decided to start small, like Mother's single rock that created an avalanche.

"I must see the king! I must see the king!" Wistala told Djaybee, the dwarf of the star-guild and the most senior of those who resided in their small house carved into the top of Tall Rock below the tower.

Djaybee looked through his off-center mask at the half-sun crawling up between the mountains to the east and scratched his underchin. "For one so insightful, you know little of the habits of King Fangbreaker—a golden garland upon him, long may he lead."

"You would deny—"

"Not deny, good dragon, not deny. It's just that he often works all night and is not to be disturbed until after the noon-bell tolls, and usually then only with his mornmeal."

"Can you arrange an audience, then?"

"We've not much influence in the king's hall—may it see no evil deed."

"Try and I will praise you to him, good Djaybee."

Djaybee bobbed down to one knee. "Then I will endeavor to get you a place in the line."

Wistala got her audience that very afternoon, though whether it was through Djaybee's exertions or the King's interest in hearing from her she could not say.

Djaybee took her across the Titan bridge and through the passages to Fangbreaker's throne room. Yellowteeth trailed along at the back in case during her wait anything needed to be cleaned up and disposed of, for she was too large to use the dwarvish comfort rooms hygienically.

The throne room was long, high, and austere, formed into a tunnel that narrowed at the top into a triangular arch like a shovel-tip. Squared-off pillars running up the sides created a series of alcoves. In each alcove stood a member of the king's bodyguard.

A long, slightly raised walkway ran from the door wardens to the steps leading to King Fangbreaker's iron throne, forged from the melted weapons of those he vanquished in single combat, or so Djaybee told her. To either side of the walkway were wooden benches of dwarf-size, positioned so the bodygard could look out over all.

Long files of dwarves filled the twin bench areas, snaking back and forth in long lines, many carrying sealed scrolls, or gifts. (Baskets of food seemed to be the most popular—Wistala smelled one surreptitiously; it was filled with sausages and cheeses and tiny bits of hard-baked salty bread.) The older or expectant mothers sat, others stood, some talked to their fellow petitioners across the raised walkway and made jokes about having joined the slower-moving line, according to Djaybee.

Upon reaching the front of one of the two lines, the petitioner would speak to a purple-garbed dwarf seated at a little half-desk. The one to the left was male, the one to the right female, her face hidden under elaborate draping. Sometimes the officials would write, sometimes they would lay a waxen seal upon the petition, and sometimes they passed gifts up to the king through his guards.

King Fangbreaker sat on his throne with his artifical leg off. He toyed with the skull-and-crystal, his heel resting on the horsehoof which had been detached somehow, and used it as a baton to point, or offer a sort of salute of acknowledgment to those who brought gifts, or to wave the very few of the petitioners up who would be granted a personal audience.

Behind King Fangbreaker sat a line of the dwarf nobles, some dozing against their fellows. She recognized a few of them from the balconies, but thanks to the masks, it was hard to tell one dwarf from another.

"I shall wait in line for you, Oracle," Djaybee said, moving for the back of the left line, which stood three-quarters of the way toward the entrance.

But King Fangbreaker turned and called to one of his nobles, who rose and hurried down the raised central walkway. He bobbed and gestured for Wistala to come directly up the center aisle.

As she approached, she noticed that one of the sets of stairs was in fact an overhang. There appeared to be a room under the dais. She saw helmets in the shadows within and some sort of war machine with a good view of those waiting in line, and especially the central walkway.

"Tala, step up! Tala, it is a pleasure to see you," King Fangbreaker said. "Are your accommodations lofty and airy enough for your comfort?"

"They are admirable, my king, and I could fill your afternoon with a thousand thanks, but I've had visions that I thought I should bring to your attention."

"Shall we speak privately?" King Fangbreaker said, his eyes narrowing.

"Oh, no, this is good news for you and all your people. But I fear I must ask that all who participate in the discussion speak Parl that I may weigh their words, for I have no knowledge of Dwarvish."

"Easily done. Do all hear?" King Fangbreaker said.

The nobles behind stirred, and the two attendants to either side set down their pens and seal-wax. All listened.

Wistala spoke loudly enough for all—at least all who could understand Parl—but she kept her snout fixed on the king: "I've had troubling dreams the last week, but I thought they only applied to me. It was of tasty dishes, gold, all things a dragon's stomach desires. But they came in one door and out the other all while I slept unawares."

"Opportunity passing you by," King Fangbreaker said. "The lowliest soothsayer could tell as much."

"Ah, but then last night came a very specific dream. I saw a great triumphant parade, celebrating dwarves, fireworks, marching up a street paved with gold toward you, Good King. I believe an opportunity is coming your way."

"Can you add anything more helpful?" King Fangbreaker asked, twirling his leg.

"The one who led the parade was a human boy, a boy of fair hair and wide-set eyes, bronze skin. But he was in manacles, my king. You embraced him, struck off his manacles, and took him to your breast, and the broken pieces of manacle turned into an ancient crown, and the boy put it on your head, but as he hesitated, the crown began to fade, and I woke up.

"I fear this opportunity may be brief, Great King."

"This is not helpful at all. There must be a million boys—"

"He was aged eleven years or so. Garbed like a barbarian, somewhat dirty about the face and hands. Perhaps he is a slave."

King Fangbreaker set his chin on his hand and thought. "Still a search for a nugget in a riverbed."

Wistala cocked her head, the way Auron used to when he had trouble understanding one of her ideas. "What do you mean—you must know the name! Is no one talking of it? Did you not hear the eagle?"

She saw the whites of King Fangbreaker's eyes. "Eagle? What eagle?"

"A most remarkable eagle flying at sunrise circled over Thul's Hardhold, my king. Purple it was—"

"Purple?" Fangbreaker thundered.

Wistala continued: "And as it circled it called the name Rayg in so mighty a voice, I can't imagine anyone didn't hear it. But now I fear it was part of the dream, as well."

"Did anyone see this eagle?" King Fangbreaker said, hopping off his iron throne and standing on one leg, using the throne-arm to balance.

"Eagle . . . perhaps . . . bird high up and far off . . . dark, possibly purple," the Lords of the Wheel of Fire said.

"A feather fell from it, and landed on my doorstep, purple it was," said one lord, falling to his knees. Another at the other end of the group slapped himself on the forehead as if to punish his wits for not being quicker.

"Hmfp! Very unhelpful, Lord Lobok, that I am only hearing this now," said the king, turning a hairy eye upon the kneeling lord.

"My wife thought it suitable to, ahem, set it in a bed of flowers, or preserve it in glass. I shall get it at once," he squeaked, and bowed himself down the stairs, and then hurried up the walkway, jumping over Wistala's twitching tail.

"A man-child. A man-child," King Fangbreaker puzzled.

"The boy's face was alive with intelligence," Wistala said. "Perhaps he will serve as an emissary, or a craftsman."

"I'd rather Hypatia come to the mountain," King Fangbreaker said. "But if we can find this boy, we'll decide then. An odd sort of vision, Tala." He scratched at his beard. "Hmfp! If it brings happiness to my people, I am satisfied. Let every one of our trading houses know to make inquiries about this boy. Say he is being ransomed through us, that none may learn his value before we acquire him. When it comes time to bring him here, I imagine I must let Lobok handle it, as the duty seems to have fallen on his doorstep along with the feather—though he is the nervous type."

"I will take no more of your time, Lord," Wistala said.

"And keep that out of my court," Fangbreaker said, fixing his eye about Yellowteeth, who lurked behind Wistala.

Oddly enough, the blighter smiled back at the king as he gave a nodding bow. Wistala might even have called the expression defiant.

Chapter 26

W istala flapped in the night sky above Galahall, a cold fall wind from the northwest helping keep her aloft as she turned circles, falling in a glide and then rising with a few hard wing-beats, wondering what transpired within.

Hammar had new hutments on the edge of his lands, the round structures of the northern barbarians with their roofs like a single-pole tent.

She accompanied the expedition at King Fangbreaker's request. He was nervous about Lord Lobok, who'd set out from Thul's Hardhold with an armed force some of the dwarvish lords laughed at as being oversize, especially considering the small amount of money borne as the agreed price for the youth.

"He never was the steadiest warrior, and always called for more axes and artillerists, whatever his situation," Fangbreaker said, watching the barges set out from his balcony ten days before.

"But the feather fell on his doorstep," Wistala said. She'd seen the purple feather, produced after some delay for the King's court; it smelled like a white one freshly dyed. "In case of treachery, would it not be better to have a large, well-arrayed force at hand?"

"This is the simplest of transactions. Why the word treachery?" King Fangbreaker asked.

"I cannot say. I speak what comes out of my mind; why it was that word instead of another is as much a mystery to me as to you."

"Hmpf," he said in return.

"Are there commanders to see that the force is well handled, whether it is a peaceful march or a warlike one?" Wistala asked.

"From anyone else I'd call that an insult, Tala," he rumbled. "But you've little opportunity to learn decent manners."

"May I hazard my manners with another question?"

"Of course."

"What happens to those gift baskets of food given to you in your throne hall? Do you eat them all?"

"I eat not a one," King Fangbreaker said. "I've a queer stomach, and mostly eat gruel a-mealtimes, which is easily digested and nutritious. And I have a terrible sweet tooth at night, which is responsible for this," he patted his paunch. "The baskets go to the poor of our city. There are many widows and orphans without a dwarf in a guild to support them. Can't have young dwarves growing up all stoop-backed and knock-kneed, coughing and feverish from malnutrition."

Wistala felt the lordly dwarves moving about her flanks, some were pointing to her underside and talked among themselves, perhaps discussing assorted methods and tactics of dragon-killing.

"How did you get the title Fangbreaker, my king?" Wistala asked.

"I was cheated by a pair of dragons," he said. "They were a wretched, misfortunate pair, who we helped restore to health and vitality with foods and metals. In return they fought for us, as some of the mercenary Ironriders do on the eastern side of this mountain, but they abandoned us to start their family without taking proper leave and asking permission to bear eggs. For we had a market for those eggs, a rich market, and they'd agreed that their bodies would be ours for a period under contract.

"Now I was not unreasonable. I just asked for one clutch. After that, they would be free to go where they wished, to the ends of the breaking earth in the west or the jeweled kingdoms of the east for all I cared, and hatch as many eggs as they liked. But I'd promised a full clutch of eggs to a buyer, and he would have them.

"The dragons argued that their services included only flying and fighting, not eggs, and when I stood firm, they fled. The laying time must have been close, for they did not flee far, though they turned up in an unexpected cave, one we'd gone to much trouble to seal from below to cut off the blighters within from the darkroads.

"I caught up to them in the end, so that I might turn over hatchlings to my buyer, if not eggs. Though that Dragonblade got overzealous in the fight and in attempting to pinion a hatchling killed it. I poked a hole in the female who'd lied to me, spilling her fire bladder and rendering her harmless and gasping, and smashed in her lying mouth with my gauntlet for defying me, turning her teeth into bloody ruin. She died cursing me through a broken jaw. Does this talk sicken you, Tala?"

Wistala, wondering how King Fangbreaker's body would dance as flame consumed it, took a deep breath. "There are good dragons and bad dragons, just as there are good and bad dwarves, Dread King."

"But so I was titled and given a place at the council table, for we managed to hunt one hatchling down and the Drakossozh killed another with his dogs."

"Bad luck, for the Dragonblade to kill two while trying for capture."

"You're a dragon yourself. You must know that it is not the easiest of tasks. But I feel for you, at the unfortunate loss of others of your kind. Would that more dragons grew up to live useful lives!"

Would that more dwarves did the same, Wistala thought.

"How can I ease your mind about Lobok?" Wistala

said. "I can go to my tower and try to force a vision. Perhaps if you gave me some personal tokens—"

"No. I wouldn't care to force a wrong reading from you. But hear! You could act as a courier between my throne room and Lobok's camp. You can bring a message in a few hours over a distance that a rider would take a day to cover."

"Nothing that would make me happier," Wistala said. "Than to be able to set your mind at ease."

So she'd gone to Lobok's camp twice carrying messages from the mountain king, carrying reassurance that all was going according to plan—and made a side trip or two to the vicinity of the Green Dragon Inn to speak to Forstrel among his honeycombs.

"I wonder why he asks for word?" Lord Lobok asked. His hands kept coming together and then running up his arms and back down again as he paced and thought, as though the right was worried that the left had eloped with an elbow.

"I do not know all the messages King Fangbreaker, high may he remain, receives. I only do my duty," Wistala said. "You have ample dwarves for a march through enemy territory."

"Enemy?" Lobok asked. "Lord Hammar is a good friend, we've had much commerce with him. The dwarves just come to guard our prize on the way back."

"I've heard he's been calling himself King Hammar," Wistala said, and flew off back to Fangbreaker with Lobok's reply.

So as she hung in the darkness over Galahall, seeing the lights go on within and the carpets laid on the doorstep, she turned and made a careful approach to the nearby stream where the dwarves were camped at the base of the ridge she'd crossed so many years ago in the company of Stog.

She asked for a meeting with Lord Lobok, busy dressing for the court dinner celebrating another successful transac-

tion, for the boy Rayg waited at Galahall to be sold to the
dwarves. She was admitted with the expediency one would
expect of a courier from King Fangbreaker, and found him
buttoning a formal robe over a chain shirt. He wore a mask
of red silk stretched under and over a decorative wooden
frame, like a child's kite.

"Lord Lobok, are you going yourself?" she asked, putting her head in his tent so as not to crowd him and the
servant-dwarf helping his lord dress.

"Of course. It's a welcoming dinner, and as leader and
emissary I'm expected. You don't—"

"The night feels wrong to me," Wistala said. "Are your
soldiers arrayed well?"

"We're on the thane's land," Lord Lobok said, fingers
fluttering against his chain shirt. "There's nothing to fear
here."

"As long as the thane is true. I've had horrible dreams,
but they must be wrong. They must be."

Lobok left off dressing, turned his silk-masked face to
her. "Why do you say your impressions must be wrong?
You are King Fangbreaker's, honors upon his name and so
forth, famous Oracle."

"Who could mistake such omens? The feather landed
on your doorstep. The Fates have chosen you."

Lobok and his servant exchanged a glance. "Of course."

"Yes. I am overwrought, seeing those barbarian en-
campments around the thane's hall. I'm imagining things."
She began to shake. "But beware, O lord; if anyone speaks
of a blood relationship between Hammar and the child you
are receiving tonight, blood will be shed. A dagger at your
back."

She let her eyes roll wildly and then flopped over, closing
the water-lids over her so that she would look glassy-eyed.

"Oh! Oh! Oh, no," Lord Lobok said, his hands clasp-
ing and unclasping, then gripping elbows tight. "Someone.
Ummm. Is it safe to dump water on dragons?"

Wistala rattled her *sii* and lifted her head. "*Nur . . .*
what am I doing here? *Ia,* I'm happy for you, Lord Lobok,
you live again . . ." She blinked, shook her head. "I beg

your pardon, my lord, were you saying something? I seem to have fainted."

Lobok gestured to his servant, took a quavering gulp of wine from a proffered cup. "You didn't have another vision, did you?"

"Oh. No, I don't think so. Hazy, so hazy. My eyes vex me. There's a mist about you, my lord. It must be the scented candles. Excuse me, I am obliged to fly back to the throne room."

She left Lord Lobok calling for more wine.

Three days later King Fangbreaker's throne room was lined with many of the most noble families in the mountains, hearing the report of Field Commander Djosh. Wistala waited for it to be read again in Parl, having begged to know what the message she carried read:

Noble King and Assembled Select and Lordly Dwarves,

I write you to report a most satisfactory outcome to an attempted treachery by Lord Hammar and his barbarians on the two hundred ninetieth of this year. I thank the Fates for the eagle and his feather landed upon Lord Lobok's door, for were it not for him not a dwarf of this expedition may be returning.

Lord Lobok insisted on our arrays being placed within hearing distance of Galahall, ready to answer a cry for assistance, and I can only marvel at his foresight, inspired, I'm told, by our lucky dragon, who sensed matters amiss.

I am told that during dinner an unusual number of barbarian leaders were present, as the infamous Hammar was building around himself a court of scoundrels. As the servants poured wine for a toast, Hammar gave some sort of code word that he was letting his illegitimate son—I shall not sully the

throne room with his coarse discourse—be sold for
little more than the song that wooed his mother. At
this there was some stirring at the priests' end of the
table and Lord Lobok let out such a shriek of warning that we would have heard it were we camped
two *vesk* away. Lobok drew blade and flung himself
sideways behind the table, knocking over a server
who was making to bring the cask of wine down on
Shieldmaster Dar's head, Lord Lobok's bodyservant
tells me.

At the calls of alarm and assistance from Lord
Lobok I sent my hardhanded dwarves forward and
they stormed through the windows of Galahall in
good order. The barbarians made some semblance
of a fight but clearly intended for the dinner to be
a slaughterhouse, not a battle hall, and seemed not
much experienced at close-quarter fighting under
roof and among furniture. Our dwarves, used to such
environs, secured the boy with some loss of blood,
almost all of it on the part of our opponents, and no
loss of the treasure we brought to purchase him, for
treachery abrogates any deal. I hope the throne will
approve.

Barbarian cavalry, long prepared to finish off the
villainy indoors, made an effort to harry our retreat,
but our catafoua made them fall back with loss.

Wistala smiled, for she'd had Lessup's mead-deliverers
start rumors of warlike preparations in the dwarf camp
where they'd just sold their honeyed brew.

I close this dispatch by saying we have lost few
dwarves as we retreat in good order for the Ba-drink.
I write to you in Lord Lobok's stead, for he travels
with the healing wagons, and is so dosed with medicines after his experiences he is currently unable to
write legibly. If you have any orders beyond return-

ing to the Hardhold with our young prize, they will be immediately carried out by

Your faithful Field Commander,
Djosh Scarchin

As the words were read in Parl, the dwarves grumbled and swore all over again, and King Fangbreaker paced before his throne.

"What do you say, Oracle?" a dwarf called.

Fangbreaker glowered. "This is a military matter, Guild-master Cyoss."

"Great King, though we would hear the dragon, you must decide, of course," another called.

Fangbreaker turned to Wistala. "What do you think, Oracle?"

"I have not a military mind. But shouldn't this sort of treachery be punished?"

The assembled select dwarves growled in agreement.

"I am very tired from my flight, and you all have weighty matters to long discuss," Wistala said. "May I be excused from council of war?"

"Of course," Fangbreaker said.

"Three cheers for the lucky dragon!" a dwarf at the back shouted.

Wistala bowed backwards out of the throne room, but she saw the fixed stare in Fangbreaker's eyes, and trembled.

Lord Lobok's expedition returned with Rayg in triumph and glory.

It must have been strange to the thin little youth, to be borne across the Ba-drink in a garlanded boat, flanked by lordly dwarves and rowed between Thul's Hardhold and Tall Rock, under a rain of tiny white mountain flowers—and bits of paper and wax wrapping—thrown from the balconies and the Titan Bridge.

Even as they returned a new expedition set out, under three of the Wheel of Fire's greatest generals.

Wistala heard from the star-guild that King Fang-breaker had decided to launch a "punitive expedition" into the barbarian lands, to teach the barbarians a real lesson for the treachery at Galahall. They were keeping their exact plans secret, but the star-guild had provided detailed maps of Kark and the Blacklake area, for barbarians from that region had been identified as among the slain around Galahall.

Wistala hung about, asked if she'd be needed to relay messages, and was told that the sight of a dragon in the sky might give away the column's presence.

When night fell, she flew away from the Wheel of Fire with all the speed she could manage and almost tore her wings off making it to the Green Dragon Inn. There she dictated a letter to be given to Hammar, and a much longer one to be sent to Ragwrist.

Lord Hammar,

You and I have had our differences in the past, but the enemies of my blood, the dwarves of the Wheel of Fire, are marching on Blacklake and Kark, intent on destruction and murder. Whether you tell your barbarian allies to move their women and children away from those areas or plan an ambush is entirely up to you.

A Daughter of Hypatia

Jessup looked at the note after he finished writing it in his chicken-run hand. Wistala pressed her librarian medallion into some very ordinary red wax he helpfully dribbled at the bottom.

"This is a dangerous game you are playing, Wistala."

She stretched her aching wings and back muscle. "It's no game, I assure you, and the stakes are beyond anything that can be placed on a table or dice-rug."

"Mod Lada would like news of her son, if you have any. She saw him seized up from table after that treacherous dwarf-lord started attacking the wine stewards and signaled his ambush."

Wistala told what she'd heard from the astronomers' guild: "I have not spoken to Rayg, but I am told he's been apprenticed to the Guild of Inventors. Evidently he showed some intelligence in the Hall of Inventions as he passed through it, and recognized some piece of artifice and its use, which much impressed the keepers there. It is a high honor, only the brightest dwarves gain an apprenticeship in that guild. I can assure her those dwarves are the best-treated of the Wheel of Fire."

Jessup pulled back a lock of his remaining hair. "It is a strange road we've traveled since that day we buried Avalanche."

"And there are still more trolls to slay."

"I'll let you deal with the trolls. I'll keep my inn and tell your story to anyone who asks about the sign."

"May it not have an end for a long time," Wistala said.

Jessup reached up, tickled her under the chin. "I've always wanted to do that. I never tire of looking at you, Wistala. There's something about dragons. All power and dread symmetry."

"I must be off. I have much more flying to do, yes, all the way to the Imperial Library at Thallia. I hope they don't panic and think I've come to burn it. I need to speak to a librarian."

"What will you do there?"

"Learn about dams."

Chapter 27

When Wistala returned to her tower a score of days later, she found all of the Wheel of Fire were aquiver. The punitive expedition had not sent communication in many days, and not a few wondered at the silence.

She received a most odd note shortly after rising the next day. Yellowteeth hurried to get her minder, who hurried to get his guild-chief, who read the note and sent for the escort Wistala requested.

So it was in the company of the star-guild that she went to meet the Dragonblade on the Titan bridge.

He stood in the center, in his armor but with sword in scabbard and cloak about him, helm hanging from his belt. His broad face was much as she remembered it, perhaps a little wearier.

"I've long been curious to meet this Oracle dragon for some time now, but was occupied on the other side of the Inland Ocean." For some reason Wistala was relieved. As soon as he said *occupied on the other side,* she feared a mention of the Sadda-Vale.

"So you've seen me, Drakossozh. Is there to be a duel here, under the eyes of the Wheel of Fire?"

"A duel? With vermin? Spare me your wit, creature."

"Then I will go about my business—," Wistala began.

"No. Walk with me. I will start no fight with you here. You have my word."

Wistala wondered if she could trust the word of an assassin.

"I must be growing old. You are the second dragon to slip through my fingers," he said.

"Who was the first?"

He turned toward the Hardhold. "Come. I wish to show you something, *Oracle*."

He led her down many sets of stairs, across chambers filled with trophies and statues, and finally down a shaft where one traveled by having the floor descend rather than going afoot. He gave a password to guards in a workshop filled with the sound of hammers and deeper pounding, and Wistala smelled hot metal and burning coal.

She passed a group of young dwarves, their faces unmasked, listening to another older dwarf talk as he pointed with a stick at various features of a hose that fed water into a series of smaller and smaller pipes, until it shot out the bottom with tremendous force. She recognized Rayg among the apprentices, the only human other than Drakossozh this far in the Hardhold.

"We're deep in the Guild of the Armorers," the Dragonblade said. They passed racks of weapons and stacked helms, with dwarves bent over workbenches on all sides. The symphony of noise was as chaotic as a battle, and the air thick with the tang of heated metal. "Have you ever wondered how the Wheel of Fire got its name?" he asked.

"You see the burning shield here and there," Wistala said. "It's an emblem."

"They were called the Wheel of Fire before that. Here, follow."

He passed into a quieter gallery. The ceiling here was wide but low, and Wistala smelled an oily smell like lamp fats overlaid with other workshop odors.

Long ranks of machines stood in little bays. Some had wooden platforms next to them, one or two had been wheeled out so the dwarves could work. A few of the workers gave Wistala a startled look as she crouched to get through the doors.

The pieces of craftsmanship were like great walls on wheels of assorted sizes. If there was an average, she would put that wheels were fully dwarf height and the walls perhaps twice that, but it seemed some walls and wheels came taller and some shorter, some wider and some narrower. But on each two spars jutted out from the axles of the wheels behind the wall, with handles at irregular intervals. Wistala watched a team of dwarves move one by having four dwarves stand at each spar and lift, then push it forward. Behind the shield were big tanks like water-cisterns, only with hoses and glass devices like clock faces fixed to the joints, along with assorted levers and cables connecting wheel to tanks.

But the objects at the front caught her attention more than anything.

Pipes projected from slits in the great wheeled shields. The slits, indeed the shields themselves, reminded her of overlarge dwarf battle-masks with their thin gaps so the dwarves could see and still have their eyes shielded.

Open-jawed dragon heads, horribly real, had been fixed to the front of the pipes, their faces forever frozen into snarling fury. Their eyes had been replaced by painted crystals, but otherwise they looked ready to come alive. There were heads with eight horns and heads with none, heads with green scales and heads with bronze, heads of hatchlings, drakes, drakka, dragons, dragonelles. . . .

Some were familiar.

The world spun about her. She fixed her eyes on the Dragonblade, who stood with hand on sword hilt, helmet cradled at his elbow. His knees were bent just a trifle, as though he were waiting to leap into action. Wistala noticed shadows, heard excited breathing, the alcoves just ahead.

"I'm not aware of all the mechanics to their operation," the Dragonblade explained from somewhere on the other side of the Endless Steppe, or so it seemed to her ears. "But the turning of the wheels forces air into one of the tanks, and that air is then used to drive flame, like dragonflame, out of the other tank and through the pipe at the front. It's ignited by a coal gas-flame there. Certainly not what a dragon is capable of, but I hear it's terrifying in tunnel warfare."

The dwarves had all frozen in their labors, watching her as though fixed by spellcraft.

"Most interesting," Wistala said. "Is there another stop to the tour, or am I done?"

"You hold your anger well. Here's another test." He extended his gauntleted palm. In it rested two ancient Hypatian coins, one of gold, the other of silver. "I found these in the jowls of a bronze I killed on the banks of the Whitewater. There was also a female hatchling there. That hatchling wouldn't have been you, would it?"

Wistala shot out her tongue, but the Dragonblade was quicker of hand, closed his fingers around the coins and withdrew them.

"Oh, I'm sorry, I thought you were offering me a treat," Wistala said. "Speaking of which, I am late for my dinner."

"A dragon who can hold her temper," the Dragonblade said.

Just, Wistala thought.

"There's something about you that frightens me," the Dragonblade said, eyebrows together. His horridly flat face wrinkled in thought. "A dragon who can keep her temper could be a deadly enemy. Or—"

"Or what?" Wistala asked.

"I won't misjudge you again," the Dragonblade said, not answering her question and crossing to the opposite gallery. "You've escaped me twice. There won't be a third."

"No," Wistala said. "I expect there won't."

"And even if I fall, I have a son and a daughter to avenge me."

"I've met your son. I hope he gets his chance."

"Ah, yes. Not his finest performance. I thought I'd try him on an easier target his first night out. I never thought you'd chew your wings open. They've grown out nicely."

Wistala took a breath. If she kept her eyes on the Dragonblade, she couldn't see the heads, except he kept strolling around so she couldn't help but view the machines.

"I wonder if Fangbreaker knows all your history," the Dragonblade said.

"I wonder if he knows you've disobeyed him, and killed when he told you to capture."

She turned and moved back through the workshops, keeping one eye on him just in case. But he stood there, helmet at his hip, chuckling. "You may walk away, dragon. Even fly. But wherever you go, you cannot hide forever. Dragons are noticed, you see?"

As she retraced her steps back dwarves seemed to be rushing about everywhere, or standing on stairways talking and gesticulating. Something had them dreadfully agitated but Wistala did not ask what. Her head hurt, perhaps from the fumes in the workshops, and she wanted to retire to her tower to sleep.

"Dhssol."

"Oracle, what do you think?" some asked, but she passed in a daze.

"Dhssol! Dhssol!" the dwarves said, one to the other. Dwarf wives wailed it from their balconies as Wistala crossed the Titan bridge.

"Who is this Dhssol?" she asked one of the leather-slippered court workers.

"Not a who, a what," he said, pulling at his beard. " 'Disaster,' it would be in Parl. An evil star is on our house."

The dwarves of the star-guild told her the terrible news when she returned to her tower. A tradesdwarf of the Chartered Company had made a rare appearance at the Wheel of Fire to bring tidings of sorrow and fear: the punitive column had been wiped out almost to a dwarf.

After a bloody march through villages where the dwarves left burned bodies in wooden cages, they'd been betrayed by their hired scouts, supposedly belonging to a rival clan to the lands they'd been traversing. The false scouts led to a flooded river, and while attempting to cross, they had been attacked during a snowstorm from both sides and by forces shooting down the river in narrow boats.

Hammar, now called the Dwarfhanger by his barbarian legion, was reputed to be on the march for the Wheel of Fire, destroying what remained of the column as the survivors retreated.

Some important voices were calling for Lord Lobok to be put in charge of the defense of the city; he'd had his share of luck against the barbarians and Hammar before.

"And he's cautious, and would not improvidently expose his troops to destruction," Djaybee said. "He can stand against this Hammar, for years if need be. The barbarians always lose interest in war after a season. It'll be over by the summer flowers. Should he assume command?" the scientifically minded dwarf, who'd never asked her advice before, wondered.

"I would like nothing better," Wistala said.

They were interrupted in this discourse by a visitor. This time Gobold Fangbreaker himself came to her, rather than going through the delay of having her brought to the Throne Hall.

"Tala, you have heard the rumors?" the king said as he arrived, surrounded by his black-armored bodyguard.

"Yes. Is it true, my king?"

"True enough," he said. "Though not quite so bad as some losing their nerve would have it. Battle Commander Vande Boltcaster has a full maneuver array of dwarves left, and they are fighting as they turn back. But they've been forced to abandon their train and are short on supplies and have no time or capacity to seek more. I've had an idea. How much do you think you can carry?"

"The weight of several dwarves," Wistala said. "Over short distances."

"This will be a long flight of short hops, then. I need you to bring him food, medicines, and above all crossbow bolts."

"My wings are at your command, Great King," she said.

"There's been talk of you being absent for some time," King Fangbreaker said. "To where did you fly?"

"To see my friends at the circus. They go into winter camp about this time each year."

"Hmpf," said King Fangbreaker, from behind his shield. "You seem the type to keep friends long. How about enemies?"

"I've set out to make no enemies, my king," Wistala said. "I made more friends than enemies with the circus. Of course, there are those who felt they were cheated—"

"I don't mean that. Ach, I don't know what I mean. I'm overwrought, imagining things. You put new heart in me. Eat a good meal and be ready to fly by tonight. The star-guild will supply you with a map based on our best information."

Wistala lowered her head to the floor, and King Fangbreaker left. She later learned he'd walked all about the city, calming the citizens on both sides of the Titan bridge, answering questions from the lowliest porter to guild-heads.

That night she came to the Titan bridge, where she was loaded with milk-powders, sugarcubes, crossbow bolts, slabs of honey, medicines, even rolls of needle and thread for stitching wounds. Dwarf wives came and stuck flowers in her scales or tied ribbons with messages inked on them about her *sii* and *saa*. She was asked to look for so many dwarves that the king's bodyguard had to push away the supplicants.

She tried a short practice flight, and returned to the bridge.

"I can carry more," she said, not altogether sure that she could. More bundles were strapped to her back and chest, everywhere but where her wings could flap.

The King himself drank a toast in her honor and gave her a heaping handful of gold coins to eat, slathered with something sweet and hard the dwarves called *cocolat*. It gave her a rush of energy, and she launched herself again, and even gliding seemed somewhat of a strain.

Behind her, they set off red fireworks.

She had to relearn to fly, laden as she was, and it was slow going until she learned to better angle her wings. After an hour she dropped, exhausted, sure she could never reach the sky again, but she did.

And so she fought her way north, an hour's flight, a half hour's rest, another hour's flight, a quarter hour's rest, another hour's flight, a drop from exhaustion into sleep that ended at daybreak.

The next day she passed over the track of the punitive expedition. The snow had covered the burned foundations, but crows poked at charred heaps here and there, extracting unburnt marrow. She'd never heard of war like this in the Hypatian books of tactics and maneuver, parley and honorable surrender. The dwarves had struck with a heavy, vengeful hand.

Or had she?

Wistala landed in a crowd of cheering dwarves the next dusk. Their eyes burned so bright behind their masks that they glowed. Beards were shorn to show loss of comrades and officers, and they hadn't had time or energy to clean the caked blood from their armor.

Battle Commander Vande Boltcaster moved with a limp, walking with the aid of a broken bow. His officers untied and distributed the messages bound on her legs and tail—many would never be read by the eyes for which they were intended.

"Can you carry out wounded?" Boltcaster asked her. "I have three hero-dwarves we've been carrying since the Norssund."

"Oh, for some wine," she said.

"Gone," Boltcaster said. "Like much else. There's toasted horsemeat and boiled entrails galore, if you like. They were to be breakfast, but there's not a dwarf here who wouldn't give you his portion."

"Can you make it back?" Wistala said. The dwarves were taking turns to slip away from their lines and write notes on everything from wrapping-paper to bits of wood, in blood if nothing else would serve, and tying it to her. She submitted, hating herself for what she was about to do.

"I'll know when we reach the Shoulder-Fell. How long before the king marches to our aid?"

"I have not seen a dwarf set out beyond the outer wall," Wistala said, honestly enough.

Some of the dwarves growled at that.

"Silence, there," Boltcaster barked. "I've still reports to send, and you have families."

"How do you move?"

"Loose march-square. If the barbarians come, we fall in tight. The cavalry hasn't been trained that can break a Wheel of Fire shield wall."

"Where are the barbarians?" Wistala asked.

"Where aren't they?" a dwarf answered.

"They mostly follow our trail, scavenging discarded metalwork and despoiling the dead," Boltcaster said. "We've had demands for surrender, and each time they've ridden from that direction. Good treatment. Ha! What do you expect, fighting savages such as these. Blighters would puke at some of their deeds."

Wistala took off down the path and winged over the dwarven defenses—felled trees, mostly—to halfhearted cheers. She saw some horses in the trees beyond and loosed some fire, more for show than for effect, and cast about until she saw tightly knit campfires. She swooped in low over the tents.

Barbarian chieftains called for their archers and pointed. A few desultory arrows sang through the air around her.

"Tell Hammar they make for the Shoulder Fell," she said, flying upside down to keep out the shafts. She repeated it again over another group of tents, before turning back for the dwarves.

They stuffed her with horse entrails before she took off the next morning, with the three wounded dwarves tied across her back. The burden seemed light compared with the supplies she'd carried in the previous day.

By the time she returned to the Titan bridge, one of the wounded had died. The other two were untied and rushed into the Hardhold.

Wistala lay on the bridge like a dead thing as the dwarves

untied the messages. One of the lordly dwarves took the courier-pouch from her neck and rushed it to the king.

Fangbreaker himself came down to the bridge to see her, stumping along on his horse hoof, which clomped on the wood planks of the bridge.

"They are in bad shape, my king," Wistala said. Some in the crowd cried out, and she heard mutters of *dhssol.* "I fear I am, too."

"Boltcaster's need is great," King Fangbreaker said. "I must ask you to fly again as soon as you've rested. He needs more supplies."

"You go," Wistala said.

"What?"

Wistala raised her head, too tired to do much but speak. If the bodyguard closed on her, it would be all she could do to roll off the bridge. "You go. Gather your forces and go to his aid."

The crowd went instantly silent.

"No," said the king. "Boltcaster must rely on his own skill and courage. We cannot take that risk. Every dwarf will be needed here."

"Or you could return with your number of warriors doubled," Wistala said.

"She's exhausted," King Fangbreaker said, loudly. "The dragon is mazed. Pay her no mind. Go, good Oracle, go to your tower and rest." He reached for a handful of *cocolat*-covered coins to place in her mouth and evidently thought the better of it. He tossed the bag down before her.

"Eat these—you'll feel better."

Wistala picked the bag up but did not eat them. Instead she bowed to the king and turned for her tower, trying to forget the masked faces of the doomed dwarves in Bolt-caster's column. They were getting what they deserved. Would she?

The bodyguard closed around the king behind her, see-ing the hard stares of some in the crowd.

Wistala slept, and ate, and waited.

The news finally came: Boltcaster and his remaining

dwarves had been defeated on the slopes of a mountain; evidently the barbarians had prepared and then rolled rocks down on them from above, breaking the shield wall just before a charge.

Fangbreaker called their end "glorious" and a credit to the Wheel of Fire. But there were mutterings against him, arrests, even an assassination or two, and suicides that some said were not suicides.

One of these was the son of Lord Lobok, who finally agreed to take command of the outer wall at the edge of the Ba-drink.

The star-guild whispered of threats to her life, and Yellowteeth grew afraid to go down for coal. Wistala shrugged off the danger. The dwarves needed every warrior who could carry a spear and would not waste any on a dragon that could be dealt with later.

Then came a dread winter morning when word spread that a barbarian horde was on the foothills below the Ba-drink. With them were Hypatian mercenaries, cavalry, even gargants. Will-making became a popular diversion, there were parties of a desperate nature on the balconies as the dwarves who would defend the walls spent one last night with their kith and kin.

Wistala watched, from her high tower, the barges creep across the Ba-drink, disgorge the dwarves for the walls, and then return for more. Control of the Ba-drink meant control of the herds on the south shores of the lake, and access to the east road for supplies, so the wall had to be held to avoid a bitter siege.

She looked at the sheer walls of Thul's Hardhold. Many were the balconies that hung black banners, mourning their losses.

Djaybee joined her at the thin window slits.

"I think you should know, there's a dozen of the king's guard at the base of the tower. They don't want you to leave," Djaybee said. Yellowteeth hung about the passage down, as if fearing a rush of footsteps, but what he could do other than slicken the steps with shovelfuls of dragon waste she did not know. "Hard words passed between us, and I was cautioned against keeping counsel with you. I fear another night of knives is coming."

"Night of knives?"

"As there was when our noble king, a curse be upon his name, claimed all power. Those who opposed him never woke again, but were found dead behind their bedcurtains."

"We'd best take turns keeping watch," Wistala said.

Her sleep was uneasy that night, and the tower went cold, for Yellowteeth was too terrified to descend the stairs to get more coal. Wistala finally let him sleep in the corner farthest from the door while she and Djaybee took turns at the stairs.

She awoke to a tickle behind her chin, dreaming that Jizara was poking her with her tail-tip. She opened her eye and froze.

Yellowteeth stood next to her neck, his shovel handle somehow transformed into a spear pressing against the interstices between her scales above her neck heart.

"Greetings from the Assassins' Guild," Yellowteeth said, his Parl-pigdin markedly reduced. "The king has a message for you as you die: Where is the crown of Masmodon, Oracle? *Where is my crown?*"

Chapter 28

Wistala smelled blood in the tower room.

Near the stair, Djaybee sat hunched over, a dark stain soaking his back. He'd never more gaze at the stars and draw maps with their aid.

Yellowteeth might have been a good assassin, but he hadn't learned all he could of dragon anatomy.

She twitched and lowered her *griff* above the spear point in an eyeblink, knocking it aside as Yellowteeth threw himself off balance trying to ram it home. The point scraped across the floor instead of burrowing into her neck.

She helped him off his feet by lashing him between the shoulder blades with her tail as she came to her fours. She put a *sii* down on the back of his head, grinding his face into the geometry of the floor.

"In my experience, a good courier always asks if there is to be a return message," Wistala said. "Will you be good enough to carry an answer back for me?"

"Mmpfh," Yellowteeth snuffled.

"How thoughtful of you. Tell Gobold to come himself and try to break my fangs, if he wishes to deliver death. Now run, before I breakfast on roast blighter."

She let Yellowteeth up, and he made better time for the stairs than he ever had running coal. If nothing else, he would muddy matters below, and he might even claim the job was done in order to effect an escape from the Wheel of Fire.

A fine cold morning of clean air and mists clinging to the Ba-drink had begun outside. She would not be taken like a rat in a mountaintop cage. The only passage out was down, but she did not want to fight her way through tunnels filled with dwarves, where she would run out of *foua* before they ran out of spears.

She needed the sky, and to learn if Ragwrist hovered at the edge of the siege or not.

On other days she'd examined her tower room, there were hours of leisure to do so, and the stone was most worn to the northwest, where the wind blew coldest in winter and ice accumulated. There were a multitude of tiny cracks in the masonry between the spaced windows.

She went to her water cistern and took a full mouthful of water, and imitating the unpleasant DharSii, spat it up and down around the masonry, did it once more with a fresh mouthful until the stone was well-wetted.

Then she employed her *foua* on the wind-chilled stone.

Loud cracks sounded through the flames. Wistala breathed through another window and smashed her tail against the wall, over and over again, as Auron had in the escape chimney, only this time a thousand times the strength was behind it.

A great piece of wall fell away between the two windows.

She could not quite squeeze through yet, but it was far easier to open it wider by pulling at the broken edges and exposed brickwork. A few more bruising tail strikes and she was out, even as footsteps sounded on the stair.

Wistala took wing above the city of the Wheel of Fire.

She roared and dived between the Tall Rock and Thul's Hardhold, aiming for the Titan bridge. She extended her claws and tail as though to land, then stopped herself with swift beats of her wings just above the bridge.

A highpoon trailing chain, fired by a mighty war-machine, shot across the bridge. As it fell the chain caught and Wistala slipped sideways to grab the links. A second highpoon lanced out from the other side, but she was watching for it, and reared out of the way.

Father, your pain was not wasted, even if your head now sits on a war-machine.

She flew into the air, as hard and as fast as she could, as other spears whizzed toward her. One pierced her wing, another glanced off her *saa*, but scale thickened by dwarf gold kept the worst of the damage out.

She swung the round iron weight at the end of the chain, back and forth, back and forth as she rose, with each swing building momentum. She let it strike the Titan bridge, breaking off a massive chunk which spun as it fell into the Ba-drink.

She flew off, flying oddly, fighting to the counterweight on the end of the chain, but her wing muscles were equal to the weight. She smashed a tower on the Hardhold where dwarves fired crossbow bolts. Two swings of the ball, and the shattered tower collapsed and slid down, smashing balcony, gallery, and garden on the way to the wharf.

Wistala noted that there were arrows sticking out of her scales and wing-leather, but in the heat of combat, she felt no pain.

She carried her burden to the far side of the Ba-drink and let the weight go at the flat part of ground by the landing. She flew over the lines of dwarves. Their war-machines were hurling missiles down the mountainside at a wave of barbarians coming up.

"*Dhssol! Dhssol!*" she wailed as she passed over the lines of dwarves at the wall. "All is lost! *Dssol!*"

And so she called over the lines of dwarves until she spotted Lord Lobok, standing with a few nobles and commanders on a prominence behind the wall at arrow-shot.

"*Oh, Dhssol*!" Wistala mourned as she landed. "I have seen it. There are too many! All is lost, see how they approach. You must fall back to the city, we are surely defeated on these slopes."

"Terrible thought," Lobok said, wringing his hands as a few ineffective arrows flew over the wall and landed near them in the rocks. "It goes badly for us, Battle Commander! These dwarves are the Wheel of Fire's last hope."

"Who needs a last hope when there's a battle being won? Your imagination has you counting each one thrice," the commander said. "Step back and let veterans command the fight. The closer they come, the more we kill, see? Our losses are but few."

But some of the troops had been unnerved by Wistala's cries, and were running for the barges.

"Hold hard there," the battle commander shouted through a speaking trumpet. "Groundholders, get those skulkers back in line. To the line!"

"Nothing can stop them, Oh, *Dhssol*!" Wistala said, as a mass of barbarians came up the hill. Many to the front fell as the dwarves fired, but others behind came on. . . .

"Shut up!" the Battle Commander insisted. "Someone muzzle this fool lizard."

"The Oracle is right," Lord Lobok shouted, lifting his own speaking trumpet. "They cannot be held here! Back to the barges, dwarves—we must fall back to the city!" He set an example to his soldiers by hitching up his robes and running toward the barges as fast as his legs would carry him.

The dwarves, many untested in battle, agreed with the sentiment, and the lines fell away like laundry carried off by a strong wind. Dwarves of all descriptions ran, even as the more experienced ones at the war-machines shouted and gesticulated at them.

The battle commander reached for his ax, and Wistala thought it best to take wing. Pebbles flew up into the eyes of the commanders and nobles as she took off.

They, too, ran for the barges as the barbarians leaped up the wall with wild cries.

The battle paused for a moment as the barges pulled away, firing crossbows at the barbarians, who fell back from the water to the wall and continued to hoot.

Wistala flew down to Ragwrist's gargants. She saw

Lord Hammar there, in a thick fur coat that hung to his bootheels, helping with the blasting kegs being handed down from gargant back.

"Place them to either side of the spillway, and on those two supporting columns, right where they join the dam," Wistala said.

"I hope this works, Wistala," Ragwrist said as the circus dwarves and riggers went forward with climbing poles and lines. "These casks weren't cheap."

"And good morning to you, too," Wistala said. "Would you rather have King Fangbreaker hunting you up and down the Inland Ocean?"

"The risks I run for my circus."

"Stop running risks then. I give Mossbell to you, if Hammar agrees."

"Hammar has other matters to attend to," he said. His beard still looked like the poor effort of a youth, even in the fullness of manhood. "First let us win the battle. Then we'll divide the spoils."

The circus folk climbed up each side of the dam and pulled and tied the blasting-casks into place. Wistala plucked crossbow bolts from her scale and nursed her javelin wounds.

"What about a fuse?" Hammar asked.

"I'm the fuse," Wistala said, licking a spear hole in her wing clean.

When all was ready, and more barbarians had the time to come up the road and array themselves behind the wall, Wistala took flight.

She saw that perhaps half the barges still dueled with the barbarians at the waterside, ready to destroy canoes or any other light boats the savages might have brought up the mountain to cross the Ba-drink. The others, undoubtedly led by Lobok, were almost at the Hardhold.

She saw that the gargants and circus folk were well out of the watercourse down the spillway, and dropped down, summoning her *foua*.

She loosed it against the dam wall, and it ran down toward the packed and tied kegs. Wistala flew up and out of the way.

The explosions came, a gentle hand shoving Wistala higher—*crack crack huhoom!*—sending rock and masonry shooting out across the mountainside, along with bits of timber and line.

For a moment after the cataclysm, all was silent, or perhaps it was just that it sounded so to battered eardrums.

Both the masses of barbarians and the dwarves in their barges left off their gesticulations and challenges, insults and catcalls, arrows, sling-stones, and bolts—frozen as though the icy wind carried a spell across all.

It seemed to Wistala that the fate of worlds hung in the balance of those few moments, as the mountaintops tossed the sound back and forth.

Nothing happened. Water still cascaded over the spill-way.

Then came more noise, a cracking, crashing sound of rocks sliding, followed hard on its heels, as wagon-wheels follow horse hooves, by the water.

When describing the scene later, Wistala always said there was no word big enough for how the water moved through the gap, opening it wider and deeper as pieces at the edge fell away—a torrent of water, an avalanche, as though the mountain had sprouted a new shoulder falling into a steep cliff.

The dwarf barges pulled like mad across the surface of the Ba-drink, but the water fell away from them, sloped under them as first one and then the next fell away, carried sideways toward the gap.

The barbarians stood transfixed as the barges fell one by one into chaos. Whether they felt for the doomed dwarves, pulling at their oars, throwing anchors in desperation, even leaping into the water to swim as though their arms could accomplish what joined oars could not, Wistala couldn't say.

The lake drained away a claw's-breadth at a time, but soon there was a path along the side of the lake to the

Hardhold. The barbarians splashed into the fresh shallows, stomped through mud, a black sea of hide-cape, helm, and round shield replacing the receding waters.

It was not a charge of ode or poetry. The barbarians came in a ragged line, a few at the front so crazed to out-race the others that they threw away their weapons as they ran, others slipped in the mud and the fortunate got up again before they were stepped on by those behind.

The dwarves did what they could, barricaded the land-ings and docks, but the barbarians climbed above to the galleries, or uprighted stranded barges and longships and climbed up the staves at the hull bottom as though they were ladders.

Screams, and over all the cacophony of steel on steel, the growled hurrahs of the dwarves matched against the wild catlike screeches of the men.

Wistala caught sight of a long, thin barge flying purple pennants, oars worked by black armored beetles, pulling away from chaos east across the receding waters, a one-legged figure at the center. She took a deep breath and went down to the landing and retrieved the ball-weight and chain.

Wistala rose into the air, all four limbs holding the bur-den to her belly. Up, up, up toward the sun, racing only herself and her exhaustion. In all likelihood, she would never have a mating flight. This would have to do. The air grew thin and cold, but she kept her eye always on the barge below, heading for the eastern road.

When she could go up no more she closed her wings somewhat and went down.

It was dizzying, a little frightening, she felt hurried by the weight of the iron ball, but she needed time to adjust her dive. The surface of the slowly receding lake rushed up to meet her at a frightening speed. She angled a little, then closed her wings more so she dropped almost straight down.

Here is your crown, King Fangbreaker—

Perhaps at the last moment he looked up from his posi-tion at the center of the barge, urging his rowing bodyguard on—Wistala didn't know, for she released her weight and opened her wings, sick from the change in air pressure. Pain tore at her joints as she leveled off, streaking across the lake surface at an impossible speed.

Kra-sploosh!

She dipped her wings and looked back. The barge had folded in on itself, and a fountain of water rose from the center like the jaws of some sea dragon shutting on a bird. Flung dwarves spun through the air before splashing down into the Ba-drink.

She flew back toward the battle, saw that flames were pouring out of some of the balconies and galleries in the Hardhold. Tall Rock seemed still to be holding, and the dwarves manned that half of the half-shattered Titan bridge.

Wistala flew with aching wings back to the outer wall. Ragwrist and Hammar stood in one of the towers with a few elderly barbarians, and she alighted next to them.

"Glorious, glorious, glorious," Hammar said, smacking his fist into palm. "Have you ever seen such a fight? Wistala, you're a marvel. With you at my side, there's no stopping me now. We'll ride your wings to Hypatia herself. 'Twas a happy day when we settled our enmity."

"It's *Nuum* Wistala, bookburner. I don't remember settling anything with you," Wistala said. She beat her wings and rose into the air, seizing Hammar by his fur cloak.

He hung there, struggling and swearing, and reached for his blade. Wistala beat him about the body with her wing-tips until he dropped it.

She flew up to the top of Tall Rock, where a few dwarves still manned war-machines, firing down at the barbarians fighting on the Titan bridge.

She swooped low between the towers, and dwarves scattered. "A parting gift from the Oracle," Wistala called. "Here's King Hammar the Dwarfhanger." She set the former thane down gently. "Dangle him from the Titan bridge or use him to negotiate, I care not."

And with that she flapped away, leaving Hammar lying bruised in a ring of desperate dwarves.

Now there was only one more account to settle on the balance sheet of her life.

The Dragonblade's home was easy enough to find. It was the only one with a dragonscale door and fire-shutters, carved under an overhanging rock that resembled a closed clam. The rest of the dwellings were humble shepherd's huts or fishermen's wharfside homes.

Wistala landed in the mud of the fallen-away lake to the barking of hounds from all around the house.

She waited out of arrow-reach and warily examined the small square windows. The flower boxes and hanging mountain ferns might hide war-machines, for all she knew.

"I call for the Drakossozh," Wistala roared. "Let him show his face if he dares."

Silence from the house.

"Well? Daylight is burning, as will this home, if I do not have an answer."

The door opened, and a long-limbed young woman stepped out. There was some of the Drakossozh in her broad face, but she had a sensitive mouth. Wistala realized she was the womanly version of the girl glimpsed watching the circus leave years ago.

She came only half out the door, seemed ready to jump back inside and slam it at the first sign of flame.

"I speak for the household," she said, voice quavering only a little. "If you've come for vengeance, my father is not here. If you've come for murder, there are children within."

"I've come for neither," Wistala said. She sat, the mud squelching against her backside. Had she ever been so tired?

"What is your name, girl?" Wistala asked.

"Adaska," she answered.

"I'm—"

"The Oracle-dragon."

"No. Well, I was. Now I'm just Wistala, a dragon who has had enough of fighting."

"What can you mean?" she asked, stepping a little farther onto her doorstep. Someone hissed at her from inside, but she ignored the comment.

"I don't know when all this started. Did my grandsire kill yours, or did yours kill mine? Your father killed mine, and I should kill yours, but I expect you or your brother would come after me. Am I right?"

"We would. But dragons must be slain."

"Must they? Size put aside, I'm not certain we're so very different."

"Dragons bring ruin and fear wherever they go; look what happens across the lake," she said. Wistala looked, the carrion birds were already gathering. She wondered if Bartleghaff or his relations were among them. "This was always a peaceful place until you came."

"As was my home cave until the dwarves across the lake came. Let us put an end to this feud. At least the one that exists between your family and mine."

"I don't know."

"You'll know when you have children of your own. Where can I find your father?"

She hesitated. "He rode with his armsmen and dogs, answering the call of the mountain king to hunt you down. He took the north trail."

Wistala sighed. "I'll make it easier for him to find me."

"You shouldn't. He will kill you."

"Perhaps," Wistala said. "Will you consider what I said?"

"Yes," she said.

"Now I go to convince your father."

With some pain she rose into the air and winged across the lake. She found a trail, an old sort of road winding along the lakeside and over little chasms on bridges and between thin, wind-bent trees. The road was nothing compared to Rainfall's, it was little more than a paved goat trail. It looked old enough for blighters to have built it. Old as war.

But also old as bridges. She alighted on one, and looked to where her eye caught a glint of metal. She retreated to the far side of the ancient bridge and waited.

The file of riders soon came over the rise and down the path toward the bridge, which leaped across a chasm to waters that lapped where her tail would reach if she let it dangle. Instead she wrapped it about the bridge; the masonry looked loose enough to be pulled apart if she exerted herself.

The men spotted her and let out halloos. They dismounted and clapped visors across helms, notched arrows into bows, and the Dragonblade came forward with spear and sword.

With a shout, one of his handlers released the dogs, who poured across the bridge in a bristle-backed river.

Wistala flapped her wings, hard, held fast by her tail. The force of the windstorm sent the dogs plummeting off the bridge into the waters below—some with a knock or two, but they swam to rocks and climbed upon them to bark up at their now impossible-to-reach prey.

The Dragonblade stepped forward, looked down at the vociferous, dripping pack, pulled back his visor and laughed loud and long. He had to lean on his spear shaft.

"Dragonelle," he said, wiping his eyes. "You are hard on my dog packs."

So he did know the name for a female dragon!

"Your daughter told me I could find you on this road," Wistala said.

The Dragonblade's face went white, and he raised his spear for a throw. His son behind came forward with a bow ready. "If you've—"

"I haven't touched so much as a winter cabbage," Wistala said. "I was all politeness to your girl."

"I will still kill you," the Dragonblade said.

"Let me speak first," Wistala insisted. "Our kind have shed rivers of blood, matched against each other. I would have the flow stopped. Shall it always be thus, one family slaughtering another, until the ending of the world?"

"Or the ending of dragons," the Dragonblade said. "Calls for peace are always made by those at a disadvantage."

Wistala hugged the road, covering her belly with stone,

readied to parry blade or spear with wing-points. "Come then," she said. "Let's start the madness afresh."

The boy raised the bow, sighted with his good eye, but his father held him back. "You must let me finish, as well." He plunged his spear point-first into the dirt beside the road. "There's been enough killing for one day. You came to my doorstep and did no harm—"

"You would believe a—," his son said.

The Dragonblade glared at him. "I believe this one. And my eyes. I see no smoke at our part of the lakeshore. And shut it, you fool hounds!"

Drakossozh looked thoughtful for a moment, and the dogs, silenced for only a moment, started up again. "The dwarves will pay no more hide-bounties, at least not for a long while. Perhaps I should take up chickens. They taste better and do not singe off one's eyebrows. You have your peace. What is your name?"

"Wistala."

"Ah. You are only the second dragon to ever escape me, Wistala. Wear that with pride, as you do that little bauble between your eyes."

"Who was the first?" Wistala said.

"A drake, a young gray."

Wistala's hearts stopped. "*What?* When?"

"A dozen years ago or so," he said. "I've heard no more trouble of him, I expect he died raiding some farmer's pigpen. No scales, you know. He would be—wait, you two must be related."

"I hope so," Wistala said, wishing the Dragonblade's dogs would cease barking. It detracted from the solemnity of the moment.

"Now I do fear to let you go. Were two such resourceful dragons to meet up again . . . but something in my heart says it will not go ill for me, or my family. Go, Wistala. No blade or arrow of mine will touch you."

The boy fired, and the Dragonblade threw up a blur of an elbow that knocked the arrow off its path. It skittered harmlessly down the rocks. Wistala gulped, it was just as well they had not fought.

"Eliam, you vex me. But we will talk at home. Go, Wistala, and let my dogs quiet, before I finish off the pack myself."

Wistala took a deep breath and launched herself into the air. She watched the spear point until she was out of range.

The old dragon proverb: *Trust, but keep an eye open.*

Epilogue

W istala sat in the old troll cave, near the entrance where the air was cleaner, and dictated her memories of the battle that destroyed the Wheel of Fire, and much of the combined barbarian power in the north, to Lada.

Of Rayg she had no happy news. A great many dwarves fled down their mysterious holes to the darkroads as Thul's Hardhold fell, and as Rayg hadn't been carried off by the barbarians or been found among the dead, she assumed he'd fled for his life with them. The barbarians had caused so much destruction, it was doubtful that he could return through Hardhold, even if he wanted to. But he was in the company of dwarves who would respect him, very different circumstances from abject slavery in the north.

The thaneship had passed to Ragwrist, of all people, as Mossbell was the largest estate in the thanedom with Galahall divided between Hammar's barbarian relations. Wistala had sold him Mossbell for a song—literally, for he had a wonderful voice. Now Ragwrist complained of his generosity to his tenants, driving him to the poverty of only drinking wines from the less renowned vineyards.

The circus went to Brok, who kept it out of barbarian lands, where dwarves were increasingly unwelcome, perhaps justifiably.

The Green Dragon Inn still stood, and tall tales had grown up around it and its sign. People in later years reached up to touch it for luck, and heard stories so bizarre and inaccurate, Wistala would have smiled to hear.

Widow Lessup retired with Yari-Tab in the modestly restored Mossbell hall and devoted herself to feeding and supervising the surviving cats, who kept the mice from nibbling the hooves of Dsossa's "north herd" of white horses.

What remained of the Wheel of Fire Dwarves came under the leadership of Lord Lobok, who, if he ever led his fighting dwarves out of the mountains again, would be assured an entertaining place in the annals of military history.

Speaking of which, Wistala had no particular desire to accomplish a war history, but the librarians had asked for a dragon's-eye memoir, and they would get one. It was the least an Agent of Librarians could do, before setting off in search of her brother.

As she talked, chose phrases, and answered the occasional question, Wistala's thoughts kept returning to the dilemma of dragons. On the one *sii,* there was the sort of grasping survival of dragons like that smelly wretch in the far north—scattering, hermitage, or worst, assassination— and on the other a useful servitude, a survival that depended on being of use to others, like the man-carrying dragons more and more sailors of the northern part of the Inland Ocean reported.

Could dragons cooperate, form an order like the old city-states of Hypat? Certainly an extended family could, as the odd dragons of the Sadda-Vale proved. And if they did, suppose a Masmodon or a Fangbreaker or worse arose at the council table? Selfishness and greed were not the least of dragon faults.

Oddly enough, she wished she could talk the matter over with that dragon DharSii. He had unpleasant manners, to be sure, and was the most arrogant creature who ever cracked an egg, but she could trust him to give an intelligent opinion. And perhaps even more important, an honest one. For in obtaining his opinion, she'd have to sum up her life and actions—she wondered if she'd done right or wrong, though why she should care what he would think of her past she did not know.

The Wheel of Fire would butcher no more hatchlings in their home cave, and Hammar's half-Hypatian, half-barbarian plot to gain power in war and conquest had vanished in the catafoua mouth, and the Dragonblade had hung up his spear, even if he wasn't exactly raising chickens. She'd kept her promises—

Save the last one to Father.

But felt little satisfaction in were-blood. Avenging her own was a grim duty, like breaking a bullock's back in a dive so that you could eat, and just as necessary to survival. Ignoring those who kill others in the hope they won't get around to you only means that when they appear to take your head and scales, they would apply all they learned in other victories, making your chances against them so much the worse.

"Does that have to go in?" Lada asked.

"What do you mean?" Wistala said, brought back to the dictation.

"The battle. Betrayals. Incompetence, even cowardice. Boats falling, mud everywhere, blood running from balconies, carrion birds poking marrow from bones, dwarves hanging from bridges, burned corpses, but worst of all, no hero whose courage and skill is put to the ultimate test."

"They asked for a history, they shall have my history. If someone else will have the battle take place on a spring-green field with pennants at the lance points and songs sung over the honored dead, let them write it thus. This history is a story of death begetting death, and should end with carrion birds, for they are the only ones who come out the better at the end.

"Speaking of which—steaks and cakes, but I'm hungry. Enough of this wordplay. Let's head over to Mossbell and eat!"

Glossary

DRAKINE

FOUA: A product of the fire bladder. When mixed with the liquid fats stored within and then exposed to oxygen, it ignites into oily flame.

GRIFF: The armored fans descending from the forehead and jaw that cover sensitive ear-holes and throat pulse-points in battle.

KAZHIN: a dragon related to you on unfriendly terms.

PRRUM: The low thrumming sound a dragon makes when it is pleased or particularly content.

SAA: The rear legs of a dragon. The three rear true-toes are able to grip, but the fighting spur is little more than decoration.

SII: The front legs of a dragon. The claws are shorter and the fighting spur on the rear leg is closer to the other digits and opposable. The digits are more elegantly formed for manipulation.

TORF: A small gob from the fire bladder, used to provide a few moments of illumination.

UZHIN: a dragon related to you on friendly terms.

DWARVISH

DHSSOL: an "evil star" or catastrophe.

COCOLAT: a dwarvish sweet made from rare tropical beans and milk.

POGT: a dwarvish curse.

ELVISH

GAR-LOQUE: a smelly but flavorful bulb of the lily family with a slightly dragonish odor.

HASPADALANESH: The final, rooted stage of an elf's life.

SENISOTE: music.

FELINE

TCHATLASSAT: a close friend.

HYPATIAN

BALAGAN: a sort of crane.

MOD: Hypatian low-priest title.

NUUM: Hypatian librarian or professor title.

VESK: a Hypatian mark of distance based on the amount of distance light infantry can cover in an hour—about three and a half miles.

YEO: an informal title for those who act as retainers for Hypatian nobles.